LORD OF THE DEAD

LORD

OF THE

DEAD

LISA A. SHIEL

 Book Two in the Human Origins Series

 Slipdown Mountain Publications LLC
Lake Linden, MI
Toll-Free: 1-877-388-5227

Lord of the Dead
by Lisa A. Shiel

First Edition

Manufactured in the United States

ISBN 13: 978-0-9746553-2-1
ISBN 10: 0-9746553-2-5

Library of Congress Control Number: 2005904681

Information: www.SlipdownMountain.com
                        1-877-388-5227

SLIPDOWN MOUNTAIN PUBLICATIONS

Shiel, Lisa A.

Lord of the dead / Lisa A. Shiel.

p. cm.

1. Science Fiction. 2. Egypt, History—To 332 B.C.—Fiction.
3. Unidentified Flying Objects—Fiction. 4. Alternative Histories (Fiction).

PS3619.H54 L63 2005
813`.6—dc22   2005904681

For Dad—
  the aviation expert

 &

For Mom—
  the expert on everything else

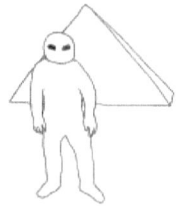

Prologue

The wind shrieked.

Akhmose tiptoed into the sanctuary behind his brother Isesi. The dust from the storm outside coated their bodies, a second skin borne of the desert. The sand burned Akhmose's eyes, parched his tongue, clung to his bare head as a wig might.

His brother led him toward the shrine. The lamplight glinted off the axe clutched in Isesi's hand.

The god's boat rested atop a dais as if drifting down an invisible river. The shrine— a wooden box seven feet tall—hulked in the center of the boat, its doors closed, the latch fastened.

Approaching the shrine, Isesi laid a hand on the doors.

"No," Akhmose said. "I have changed my mind."

"We are dying. The fields have turned to dust, the canals have dried, and the wells are nearly drained. Yet each day we bring oil to the temple so the high priest may anoint the god's image. Even as we starve, we offer food to the god's image." Isesi lowered his voice to a whisper. "The legend tells—"

"You cannot believe a legend."

"Our father was a priest of Djehuty, like us. He believed."

"The gods will punish us."

"My brother, the gods do not exist. If they lived, they would save us."

Isesi climbed into the god's boat. He unhooked the shrine's latch and parted the doors. The golden statue of Djehuty gleamed in the flicker of the oil lamps. While the body was rendered as a mummy with hands folded over its chest, the face displayed a fullness far from the gaunt figures he had passed on the journey here. Far from his own wasted form.

Isesi swung the axe backward.

The god's eyes, painted so vividly they seemed alive, stared at Akhmose as if the great one knew his thoughts. Akhmose shuffled closer to the shrine.

Isesi hammered his axe into the statue. The gold chipped. He hacked at it until sweat stained his clothing, yet even then he did not stop.

Pfft!

They froze. The side of the statue had cracked. A cold draft emanated from the breach.

Isesi's chest heaved. He dropped the axe.

Akhmose stumbled to the shrine. Leaning over the boat's hull, he squinted at the crack in the statue. The figure was a hollow shell. He inserted his fingers through the gap and pulled. A hinge groaned. The front half of the statue swung open.

A body tumbled out onto the floor.

Isesi gasped.

Akhmose knelt beside the body. Wrapped in linen with the arms crossed over the chest, the body resembled a mummy. Steam rose from the corpse. He touched the bandages. Cold. He prodded the body with his finger. Soft.

Inside the statue, behind where the body had stood, Akhmose noticed a cylindrical object. A papyrus scroll. Bound with a gold ribbon.

He snatched the scroll. The ribbon bore the seal of the great god Djehuty.

The hairs on his body stiffened. A strange tingling rushed over him.

Lightning exploded before him. In its wake, a man hunched. The lamplight set the man's red hair afire.

The stranger strode toward Akhmose. He extended a hand. "Give me the scroll."

Akhmose hugged the scroll to his chest.

"Do not," Isesi rasped. "Its wisdom will save our people, as the legend foretells."

The stranger scowled at Akhmose. "Relinquish the scroll."

Akhmose gaped at the stranger. He let his jaw fall open, for he could not hold it shut.

"Y-you," Akhmose said. "You are the god—"

"I am chaos. That is all you need to know."

The god stepped toward him. Akhmose scuttled backward.

With a shout, Isesi rushed at the god. He rammed his head into the god's gut. When the god struck his jaw, Isesi wrestled him to the ground. Limbs flailed. Cries echoed off the limestone walls.

Akhmose bolted out the sanctuary door, into the antechamber, through the columned hall, past the pylons into the sandstorm that had settled over the town. The wind tore through the streets. It battered him until his flesh ached.

He glanced backward. A light, larger than a hundred suns, hovered above the temple. Flames devoured the temple's roof.

Akhmose hurtled through the storm.

Lightning burst behind him. He ran faster, the scroll clutched to his chest, the sand scouring his breaths. Ahead, lightning erupted. A woman shrieked.

Out of the dust something rolled toward him. He tripped over the woman's body.

Her eyes stared up at him without seeing. Blood streamed from wounds on her chest.

A knife gored his back. Pain wrenched through his body. He lurched forward. The assailant tore out the blade and plunged it into him again. He gasped for breath. The pain wrung his body like a fist, and his knees buckled. He collapsed onto the ground. The scroll slipped from his hand, rolling away into the storm.

His assailant stabbed the blade into his back. As his *ka* flowed from his body on a river of blood, he glimpsed a woman fleeing past him. She clasped the scroll to her chest.

Screams echoed through the town.

His assailant thrust the blade into him one last time.

Akhmose whispered a prayer to Ra—and then he died.

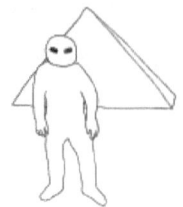

Chapter One

Glacier Peak Wilderness
Wenatchee National Forest, Washington State
Wednesday, October 15

One year ago she'd found a 100-million-year-old human footprint.

Today she was looking for a really big rock.

Katy Bergren hopped over a foot-tall clump of stinging nettles. She halted beside a hemlock tree to adjust the straps of her metal-frame backpack. The hemlock towered over 100 feet tall, with a girth of three feet at its base. She leaned her shoulder against the tree and, pulling a Kleenex from her pocket, blotted her forehead. Despite a temperature in the upper forties, sweat moistened her skin. An hour ago she'd taken off her jacket. She rolled up the sleeves of her flannel shirt. The wind tugged at her canvas hat. She wiped her hands across her thighs, smearing sweat on her blue jeans.

She wasn't used to the altitude. She estimated they'd hiked to less than 2000 feet, but back in Michigan she never got even that high.

A gust roared through the trees.

The hairs on her neck prickled. She patted the fanny pack strapped around her waist to feel the lump of her Taurus .357 revolver inside it. Unlike most hikers, she knew what dangers lurked in the forest. Big, hairy, bipedal dangers. The press had given the creatures the innocuous nickname "Bigfoot." She knew first-hand how the creatures turned violent when they felt threatened.

Breaking into their home could be construed as threatening. The big rock she sought marked the entrance to the tunnels the creatures called home. She must break into the tunnels to find what she needed.

Ahead of her Rick stopped. A series of beeps issued from his direction as he checked their position on the GPS unit. They'd adopted a zigzag pattern for their search which had thus far netted them nothing.

Rick glanced back at her around the body of his metal-frame backpack.

The trees swayed in the wind. A light flashed overhead.

Katy jerked her head back to look up at the light. The sun, of course.

"It's almost noon," Rick said, "and we've only gone seven miles from the trailhead. At this rate we'll need a month to find whatever it is we're looking for."

"A big rock by a Y-shaped tree, uphill from the stream. Under that, we'll find a tunnel."

"And in the tunnel, a stela explaining the truth about human origins." Rick strode to her. "I still get the willies every time I think how human beings have been around for half a billion years."

"Maybe longer."

"Great, I feel much better." He frowned. "We're looking for a pine needle in a forest, Katy."

She blotted her temples with the Kleenex. Where had humans come from, since they hadn't evolved from the ancient hominids as evolution said? Today, she and Rick intended to find out.

Seven miles in four hours—not exactly record time. From the trailhead at Downey, they'd driven their rented Ford Explorer down the four-wheel-drive road that paralleled Downey Creek. Six miles from the trailhead, at Bachelor Creek, they'd parked the Explorer and taken off on foot. Searching every shady spot, dip, and stream they encountered slowed their progress.

Rick tucked the GPS unit into a pocket of his vest. The vest hid his shoulder holster, which housed an old service issue .45 auto. The shoulder strap of his backpack rode just above the holster.

"Let me see the map," Rick said.

Katy reached into her jeans pocket. She withdrew a folded sheet of paper, wrinkled from its captivity in her pocket. It was a satellite photo of the Glacier Peak Wilderness that she'd printed out from a website. A black circle marked an area of the wilderness. She handed Rick the map.

He pointed at the circle. "This is where we are. But the circle covers a six-mile area. We've gone about two miles into the circle."

"We keep going then."

He handed the map back to her. "I can't believe we're following directions given by a Bigfoot."

"Garfield's smart. He understood what I wanted from him."

Over the past year, Katy had developed a friendship with Garfield. In spite of that, he'd waited two months after his trip in a UFO to tell her about it. He remembered flying over North America to a spot near "the great western river." After showing him some

5

maps, she'd figured out he meant the Pacific Ocean. The ufonauts, who called themselves the Planners, had taken Garfield into an underground tunnel system. There he met other Bigfoot or, as Katy called them, hairy hominids. Most importantly, he'd seen a stela. The standing stone mentioned the origins of man.

The Planners had stopped him from getting close enough to see any more. By showing Garfield satellite photos of the US, Katy had determined the Planners brought Garfield to Wenatchee National Forest in north-central Washington State. Specifically, they brought him to a 700-square-mile area called the Glacier Peak Wilderness, in the northern end of the park. Nearby, Glacier Peak mounted over 10,500 feet into the heavens.

The wind gusted. Dead leaves, strewn across the forest floor, crackled.

"Maybe Garfield got confused," Rick said.

The wind gusted again, harder. Branches twisted and bobbed. Peripherally, Katy spotted a flash of gray.

She spun toward the flash. Between gusts, the branches settled down. They masked whatever she'd spotted.

The wind kicked up. Branches flapped. Low to the ground, gray flashed.

Thirty feet straight ahead. Beyond a pair of spruces. The trees jutted upward at inverse angles. Three feet off the ground, the trunks of the spruces merged.

Katy leaped to her feet. She pointed at the trees. "There it is!"

"I'll be darned," Rick said.

Katy bolted toward the tree.

The wind blustered. Branches dipped down toward her head. Ducking, she hurtled through the forest toward the Y-shaped spruces. Her backpack caught on a branch. She jerked it free and charged onward. Behind her, Rick's boots clomped. Leaves crunched beneath both their feet. She swerved around the spruces.

Her legs crashed into a two-foot-tall boulder.

Her feet flipped out from under her. She tumbled over the rock. The weight of her backpack propelled her forward. Face-first, she hit the ground.

Rick hurdled over the rock. He landed on both feet, right beside her.

Katy unhooked the straps around her chest and waist that secured her backpack. She shoved the pack off her shoulders onto the ground, scrambling to her feet. At two feet tall and three feet wide, the boulder could seal off a tunnel entrance. The hairy hominids added back entrances to their caves, cut out of the ground, with boulders to seal them off in case of emergency.

Four feet to the left of the boulder sat an earthen plug, rectangular, three feet wide by two feet long and six inches thick. A wooden peg protruded from one side. The plug rested next to a hole of matching dimensions. A portal into the caves.

Rick dropped his backpack on the ground. He squinted at the portal.

Katy bent down. She tore open the zipper of her backpack and pulled out her digital camera. From a side pocket, she dug out a flashlight.

"Oh no," Rick said. "Wait a m—"

She ran for the portal, jumped in feet-first. When her boots struck the floor, she scuttled sideways. She flicked on the flashlight. Light flooded the corridor. The passage dead-ended to her right, but stretched into darkness to her left.

Rick dove into the tunnel. *Whump.* He landed beside her.

"Thanks for waiting," he said.

"First doorway on the right," she said. "That's what Garfield told me. Which must mean we go left, then find the first doorway on the right-hand side of the passage."

She angled leftward.

Rick swiped the flashlight from her. Pushing past her, he marched down the corridor. Thirty feet later, they found a doorway on the right. It led into an oval room 15 feet long by ten feet wide. The walls bore no paintings or inscriptions. At the farthest end of the room hunkered a stela, a standing stone three feet tall, etched with symbols.

Katy trotted to the stela. The inscription was written in ancient Egyptian hieroglyphs. She kneeled before the stela. As she skimmed her fingers over the opening lines of the inscription, she translated them silently.

Her heart thudded. Blood thundered behind her eardrums.

She whispered, "We found it."

Rick lingered in the doorway, halfway across the threshold. The .45 in his hand, he watched down the corridor.

"What's it say?" he asked.

She swallowed the mass in her throat. "Here lies the Master of Secrets, he whose identity is hidden, whose ancestors lived in the first house of man. The second house of man was born here…a thousand million years before the First Time. This is the tale of our birth."

Katy sat back on her heels. She bit her bottom lip.

Rick looked at her. She looked at him.

"A thousand million years," Rick said. "That's one billion years. Human beings were born over a billion years ago?"

"Yes, and I have an idea of where." She placed her fingers in a V, one fingertip under each of two hieroglyphs. "These are the symbols for star and sky. They're right after the phrase First House of Man."

She looked at him. "We came from another planet."

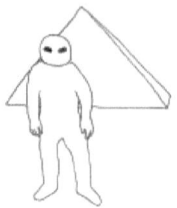

Chapter Two

She photographed the stela's face from every angle. While the stone preserved the opening lines intact, the remainder survived in fragments. Bits had flaked off the face of the rock, taking the hieroglyphs with them. A full translation would have to wait until she and Rick got home.

On her knees beside the stela, she tilted sideways to peek around it. The backside consisted of three steps—the bottom one wider and low to the ground, the middle one narrower and five times higher, and the top one the narrowest of all. The top step featured a carving of an eye with lapis lazuli inset for the pupil and iris. Nothing else adorned the backside.

She shot five photos of the backside.

Six inches behind the stela, a pile of dirt adjoined a rectangular pit whose length stretched away from the monument.

Katy glanced at Rick. He lingered in the doorway, the .45 in his right hand, arm crooked in front of him. He swiveled his head left and right to observe the corridor. Furrows creased his forehead.

Looping the camera strap around her neck, Katy rose and walked to the pit. It measured six feet long by two feet wide, with a depth of three feet. Someone had sprinkled dirt over the pit's floor. The disturbance looked recent. She crouched beside the dirt pile and sniffed it. Smelled recent too.

Stones set into the dirt encircled the pit. One stone—larger than the others, painted with pictographs—marked the head end of the pit, across the gulf from the stela.

Katy crouched by the stone. She pried it loose from the dirt. The symbols depicted a red pyramid behind a figure in a loose-fitting jumpsuit. The figure's helmet, a perfect sphere, had black, almond-shaped eyes. A pair of ovoid UFOs flanked the figure. The rock served as the headstone for a grave.

She and Rick had seen a similar grave in Michigan last year, inside the hairy hominid caves. The Michigan grave had held the remains of a human being named Ranefer. He hailed from an advanced culture that had flown UFOs while the rest of humanity struggled through the ice age.

Katy flipped the headstone over in her hand. Although dirt encrusted the backside, she saw hints of pictographs beneath the grime.

"Hurry up," Rick said.

She snapped a picture of the grave. The headstone she slipped into her pocket.

She hopped down into the pit. In a crouch, she brushed aside the loose dirt at the foot of the grave. A white object emerged from the covering. A human skull.

"A Planner was buried here," she told Rick. "Somebody dug him up."

"Garfield and his buddies dug up a Planner," Rick said, still focused on the corridor. "They made him a doormat to scare humans away. Maybe these guys did the same thing."

"They left the skeleton *in situ.*"

Ranefer's grave had lacked a funerary stela. The person buried here had warranted a stela, yet those who buried him robbed him of his name. To rob a man of his name meant to rob his soul of eternal life.

Katy wiped the dirt from the skull's mandible. The jaw retained a full set of teeth.

Grumbling echoed down the corridor like distant thunder.

"Time to go," Rick whispered.

Katy grasped a molar and jiggled it. The tooth inched out of its slot. She jiggled the molar back and forth as she eased it upward out of the jawbone.

Rick stomped to the stela. He bent over the monument, leaning down into the pit to scowl at her. In the corridor, the grumbling segued into growls. The bare feet of hairy hominids whomped on the earthen floor.

"We have got to leave," Rick said.

"One second."

Grrrrrrrr. Whomp, whomp.

"What the hell do you want with a tooth anyway?" Rick demanded.

"A sample for carbon dating." She prized the tooth free. "Got it."

She stuffed the tooth in her pocket. Grabbing her hands, Rick hoisted her out of the pit.

At the doorway, they hesitated. Together they peeked around the threshold into the corridor. Twenty feet to the right, red eyes twinkled. She counted the pairs. Two, three, four, five, six.

Grrr-rrrr-rrrrr. The growls from multiple voices overlapped each other.

Goosebumps prickled her skin. A chill slithered up her spine.

Rick charged into the corridor. "Go!"

Katy sprinted out the door, left down the corridor, toward the portal. Rick's footsteps clapped after her. Behind him, hominid feet pounded.

A shaft of sunlight, dimmed by the forest canopy, streamed through the portal.

Katy leaped off the floor. She stretched her arms up, clawing for the portal's walls. Her fingers met air, and she thwumped onto the floor.

Knees bent, Rick linked his hands into a stirrup. She planted her right foot in his hands, stepping up as he heaved her off the floor. The crown of her head cleared the portal. She threw her arms out to either side. Rick thrust against her heels.

She sprang out of the portal. Face first, she flopped onto the ground.

Rick vaulted through the portal. He grasped its rim, his body dangling through the opening, and swung his legs out onto the ground.

They charged toward their backpacks, eight feet away. Rick boosted hers onto her shoulders. She jammed the strap closures into place while he hefted his own pack onto his shoulders.

A grunt resonated from the portal. The breath trapped in her throat, Katy stared at the portal.

A pair of hairy hands grasped the portal's lip. The creature bobbed his head out of the hole like a prairie dog. A mutant monster prairie dog.

The creature met Katy's gaze.

He shrieked.

Straight ahead, twigs snapped.

Moving only her eyes, Katy looked toward the sound. Behind the branches of a fir tree skulked a dark, humanoid shape. The silhouette lacked a neck. Sunlight glinted in the creature's eyes.

Katy ran. Rick took off after her.

They rocketed through the woods, downhill toward Bachelor Creek a mile away. If she remembered the direction right. If she hadn't gotten turned around in their zigzag search.

"Eh-eh-eh."

She glanced back. Rick was an arm's length behind her. Two hairy hominids galloped three yards behind him. They grunted in time with their footfalls, eh-eh-eh-eh.

Katy tripped over a branch. Her hip hit the ground first. She rolled onto her back. Rick tripped over her legs, belly-flopping onto the dirt. A wedge of sunlight pierced the canopy overhead to stripe them in sunlight. Katy winced at the brilliance.

A hairy hominid barreled toward them. Katy yanked the Taurus out of her waistband.

Rick rolled over. He groped for the .45, yanked it out of its holster.

The hominid slid, threw both arms out for balance, stumbled forward a step. He stopped six feet from Katy.

His compatriot careened through a sapling behind him. The second creature rushed past the first toward Katy.

She swung the gun up in the creature's face.

The first hominid seized his compatriot's arm, yanking him backward. The second creature snarled, his lips peeled back to bare his teeth.

Katy curled her finger over the trigger.

The first creature gestured at her. He grunted, "Aset. *Neteret a'a.*"

Great goddess. He'd called her Isis, Aset in ancient Egyptian. The great goddess Isis. Garfield called her Isis too.

The hominid repeated, "Aset, *neteret a'a.*"

The second creature looked at her. His eyes widened. He barked, reeled around, and scurried back toward the cave portal. The first creature loped after him.

Katy set down the gun.

"What was that about?" Rick asked.

"No idea."

When the creatures had disappeared from sight, and their footfalls faded into silence, Rick clambered to his feet. He helped Katy stand. From his pocket, he retrieved the GPS unit. He punched buttons. The unit beeped.

"This way," he said.

They hiked back to Bachelor Creek.

Twice she thought she glimpsed a bright object in the sky. She tried not to think about it. But she knew they watched.

They always watched.

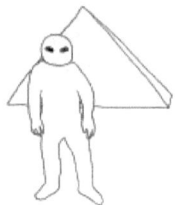

CHAPTER THREE

Anameka, Michigan

Rick towed the suitcases up the last step, across the threshold into the porch. Katy fumbled with the keys to the inner door. The outer door banged shut behind her. Once Rick had opened the door, he lugged the suitcases across the threshold into the cabin. Katy followed him inside.

The cabin was dark. The digital clock in the kitchen read 9:15.

Katy flipped on the overhead light.

The layout of the 900-square-foot log cabin created the illusion of space. The front door opened into the living room, with its high ceiling. To the left, a bar split the combination kitchen and dining area from the living room. On the right, stairs led up to the loft and down into the basement. The sofa stood flush against the rail of the basement stairs. Straight across from the front door, the back door exited onto a porch that overlooked the steep slope of the hill against which the cabin nestled. Pines and birches loomed on the hillside and all around their property, except on the four treeless acres in front. The bathroom filled the space behind the kitchen, alongside the back door.

Rick stowed the suitcases on the floor by the sofa. He hustled toward the back door. Easing the door open, he peeked outside.

Katy shuffled in a circle to survey the cabin. No broken windows. No rifled drawers. The computer, a laptop that required a password for access, sat on the desk in the corner, its lid shut. She had also removed its battery and hidden the AC adapter to prevent unauthorized access. No juice, no use.

An upward glance revealed the loft as she'd left it, bed made, curtains parted.

She headed toward the basement stairs.

Rick crossed the living room in three steps. As she placed her foot on the second step, he clasped her arm. She scrunched her eyebrows. He raised a hand, palm out. She shrugged.

He let go of her arm. She waited on the second step. He dug the Taurus out of her purse. The gun was hers because she'd bought it before she met him and because it fit her hand. In his hand the revolver, with its short barrel and concealed hammer, looked like a toy.

He sidled past her. She shadowed him down the stairs into the gloom of the basement. Halfway down, he stopped. She bumped into him. He wobbled, grabbing the handrail. She slapped a hand on the wall for support.

His watch ticked. Below, silence and darkness reigned.

Rick crept down the stairs, around the corner into the hallway. To the right the hallway extended toward the laundry nook and a storage room, but to the left it ended at the door to the woodshed. The light switch was near the door. Rick leaned left to flick the switch. The lights buzzed on. He veered right.

No one lurked in the laundry nook.

At the storage room door, Rick flattened against the wall. The Taurus in his right hand, he grasped the door knob with his left. He hurled the door inward, rushed inside, and hit the light switch.

No one hid in the storage room.

Rick lowered the gun. He sighed. His shoulders sagged.

When they returned from a trip, they always searched the house for anything amiss. Their quest to prove the true origins of humanity had earned them enemies—the kind without a conscience, without mercy, without qualms.

Back upstairs, Katy reattached the battery to her computer. She booted up the laptop. No one had erased the hard drive or deleted any files. All her CD-ROMs were stacked beside the computer.

Rick strolled up beside her. "How's the computer?"

"Feeling neglected but otherwise fine."

"Let's check the security system."

Katy trailed Rick onto the back porch. He whistled the sort of high, piercing whistle most people reserved for football games. They'd discovered it worked well for activating the security system. Except Katy couldn't whistle like that.

The moon bathed the hillside in pale luminance. A shadow rippled halfway up the hill. A hairy shape separated from the darkness, tromping down the slope toward them.

Garfield, a black-haired hominid, lumbered to within a few feet of Katy and Rick. Katy waved. Garfield grunted.

The media, and most scientists, labeled the creatures Bigfoot and ridiculed the notion of their existence. Katy had known for years they did exist. At first she'd called them hairy hominids but, on the four-day hike that had changed her life, she'd discovered their true identity: *Homo sapiens*.

The creatures weren't related to humans. DNA testing had proven they represented, instead, the true descendants of *Homo erectus* and *Homo heidelbergensis*. Hence, they—rather than humans—deserved the title *Homo sapiens*, since it designated the species who had evolved from the ancient hominids. Humans had not evolved from the hominids. Humans did not belong.

What humans were, how we had gotten here, Katy had yet to learn. Which explained the trip she and Rick had taken to Washington. They needed to know. The stela offered a morsel that wetted her appetite.

Garfield grunted.

Katy spoke to him in ancient Egyptian, the language his kind had learned from the Planners. Katy had learned enough ancient Egyptian to converse with Garfield, although sometimes she needed Rick's help.

While the creatures could speak, their words resembled grunts. Most people mistook the grunting for meaningless vocalizations. After all, "apes" weren't supposed to talk.

She asked Garfield for his report.

"Good," he said.

"Did you see anyone?" she asked.

"Half people," he mumbled.

She'd explained to Garfield that the house across the field from theirs was a summer home. The people who owned it lived in Chicago the rest of the year. He hadn't quite understood. Her attempt left him with the notion the summer people lived on Earth half the year and in the *duat*, the Egyptian underworld, the other half. Hence, he called them half people.

She'd also tried to teach him English. While he excelled at ancient Egyptian, and even charades used as communication, he failed at basic English. Maybe she was a bad teacher.

Rick leaned close to her. "I can't believe how fast you learned ancient Egyptian. I needed twenty years, but you licked it in one."

"Sorry, honey, I'll try to be less competent."

She smiled. He slipped his arm around her waist and kissed her.

Garfield grumbled.

Katy thanked Garfield. Flashing a smile, he plodded up the hill to the spot he'd chosen two months ago as his guard post. For the past two months he'd haunted the hillside day and night, with breaks to catch meals and relieve himself. When she queried him, he would say he sensed danger yet refused to explain.

Something was up. The Planners had returned around the same time—to take Garfield on a field trip to Washington. But she hadn't seen their craft in the night sky, glowing like false moons.

Not yet.

Grasping Rick's hand, Katy ushered him into the house. They collapsed onto the sofa. She snuggled against him.

Rick lifted his feet onto the coffee table. He shifted his weight, pressing his hip into Katy's. A hard lump in her pocket dug into her flesh. She pulled out the lump.

The headstone. She scraped at the dirt encrusted on its backside. Bits crumbled away. She spat on the stone, rubbed it, spat, pecked at the dirt. In under a minute she'd cleaned the stone. The hieroglyphs incised on its back stood out white against the black basalt.

"Sahor-Imsety," she read aloud. "Master of secrets, son of the king's body, the justified."

Rick sat up. "I know that name."

In the Michigan caves, Garfield had shown them a sacred room on the walls of which the Planners had carved a history lesson. The text told of the catastrophe that forced them into hiding 12,000 years ago. The king who had ruled over the Planners during that time was named Sahor-Imsety.

Katy shoved her hand deep into her pocket, withdrawing the tooth she'd stolen from Sahor-Imsety. Was he the same Imsety? Carbon dating the tooth would tell them when he'd died, which would either refute or verify his identity as Pharaoh Imsety of the Planners.

She traced the outlines of the hieroglyphs. "The stela said his name was hidden. So why does the headstone give his name?"

"The hairy hominids made the headstone."

The creatures had made the headstone for Ranefer's grave. But they'd also buried Ranefer. The Planners had buried Imsety. Maybe one Planner, a friend or relative of Imsety, instructed the creatures to place a headstone on the grave, thereby restoring Imsety's name to him.

She handed Rick the tooth. "Can you pack this up? Tomorrow we'll send it to Victor for carbon dating."

Rick nodded and took the tooth. He rose, stretched, and trundled downstairs.

The wheels of Katy's suitcase stuck out from beside the sofa. She rolled the case in front of her. Its wheels click-click-clicked on the wood floor. Unzipping the main compartment, she fished out the digital camera. The photos of the stela text needed translating.

At the desk, she sat down in the chair. She set the headstone on the desktop beside the stapler. While she waited for the computer to boot up, she pulled out the left-hand drawer. Cables clustered inside the drawer, their bodies entwined like snakes mating. Rubber bands lay clumped in the corner of the drawer. Rick coiled the cables and fastened each with a rubber band after he'd used them. She crammed them in the drawer loose.

Burrowing through the mess of cables, she found the one for connecting the camera to the computer. She disentangled it from three other cables and dumped it on the desktop.

Her computer chimed. Windows had loaded.

She flipped up the laptop's lid. The screen switched on. She plugged the cable into the camera and computer. Thirty seconds later she'd transferred all the photos onto the hard drive. With the images open in one window, she typed the translation in a separate window. The missing sections of the text she wrote as ellipses inside brackets. So much of the text was missing that her translation looked like a connect-the-dots puzzle.

Footsteps thumped on the stairs. Rick stopped at the head of the stairs.

"Time for bed," he said.

She zoomed in on a section of the text.

Rick waved a hand in front of her face. "It's ten o'clock. We've been up since five."

"I need ten minutes." She smiled at him. "Tops."

He frowned at her. With a sigh, he walked upstairs to the loft.

She focused on the computer screen. The floor of the loft creaked. The refrigerator hummed.

Done with the translation, she leaned back and rubbed her temples. The translation filled the screen. Clicking the print button, she reread the translation. The first line announced the date of the stela's dedication.

In the second month of Inundation, day 12, in Year 6 of the king of Upper and Lower Egypt, lord of the Two Lands, Sahor-Duamutef. Here lies the Master of Secrets, he whose identity is hidden, whose ancestors lived in the first house of man. The second house of man was born here [...] a thousand million years before the First Time. This is the tale of our birth. [...]

Here a long segment had broken off the stela. No amount of squinting, zooming in, or digital enhancement could restore it.

[...] came to the Land of the Hoe, where they flourished. Osiris-Khentiamentu, lord of the Two Lands, brought life to the land and ruled justly. [...] the secrets that live on in the wisdom of Thoth, hidden [...] He who protected Thoth's wisdom lies in this tomb far from his birthplace where the Condemned One may never find him.

Land of the Hoe referred to Egypt. The Planners, like the ancient Egyptians, had called their land by many names—Kemet, Land of the Hoe, the Two Lands. Who had come to Egypt? When? Why?

She'd thought that, after she translated the full text, she would know the true origins of humanity. Damn. The truth dodged her again.

Katy glanced at the computer's clock. It was 11:50.

She shut down the computer. The answers she sought existed somewhere out there.

But where?

Thursday, October 16

He woke in bed, alone. The alarm clock gave the time as 8:07.

Rick jumped out of the bed. He rushed into the walk-in closet with the sheets dragging after him. No Katy. He tore down the stairs into the living room.

Katy slumbered on the sofa, hands folded across her belly.

Her breathing was regular. Her face was slack. She'd left her boots on, the barrette in her hair, her watch fastened around her wrist. He knelt beside her and prodded her arm. Nothing. He shook her shoulders. She opened her eyes a smidgeon.

Yawning, she asked, "What time is it?"

"Eight."

She raised onto her elbows. Her eyes were bloodshot. She frowned.

"What's wrong?" he asked.

"Not sure. I was shutting down the computer when I heard a noise out back."

He sat down on the floor, his knees bent in front of him. "You opened the back door, of course."

"I heard a hissing, then I blacked out."

She blinked as if clearing grit from her eyes.

"You feel okay?" he asked.

"Fine. A little groggy, that's all."

Acid churned in his stomach. His jaw tightened as if steel wires clamped it shut.

She looked okay. She claimed she felt okay. If he suggested she have a doctor check her out, she'd run out back to hide with Garfield. Without evidence that anyone had harmed her, he had no recourse but to accept her statement. She was okay.

"You take a shower," he said, "I'll check for missing stuff."

While Katy shambled into the bathroom, he hurried upstairs to pull on jeans and a flannel shirt, socks and a pair of Nikes. Downstairs again, he inspected the living room and kitchen for missing items. In the basement, he searched the laundry room, storage room, and woodshed, less for missing items than for signs of the intruder. He found nothing, so he investigated the back porch, the driveway, the front acreage. The intruder had left no trace.

He tramped around back to the porch. Since it had no roof, he could stand on the porch to survey the slope from its base to the summit. He scrutinized the hillside up to the spot Garfield had occupied for two months. Instead of Garfield, he saw parallel lines etched in the dirt. The marks wound uphill toward the shadows halfway up the slope. Rick jogged toward the marks.

They began in the center of an area where the grass had been tamped down, probably by feet. Though the footprints overlapped until they became inseparable, the parallel lines traced a clear path up the hillside. They were more than lines. They were drag marks. Someone had dragged a body up the hill.

Rick tracked the marks. They ended at the base of a birch tree. Its branches fanned out over the figure sprawled on the ground. Rick bent over Garfield.

The creature lay still, eyes shut, arms splayed at his sides, with his right foot wedged under his left leg. His head lolled sideways, mouth open. Saliva dribbled down his chin.

Garfield opened his eyes. He shrieked.

Rick stumbled backward into a tree.

The beast really did hate him. Garfield had adored Katy from the start. He called her Isis and sat on the hill protecting her—from the bad guys, Rick had thought, though possibly from him too. Not that he blamed Garfield for adoring Katy.

Garfield sat up. He coughed three times, rubbing his nose.

Rick trod closer to the creature. Garfield stood up. He towered over seven feet tall, a foot more than Rick, while his shoulders spread to twice the width of Rick's. At its apex, his head tapered into a cut-off cone. The black hair that covered his body grew longer on the shoulders, but no hair grew beneath his eyes, over his nose, or around his wide lips.

Garfield cracked the knuckles of his stubby fingers.

"What happened to you?" Rick asked.

He could manage a conversation in ancient Egyptian, although sometimes he needed five or ten seconds to decipher a phrase. His skills improved each time he talked to Garfield.

"Bad breath," Garfield replied.

In English, Rick said, "If that means something else in ancient Egyptian, I don't have a clue what."

Garfield crinkled his nose.

Rick slipped back into ancient Egyptian. "What did you see?"

The creature pointed down the hill at the cabin. "Bad breath."

"I don't have time for this."

Realizing he'd spoken English, Rick translated the sentence into Egyptian. Garfield answered with a grunt. Rick grunted back. Garfield plunked onto his butt on the ground, turned his head away.

Rick dismissed Garfield with a wave of his hand. He trotted back to the cabin.

In the kitchen, Katy mulled over a box of Frosted Mini-Wheats.

He'd thought she might've heard Garfield's scream. In her state, she wouldn't hear a nuclear warhead if it detonated in the living room.

He stopped at the bar. "Whatcha doing?"

She jolted, yelping.

"From now on," Rick said, "we go to bed at the same time."

"Good idea. That way we get abducted together."

"Guess you're not groggy anymore."

She smiled. The sunrise filtering through the window glittered in her green eyes, deepened the pink in her cheeks, ignited red streaks in her chestnut hair. The tightening in his chest reminded him why he put up with her bullheaded, reckless behavior. Why she put up with him remained a mystery for the ages.

Katy decanted Mini-Wheats into a bowl. She poured milk over the cereal.

Rick reported the results of his inspection.

"I don't get it." Katy swallowed a mouthful of cereal. In mid-chew, she hesitated. "The photos."

She banged the bowl onto the counter. They both ran to the computer.

The digital camera had moved from the right corner of the desk to the left. As Katy booted up the computer, Rick switched on the camera. No one had erased the photos.

Katy, hand cupped over the mouse, inspected the files on the computer's hard drive.

"No damage," she said.

Anyone could've browsed the files on the hard drive without leaving a trace. The computer required a password, which ought to preclude tampering. Ought to. He didn't claim to understand the nuances of computer security but, the way Katy explained it to him, nothing was foolproof—especially with computers. She backed up all the files twice a week, on two different disks, and did something called a "drive image backup" once a month. The drive image thingamajig swallowed up a dozen disks, which she stored in the basement safe.

A printout of the stela text, with translation, lay on the desktop where she'd set it last night. Rick picked up the printout.

He read the translation. Not exactly clear-cut. With a bit of work, a lot of time, and some luck, they might figure out what it meant.

Katy groaned.

Rick peered over the printout at her. She stared at the upper left corner of the desk, where the stapler sat. She exhaled. Loudly.

"They stole our staples?" he asked.

"They took the headstone."

"Got any idea what the Planners want with Imsety's headstone?"

"Not a clue."

Rick started to turn off the camera, froze. The LCD screen on the back displayed the last photo taken in the Washington caves, of the stela's backside. Katy had snapped the photo from the side, highlighting the stela's profile.

Katy pushed up out of the chair, onto her feet.

"Did you notice this?" he asked, tipping the camera toward her. "The stela is in the shape of the Egyptian hieroglyph *set*, which meant seat or place."

She squinted at the tiny display. "Oh yeah."

"I've never seen a stela shaped like that."

Katy pursed her lips. Glanced at the computer.

She plunked down in the chair and reopened the image files, scanning them until she located one that showed the stela's backside head-on. She zoomed in on the top. An eye, with a blue iris formed by lapis lazuli, crowned the stela.

Rick peered over Katy's shoulder at the photo.

An eye. The seat glyph.

He snapped his fingers. "Osiris."

"Of course. The eye with the seat glyph stood for Osiris' name—Wesir in ancient Egyptian. Think it's important?"

The god Osiris ruled the kingdom of the dead. The deceased was even called the Osiris. The god played a vital role in the deceased's journey from this world to the next. Tomb inscriptions often mentioned him. Offerings were made to him.

Elation flooded out of Rick like water from a crumbling dam. The stela's shape was unusual. Referencing Osiris in a tomb wasn't.

"No," he said. "I doubt it's important."

While Rick retreated to the sofa, Katy logged onto the Internet, navigating to the website for their organization, the Human Origins Project.

Rick's father, Charlie, had founded the project seven years earlier. Katy had joined him three years ago, back when no one else believed in or cared about it. They investigated hairy hominid and UFO sightings, collected evidence that human beings had existed for millions of years, and endured ridicule from every yahoo in the United States.

For the past year, since Charlie had gone away, she'd continued the quest with Rick.

Gone away. She bit her lip. He hadn't died—she thought. She didn't really know.

Her email program bonged, announcing new mail. She opened the program.

Seventy-five new messages crammed her inbox. All bore the same title: "Sighting Report Submission (UFO)."

These days the project collected UFO sightings more to track the Planners movements than to unmask a mystery. For the past year, since she and Rick first encountered the Planners, UFO sightings had remained sporadic. A wave here and there. Nothing spectacular. Just the Planners showing off their superiority.

Until today.

Normally, the project received a handful of UFO reports each month. All 75 of the new reports had been submitted since 11 o'clock last night.

Katy skimmed through them.

It was a glowing sphere, 200 yards in diameter...a ball of light bigger than my house...static electricity all over my body...couldn't move...the bright globe sped away faster than any airplane...

The descriptions were identical. The glowing orb hadn't abducted anyone, or mutilated any cows, or bestowed revelations on the witnesses. The craft simply drifted overhead, paused, then sped away at incredible velocity.

They wanted the witnesses to get a good look. To make sure they'd report it.

To make sure she and Rick would find out.

The first sighting occurred in New Jersey. From there, the craft had traveled inland, across Pennsylvania and Ohio, over Lake Erie into Michigan, and northwest through the center of the state. The last sighting had happened in Anameka—one hour ago.

Last night, an intruder gassed her in order to steal an ancient headstone. At the same time, the Planners left their hideout at the bottom of the ocean, flying straight to Anameka.

She spun her chair toward the sofa. Rick looked at her.

"We'd better figure out that stela," she said. "Fast."

Meidum, Egypt

The wind twirled sand into the air, then dropped it as if the heat had scorched its hands. The sun baked the ground—and his head, through the canvas hat he wore. He sympathized with the wind.

Bob Hanover crouched at the end of the causeway, a path created in ancient times by the Egyptians. The causeway led to the ruined pyramid attributed to Sneferu, predecessor of the builder of the Great Pyramid, Khufu. Even if he accepted that Khufu and Sneferu had built the pyramids credited to them, he harbored reservations about the orthodox chronology. More than reservations. He lived in a suite at the Not-Bloody-Likely Hotel.

Flat desert stretched out on three sides. Behind him, past the end of the causeway, the Nile nourished trees and grass. Further ahead a stepped tower, all that remained of Sneferu's pyramid, projected from a pile of rubble. Before him loomed two stelae,

14-foot-tall slabs of stone with rounded tops, their bases buried in the sand. Most stelae boasted inscriptions commemorating a pharaoh or an event. These stelae were blank. Egyptologists had never puzzled out why.

Bob mopped a skin of sweat from his face. The temperature had warmed into the mid-eighties. In the sun, though, the air felt superheated.

"Show me the break," he said to the man beside him.

Halim stooped beside Bob. His robes billowed around his legs. A scarf swaddled his head and face to block the sand cast about by the wind. Halim, an Egyptian, stood six inches taller than Bob, his frame wiry rather than stocky like Bob's. When the sun struck his hazel eyes, the gray and gold undertones sparkled with a luster akin to the painted crystals the ancient Egyptians had used for eyes in many statues.

Halim indicated the back of the stela.

"That is where it broke," Halim said. "I was trying to clear its base when I slipped and the shovel broke the corner. I should have been more careful. I hope Lord Sneferu is not watching."

"Lord Sneferu is dead."

"His mummy has never been found." Halim grinned. "Perhaps he still lives, as in those American films, craving revenge."

"My countrymen also made films of that nature." Bob hopped around the back of the stela. "Poppycock is what they are."

"But quite entertaining."

"I prefer westerns."

A slab had broken off the bottom-left corner of the stela, where Halim had tried to clear the base. Bob explored the gash with his fingers. The surface had cracked, which created the illusion a layer of stone had separated from the stela. Bob withdrew a hammer and chisel from his tool belt. He chipped at the stone around the break. Chunks fell away, revealing more stone beneath. The separation was no illusion. Like a tablecloth, the blank surface covered a core block. The core had no inscriptions either.

He hacked at the rock. His face reddened. He puffed out a breath with each concussion. Picking up his hammer and chisel, Halim chopped at the front of the stela.

Two hours passed. The sunlight waned. Sweat oozed from Bob's pores.

Halim had stopped chipping. He whispered in Arabic.

Bob crawled around the stela. Halim squatted before the stela, touching its surface, eyes wide. He had cleared the front of the stela to reveal the core. Hieroglyphs packed its 14-foot height. Vertical lines organized the symbols into registers. The Eye of Horus gazed outward from the apex, the symbol as wide as the stela. Two goddesses—the sisters Isis and Nephthys—flanked the registers, each ten feet tall. They faced each other, hands raised. At the bottom, beneath the registers, a single line of hieroglyphs stretched across the stela horizontally, between the goddesses' feet. A line of star glyphs separated the final line from the main text.

Never in his 38 years of excavations had Bob seen such a contraption. One stela hollow, blank, covering a second, inscribed stela. Why conceal the text?

The ancient Egyptians had, several times, attempted to erase the past by destroying inscriptions. They erased names from king lists, hacked out the faces of figures in temple carvings, scratched out the cartouches on coffins. To erase the name meant to obliterate the person—forever.

But to hide a text…

Bob read the first register of hieroglyphs. "Dear God."

From inside his rucksack, he unearthed his digital camera. He photographed the entire stela before stepping closer to capture the lines of text. Katy Bergren would want to see this.

He must translate it. Get the results to Katy along with the digital images.

After he'd photographed the stela, he sat cross-legged in front of it with his computer on his lap. He translated the text as he typed.

Soon the sun relinquished Egypt to the night, and the stars took up their stations in the sky. Halim held a propane lantern above Bob's head.

The moon rose behind the pyramid's tower. Seated off-center from the stela, Bob could see the tower and the moon. His gut tightened. He couldn't explain the tension that prickled through him at the sight of the moon. Neither could he explain the thought that entered his mind at that moment.

Run.

One register remained to translate. He copied the text file and the digital images onto a disk. Glanced up at the pyramid. The light floated higher.

The disk drive ceased whirring. He popped out the disk. Looked at the light.

The hairs on his neck bristled.

Bob thrust the disk at Halim. "Take this to Tony Edwards. He'll know what to do."

"Yes, we should leave. Evil draws near."

"Oh don't be so melodramatic, Halim. I'll stay to finish the translation while you deliver the disk."

"I will not leave you."

The object swelled to twice the width of the tower's cap. The radiance that camouflaged its shape glittered. Static electricity prickled over Bob's skin.

"Take it now," Bob urged. "Please."

The Egyptian stared at him for a moment, hazel eyes narrowed, brow tightened by lines.

Halim grabbed the diskette. "I will come back, my friend, once I have delivered this."

He slid his knife from the sheath tied around his calf. He handed Bob the blade. Bob accepted it.

Halim darted past him toward the Nile and their boat moored at its banks.

Bob faced the pyramid. He knew what the light meant. He knew what they wanted. He knew they would get it.

The light pulsed. It ballooned until its brilliance dwarfed the pyramid, rubble pile and all.

Bob set his computer on the ground. He pushed onto his feet. Lord Sneferu had come to reclaim his property.

Perhaps not Lord Sneferu. Someone more powerful than any pharaoh.

The gods had come for him.

Anameka, Michigan

An owl hooted.

Katy rocked in the chair, her attention fixated on the computer screen. The clock in the lower right-hand corner of the screen read three minutes past ten.

Katy yawned. Three minutes past her bedtime.

Around one o'clock, she and Rick had driven into town to mail Victor Oberman the tooth she'd ripped out of Imsety's mouth. Radiocarbon dating would give them an idea of how long ago Pharaoh Imsety had reigned. The information had no bearing on their search for the truth about human origins. If the remains they'd found belonged to the same Imsety mentioned in the hominid caves, they'd discovered a Planner's grave.

Which also had no bearing on their search. Ugh.

Katy checked her email.

The inbox held one message from Warner, their financial backer, friend, and mercenary advisor. These days Warner sweated in the field, a bona fide member of the project, uncovering anomalous evidence while his underlings ran his conglomerate for him. The message he'd sent was encrypted. Katy insisted members of the project encrypt all communications. They used an off-the-shelf program for encryption and decryption. Although she would've preferred a program designed just for their group, she lacked the skills to write one. Maybe one day a hacker would join their group.

To date, their network boasted five members. That tally included herself, Rick, Warner, and Victor Oberman, the paleopathologist at Warner's museum in Chicago. Recruiting members had proved as difficult as teaching Garfield English.

She opened Warner's message. The first line said, "URGENT: must meet tonight 2330 hrs." The second line consisted of GPS coordinates.

Something about the message niggled her brain. For Warner to request a meeting at short notice, without giving a reason…

She examined the source code for the message. The "from" field listed Warner's email address. But the "received from" information didn't correspond. Someone else had sent the message, and forged Warner's email address. Who?

One way to find out.

Katy printed the message, shut off the computer. She retrieved the GPS unit from Rick's suitcase, which still sat by the sofa.

Rick slumped on a stool at the bar, studying his fingers as if fascinated by the cuticles. His right arm lay on the bar. He rested his left hand on his thigh, his fingers crooked, the tendons on the back of his hand taut. Katy padded across the living room to him.

She looped her arms around his neck. "Thinking about Charlie?"

"He's dead."

"The Planners said they wouldn't hurt him so long as we kept our mouths shut about the DNA evidence."

"They said he could visit twice a year too." He clenched his jaw. "That was a big, fat lie."

"He's okay. Trust me."

23

He arched an eyebrow at her. She kissed his forehead.

His expression went stony. She waved a hand in his face. He blinked, looked at her.

"Just reminiscing," he said. "About our first date. A year ago yesterday."

"A life-or-death trek into the woods hardly counts as a first date."

He smirked. "With you, it does."

She made a face. He slipped an arm around her waist.

Turning on the GPS unit, she punched in the coordinates sent by "Warner." The screen displayed the location—a beach near the Mackinac Bridge, about an hour north of Anameka.

Katy swiped Rick's keys from the bar. "Let's go for a little drive."

Fort Michilimackinac State Park
Mackinaw City

"This is the dumbest thing we have ever done."

Katy glanced at him sideways. "Really."

They clomped down the beach, past the walls of the reconstructed 18th-Century fort, now the centerpiece of a park. The Mackinac Bridge towered over the fort, whose visitor center snuggled under the approach.

The bridge stretched five miles across the Straits of Mackinac to connect the Upper Peninsula with the rest of Michigan, while the straits united Lakes Michigan and Huron. The main towers of the suspension bridge soared 552 feet above the water. Lights on the suspension cables sketched out the bridge's silhouette in the darkness.

Rick halted. "We have no idea who sent the email. It could be a trap."

"We'll find out soon enough."

She risked pressing the button that illuminated her watch's face. 11:20. Ten minutes to go.

Rick consulted the GPS unit. He led Katy to a spot 15 feet from a cannon, an artifact from the Revolutionary War.

Katy sat down cross-legged with the Taurus on the sand beside her. Rick crouched on the other side of her, one hand clamped around the .45.

A twig cracked.

Katy held her breath. She tipped her head toward the sound. Nothing. She swiveled her torso to study the shadows around the fort.

A phantom moved. She felt for the Taurus.

A deer bounded out of the shadows. The doe scampered around the fort into the trees.

Katy let out the breath she'd held. She sagged her shoulders.

Seconds grew into minutes. She checked her watch again. 11:29.

Traffic whirred across the bridge. A chill infected the breeze. Katy zipped up her jacket. 11:30.

A light glanced out the corner of her eye. She looked northeast, past the bridge.

A glowing orb rose behind the trees. It glided up over the treetops.

Katy hopped up. She nudged Rick. He jumped to his feet.

The light surged closer. It drifted toward the bridge, passing between the main towers. There, the craft stopped. It hovered 200 feet above the roadway.

Tires screeched. Horns blared.

The craft descended. Fifty feet above the roadway, it leveled off.

Crunch. Bang. Vehicles collided.

Katy's eyes burned. For the first time in over a minute, she blinked. Static electricity tingled over her body.

Her cell phone warbled. She ignored it.

The ringing stopped. A heartbeat later, the phone trilled again.

Katy dug the phone out of her pocket. She flipped it open.

She hissed into the phone, "Call back later."

"Do we have your attention?"

The voice was male, lilted by an exotic accent. The accent of a Planner.

Katy clutched the phone. "Who is this?"

Rick pulled Katy close, their heads together, and tilted the phone to listen into the conversation.

"We have something of yours," the voice said. "If you want him back, listen carefully."

On the bridge, an 18-wheeler veered around a collision. The truck skidded. Its trailer fishtailed, sideswiping an oncoming car, shoving the car sideways into the guardrail.

Katy shut her eyes. "I'm listening."

"We led you to the Osiris Imsety. Now you will lead us to what we seek."

"Which is?"

"Bring us the book."

Katy looked at the bridge.

Drivers clambered out of their cars. Shielding their eyes, they gaped up at the craft. A woman screamed. Inside a station wagon, children wailed.

"What book?" Katy asked.

"The Book of Thoth. Find it, or he dies."

Click. The caller had hung up.

Katy lowered the phone. She couldn't avert her gaze from the bridge. Her muscles refused to obey her commands. Beside her, Rick said nothing.

The craft whooshed straight up. The light shrank into a pinpoint and winked out.

People milled about on the bridge. They babbled, gestured at the sky, inspected damage to vehicles, aided the injured.

Katy and Rick trudged down the beach, away from the bridge.

Five minutes later, they climbed into their pickup, a Dodge Ram that had belonged to Charlie before the Planners took him. They'd parked along a side street, in the shadow of an elm tree that had yet to shed its leaves.

As Katy slammed her door, Rick jammed the gear shift lever into reverse. He gunned the engine. Katy pitched forward. Gravel sprayed up from the tires as the Ram zoomed backward. Rick twirled the steering wheel. The Ram spun left into the street.

"Slow down," Katy said.

Rick braked. She lurched back into the seat. Her head knocked against the headrest.

"Take it easy," she said.

"You know they'll kill us once we find this book they want."

"We have the DNA evidence. They don't want the world to know hairy hominids are real."

"Assuming anyone believes us. Assuming they haven't figured out your little computer program is a sham."

Last year, she'd concocted a computer program designed to send emails to every scientist in the world if she didn't enter the password every 24 hours. The email detailed their findings about the hairy hominids, as well as providing GPS coordinates to the hominid caves in Michigan.

Theoretically, the program worked. In practice, however, she had no clue if it would work. Even if she could find the email addresses for all the millions of scientists in the world, she couldn't guarantee a single one of them would believe the email.

Her bluff had worked because the Planners knew nothing about the technology of everyday people—non-Planners—whom they called the Low Ones.

The Planners had faked an email and contacted her via cell phone. While a year ago they'd known nothing about Low Ones' technology, they must've learned.

Who taught them? Charlie knew as much about computers as she knew about building space probes. Someone else must've taught them. Which left two questions.

Who had aided them? And why would a Low One conspire with the Planners? Whoever aided them must be a Low One, because only a Low One could teach them what they needed to know.

As for the show they'd put on over the bridge, it served as a reminder of their superiority. On the canvas of the night sky, they'd painted a masterpiece for her. In shades of fear and foreboding, they'd illustrated their power.

She'd seen the painting. She'd read the message hidden in its brush strokes.

"We can safely assume," she said, "the Planners have learned a thing or two lately."

"Great."

"We have to trust they won't do anything until we find the Book of Thoth."

Rick snorted. "You can't trust bastards in spaceships."

"We have no choice." She dug out the cell phone. "Better give Warner a heads-up."

She dialed Warner's mobile number. After five rings, the call forwarded to his voice mail. She disconnected. Next she dialed his home number, but got his answering machine. She tried the last number she had for him, his office in Chicago.

Sorry, Warner Industries is closed for the day. Please call back during normal business hours, 8 AM to 6 PM Central time, Monday through Friday.

Katy turned off the cell phone. Rick drove down the street, heading toward the freeway onramp.

"You're right," she said, "The Planners just called our bluff."

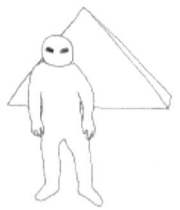

CHAPTER FOUR

Anameka
Friday, October 17

Rick ambled downstairs into the living room.

Katy had squished herself into the corner of the sofa, legs curled under her. She contemplated the sheet of paper that draped over the sofa's arm. Elbow propped on the arm, chin supported by her fist, she gnawed on her lip.

As he bypassed the sofa, Rick glimpsed the text on the page. The stela inscription.

Moseying into the kitchen, he said, "Morning."

"Mm," she said.

He opened the cupboard. No cereal. A container of oatmeal stood alone inside the cupboard. He picked up the container and popped off the lid. A handful of oats. Replacing the oatmeal, he checked the other cupboards and the fridge. He found peanut butter, rice, and frozen chicken. Yum.

Better go to the store.

Katy mumbled, "I'll stay here."

Rick turned around slowly. Katy, focused on the stela text, grazed her finger across the paper.

She glanced up at him. "Get milk."

Had he spoken without knowing it? Sure, he was tired but…no, he knew without a doubt he had not said a word since "morning."

He folded his arms over his chest. "What the heck are you talking about?"

"You said we better go to the store."

"I didn't say it. I *thought* it."

Her face flushed. She tried to smile, faltered, bit her fingernail. Clearing her throat, she squared her shoulders and met his gaze.

"I saw you looking for food," she said. "I figured you'd suggest we go to the store."

"Uh-huh."

Rick fidgeted. He scratched his neck. The itch he felt originated inside his chest, in that spot where intuition tickles your gut.

"I hate when you do that," he said.

"Do what?"

"Say what I'm thinking. It's unsettling." Hands on hips, he puckered his mouth. "Maybe you should see a doctor."

Grimacing, Katy rolled her shoulders back. She held up the printout of the stela inscription.

"What do you know about Thoth?" she asked.

"Katy."

"Wasn't he the god of writing?"

Rick sighed. He walked to the sofa and sat down beside her. "Thoth was the god of writing and wisdom."

Early on, the Egyptians had worshiped Thoth as a moon god. Throughout their history, they continued to associate him with the moon. Often he was shown as a man with the head of an ibis. He served as benefactor of scribes, as well as patron of science, medicine, and inventions. The myths credited him with inventing writing, which he bequeathed to the Egyptians. For that reason, they called their language the Words of the Gods.

He and Katy knew better. The Planners had given the hieroglyphic language to the Egyptians. The Low Ones of Egypt had adopted the culture, beliefs, and symbolism of the Planners. Whether the Planners knowingly conferred their language to the Egyptians, or the Egyptians simply picked it up from the hairy hominids, remained unclear.

As for Thoth, the myths described him as the keeper of the gods' archives, a capacity in which he both chronicled pharaonic history and recorded his knowledge in the Book of Thoth. In his role as judge, he supervised the coronations of pharaohs. To round out his duties, he recorded Osiris' judgments of the deceased.

Thoth was a busy guy.

"The inscription," Katy said, "claims Imsety protected the wisdom of Thoth. Could that mean the Book of Thoth? What if the book was buried with Imsety?"

"Then the Planners would have it already. They sent us to Washington, remember?"

"Which explains why they took Garfield there. They wanted him to tell us about it."

"So we'd find the stela."

"And decipher the inscription. They can speak the old language, but they have trouble with the nuances—the metaphors, what's written between the lines."

Rick nodded.

He'd read about the Book of Thoth somewhere. The memory refused to surface. He could've read it in a magazine, a book, on the Internet. Dang.

Katy set the printout on her thigh. Rick read through the translation. Katy believed the text referred to another planet, based on the star and sky hieroglyphs tagged onto the phrase "First House of Man."

Was she right? She had learned ancient Egyptian at light speed, yet deciphering a text as complicated and disjointed as the stela inscription required experience. Did Katy understand the nuances of the language well enough to determine the meaning of the star and sky symbols?

Did he?

Twenty years of study ought to give him the background and experience. Twenty years of intermittent, self-taught study. Any Egyptologist would laugh at him. Of course, they snickered at anyone who evinced an interest in alternative theories about ancient history. Why did he care what they thought?

Screw them.

The star and sky symbols seemed to act as determinatives, hieroglyphs used to emphasize the meaning of a word, to distinguish between the multiple meanings a single word could represent. To know for certain, though, he had to rely on intuition.

He trusted Katy's intuition above his own, because he'd learned her intuition outshined his by a million candlepower. Sometimes the accuracy of her instincts disturbed him.

She knew what he thought.

He pushed up off the sofa. Time to go to the store.

Katy shot a sidelong glance at Rick. The store. She didn't want to go anywhere until she'd figured out what the stela inscription meant. They had to find the Book of Thoth.

She traipsed to the desk and parked herself in the chair. Cupping her hand over the cordless mouse, she skated it around the desktop. A red light flashed inside the mouse, tracking its motions in lieu of a ball. The mouse pointer flitted around the screen.

She felt Rick behind her before his shadow descended over her. She knew what he wanted too.

"I'm staying here," she said.

He whirled her chair around, slapped a hand on either side of her head. She raised her eyebrows. He pushed down on the headrest until the chair thumped into the desk. Her feet lifted off the floor. He slanted forward, his nose a millimeter from hers.

He locked his gaze on hers. "I am not leaving you alone."

"I'll be fine."

"Right, and I'll come home to find you unconscious on the sofa. Or worse."

She stared at him. He stared at her. His blue eyes twinkled like faceted sapphires, the color as luminous as gems. Strands of gold shimmered in his chocolate-colored hair.

"You're coming with me," he said. "Like it or not."

"You have to let me out of this chair first."

"I don't know, I think I like this. You can't take off on me."

He smirked. She knew no one else who could make a smirk endearing.

"Okay," she said. "I surrender."

She hooked her arms around his neck. He slid his arms around her waist and scooped her out of the chair onto her feet. Her foot brushed against a hard lump attached to his ankle. Bending down, she pulled up his jeans leg. A holster strapped the .45 to his ankle.

"Highly illegal," she said.

"Highly necessary." He strode toward the bar, where he grabbed his keys. "Long as my wife insists on sticking her head in the lion's mouth."

"How else can I count his teeth?"

"You could at least pretend to be cautious."

Katy pulled on her boots, tying the laces with a double knot.

"Tell you what," she said, "I'll promise not to leave your sight. Ever. You're stuck with me twenty-four hours a day until I die. How's that?"

"Better."

Rick marched out the door. She marched after him.

As she climbed into the Ram, motion flashed out the corner of her eye. A flourish of dark hair. She glanced at the porch of the half people's bungalow. No one there.

She shut the door. She couldn't shut out the feeling.

Someone was watching.

An hour later, she leaned against the Ram's bed while Rick tucked their grocery bags behind the seat. She observed the other cars in the parking lot. A Hummer parked in front of the store's entrance, blocking both lanes. In the next aisle over, a black Buick sedan detoured around an elderly woman. Aligned with Katy, the sedan paused. A dark-haired woman, cloaked in shadows, regarded Katy from behind the steering wheel of the Buick.

A shiver skittered up Katy's spine.

The woman looked away. The Buick rolled down the aisle, out of the parking lot.

Katy ducked inside the Ram, buckled her seatbelt, chewed the inside of her lip.

Without a word, Rick got in and pulled the door shut. He started the engine.

Katy glanced over her shoulder. No sedan.

Rick backed out of the parking space. Exited the lot.

Katy peeked in the side mirror. No Buick behind them.

As they drove home, Katy checked the mirror twice more. Silly. The woman's gaze meant nothing. Strangers often looked at each other, even smiled or nodded. Gee, sometimes complete strangers said hello to her without provocation or reason. It was called common courtesy.

She'd inflated a simple glance into a sinister act. *Jeez, Katy, get a grip.*

So the Planners wanted to kill her. Didn't mean everyone in the world was out to get her.

Rick turned into their driveway, steering the Ram around the circular drive to park in front of the woodshed. Katy gazed across the four-acre field at the woods.

"Who the hell is that?" Rick asked.

"What?"

As he nodded at the porch, Katy swiveled her head toward the house. A man of about 40 slouched on the top step, arms on his thighs, hands dangling over his knees. He wore khaki pants, a denim shirt with the long sleeves rolled up, and hiking boots whose leather had cracked and scuffed. His head was bowed, the brim of his canvas hat masking his face. A rucksack slumped on the step beside him.

Rick jumped out of the Ram. While Katy climbed out, he strode toward the stranger on the steps.

The man rose, brushing dirt from his wrinkled pants, and removed his hat.

"Hello," he said, his accent British. "Sorry to barge in like this."

"Tony Edwards," Rick said. "What are you doing here?"

"I've come on behalf of Bob Hanover."

Tony proffered a callused hand. Rick eyed the man's hand.

"I know I was rather rude," Tony said, "last time we met. I'm sorry."

Rick huffed. "You accused us of corrupting an old fool with delusions of self-importance."

"Called us crackpots too," Katy interjected.

Tony ducked his head, fingered his hat's brim. His expression darkened as he looked up at them.

"I'm sorry," he said. "Last night I saw something that...suggested I may have been mistaken."

Tony extended his hand again. Rick refused to shake it.

Bob Hanover had first contacted them six months earlier after seeing the website for the Human Origins Project. He evinced doubts about the orthodox version of history, and a willingness to search for the truth, no matter what the cost to his reputation. After all, he'd said, his reputation had gone in the dumper five years ago, after he presented a lecture about the fallacy of attributing the Meidum pyramid to Sneferu.

When Bob joined the project, he'd asked her and Rick to invite Tony into the group as well. He had been amenable to the notion—until they mentioned UFOs and hairy hominids.

Rick had once denigrated the project, and ridiculed Katy for believing in the quest. She hadn't given up on him. Tony deserved a second chance too.

Tony started to retract his hand.

Katy grasped it. "Apology accepted."

Rick glanced at her. Lips screwed up. Head tipped to the side.

She rolled her eyes in Tony's direction.

Sighing—loudly—Rick shook the man's hand.

Tony surveyed the front acreage, the gravel road, the Thompson bungalow across the field. He gripped his hat so firmly the brim warped.

"Could we talk inside?" he asked.

Rick led the way into the house. As Katy trailed the two men, she glanced back at the Thompson bungalow. Steam curled up from the furnace vent. The hairs on her neck stiffened. Summer houses were heated all winter. The steam meant nothing.

On the bungalow's porch, the shadows shifted.

The hairs on her neck electrified. She tensed.

A squirrel scampered off the porch to a nearby tree.

"Katy?"

In the porch, Rick waited for her. He held the inner door ajar.

She walked toward him. When she moved to bypass him, he grasped her arm.

"You sure we can trust this guy?" he asked.

"You used to be like him."

"I wasn't as obnoxious as Tony."

She raised an eyebrow.

"Was I?"

"Of course not." She kissed his cheek. "Your condescending remarks were endearing."

"Thanks. I think."

She glanced through the doorway at Tony, who loitered by the wood stove.

"Bob trusts him," she said. "That's good enough for me."

They crossed the threshold into the living room. Rick closed the door. He motioned Tony onto the sofa, and seated himself at the bar.

Katy locked the door. Tested the knob. The lock held. The tingling she'd felt outside had faded, yet the tension in her muscles lingered. She felt...observed. Although she'd never believed in a sixth sense, she could no longer dismiss all the twinges as paranoia. Maybe you could sense danger approaching, feel another's gaze tracking you, know when your world had tilted out of alignment. Just *know*.

Ridiculous.

She boosted herself onto the stool beside Rick's.

Pinning her gaze on Tony, she asked, "Why are you here?"

He flopped his hat down on the table. "Doctor Hanover has gone missing."

"You need the police."

"They can't help." Tony leaned forward, drumming his fingers on the table. "After our disagreement six months ago, Bob and I parted ways. I signed up with a dig at Dahshur, and I haven't spoken to Bob since. But last night his assistant, Halim, showed up at my flat in quite a state."

Tony dug through his rucksack, pulling out a CD-ROM in a slim plastic case. He set the disk on the table next to his hat.

"Halim gave me this disk," Tony said. "Bob told him I'd know what to do with it. After I looked at its contents, I knew I had to bring it to you. "

Katy studied his face. If he was lying, he had a real talent for it.

"Recently," Tony continued, "Bob and Halim had begun studying a pair of blank stelae near Sneferu's pyramid. Digging down to their bases, hoping to uncover a secret chamber or God knows what."

"Did Halim say what happened to Bob?" Rick asked.

Tony hesitated. "He ranted about lights in the sky and Lord Sneferu coming down to reclaim his land. I didn't know what to make of it, so I had him take me to Meidum. I thought perhaps there had been an accident."

"You didn't find Bob," Katy said.

"No." Tony raked a hand through his red hair. "And the inscribed stela had…vanished."

"Somebody took it?"

"Those stelae were over three meters tall—nearly fourteen feet. How could anybody steal one?"

How indeed. Katy glanced at Rick, though he kept his gaze zeroed in on Tony.

The Planners had abducted Bob. Halim and Tony they allowed to escape. The Planners played a gigantic game of chess, with Low Ones as the pieces, the Earth as their board, and rules they kept secret from their opponents. From her and Rick.

"How was the trip from Egypt?" Katy asked.

Tony twisted his mouth in a sour smile. "You're wondering how I escaped from Egypt unharmed. Can't say, really. I suppose whoever took the stelae and took Bob must not know about the disk."

Oh, they knew all right. The Planners wanted her and Rick to have the disk, and whatever information it contained. Otherwise, Tony Edwards would've suffered a tragic accident on his journey to America.

"What's on the disk?" Katy inquired.

"Photos of an inscription found on one of the stelae, plus Bob's partial translation of it."

"You said the stelae were blank."

"The blank face hid an inscription."

Katy hopped off the stool. She moseyed to the table, picked up the CD, tapped it against her palm. The disk had no label.

To Tony, she said, "You mentioned something happened that made you change your opinion of us."

"On the flight over, I saw a strange light shadowing the plane. It wasn't the moon."

"No, it wouldn't be."

"I've never believed in UFOs, but…I don't know."

Katy took the disk to the computer. She inserted it into the CD drive.

The computer loaded the files from Tony's disk. Katy opened the first file from the disk, a compressed image. A stela filled the image from top to bottom, though photographing its whole 14-foot height had forced Bob to stand back so far that the inscription became unreadable. The Eye of Horus dominated the stela's pinnacle. Along either edge, Isis and Nephthys guarded the stela. The next image showed the stela's top third, while subsequent photos revealed the middle and bottom thirds. The last file, a text document, contained Bob's translation. Katy returned to the third image. She zoomed in on the inscription.

Locating the spot where Bob stopped, she typed the remainder of the translation into the text file.

The inscription talked about a queen named Nitiqret, whose "ancestors lived in the first house of man." Nitiqret had erected the stela as a memorial to those who died in an unspecified disaster at someplace called Bakhu. The main portion of the text echoed the Washington stela.

The second house of man was born here, it stated, *in the time before the Spirits of the Dead arose, a thousand million years before the First Time. The great god Thoth, lord of Bakhu, recorded the tale of our birth in the book of his wisdom. The Sons of Horus protect his wisdom, a secret sealed with the blood of Bakhu.*

She knew from the inscription they'd discovered in the hairy hominid caves that, for as long as the Planners could recall, two types of humans had shared the globe. The Planners possessed the advanced technology, while the Low Ones lived as primitives. The next section seemed to explain how the human race had segmented.

After many years, the Second House of Man had spread across the earth. Some became separated from their brethren. Alone, without purpose, they regressed into a state like that of animals. The Spirits of the Dead then went forth to tame these Low Ones and, thus, they came to the Land of the Hoe, where they flourished. This age was named the First Time.

The secrets of the First Time, and all ages before, live on in the wisdom of Thoth, hidden forever like the face of Amen-Ra. Those who protect Thoth's wisdom must die without their names.

Old Imsety must've protected Thoth's wisdom. Hence, he died "without his name," interred in a nameless grave marked by a stela commemorating that which he defended. The story of humanity.

The Book of Thoth.

The balance of the inscription listed the names and titles of 148 people, including two priests named Akhmose and Isesi, who died on the same day in Bakhu: the third month of Harvest, day 20, Year 1 of Nitiqret. The text declared the "wrath of the Condemned One" had claimed their lives. Perhaps they had provided the "blood of Bakhu" that protected Thoth's secrets.

"Well?" Rick asked.

She read the translation aloud.

Tony paced the living room, between the front and back doors. Rick made faces at the floorboards.

Katy printed out the translation. She saved one copy onto a CD and another onto the web server. She also emailed copies to Warner and Victor Oberman.

Nitiqret, like Imsety, descended from a family "whose ancestors lived in the first house of man." Did that make them Planners? Aliens? Something else?

The inscription referred to Bakhu twice. Thoth had served as "lord," or god, of Bakhu. Therefore, Bakhu must be a town or settlement. If the "blood of Bakhu" had guaranteed the secrecy of Thoth's wisdom, logic suggested they would find the Book of Thoth there. At least it gave them a place to start.

But where was Bakhu?

The computer chimed. New mail. She switched to her email program.

The message to Warner had bounced back as undeliverable.

"Nitiqret," Rick said. "I think she ruled at the end of the Old Kingdom, right before the First Intermediate Period. Sneferu's pyramid was there before the stela." He tapped his toes on the floor like a drum roll. "The Spirits of the Dead were the gods who ruled on Earth

34

long before ancient Egypt existed. Osiris was one of them, he ruled as the first pharaoh. They could've been Planners."

"What about Bakhu?"

"Legend says it was a mountain range on the western horizon, the doorway to the kingdom of the dead."

Tony yelped. At the window, beside Katy's desk, he dropped into a crouch. Peeked over the windowsill.

"What the hell is that?" he asked.

Katy looked outside. Garfield knelt on the hill, peering down at the cabin.

The creature turned and lumbered uphill, out of sight.

Tony stared after Garfield, his eyes widened to the verge of popping out.

"That," Katy said, "was a hairy hominid. "

"They're—they're real?"

Katy shrugged. "Welcome to the asylum."

Cairo, Egypt

Bob reclined on the bed, hands interlocked over his belly. The flat pillow, although swaddled in a new case that matched the new sheets, stank of body soil. He peeked under the pillowcase. Yellow and brown splotches stained the pillow.

He locked his hands behind his head. The bed frame creaked. The stench of mildew mixed with urine wafted up from the mattress. He breathed through his mouth.

The blanket beneath him was soft acrylic. Rugs decorated the walls, their hieroglyphic patterns woven in shades of red, blue, and gray. His captors had turned the 10 by 12 cell into a duplicate of his own flat in Cairo.

An hour ago he'd woken from the slumber induced by whatever drug his captors had given him. Next time they offered him a glass of water, he'd decline. Once the haze cleared from his mind, he'd gone to the window to peek out between the slats of the shutters. He was in Cairo. He'd spotted the peaks of the Giza pyramids in the distance, at the periphery of Cairo's suburbs.

Sunset had crested and ebbed as night broke over the city. He lounged on the bed because he'd given up escaping. The shutters were nailed to the outside wall. On the inside, metal bars blocked the window. The door was locked, the hinges on the outside. Since few doors opened outward, he assumed his captors had switched the door to prevent what he'd hoped to do. Pop out the hinges, pull the door down, and escape.

Had Halim made it to Cairo? Had he given Tony the disk?

If so, Katy and Rick must have the disk by now. Unless his captors had intervened.

The heat pressed down around him. He'd unbuttoned his shirt earlier. He shrugged it off and tossed it onto the foot of the bed. He glanced at his torso, pale and soft like a Christmas goose before baking. Sweat dribbled down his balding head, soaking the fringe of hair that endured. He wiped a hand across his forehead. No one would mistake him for Cary Grant.

The door hinges squeaked. He struggled into a sitting position.

An Italian-looking fellow entered the room. When the man shut the door behind himself, the guard outside chunked the lock into place. The man hobbled into the center of the room. Rather than favoring one leg, he shuffled along as if he'd injured both feet. His heels dragged a bit.

The man's black hair, trimmed short, matched dark-chocolate eyes. Sunlight, strained through the shutters, brought out sallow undertones in his complexion. The chap wore charcoal slacks, a long-sleeved white shirt, and black loafers. Yet he didn't sweat.

Perspiration stung Bob's eyes. He rubbed them.

"Rise," the man commanded.

"I prefer to die lying down."

"You are not scheduled to die—yet."

An accent colored his speech. The inflection sounded not quite Italian, not quite Indian, not quite Israeli. In fact, his accent resembled every accent Bob had ever heard. But not quite.

"Clothe yourself," the man said. "We have much to do."

"I'm on sabbatical."

The man sauntered to the bed. With one finger, he plucked up Bob's shirt and held it out to him. Bob took the garment.

The man wiped his finger on his slacks. "The stelae will lead me to what I seek."

"I won't translate one syllable for you."

"You do not need to. The Bergrens will find the Book for me."

Bob slipped on his shirt. As he buttoned it, he asked, "Then what am I doing here?"

"You are my...backup plan."

Hands frozen in mid button, Bob stared at the man.

"Is that not the phrase?" the man asked.

"Yes," Bob said, fastening the last button. "That is the phrase. I don't understand what you mean by it, that's all."

"You will confirm the Bergrens are truthful with me. And if they fail to find the Book, or die in the effort, you will find it for me."

"If I refuse?"

The man smiled.

A chill frosted Bob's spine. The man imbued a simple smile with the venom of an asp.

Bob unbent his back, lifted his chin, aligned his shoulders. He got to his feet. Sweat trickled down his spine.

The man ushered Bob toward the door. He knocked twice.

"Who are you?" Bob asked.

"You may call me Intef."

The lock chunked. The door swung outward. The guard stood straight as a granite colonnade in the hallway. Intef motioned for Bob to exit first.

Bob stepped into the hallway. The guard headed down the corridor toward a stairwell. Bob followed, with Intef close behind him.

Thirty-eight years of excavation, study, and sweat. Sacked from his professorship at Cambridge, banished from academia altogether. Five years in exile, struggling to find sponsors willing to fund an independent Egyptologist with a proclivity for the alternative. Now what had he become?

A backup plan for spacemen.

They weren't spacemen. Katy had chastised him for using the term. They seemed to shy away from space travel, for some reason, preferring the cold and dark of the oceanic abyss.

Yet what did Intef need with a backup plan, when he had Katy and Rick to labor for him? They had the minds for riddles. They understood the Planners. He had come to the project recently. Before yesterday, he'd never seen a UFO, or met one's commander. His doubts about the accepted chronology of civilization stemmed from intellectual analysis, not personal experience. Until the moment he and Halim had cleared the stela at Meidum, revealing its hidden core, he had never touched the truth.

Bob halted.

Intef stopped beside him, that serpentine gaze searching his.

Bob looked straight into the cobra's eyes. "What do you really need me for?"

"I explained."

"I don't believe you. If you think I can find the book, why bother with the Bergrens?"

"To make them do my will pleases me."

He glanced down at his feet. When he looked up at Bob, a sneer twisted his whole face. "Most of all," he growled, "I wish them to suffer."

Intef slapped a hand on Bob's back, propelling him down the hallway. So, he was a contingency scheme for the Planners.

At least they could've made him Plan A.

Anameka, Michigan

Tony Edwards paused at the bottom of the steps. The midday sun bathed his tanned face in gold. He squashed his hat onto his head, looping the strap of his rucksack over his shoulder.

A taxi waited in the driveway.

Rick and Katy watched him from inside the porch doorway.

"Sure you'll be okay?" Rick asked.

"Positive," Tony answered. "I've got a friend in Toronto. I'll hide out there for awhile."

Katy suppressed the urge to ask for his help in finding the Book of Thoth. They had just pummeled him with the facts about hairy hominids, the Planners, and the Precambrian origins of humanity. To expect him to relinquish his death grip on the orthodox so soon, and plummet into the cold depths of reality without a wetsuit, seemed harsh. Rick had clung to the mainstream his entire life, until he met the forbidden truth face to face—in the form of hairy hominids.

She could recall the last time she'd believed what they taught in school—that humans evolved from apelike creatures about 200,000 years ago, that civilization began no more than

5000 years ago, that ice-age humans possessed nothing more advanced than spears—but the memory dimmed more each day. By the time she graduated from college, the orthodox had lost its stranglehold on her psyche as she developed a voracious appetite for information. The more she read, the less she believed what "the experts" told her. When she'd met Charlie, he not only encouraged her interest in the past, he gave her a mission in life.

Reveal the forgotten history of mankind. Whatever the cost.

The cost had become too high. But she no longer had a choice. The Planners had stolen all her options.

Tony ducked into the taxi. The driver maneuvered around the circular drive, down to the road, and swung right toward town.

The latter half of the day lay before them. Time enough to find the Book of Thoth?

Rick kissed the top of her head. "We'll find the Book, don't worry."

"You just did it."

"Did what?"

"Said what I was thinking. The freaky thing you hate for me to do."

He backed up and shut the door. "No I didn't."

The phone rang. Katy trotted through the inner door into the kitchen. She grabbed the receiver, muttering hello.

A gravely voice asked, "Is this the Institute for Far-Out Studies?"

"No, this is the Lunatic Fringe Society."

Dr. Victor Oberman chuckled. "My mistake. I have news about Deena."

"You know better than to gossip about your girlfriend over the phone."

"She mailed you a present."

Per her instructions, Victor spoke in code when forced to discuss project-related matters over the phone. Deena meant DNA. They'd told Victor to perform radiocarbon dating on the tooth, not DNA analysis.

"I didn't want a present from her," Katy said. "I need time, not gifts."

"That's the beauty of it. Deena sent you a clock."

Katy groaned. She glanced at her computer. "Victor, have you heard from Warner lately? He's not answering at any of his numbers and his email bounces back."

"Haven't seen him in a few days. The corporate server got hacked yesterday, email's shut down. Times like this, I wish the museum's website weren't hitched onto the Warner Industries wagon."

"If you see Warner, tell him to call us."

"Will do."

Click. The dial tone buzzed in her ear.

Hanging up the phone, Katy dragged herself to the computer. She retrieved her email. One message, from Victor. She decrypted the email. Deena's clock displayed on the screen. The calibrated radiocarbon test dated the tooth to between 10,350 BC and 11,000 BC. The DNA, in Victor's words, was "human, human, human…how boring."

Imsety was over 12,000 years old. He'd died over 7,000 years before the dawn of Egyptian civilization. If you bought the mainstream story.

The date for his death coincided with the date they'd obtained from textual evidence in the hairy hominid caves, from the inscription King Imsety had ordered his royal scribe to create. The first line dated the text to a period when the constellation Orion aligned with the Giza plateau, which last happened around 10,500 BC. The Imsety buried in Washington must be the same one who ruled as pharaoh.

She relayed Victor's findings to Rick.

"Sounds like the answers are in Egypt," he said.

"That narrows it down."

Katy sank into the desk chair. She opened Bob's photos of the stela. Zooming in, zooming out. Squinting. Frowning. Crooking her neck.

I missed something. She enlarged the image until it separated into pixels. Helped a lot. She zoomed out a little. Where was it?

Where was what?

Rick strolled up behind her. He rested an arm on the chair behind her head and bent over her to look at the screen.

"How can you stare at blurry squares?" he asked.

"It grows on you."

Zoom in, zoom out. She increased the contrast on the photo. Zoom in. Her eyes burned. She squeezed them shut.

"You're turning cross-eyed," Rick said.

She panned down to the bottom of the image.

There it was. Duh.

A row of stars isolated the last line, which stretched horizontally across the stela rather than vertically, like the rest.

Rick slanted over her. Fixated on the screen, he moved his lips as if reading to himself.

He straightened, rubbing his eyes. "I don't get it."

Katy read the line aloud. "Five rivers, seventy-four rods, ten cubits, three fingers. Horus flies toward the Marsh."

"Measures of distance. Except for the part about Horus."

"Distance? Can you convert it into feet, miles, whatever?"

"Need a book from the basement first."

He trotted downstairs.

Katy printed out the translation.

At the bottom of the stairs, Rick angled right toward the storage room. Inside the room, he switched on the light—a 75-watt bulb, sans fixture. Plastic storage bins, stacked in columns three or four high, crammed into the back corner. He pulled down a bin on which Katy had scrawled the words "Rick's books" on a piece of masking tape.

On his knees before the bin, he flipped up the lid. Rooting through the books heaped inside, he kicked up a musty odor that enveloped him. He sneezed. The ceiling creaked. Katy was walking around upstairs.

In a minute he'd unearthed the book he needed, a survey of the hieroglyphic language. The book included a chapter on numbers that explained measures of distance. The ancient Egyptians had used as their standard measure the cubit. Rivers, rods, palms, and fingers all derived from that base. One cubit equaled 20 and some odd inches. His recollection ended there.

He thumbed through the book. A drawing flashed past, a man with an ibis head.

Wait. He flipped back to the page. Thoth. The drawing depicted the god, but the text mentioned him only in passing, within an inventory of ancient Egyptian deities. Before, when he'd heard the phrase Book of Thoth, he'd felt certain he had read about the Book somewhere.

He set aside the hieroglyphs book.

As he skimmed through five books, he checked the indexes for references to Thoth but found nothing of note. He sat back on his heels. It had to be here.

Three books later, he found it. The index listed a subentry under Thoth: "Book of, 184." He fanned through the pages until he found 184.

The heading read, "The Book of Thoth & The Legend of Setna."

The Book of Thoth, the text said, was rumored to hold the knowledge of the gods, magical spells that endowed the reader with immense power. Egyptologists believed the Book expounded information on the sciences, including astronomy and medicine, as well as religion, philosophy, and astrology. No one had found more than fragments of the Book, reproduced elsewhere.

The section recapped a legend first told hundreds of years after the reign of Ramses II, about a scribe called Setna, Son of Ramses. Egyptologists assumed the title meant Ramses II, and that it implied a blood relationship rather than a symbolic one. Setna, a brilliant scribe, could read the old texts that no one else understood, as well as perform great magic gleaned from those texts. Despite his wealth and status, he thirsted for more.

In an old scroll he read about the power of the Book of Thoth. The scroll talked about a scribe named Nefrekeptah—the son of an earlier pharaoh, Amenhotep II—who had discovered the Book of Thoth buried in the Nile. Nefrekeptah had exploited the Book's secrets to make himself the greatest magician in the land, more powerful than the gods themselves.

When Setna read the story, he knew he had to have the Book for himself.

Since Amenhotep had buried the Book with Nefrekeptah, Setna traveled to the Memphis necropolis—the city of the dead—where the great magician had been interred. He broke into the tomb. Crawling through rubble and muck deposited by centuries of floods, he broke into the burial chamber. At last he would have the Book!

But the tomb's guardians had other ideas. The spirits of Nefrekeptah's wife and son, imprisoned in their *ka* statues, spoke to Setna. Nefrekeptah's wife told how her husband had become the greatest magician in the land, with the Book's help, but that his misuse of Thoth's wisdom had cursed him to suffer for eternity. Nefrekeptah had watched his wife and son drown themselves in the Nile, coerced into suicide by an irresistible force. Bereft,

Nefrekeptah buried his wife and son at Koptos, where he had discovered the Book, and sailed for home.

He arrived dead, the Book clutched to his chest. Amenhotep buried Nefrekeptah at Memphis, far from his wife and son.

Undaunted by the story, Setna had outwitted the spirits via his magic and escaped with the Book.

Soon visions of his terrible fate plagued Setna. He saw himself meeting a beautiful woman, divorcing his wife and murdering his own children to please her, only to discover she was nothing more than a rotted corpse. He couldn't ignore the truth. He had to return the Book to Nefrekeptah's tomb before his visions came true.

On hands and knees he entered the tomb. The spirit of Nefrekeptah spoke to him, agreeing that he would be forgiven if he completed one task. He must find the bodies of Nefrekeptah's wife and son, bring them to Memphis, and bury them with Nefrekeptah. When Setna had obeyed, the gods absolved him.

But Setna knew he had to protect the Book's power. With the Book inside the tomb, he sealed the crypt's door with a magical incantation. With another spell he conjured a sandstorm that buried the tomb.

Within the tomb's walls, the Book of Thoth waits for the Day of Awakening, when Osiris will return from the underworld to reclaim his throne.

During the later New Kingdom, the Egyptians had regarded Setna as the greatest magician and scribe, a hero for the ages, revering him almost as a god. Because of their reverence, as well as the fantastic quality of stories about him, Egyptologists dismissed the story of Setna and the Book of Thoth as myth.

Modern people had trouble seeing ancient legends as anything but fantasy. But most myths had their roots in truth. Setna probably hadn't chatted with the spirits of Nefrekeptah, his wife, or his son. He could've found the Book, though. He could've hidden it because its knowledge was forbidden.

"What are you doing?" Katy shouted down the stairs.

"Coming," he hollered.

Rick closed the book. His finger marked the pages about the Book of Thoth.

He ran upstairs.

Rick plunked a book on the desk in front of her. The book fell open to the page his finger marked. The Book of Thoth and the Legend of Setna.

"Read this," he said, "while I convert those numbers."

Katy handed him the printout of the translation.

He grabbed a calculator and pen from the desktop. Taking the printout, he started scribbling numbers on the sheet.

While he computed the distance represented by rivers and fingers, Katy yanked open a drawer. She burrowed through a heap of papers until she located one folded several times. She opened out the sheet, a map of Egypt three feet tall, half as wide. Flattening the sheet on her desk, she slid her finger down the map until she found Meidum, on the Nile's western edge south of Cairo.

Hunched over the desk, Rick punched calculator keys.

Katy read the legend of Setna.

Rick slid the printout toward her. "Done. It's thirty-five miles, give or take a few fingers."

"The text says Horus flies toward the Marsh. "

"The Marsh means the Nile delta."

"So Horus flies north thirty-five miles. "

"From where? We need a starting point."

She closed the close-up photo of the stela's bottom. Another image came into view. The photo of the entire stela, with the ruined pyramid behind it.

Katy tapped the screen. "There's our starting point. Meidum."

The map had a scale of 25 miles per inch. Katy extricated a ruler from the drawer, then nabbed a pen from a mug on the desktop. She placed the ruler's end at Meidum, aligning it due north, and drew a line 1⅖ inches long, from Meidum to…

"Saqqara," she said.

Rick laid his finger on Saqqara. "The legend of Setna says the Book is buried in the Memphis necropolis, which just happens to include Saqqara."

"We have our destination."

"The measurements go down to inches. They must lead right to the tomb." He folded the printout, stuffed it in his hip pocket. "We go to Meidum first."

"But the Planners took the stela."

"The other one's there. It'll have to do."

Katy's email chimed. One message, unencrypted, stamped with Warner's forged address. The message contained one line.

TURN ON THE TV.

She sprinted to the coffee table, snatching up the remote. She switched on the TV.

A live feed focused on a female reporter. Behind her, lights from police cars, fire engines, and ambulances strobed. A banner across the bottom of the screen announced, "SPECIAL REPORT: Plane Crash in Chicago."

"—private jet has crashed outside Chicago," the reporter intoned. "The Warner Industries jet plummeted from the sky forty-five minutes ago. Authorities won't speculate on the cause of the crash."

Katy dropped the remote.

The reporter assumed her somber face. "All four people on board were killed."

Every muscle in Katy's body petrified. She heard the blood rushing through her body, yet she felt cold as a fossil buried under a glacier.

The camera panned over the wreckage. Gnarled lumps of metal scattered across a field. A hunk of fuselage here, a scrap of tail there. Flames billowed smoke.

A hand squeezed her shoulder. She jumped.

Rick released her shoulder and picked up the remote.

The camera pivoted left. Two paramedics carried a body bag to an ambulance.

Rick shut off the TV.

The computer dinged. Katy stumbled toward it. A lone message awaited her perusal, received from the same phantom address. Her heart skipped.

She opened the message. The words glared back at her.

FIND THE BOOK.

Saturday, October 18

Rick woke with a twitch. He glimpsed the alarm clock: 6:30. Katy's side of the bed lay empty. The blanket was pushed over, lumped behind his back. The rumpled sheet and pillow preserved her outline.

Her voice carried up the stairs from the living room.

Pulling on jeans and a flannel shirt, Rick jogged downstairs. At the bar, phone to her ear, Katy murmured agreement to the party at the other end of the conversation.

"A-S-A-P," she said, and hung up.

In the kitchen, Rick poured a glass of orange juice for himself and another for Katy. He slid the glass across the counter toward her.

"Grab a granola bar," she said, "we leave in fifteen minutes."

"I hate granola."

"Eat a banana instead."

"What's the rush?"

She sipped orange juice. "The Planners killed Warner. It's a message."

"Meaning..."

She downed half the orange juice. "Get your butts in gear."

Pressure. Great, he needed more of that.

Why did the Planners need him and Katy to find their own damn book anyhow?

He knew the answer already. Sure, the Planners descended from the forefathers of ancient Egypt. But that didn't mean they knew all the ancient secrets. Whatever the Book of Thoth contained, whatever had happened in Bakhu, the Planners knew as much as—or possibly less than—he and Katy did.

They dug up Imsety in the hope that the Book was buried with him. Wrong. His job as protector of the Book apparently ended at death.

Rick gulped his orange juice. He slammed the glass down.

The Planners killed four people, three of whom knew nothing about the Planners or their damn book. Four people dead, as a message.

No. A threat.

Rick looked around the cabin. Though he saw nothing unusual, he had the strangest feeling someone had overheard their conversation. Jesus, he was getting paranoid.

Of course, they had fallen victim to eavesdropping before. Warner had spied on them last year, when he thought he had to threaten them to gain their cooperation in keeping secret the hairy hominids' existence. Back then, he'd protected the secret to keep his logging and mining empire intact. If the hairy hominids became public knowledge, a scientifically-accepted species, they would also become an endangered species. Bye-bye forests, hello Bigfoot sanctuary.

Warner had spied on them from inside the vacant house across the—

The Thompsons had left two weeks ago. Rick knew, because Mrs. Thompson had called last week to ask if he and Katy could pick up the newspapers, since they'd forgotten to cancel the service before leaving for the winter.

Garfield said he'd seen the half people. Garfield wouldn't know the Thompsons from the Jetsons. He saw people. At the vacant bungalow.

He strode to the front windows. The bungalow across the field sat dark, the shades drawn, the driveway empty. The knot in his gut cinched tight.

He glanced at the bar, where the .45 lay in its holster. A rifle case leaned against the wall beside the back door.

Dad's Remington .30-06. He cleared his throat, stared out at the bungalow.

Screw the spies, whoever they were. He faced the living room.

Katy hopped off her stool. She gestured at the suitcases still stowed by the sofa.

"Least we're still packed," she said.

He crooked a finger at her.

She sashayed to him, hooking her arms around his waist. She hugged him, kissed his cheek, and pulled away from him.

He pulled her back. She scrunched her face. He leaned down to whisper in her ear.

"We've got bugs," he said.

She met his gaze. Without a word, he knew she understood.

"I'm going for a walk," she announced. "Get the blood flowing before we take off."

Clasping his hand, she dragged him toward the back door. As they passed the bar, he tore the .45 from its holster. At the door, Katy released his hand. She retrieved her Taurus from a desk drawer, along with two speed loaders.

After she'd checked the cylinder, and found six rounds snug inside it, she jammed the speed loaders into her pocket.

They walked outside onto the porch. Rick shut the door.

"Stay here," he said. "I'll check out the Thompson place."

"I'm going with you."

"Uh-uh."

She tucked the Taurus inside her waistband. "If any creeps jump out at me, I'll shoot first and sort out the bodies later."

"Comforting."

He could tie her to the porch swing, or ask Garfield to hold onto her until he got back. Other than that, he had no power to make her stay put.

Garfield would sooner eat him than do as he asked. And he didn't have any rope.

He sighed. "Come on."

Half crouching, they skulked into the woods.

The dark-haired woman strolled into the kitchen.

Jed and Chin slouched on either side of a wood table, in matching wood chairs, their attention centered on the electronic equipment on the table. The equipment included a radio receiver, a tape recorder, earphones, and a portable computer. Jed fiddled with the receiver while Chin typed on the computer.

Primitive equipment, but she had no choice. Isolation forced her to use the technology at hand. They had taped cardboard over the windows, behind the curtains. Nevertheless, she bumbled in the darkness each night to prevent the lights from alerting the Bergrens to her presence. She conversed with Jed and Chin in whispers. None of them wore shoes, though at night the wood floor chilled her soles through her socks as if she trod on a frozen pond. She endured days spent in seclusion, in a house so like a tomb that she felt herself dying from lack of oxygen and sunlight. Like a lotus flower, she hungered for sunlight and water and fresh air.

Chin, the Asiatic with shoulder-length hair, stumbled out of his chair. He joined his hands behind his back. The olive-skinned Jed wore his brown hair cut short. He rose from his chair like a cobra rising for an attack, and linked his hands before him. Both men wore khaki pants and earth-tone shirts. Both stood erect, stiff, heads bowed.

She nodded to them. A lock of hair tumbled over her shoulder, the ringlet draping down to her elbow. She flicked the lock back over her shoulder.

"Sit," she said.

As the men sat down, she leaned against the counter. "Jed, how was your journey?"

"My contact knew nothing. I am sorry, my lady."

"I hope you were not too forceful in your questioning of him."

Jed started to smile, then thought better of it. He propped an elbow on the table, fisted his hand, and rested his chin upon the fist.

She gestured at the equipment. "What have you learned?"

"The Bergrens have a lead," Chin said. "Saqqara. Something about a tomb."

Her heart fluttered, her ears rang, her hands trembled. She tucked her hands behind her buttocks.

"Have you nothing else?" she inquired.

"No, nothing."

His expression, one of pity, fueled the flame of anger inside her. She gripped the countertop until her fingers ached. At least the anger quelled the trembling. Releasing her grip, she stalked past the men into the living room. No fire sizzled in the hearth. Though the house's owners left the furnace running, the device maintained a lukewarm temperature that failed to eradicate the chill in the air. She settled into a high-backed chair near the hearth. Or perhaps the chill resided in her. The chill of death.

These days she called herself Asru, after a mummy autopsied in England three decades earlier. Whether they hailed from the High Andes of Peru, the tombs of Egypt, the deserts of China, or the ancient bogs of Europe, mummies fascinated her. She felt a kinship with them, a bond deeper than curiosity. Perhaps her obsession stemmed from the loss of her husband, or the near-loss of herself. Perhaps the idea of anyone outwitting the forces of nature appealed to her. Perhaps she had developed a taste for the morbid.

After two years the loss still tugged at her soul, weighted down her stomach, tainted her tongue with the sourness of blood. Her own blood. Her husband's blood.

She had re-christened him as well, because neither of them belonged to their birth names anymore. She called him Ben after the *benu* bird, the Egyptian version of the Phoenix, for like the *benu* he would rise from death. She must resurrect him, if only in memory, for his memory ensured his soul's survival.

A clock ticked mercilessly in her mind. She must find him before the forces of nature devoured what remained of him.

A golden amulet hung on a chain around her neck, tucked inside her blouse. She fingered the amulet through the fabric. The scarab beetle, shaped from gold, spread its wings across her chest. The wings were inlaid with carnelian and lapis lazuli. The deep blue of the lapis stones, the scarlet of the carnelian, highlighted the gold's luster.

The amulet protected her. With its magical help, and the earthly aid of the Bergrens, she would reclaim her life.

The others interfered. She must find the Book before them. Perhaps it led to her destination, to that unknown place where she would find what she had lost. The Book belonged to her after all, for no one else understood its secrets. She had vowed to protect it in life and beyond.

Words possessed the power to heal as well as to destroy. A vow written on a scrap of paper wielded the power. But a vow spoken aloud brandished the greatest power of all, the power of life, of time itself. The power to alter the past.

Huddled in her self-made tomb, clutching the amulet, she uttered a new vow.

"I will find you, my love," she whispered. "I will find you."

Garfield was gone.

A trail of tamped-down earth wended uphill from the spot he'd occupied for months. The grass had worn away in the shape of his buttocks. His 18-inch prints followed the footpath up the hillside. A handful of branches had bent at acute angles. Three had snapped off, their flesh showing pale, fresh. The split pieces lay scattered across the ground.

Katy knelt beside the footprints. Visually, she tracked the prints up the slope past Garfield's lookout point. The first prints looked deformed—his heel had slid out as he fled at top speed. Beside the footpath, five feet from the lookout point, dirt smeared the weeds. Katy frog-hopped to the spot. The weeds were bent. Underneath the stalks, she found a handprint.

Stubby fingers. Wide palm. Deep impression. A hairy hominid handprint.

Garfield had taken off so fast he tripped, catching himself with his left hand.

An arm's length from the lookout point, claw marks scratched the earth. On hands and knees Katy crawled to the site. Fingernails, not claws, had scored the marks into the dirt. The scratches formed symbols, a series of hieroglyphs. Garfield had left them a message.

The Spirits of the Dead have risen.

46

Katy grazed her fingers over the hieroglyphs.

Rick stooped beside her. "What's Garfield trying to tell us?"

"You said the Spirits of the Dead ruled Egypt long ago."

"It's a myth."

"Myths often contain a smidgeon of truth."

In lieu of words, he responded by grasping her hand. Together they sneaked through the woods toward the rear of the Thompson bungalow. At the field's perimeter, they dropped onto their bellies and crawled through the knee-high grass.

Overhead, the sunrise unfurled streamers of gold, pink, and purple against a backdrop of stratus clouds. The morning had unleashed a wind, 20 miles per hour or more, that disguised their movements—the rustling of the grass, the jostling of the stalks. When they reached the bungalow, they rose into a crouch, backs to the house's wall.

Curtains veiled the windows, their fabric crushed against the glass. Through a half-inch gap between the halves of the curtain, Katy spied a strip of brown cardboard. Someone had sealed the windows.

They slunk around the bungalow's side. Each window sported a cardboard covering behind the curtains. Her stomach churned. While the cardboard over the windows blocked the view both into and out of the bungalow, their watchers might've posted a sentry outside.

At the corner, where the porch jutted out from the bungalow's front, they paused. Rick stole a glance around the corner. Katy peeked over his shoulder.

The roofed porch stood vacant. A cement path curved across the yard to the driveway. Despite the distance, she had no trouble spotting the tire tracks incised in the gravel drive. The tracks led straight into the garage, under the closed door.

No railing enclosed the porch. Rick swung his left leg, then his right, onto the floor of the porch. On his belly, he shimmied sideways until he'd swiveled parallel to the wall. He pushed up into a squat.

Katy seized his pants leg. He squeezed her hand, released it, and crept toward the front door.

She bit her lip.

Rick stopped beside the door.

Katy slithered onto the porch. On all fours, she wriggled after Rick.

Sunrise brightened behind the house, yet in front the house's shadow overcame the glow. The porch roof deepened the murk to virtual night. Behind Rick now, Katy clenched a handful of his shirt. He patted her leg as he pressed his ear against the wall. She mashed her own ear to the house.

Voices murmured, muffled like a furnace running in the basement. She opened her mouth a little, held her breath. The voices hushed. Thump, thump, thump.

Her heart skipped. *Footsteps.*

She yanked Rick away from the door. He shrugged off her hand. She grabbed his shirt collar and jerked him backward. He batted her hand away.

Her heart jackhammered inside her chest. Her pulse roared in her ears. What if the pounding transmitted through the wall into the house? Ridiculous. Yet she peeled herself away from the wall.

Thump, thump. The footsteps clapped louder than her heart.

Sweat trickled down her temples. She tugged Rick's sleeve.

Six inches from his head, the door knob clicked.

Rick spun on his heels. The knob rotated. He grabbed Katy, hurling them both off the porch onto the grass below. *Thud.* They touched down an instant before the door creaked and swung inward. Katy and Rick scrambled past the porch to huddle against the house.

Footsteps rapped. The floorboards groaned under the newcomer's weight.

Too late to run. Katy tried to calm her breathing. Didn't work. She risked a peek around the corner.

A man lifted a thin stick to his mouth. Scritch. A flame erupted near his other hand. He lit the cigarette. Its tip smoldered orange in the false dusk on the porch.

Smoke wafted over Katy. Her stomach lurched. She gritted her teeth.

From within the bungalow, a voice hissed, "Get inside."

The man turned toward them.

His body went stiff. Even in the gloom she recognized the tension. The orange tip of the cigarette flared as he suckled it. He dropped the cigarette, snuffing it out with his heel.

The man sauntered into the house.

Katy and Rick waddled into the field. They belly-crawled into the woods, segueing into a trot once inside the sanctuary of the trees.

Rick hopped onto the porch. The floorboards groaned. The wind whined as it funneled under the eaves. Behind that sound, footsteps crunched dead leaves. The sound issued from the right, alongside the cabin.

Katy sprinted around the house. No one there. She glanced across the field.

Near the road, a figure dressed in camouflage ducked into the trees.

Katy looked at the Thompson bungalow. A light flashed in the nearest window. Sunlight glinting off glass. Binoculars, eyeglasses, telescope. A watcher monitored their escape.

The watcher who had allowed them to escape in the first place.

A question flitted through her mind. She let it go. Questions helped her none. She needed answers. Time. Instead she had orders.

Find the Book.

Cherry Capital Airport
Traverse City

Asru wandered through the baggage claim section into the waiting area. People stared at her, as if they knew she did not belong.

Chin had recommended she adopt the dress of the day, but she had no desire to don baggy pants with floppy pockets, military boots, and a too-small shirt that stopped above

48

her belly button. By Chin's advice, she could also have opted for a skirt that squeezed her thighs in a death embrace, disallowing movement, and complemented it with a tight t-shirt held up by two spaghetti straps.

And people found her attire strange.

Admittedly, no one she'd seen thus far dressed as she did. Her hair draped down her back to her waist, curling into loose ringlets. Her dark hair and eyes contrasted her fair skin. She wore an ankle-length skirt that swished around her legs as she moved, a peasant blouse, and leather boots the shade of molten copper. A gold-chain belt draped low around her waist, fastened with a square buckle. On the buckle, an intricate design of coiled snakes encircled a falcon. Her necklace, an amulet shaped like a winged scarab beetle, hung below the neckline of her blouse, the amulet against her skin.

Men glanced at her in surprise. Women glowered at her.

She ignored them all. They meant nothing. In the cycle of life, these people impacted the world less than an ant affected a tree by carting away one leaf. Despite their actions, the sun set each evening and rose each morning. The old died. The young grew. The cycle continued.

She stopped to survey the waiting area.

The Bergrens dawdled at the end of a line of seats. If they turned toward her, they would see her.

Asru ducked behind a burly man. Engrossed in a newspaper, he disregarded her. She took half a step sideways to glance around the man.

Rick Bergren embraced his wife.

Her throat constricted. Asru averted her gaze. Her lips trembled. Tears stung her eyes. She had no time to waste on the feelings, or the thoughts they engendered—thoughts that poisoned her mind.

Raising her chin, she blinked away the tears.

A man approached the Bergrens. After they exchanged words with him, the Bergrens followed the man out of the waiting area, through a doorway to a Warner Industries jet.

Exiting the airport, she drove back to Anameka. As she turned onto the road that wound through the woods toward her temporary home, the phone in her pocket rang. She slowed the car, brought out the phone, flipped it open. She muttered hello.

"It's done," Chin said. "This dump is cleaner than a hospital."

"Excellent. I will arrive soon."

She disconnected the call. Tossing the phone onto the passenger seat, she guided the Buick around a curve toward the cottage she had called home for the past two weeks. A picture flashed in her mind, a memory of her true home. She could never return to it.

The tears burned in her eyes once more. She clenched her jaw. No tears. No weakness. She must show no emotion other than anger, for anger helped her achieve her goals. The others thought her frail, vulnerable. What phrase would Katy Bergren use?

They thought wrong.

Yes, she was adapting nicely.

A figure darted across the road in front of her. She jammed her foot on the brake. The tires squawked. The force shoved her forward, rasping the seatbelt against her neck.

The creature halted in the middle of the road. Covered from head to toe with brown fur, the animal pivoted his torso to gawk at her.

She rolled down the window. In a language she knew the creature understood, she said, "Get out of the way."

The creature blinked. She leaned out the window, repeating the phrase. The creature's eyes widened. He honked and bolted into the trees.

She continued to the cottage.

The Bergrens had departed in a Warner Industries jet. She knew of their link to Warner, how he funded their network and granted them his jet. Thanks to her eavesdropping, she also knew where they would go. She should follow.

Shortly, she would. Unlike the Bergrens, however, she possessed no jet to whisk her away to her destination. Alienation from her brethren forced her to use the commercial transport system. Her flight left in two hours. The travel time, compounded by stopovers in Detroit and New York, gave her little time in which to relocate the Bergrens once in Egypt.

Time sifted away from her, inexorable in its passing. Yet time failed to frighten her. She had more time than she wanted, more time than any human being could use.

She had eternity.

Chicago, Illinois

Rick parked in front of the house.

Warner's mansion nosed its two-story head above the treetops. Gargoyles squatted at either corner, where the first floor met the second. In the center of the façade, marble steps scaled four feet up to a pair of bronze doors. A vulture, carved in raised relief, spread its wings across both doors. Above the bird, frosted glass filled a window two feet square.

After detouring to Chicago en route, they'd borrowed a car from Warner's pilot in order to visit the mansion half an hour's drive from the airport. Along the way, they'd passed the Museum of Prehistory. Warner's museum.

Katy gazed up at the house. The interior was dark. Inert. Silent.

The gargoyles pierced her with their gazes, sharp as the talons on their gaunt hands and feet. The sunlight gleamed on their muzzles like saliva.

The passenger door clicked.

Katy jumped.

Rick opened the door.

She stepped out onto the asphalt. "The castle of doom."

"Betcha he's got a mummy in his drawing room."

They mounted the steps to the front doors. Rick knocked. Nobody home, naturally. Warner had no wife, girlfriend, children, living relatives, or close friends, other than the two of them.

Rick clobbered the door. The pounding reverberated through the house.

Behind the door's window, an apparition quavered. The pale specter rippled. Its eyes glittered white. Dark hair cascaded around the face.

Katy touched the glass. The apparition raised a hand.

Katy waved. The apparition waved in unison with her.

Jeez, it was her own reflection. She groaned.

Rick rubbed his knuckles. "Can't kick it in, these doors must be a foot thick."

The doorknobs emulated talons. She clamped her hand around a knob.

"Katy, he wouldn't leave it open."

She twisted the knob. It turned, unlatching the door. She pushed the door open.

A cold draft sluiced over her.

Rick strode inside. Katy hurried behind him.

They crossed a vestibule whose ceiling arched into a dome high above their heads. On the left a staircase spiraled toward the second floor like the double helix in a strand of DNA. Straight ahead, a hallway extended into the gloom. On either side of the vestibule, closed doors concealed their contents.

Rick tugged the .45 out of his ankle holster. Katy slid the Taurus out of her purse. Together they explored the mansion.

They found nothing, not even a mummy in a drawing room. On the second floor, they located Warner's bedroom. A pair of fluffy pillows formed mountains under the comforter. A suitcase lay open on the foot of the bed. Inside the case, Warner's clothes were pressed, folded, stacked in geometric order. A pair of hiking boots fitted into the space between stacks of shirts and pants. In the upper half of the suitcase, three nylon straps secured a leather jacket that padded a Glock 9mm pistol, berthed inside a shoulder holster.

In a rush, Warner might've abandoned his clothes. He would never have left his Glock.

Rick walked to the bedside table. He pulled out the drawer. Picking up a little notebook from inside the drawer, he flipped it open. His forehead crinkled as he contemplated the notebook's contents. He grunted and slapped it shut.

He tossed the book to her. "Bugger's in German."

Katy caught the notebook. She skimmed through its pages. Warner had jotted down his appointments, important dates, and reminders to himself—all printed in block letters, crisp and neat. She flipped to the last notation, on the page for October 17th. Yesterday.

No mention of his ill-fated flight. Instead, he alluded to a meeting with someone identified as "J," whom he'd met at the museum last night, two hours before the jet crash. The note ended with a word she recognized.

Thoth.

She clapped the notebook shut.

"Nothing here," she said, as set the notebook on the bed. "Let's go."

Rick shepherded her out of the mansion. As they neared the car, a light burst in the sky.

Katy threw her head back. The sun radiated in a field of blue. The light flared again, closer. The object banked toward her, the sun gleaming on its metal surface.

The airliner's engine whined. The sun had flashed off its fuselage.

Rick opened the car's door for her. She plunked into the passenger seat. As he shut the door, and jogged around to the driver's side, she eyed the sky.

Not every light in the sky was the Planners. But she knew, somewhere out there, they watched. And waited.

They wanted the Book of Thoth.

Fine, she'd get it. To save Charlie, Rick, and herself. For Warner and the three others who died on his jet, she could do nothing, except make sure no one else died.

The blood of Bakhu had sealed the Book's secret. No more bloodshed.

Unless the blood flowed from a Planner's heart.

As the car rolled around the circular drive, Katy glimpsed movement in the shrubbery alongside the house. Though she'd seen it peripherally, she didn't bother to look straight at the spot. No one would be there, of course. She'd let stress chafe her nerves raw.

Oh yes, she'd find the damn Book. But she'd dive into an erupting volcano before she'd hand the Book over to the Planners.

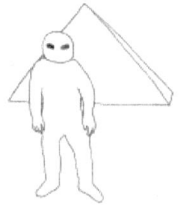

CHAPTER FIVE

Meidum, Egypt
Sunday, October 19

The blank stela towered eight feet above their heads. Adjacent to the stela, an oblong hole marked the spot where its twin had resided until three days ago.

Katy and Rick stood behind the stela, inside its shadow. Across the Nile, the sun—the god Ra to the ancient Egyptians—nudged above the horizon. Ra outstretched his arms to the river, embracing the fertile valley in his warmth. Light and life, fresh from the underworld.

Beeps fractured the silence as Rick fiddled with the GPS unit.

Katy craned her neck back. The stela bore no tool marks, no trench around its base, nothing to indicate Bob and Halim had attempted to excavate it. Did this stela conceal an inscription, like its twin?

The Planners had taken the inscribed stela, but abandoned its mate. Either they thought the second stela hid no inscriptions, or they failed to realize the first stela had possessed a covering stone that disguised the inscribed surface. Since they kidnapped Bob, they must've known—unless they'd shadowed everyone associated with Human Origins Project in the belief someday they might uncover an artifact worthy of a cover-up. The Planners knew nothing about the history of Low Ones. Yet even their own history seemed to baffle them.

Screwy people.

Of course, advanced technology didn't make you smarter or better than more primitive people, a fact the Planners attested with their attitude and actions. For countless millennia, the Planners had possessed advanced technology which they refused to disclose to the rest of humanity—the Low Ones, creatures unworthy of life. Because they despised Low Ones, the Planners sequestered themselves from the world. Occasionally, they emerged from hiding to interfere in the affairs of Low Ones, like when they'd discovered the Michigan hairy hominids sharing their tunnels with Low Ones. The Planners incited the creatures to massacre the humans in order to keep the species separate, instilling in the hominids a fear of humans that persisted today. The Planners preferred killing or causing the deaths of Low Ones to matriculating with them. They wanted all evidence of mankind's antiquity covered up to preserve the secret of their own existence. They covered up the truth for another reason too, she suspected, though she had no idea what.

Via the creatures, the Planners had accidentally kick-started ancient Egyptian civilization. The hairy hominids, who learned the Planners' culture from the "gods" themselves, had taught the people of archaic Egypt what they knew. Soon Egypt resembled a clone of the Planners' society, minus the advanced technology. As far as she knew, however, the Egyptians knew of the Planners only from stories told by the hairy hominids, tales of beings with technology so advanced they must've sounded like gods. No wonder the Egyptians built their religion around the Planners, just like the creatures had done.

Thousands of years before the advent of ancient Egypt, the Planners had employed the hairy hominids as workers in construction projects from temples to pyramids. About 12,000 yeas ago, with a volcanic cataclysm imminent, the Planners disseminated the creatures into prefab caves throughout the world. Safe underground, the hairy hominids survived. The Planners also survived, in their crafts hidden at the bottom of the ocean. The Low Ones they left to die.

If she'd spent thousands of years on the ocean bottom, confined to a flying saucer, she might lose track of history too. A volcanic cataclysm could blot out the sun for decades, perhaps centuries, inducing a nuclear winter. Despite their advanced technology, the Planners couldn't overcome an obstacle like that. So if the disaster had stranded them below the ocean for centuries...well, no wonder they were so nutty.

Voices chattered in the direction of the river. Katy shuffled sideways, into the sun.

A hundred feet away, four men meandered toward the stelae. The quartet lugged equipment under their arms, packs on their backs. One man removed his hat to wipe sweat from his forehead and smooth back his red hair.

"Got it," Rick said. "Let's move out."

"Wait."

Katy waved at the men, who approached within 50 feet.

Tony Edwards waved back. He mashed the hat down over his red hair.

Rick stepped in front of her. "What's he doing here?"

"I don't know." She yelled to Tony, "Rick wants to know what you're doing here."

Tony and his companions strolled up to the stelae. While his buddies gawked at the hole where the missing stela had rested, Tony faced Katy and Rick.

54

"Not sure," he said. "What I'm doing here, I mean. I planned on flying to Toronto to stay with a friend, as I told you, but when I thought about Bob…I don't know. I had to see this place again."

Rick slipped the GPS unit into his pocket. "Do you know if this stela has a cover stone, like the other one?"

"Not a clue."

Katy glanced at the monolith. "Maybe we should check it out."

"These gentlemen can help," Tony said. "Chums from the dig at Dahshur. Meet Theo, Yves, and Ethan."

Tony indicated each man in turn. Theo, the elder of the group, scratched his head, intent on the hole in the sand. A rubber band tied his gray hair behind his head in a ponytail. In blue jeans, sneakers, and a yellow t-shirt, he cradled a red metal box in his arms. A metal rod, wedged under his arm, stuck out behind him. The rod connected to the box and featured a handle on its extremity. A wire draped from the red box to a blue-gray control unit held by Theo's young friend, Ethan.

Ethan shook his head as if unable to believe his eyes, which he focused on the hole. Clad in faded jeans, cowboy boots, a plaid shirt, and a straw cowboy hat, he hugged the control unit—a type of computer—to his chest.

"What is all that stuff?" Rick asked.

Yves replied, his voice thickened by a French accent. "G-P-R—ground-penetrating radar. Tony felt there might be a cavity under the stelae."

"And what, Bob fell into it?"

Tony blushed. He tugged the brim of his hat down to shade the pink in his cheeks.

Yves jammed his left hand into the pocket of his pants, amusement curling his lip. A smattering of light brown hair ringed his head. The Frenchman had adopted a variation of the Indiana Jones look, minus the bullwhip and gun: khakis with boots and a fedora. The hat he clenched in his right hand. On a cold day, he probably wore a leather jacket too. Aside from the clothes, Yves sported the muscles required for his role as movie-star archaeologist. He had the looks too.

Ethan ambled to the hole. He kicked sand into it.

"Bob's not in there," Katy said. "Will you help us check out the stela, though?"

"Of course."

Theo set down his load. Ethan did the same. From his backpack, Theo produced chisels and hammers. Ethan and Tony chipped at the stela while Rick, Theo, and Yves excavated around the base.

Katy kept watch on the sky, the river, the desert, as if she could stop their enemies if the creeps showed themselves.

Twenty minutes later, the men gave up. They'd unearthed the stela's bottom, and transformed the monolith into abstract art, but discovered no inscriptions.

"Solid rock," Theo announced.

The others murmured agreement.

Katy sighed. She looked behind her at the pyramid, or what remained of it. Her shoulders slumped lower than the rubble pile around the pyramid.

Rick extracted the GPS unit from his pocket. "Back to Plan A."

"What are you after?" Tony inquired.

"Nothing much. Just a tomb that disappeared three thousand years ago."

Rick told them the story, minus the part about the Planners, concluding with their task at Saqqara. Instead of guffaws, silent nods ensued.

Tony herded his buddies out of earshot, where they engaged in a discussion replete with waving arms, shaking heads, and pursed lips.

A few minutes later, the quartet returned.

Theo shrugged. "You can use our G-P-R if you want."

"Really?" Katy said.

"Provided you take us with you."

Rick extended a hand to Theo. "Deal. Can you give us a lift too?"

"Sure thing."

The archaeologists led the procession back toward the river, where a jeep awaited them near the main road. The vehicle lacked a top. It sported a coat of dust, along with black mud dried onto the tires and wheel wells. The paint, what little of it remained under the grime and rust, was pea green. Dents and nicks scarred the exterior. The seats were ripped.

Theo and Ethan stashed the GPR equipment in the jeep's rear, behind the backseat.

Ethan took the driver's seat, with Theo riding shotgun. Yves and Tony climbed into the rear, squeezing themselves in around the GPR. Rick and Katy took the backseat. The seats creaked under their weight.

Ethan turned the key in the ignition. The engine stuttered. He cranked the key twice more. Finally, the engine sputtered to life. He gunned the engine. The jeep rocketed out onto the main road, jouncing over a pothole.

Theo chuckled.

Katy clung to the door. Rick ground his teeth.

Ethan swerved around a mob of pedestrians. A man gesticulated at the jeep, venting in Arabic. Ethan smiled and waved. The man spat at the jeep.

The junior archaeologist stomped on the gas. The jeep shot forward. Pedestrians cursed Ethan, yet he waved and grinned at them, hollering apologies out the window.

Yves leaned over the backseat between Katy and Rick. "You drive like a drunken cow, Ethan. You're frightening our guests."

"We're fine," Katy said. "You should see how Rick drives in the snow. It's more like a runaway sled than a car."

Rick glanced at her sideways. "Least I don't run after hairy monsters."

Theo twisted around to peer into the backseat. "Hairy monsters?"

"Long story."

The jeep hit a bump. For a second, the vehicle sailed through the air.

"When I asked for a lift," Rick said, "I didn't mean it literally."

Ethan glanced back at Rick. "If you think the jeep flies, you should see my little baby."

56

"Your what?" Rick asked.

Theo rolled his eyes. "Ethan thinks he's a pilot. Say, what are you guys after in this tomb anyhow?"

Elbow resting on the window frame, chin supported by her fist, Katy grimaced at the wind that buffeted her face. Eyes half closed, she tapped a finger against her jawbone.

Rick fidgeted. "Looking for an ancient relic."

"Got permits to dig?" Theo asked.

"Not exactly."

Katy turned her attention to the men. Nobody in their right mind would believe the details about the Planners, or how they'd ordered her and Rick to find the Book of Thoth. No archaeologist with a grant and tenure at a university would swallow a story about modern humans existing for millions of years or ancient Egyptians flying UFOs.

The *ancestors* of ancient Egyptians flying UFOs. Whatever.

"I like stories," Theo said. "Give me the Cliff's Notes version."

Rick told them everything.

When he'd finished, he took a deep breath. "Basically, we're looking for a book that doesn't exist in a tomb that doesn't exist while being chased by people who don't exist." Rick laid his arm across the seat behind Katy's head. "You know, the usual."

Ethan veered around a man leading a camel.

No one spoke for several minutes. Dust kicked up by passing vehicles swirled around them, sandblasted their faces. Katy wiped the dust off her sunglasses. Theo watched Rick with an expression as unreadable as her own handwriting. Yves whistled the theme from *Mission: Impossible* as he took in the scenery outside the jeep.

Katy coughed. "If you want to back out, we'll understand."

Theo poked Ethan's side. "Want to back out?"

"Heck no."

Yves and Tony voiced their agreement, muted by the wind.

Rick closed his eyes. He rested his head on his arm.

Great, he spilled the details then went to sleep.

"I've got a hankering for excitement," Ethan added. "Our most thrilling moment so far was when Yves cussed out the hotel manager in French because they lost our reservations."

Rick kept his eyes—and mouth—shut. His arm had gone slack behind her head, his fingers draped onto her shoulder. Pretty soon he'd start snoring.

Katy jabbed him in the gut. He jerked upright, eyes wide.

"Where do we start?" Ethan asked.

"Saqqara," Katy answered. "We have GPS coordinates."

"The ancient Egyptians had GPS?"

"No, it's—"

"A long story."

Ethan decelerated to turn a corner in an almost leisurely manner. Katy pried her fingers free of the door handle.

The kid jammed his foot on the gas. The jeep launched down the road, pinning her against the seat. She grabbed the handle.

Rick rubbed his eyes, yawning. "You should know the odds are we'll all die."

"Doesn't scare us." Ethan lifted his chin and declared, "We've been shot at by terrorists."

Theo tousled the kid's hair. Yves whistled an encore of *Mission: Impossible*.

Rick warped his mouth into a lopsided frown. Katy patted his leg.

Ethan grinned. "Bring on the aliens."

Saqqara

Asru leaned against a palm tree. In the distance, beyond the cultivations, a stepped pyramid projected above the desert within the ruins of an enclosure wall. Scholars believed the pharaoh Djoser had ordered the structure built as his tomb. He may have.

Even if he had, the fact proved neither that pharaohs had built every pyramid in Egypt nor that the pyramids served as tombs. Modern techniques for dating artifacts failed when applied to edifices constructed entirely from stone. She had learned as much in her readings. A few individuals, whose numbers grew slowly, recognized the fallacies embedded in the modern version of history, especially prehistory. The Bergrens counted themselves among those few.

Smaller pyramids clustered around the Step Pyramid. One, the pyramid attributed to Unas, housed inscriptions on its walls, magic spells known as the Pyramid Texts. None of the supposed tombs harbored mummies, though countless tombs—crypts sunk into the sands—surrounded the structures.

Asru raised binoculars to her eyes.

The six figures still looked tiny. It must be the Bergrens. And who else?

They had spoken of Saqqara before leaving Michigan. Yet she had waited five hours for the Bergrens to arrive. No matter. They had come, however long their journey took.

Asru lowered the binoculars. A serpent of ice rattled its tail inside her gut. She curled the chain of her belt around her fingers.

The Bergrens knew more than she about ancient history, especially the language of ancient Egypt. The riddles woven into the inscriptions on the stelae from Meidum and Washington challenged their minds, yet they overcame each obstacle with a speed that Asru herself could not rally. Neither she, Jed, nor Chin could decode the riddles. For her, the grammar of the texts seemed familiar yet perplexing, the phrasing strange, the symbolism infused into the words alien. If she'd lived longer, she might comprehend the inscriptions.

She needed the Bergrens. As did the others.

Thirty feet distant, a man emerged from behind a palm tree. He faced the desert, his body in profile. Recognition twanged the strings of her mind, eliciting a dissonance that vibrated her nerves. She clutched her amulet. The wings dug into her flesh.

Since last she encountered him, he had altered his appearance with modern attire and black hair. His demeanor she knew all too well. The squared shoulders, the tension spiraling through him, how he flicked his fingers as a scorpion snaps its tail. He held his chin up, arms slack at his sides.

She spoke his name. Her throat choked off the sound.

Pivoting on his heels, he centered his gaze on her. Recognition summoned a sneer to his features.

A shudder rippled through her. She had known him better than she wished—he, the one who had taken Ben from her, who wished to steal her very soul.

He strolled toward her.

She slipped a hand under her blouse, caressing the leather sheath harnessed to her side, which sheltered a steel blade. She moved her hand up the sheath to the wooden handle that capped the blade.

Ten feet away, he halted. He flicked the fingers of his right hand.

She clenched the knife's hilt.

He scanned her body with his gaze, a medical machine examining her for defects. She felt his gaze penetrating her flesh like an x-ray.

"*Neferet*," he said, "you are as enchanting as I remembered."

"I am not your *neferet*."

He bowed his head, looking up at her. "As you wish."

His lips twitched at the corners. He raised his arms to his chest, crossed at the wrists in imitation of the position in which embalmers had posed pharaohs' mummies.

The darkness of his eyes matched his soul. She slid the knife out halfway.

"What do you call yourself?" she asked. "Surely not your birth name."

He straightened. "We both shed our birthrights, did we not? Today they call me Intef."

"How common. I would have thought Ramses or Khufu."

"What do you call yourself, Nefertiti?"

"Asru."

"Lovely." He dropped his voice to a whisper. "The Bergrens will find the Book for me. You have no hope of reaching it first."

"I have ways."

He snickered. "Your ways are dead."

Intef spun on his heels. He swerved behind a stand of trees, out of view.

Jed and Chin dashed up behind her.

"We saw Lord Intef," Jed told her.

She ground her teeth. The serpent in her gut whipped his tail.

"I have told you," she hissed, "Intef is neither your lord nor mine."

"Of course. I am sorry, Your Incarnation."

Jed bowed his head.

Her knuckles ached. Pain lanced through her jaw. She slid the knife back into its sheath and relaxed her jaw.

She placed a finger under Jed's chin and raised it for him. "You are not my servant. Call me by the name I have chosen for myself."

"I cannot."

"If you honor me, you will." She glanced at Chin. "Both of you shall."

With a slight smile, Chin nodded.

Jed hunched his shoulders. Face pinched, he frowned.

Asru stared at the tree behind which Intef had gone.

Why did she tell him her new name? He had asked and she had responded. Had she become a *shabti*, a figure of clay that did Intef's bidding? She had granted him the power of knowing her, for knowing the name meant knowing the woman who answered to the name.

Knowledge is power. Yes, she liked that maxim. Another ancient belief filtered through the lens of modernity. She had given Intef that power. He had granted her the same power. He told her his new name. She also knew his birth name. They wielded equal power, as before, yet she must turn equality into advantage. She must destroy him. To do so, she must have the Book. She could not find it without the Bergrens' assistance.

She looked through the binoculars. The tiny figures advanced past the pyramid.

"Come." She handed Jed the binoculars. "We must safeguard our past—and our future."

Ethan parked the jeep amongst the sand dunes along the eastern side of Djoser's pyramid complex. A hillock separated them from the roadway, thereby screening them from onlookers.

The portion of the Memphis necropolis known as Saqqara encompassed 2 ¼ square miles of a plateau, just off the fertile corridor along the Nile. Other pyramids adjoined Djoser's, all attributed to later pharaohs. To the northeast, Userkaf's pyramid had sloughed off its casing. Across a roadway, on a diagonal with Userkaf's monument, a stump designated where Teti had built his pyramid. To the southwest, rubble slumped in heaps on the sites where Unas and Sekhemkhet had erected their pyramids. Low, flat crypts called mastabas hunkered in the desert around the pyramids, while pits dug by past explorers, in search of shaft tombs, pockmarked the sands.

As the jeep rolled to a stop, Katy shoved the door open. She plopped down onto the sand.

If Setna had stashed the Book in Nefrekeptah's tomb at Memphis, exactly where he'd found it, then there it should have remained.

Unless tomb robbers stole it. Or a flood disintegrated it.

Stop it.

Rick disembarked on the opposite side. He trotted around the jeep to her.

The archaeologists had stocked their jeep with equipment for excavating: shovels, crowbars, oil-powered lanterns, etcetera. Theo had brought a Polaroid camera to document anything they found at Meidum. Now he wanted the camera to document the rediscovery of Nefrekeptah's tomb. She'd told him the Planners would destroy the tomb once the Book had been found. He had insisted, however, that he must record the find "for the benefit of future generations."

She didn't tell him the Planners intended to annihilate those future generations of Low Ones. Any descendants of the Planners would care nothing about Nefrekeptah or the intrepid explorers who unearthed his tomb after 3,000 years.

Rick gave her the GPS unit. "Start looking while we unpack."

He marched around back, where the archaeologists were unloading equipment.

Katy punched up the location on the GPS. She marked the jeep's position as a waypoint, in case a sandstorm or Plannerian siege should isolate them from the vehicle. Next she called up the coordinates Rick had guesstimated based on the data from the Meidum stela. Once they'd found the vicinity, they would use the GPR to pin down the tomb's location.

The men had finished unloading. Each hauled a backpack, stuffed full of equipment, on his shoulders. Yves deserted his backpack, opting to haul just the GPR antenna with its digital control unit.

Katy consulted the GPS. She set out, with the men in tow.

They slogged southward through the sand parallel to the Step Pyramid, toward the ruins attributed to Unas and Sekhemkhet. Katy looked back at the roadway north of the Step Pyramid complex. Without a permit, they had no defense if cops, other archaeologists, or anyone from the Supreme Council of Antiquities questioned them. Thus far, no one seemed to notice or care about their activities.

They stopped in line with the pyramid's southeast corner. In antiquity, a 34-foot wall had enclosed the complex, though little of it remained. After referring to the GPS for guidance, Katy hiked southward beyond Djoser's complex, detouring behind Unas' pyramid. The men flocked after her as she set off from into the open sands southwest of Unas' pyramid.

In an empty expanse, she ended the parade.

"This is it," she said. "Near as I can tell."

Theo extracted a wad of ropes from Ethan's backpack. As Tony and Yves discussed where to start the GPR sweep, Ethan untangled the ropes.

"Think it'll work?" Katy asked him.

"I'm hopeful."

"How long will this take?"

"We can see the results right away on the control unit screen. It'd be better if I had time to clean up the reflection profiles on my computer—"

"We're in a hurry, Ethan."

"Right." He unraveled a fist-size knot. "The raw data will have to do."

Several yards away, Yves slouched with the GPR antenna at his feet, one arm on the unit's handle. The control unit hooked onto a wide belt similar to a back brace, which he wore around his waist. Shoulder straps secured the belt and provided an anchor for the two straps that stabilized the control unit.

Behind Yves, Theo, Tony, and Rick hammered stakes into the sand, stringing a rope between them to delineate a square sector for the GPR sweep. Ethan had explained that they swept a sector in transects—straight lines—like a lawnmower trekking back and forth.

Sweat oozed from under her hat's sweatband. Katy blotted it away with her sleeve.

Rick drove in the last stake. Theo knotted the rope around it. The men strode to Ethan and Katy. The sector they'd roped off measured 225 square yards.

Ethan pointed at Yves. "Go."

The Frenchman dragged the GPR antenna along the ground, aligned with the long side of the perimeter. Head down, he concentrated on the control unit screen.

"And Yves," Ethan said, "could ya hotfoot it with those transects?"

Ethan winked at Katy.

Yves muttered in French.

When Ra dunked his chin below the horizon, Yves had concluded his sweep of the third sector Theo and Rick had roped off for him. Around them, the desert burned a golden red in the inferno of sunset. The neighborhood seemed lifeless, save for the six souls who conducted an illegal dig in the vicinity of Sekhemkhet's pyramid.

Yves completed the last transect within the sector. He shook his head.

Katy slumped her shoulders. Rick's hand, stiff as a mummy's, cupped her elbow. His expression matched the tension in his body.

Yves angled the control unit so his comrades could examine the readout. Katy glimpsed the screen. In the multicolored profile, bubbles interrupted wavy lines. Though it must've been the readout from the GPR, it might as well have been the DNA sequence from an alien organism.

Questions boiled in her brain. She slapped a lid over them.

Her watch ticked off two more minutes.

"Set up a new perimeter," Theo said.

Katy pitched in as Rick, Tony, Theo, and Ethan relocated the ropes to form a new square. They left one perimeter of the old sector intact as the backbone for the new grid. The sunset dimmed while they worked until, when they'd marked out the new sector, the solar blaze had faded into a glow along the horizon. They lit the lanterns, situating them at intervals around the sector. Ethan reserved two lamps for himself, one at either side of his computer.

Yves carried the GPR antenna into the new sector. He commenced the transects.

Twenty-five minutes later, he finished. Ethan, Theo, and Tony jogged over to Yves, and all four fretted over the radar profile on the control unit screen. Theo chomped on a Snickers. Yves massaged his low back. Ethan bobbed on his tiptoes.

Katy sat down, folding her feet under her, but Rick insisted upon standing.

Ethan gave them the thumbs-up sign. "Got an anomaly."

Katy jumped up. "Where?"

"Two meters north of the south perimeter, four meters west of the east perimeter. Cavity looks to be three-by-three, at a depth of about one meter."

"Let's get digging," Rick ordered.

Theo distributed the shovels and the men jogged to the area they'd isolated with the GPR. Rick plowed his shovel into the ground.

"What should I do?" Katy asked.

Rick met her gaze dead-on. He hooked a thumb skyward. "Watch."

She turned toward the Step Pyramid. Behind her, the men's shovels scraped in the sand. Their breaths huffed.

In the final flush of sunset, the pyramid loomed as a shadow, an echo of a culture that perished more than 2,000 years before her birth. The Planners had thrived still deeper in the past, in a time when convention asserted humans had yet to coalesce into cultures, much less global empires. The evidence existed—archaeologists covered it up, misidentified it, decried it as forgery. As unwitting collaborators, they abetted the Planners. Whether they distorted the past to protect the precious theories on which they'd based their careers, or to eradicate a truth that terrified them, mattered less than the aftermath of their centuries-old conspiracy.

What didn't they want us to know?

What didn't the Planners want us to know?

The Book of Thoth would spill their secrets. She hoped. She prayed. If they strove to find the Book only to discover it contained nothing more than Thoth's secret recipe for fruitcake, she'd chuck her quest into outer space. Let the Venusians figure it out.

A breeze chilled her arms. She folded them over her chest, hands tucked into her armpits.

Nut, goddess of the sky, arced her star-spangled body over the plateau. Ra had relinquished his kingdom for the night.

No moonlight quelled the dark. Thoth had forsaken them.

The digging sounds ceased. Katy shuffled in a circle.

The men had dug a pit ten feet around and three feet deep. Ethan, Yves, and Rick stooped inside the pit shoveling sand into a mound that bordered the ditch. Theo spooned the mound aside with his shovel. He wheezed with each effort, panting in between exertions.

Tony took the shovel from him. Despite his protests, Tony waved Theo away and scooped the mounded sand to the side.

Katy watched the sky, the desert.

The stars inched across the heavens. The pit enlarged to 12-by-12 around, three feet deep.

The western desert, invisible in the night, unfolded around her. To the north, the Nile fanned its fertile corridor out into the Delta, while south of Saqqara the river leaked its fertile soil westward across the Faiyum to Lake Moeris. This was the land of Osiris, lord of the dead, mythical first king of Egypt whose son Horus had bestowed kingship on the first pharaoh and whose brother Seth had murdered him out of jealousy. In ancient times, the Memphis necropolis had welcomed souls on their voyage into the *duat*—the underworld ruled by Osiris where Ra journeyed each night.

The dead surrounded her. How many tombs, as yet undiscovered, lay beneath the sands? Within each tomb, a mummy rotted into a skeleton. Its bandages hardened from the resin used to glue them. The flesh crumbled to dust. A *ka* statue, the embodiment of the deceased's life force, guarded the crypt.

Rick pitched a load of sand out of the pit. Tony shoveled the sand aside.

Disturbed by the digging, the *ka* statue claws through the tomb's ceiling. Burrows up through the earth. A hand, sculpted from wood, surfaces from the sand. Fingers grope at the air.

Katy spun around. No wooden hand. No statue animated by rage. Christ, she was jumpy. Excavating a lost tomb in the dark would unsettle the most stoic of people.

63

Thunk.

Everyone froze.

Rick knocked his shovel on the spot he'd just hit. The metal thumped on stone.

Kneeling, he pawed the dirt away with his hands. Katy grabbed a lantern, bent over the pit's edge, and held the light above Rick. He brushed the earth away with the side of his hand. A solid surface emerged.

A granite slab.

Tony tossed Rick what looked like a make-up brush. Using the brush to sweep the edges of the stone clean, Rick cleared the slab. The block was square, four feet wide, set flush into the bedrock. Carved into its smoothed surface, hieroglyphs spelled out the throne name of Amenhotep II inside a cartouche, an oval that enclosed pharaohs' names.

They'd found the door.

Yves whistled the Indiana Jones theme. Theo snatched his camera from his bag and leaped into the pit. The flash pulsed. Dark ghosts danced in Katy's vision.

Ethan whooped. Tony rolled his eyes at the youngster.

On all fours Rick examined the slab, puffing on it to liberate sand that had clumped in the carvings. Katy deposited the lantern along the pit's edge. She hopped down into the ditch beside Rick.

He scratched at the stone below the cartouche. Dirt popped out of grooves in the slab. The encrustation covered more hieroglyphs, a line of text below the cartouche.

Katy read the inscription aloud. "He who violates this tomb shall have his heart fed to Amaunet the Devourer."

Despite what Hollywood said, few tombs had curses attached to them. Amenhotep must've wanted extra protection for the Book of the Thoth. Anubis weighed the deceased's heart against the Feather of Maat, symbol of truth and order. If the soul weighed more than the feather, the deceased flunked the test.

And got eaten by a hideous creature—Amaunet the Devourer.

In spite of curses, the ancient Egyptians had broken into the tombs of their own kings and nobles. If they survived curses, she'd risk it too.

Ethan had collapsed onto his knees giggling. Theo, done photographing the scene, gazed at the slab as if it contained on its face the secrets of the universe.

Rick snagged a crowbar from the pit's rim. He dropped onto his knees by the slab.

Yves, Tony, and Ethan climbed out of the pit. Theo perched on the ledge that surrounded the ditch with his legs dangling into the chasm. Katy trotted behind Rick. He jammed the crowbar into the seam and pushed down against the slab's weight. The block wobbled. Setting one foot on the crowbar, he pushed with both hands as he half stood on the bar.

The slab lifted.

Rick's foot slipped. He stumbled sideways, fell onto his knees. The crowbar jerked out of his hands. The slab skated to the side, out of its slot. The stone teetered with a thrump-thrump-thrump. It came to rest propped on two sides of the hole it had vacated, balanced a few inches off-center.

Tony, Yves, and Ethan rushed into the pit. The archaeologists each seized an edge of the slab. As they pulled from one side, Rick thrust from the other. The slab grated over the stone frame that had housed it, away from the opening. The quartet heaved once more. The slab whomped into the sand near the pit's wall.

The four men wilted onto the sand, panting, sweating though the temperature had plummeted. Katy retrieved water bottles from one of the backpacks. As she handed them out, she couldn't help looking into the void the slab had concealed, a chasm lightless as a black hole. A draft emanated from the hollow. The airflow intensified her chill, and she rubbed her arms. Crinkled her nose. The hole emitted a stale stench.

No one had entered the crypt in millennia. The air escaping its depths had remained trapped inside for longer than most civilizations lasted. No wonder it stank.

The slab served as more than a door to a tomb. It functioned as a portal into the past.

Katy crouched at the tomb's mouth. No wooden hands reached out to crush her throat. She sat back on her heels.

Rick rubbed his neck.

Theo and Ethan whispered to each other. They gesticulated at the tomb, eyes wide, faces pale. Yves leaned against the wall at the far end of the pit. Hands in his pockets, he pondered the stars overhead.

Tony huddled on the sand above, a few feet from the pit. The lamplight silhouetted him.

Katy combed her fingers through the sand.

Rick swiped a lantern from the pit's lip. He flapped a hand at her, and she backed away from the opening. At the hole's periphery, he held the lantern out in front of him. The lamplight dissipated into the darkness below.

Tony joined them in the pit. Six bodies crowded around the opening. No one spoke.

"Get the ropes," Rick ordered.

Ethan, Tony, and Yves vaulted out of the pit to collect the ropes from the perimeter. Theo didn't move. He clucked his tongue as he scrutinized the gloom in the shaft.

Yves, Tony, and Ethan returned with the ropes and another lantern. Tony and Ethan dropped the pile of ropes into the pit. Theo gaped into the chasm.

"Move your ancient relic, Doc," Ethan teased.

Yves grasped Theo's shoulders, towing his colleague away from the opening.

Rick selected a 25-yard length of rope from the pile. Yves nailed a tent stake into the ground next to the portal. When Rick handed him an end of the rope, he fastened it onto the stake with a knot that looked strong enough to tether a continent. He tested the apparatus by looping the rope around his waist and leaning back with all his weight.

Satisfied, he un-roped himself.

Rick tossed the rope into the shaft. He tied a lantern onto his belt. Slinging his sack over one shoulder, grasping the rope in both hands, he jumped over the edge.

The lantern Yves and Ethan had brought perched on the brink. Its light diffused into the chasm. Rick's head receded into the gloom as he shimmied down the rope toward the floor. Katy peered into the abyss. Soon he had retreated from the lamplight altogether. The fire from his lantern, however, alerted her to his position, even as it shrank into a distant star.

65

From far below, Rick's voice reverberated. "Come on down."

Yves stepped toward the rope.

Katy pushed past him. She clutched the line and launched herself over the edge. Her knees smacked into the wall. Her fingers slipped, rasping against the rope's fibers. Her knees throbbed. Her fingers stung. Below, the flame of Rick's lantern flickered. She hung onto the rope, gritted her teeth, and lowered herself hand-over-hand into the murk.

Her biceps twanged. Sweat drenched her shirt, greased her skin and hair. Rick's lantern glimmered brighter as it enlarged into a cone of light on the floor. Rick loitered at the cone's margin until she descended to within a yard of the floor. Then he reached out to support her as she dismounted the rope.

Yves and Ethan shimmied down next. Ethan had tied a lantern to his belt loop with a strip of cloth. Tony descended third and Theo, last in line, leaped from the rope to land with a thud and a grunt.

Theo dusted off his clothes. "Floor's hard as—well, a rock."

The builders had composed the floor from compacted dirt. Nonetheless, the floor did feel as unyielding as granite. The builders had hewn the shaft right out of the bedrock, leveling its walls and perfecting the corners into 90-degree angles. No reliefs decorated the walls. At its eastern extremity, a granite slab plugged the chamber.

Rick reclaimed the pickaxe from his sack. He strode toward the granite plug.

"Um," Katy said, "you might not want to—"

He drove the pickaxe into the granite. Metal thwacked into stone.

Rick shouted. He dropped the pickaxe. Cradling his arm, he hobbled backward. His face crimped into a grimace.

"You okay?" Katy asked.

He shook his arm. "Fine."

"I was trying to tell you," she said, "granite is extremely hard."

"No kidding."

The axe had scraped the granite plug. Rick had inflicted no other damage.

Katy walked to the plug. It rested inside a slot with its edges tucked inside the limestone of the wall. The Egyptians must've lowered the plug from above. Most of the tombs in Saqqara comprised a mudbrick core with a limestone revetment to cover up the brick. While she had no doubts the workers cut the exterior walls of Nefrekeptah's tomb from the bedrock, they might've constructed the interior walls from mudbrick reinforced with limestone revetments.

She handed Rick the pickaxe. "Try the limestone."

He massaged his shoulder. "You sure?"

She smiled. "Positive."

"When you smile, I get nervous." He grasped the pickaxe in both hands. "Get back."

She moved behind him. He repositioned himself parallel to the wall, alongside the plug.

Katy corked her ears with her fingers.

Rick pounded the axe into the limestone. Shards spewed in every direction. The tiny missiles embedded in the walls, nicked skin, showered onto the floor, stuck to clothing.

Rick slashed chunks from the revetments. The slices he sheared off the walls smashed into each other on the floor. Dust enveloped him.

Katy pulled her shirt up over her mouth. Her eyes watered. She wiped away the tears with the back of her hand.

The pounding ended. The cloud dispersed.

A three-by-four-foot hole breached the wall. The ragged boundary of the limestone exposed the mudbrick beneath it. Rick shined his lantern through the gap.

Behind the mudbrick, a second revetment glowed white in the lantern light.

Katy took the lantern.

Rick chopped at the stone. Limestone crumbled out, gradually clearing the way. Rick kicked at the mudbrick to widen the hole. Debris scattered inward onto the floor of the chamber beyond the wall.

Katy raised the lantern into the hole. Light spilled a few feet past the opening. The glow painted the naked walls within the chamber yellow. Through the rift, time had frozen in its tracks.

Rick grabbed the lantern from her. He ducked through the opening.

She half expected him to vanish through a time vortex. Instead he tripped, reeled headlong into the chamber, and flailed a hand out to bar his fall a millimeter before his skull bashed into the floor.

He sucked in a breath. Pushing onto his knees, one hand clamped around the lantern's handle, he stood.

Katy squeezed through the opening. Rick let out the lantern wick. Light inundated the chamber. A doorway led through the eastern wall into another chamber whose bowels resisted the lantern's glow. The chamber in which they stood, an antechamber for the tomb, retained the same width and breadth as the shaft. Its ceiling rose eight feet high, rather than 60.

The artisans had smeared plaster over the walls yet left them undecorated. Food offerings crowded against the north wall—clay jars of beer, bread loaves, a fruitcake, wine. Someone had donated a mummified falcon, its wrappings darkened by the resin applied to seal them. A table along the south wall accommodated an army of *shabti*, tiny statues designed to answer for the deceased in the afterlife. Life after death emulated life itself. In a paradise version of Egypt, the deceased carried on with life as usual, which meant someone had to tend the fields, mill the grain, brew the beer, bake the bread. To ensure a peaceful and restful afterlife, the *shabti* performed those labors for the deceased. These *shabti* had been fashioned from blue faience, a ceramic with coloring so delicate it appeared translucent.

Rick stepped over the threshold into the second chamber. Katy tramped after him.

A sarcophagus abutted the eastern wall. At nine feet long and three feet wide, the stone box took up three-fourths of the room. Carved from rose granite, with its lid intact, the sarcophagus showcased raised reliefs of the goddesses Isis and Nephthys, each of whom embraced an end of the sarcophagus in her wings. A pair of wooden statues, their backs to the east wall, flanked the sarcophagus. One embodied a boy, the other a woman. Blue and white paint enlivened the eyes. The *ka* statues strode one foot forward as if about to vacate their platforms to join Osiris in the *duat*.

A shiver jangled her spine. In the Legend of Setna, the statues had come to life. Their discoveries had validated parts of the story. What other truths might the myth include?

Don't be stupid.

Katy shambled to the sarcophagus.

The coffin came up to her chest. She perched on her toes to inspect the reliefs incised on the lid. Hieroglyphs marshaled into registers, pictographic soldiers who guarded the mummy inside. The inscription began with a chapter from the Book of the Dead, followed by an invocation offering to Osiris meant to ensure the deceased admission into the afterlife. The first line dated the text to the reign of Amenhotep II. The offering itself described the deceased as the son of the king's body, chief scribe, "he who knows the secrets of Thoth." The symbols that formed his name had been chiseled out. The tomb must belong to Nefrekeptah. What other son of Amenhotep knew Thoth's secrets?

Rick ran his hand over the granite. A smile, half suppressed, curved his lips.

Katy squeezed his forearm. "This is it."

"I hope so." He traced the hieroglyphs with his fingertip. "I've never seen a sarcophagus *in situ* before."

The archaeologists crept into the burial chamber. They advanced toward the sarcophagus in silence. Theo looked at Ethan, who looked at Yves, who arched his eyebrows at Theo. The air felt warm and damp from the moisture the ground had imbibed.

"Where's Tony?" Katy asked.

Theo pointed at the ceiling. "Went up to get my camera."

"The old coot forgot it," Ethan said. "They say the memory's the first to go."

Theo wagged a finger at him. "Respect your elders, son, or they might come back to haunt you. Literally."

Rick pulled the crowbar out of his sack.

Katy backed away past the sarcophagus' foot.

Rick and the archaeologists levered the lid from its slot. Rock grated against rock. The lid gyrated atop the sarcophagus. Theo and Ethan dove sideways.

The lid scraped to a halt. Its trajectory had skewed it halfway off the sarcophagus, semi-suspended in front of Katy. On the far side, diagonal from Katy, the corner had wedged itself against the wall. The head end angled across the sarcophagus.

Inside the cavity lay a wooden coffin.

The wood had decomposed into strips that enshrouded the mummy. Gaps between the strips exposed a cartonnage, a painted mask placed over the mummy's face. The cartonnage portrayed Nefrekeptah as a youthful man with thin lips, a narrow nose, plump cheeks, and a rounded chin.

Rick gazed down at the mummy. The corner of his mouth curved up as his lips parted.

The archaeologists crowded around the sarcophagus. They murmured to each other— ooh, ahh, fabulous, amazing.

Katy folded her arms on the sarcophagus. No book.

The burial chamber held nothing aside from the sarcophagus and the *ka* statues. No inscriptions on the walls. No funerary equipment. No offerings. Either Nefrekeptah had fallen out of favor with his father or robbers had looted the tomb in antiquity.

Why loot and leave behind the *shabti*? The figurines would fetch a good price on the black market, even the ancient black market. Perhaps pharaoh's soldiers had interrupted the robbery, saving the statues, after which they resealed the tomb.

Statues.

She gripped Rick's arm. "The Legend of Setna said the statues spoke to him."

"Katy, statues can't talk."

She approached the female statue. "A statue doesn't need to talk to speak to us."

"Talking and speaking are the same thing."

"Honey, don't be so literal."

Kneeling, she probed the statue's surfaces for inscriptions. On the platform, between the woman's feet, she located hieroglyphs painted onto the wood. The text identified the woman as Ahura, beloved wife of Nefrekeptah the scribe and magician. On the boy's statue she located a similar inscription naming him as Merab, son of Nefrekeptah the scribe and magician. Standing, she examined the statues' posture. Perhaps the position of the limbs imparted meaning.

She shoved her hands in her pockets. They looked like two people taking a stroll. Both mother and son held walking sticks. Their mouths closed, they assumed placid expressions fit for eternity in paradise.

The statues' backs offered nothing either.

"If the statues don't speak," Rick said, "maybe old Neffie does."

He bent over the sarcophagus. A thumb on each of the mummy's lips, he pushed one lip up, the other down. Nefrekeptah kept his mouth shut. Rick shoved a finger between the lips. Neffie's teeth barred passage.

In a flourish Rick whipped out his pocket knife and snapped it open. He slipped the blade between the mummy's lips. He hammered the hilt with the heel of his hand, forcing the blade between the teeth. The blade got stuck. He rocked it side to side. The blade wouldn't budge. He pounded the heel of his hand against the knife's hilt. Nothing.

He struck the hilt twice more. On the third strike, the knife popped through. The teeth separated a sliver. Rick poked around with the blade. He muttered "hmm," withdrew the knife, and handed it to Katy. Then he eased two fingers into Nefrekeptah's mouth.

The teeth parted a quarter-inch more. Rick thrust his fingers deeper inside the mummy's mouth.

Katy folded his knife. She tilted sideways. Rick's arm blocked her view of whatever he was doing inside the mummy's mouth.

He stood up. Between his fingers he held a tiny scroll.

Katy traded him the knife for the scroll. She fingered its banded surface. The Egyptians had created papyrus paper by gluing strips of the reed together, which created a striping across the paper. About three inches long, this papyrus had been rolled tightly, secured with a gold thread. She snapped the thread. The scroll unfurled in her palm.

She translated the text aloud. "He shall not speak."

"That's it?" Rick said.

"Yep."

Katy leaned over the sarcophagus' lip. Spells adorned the mummy's wrappings, verses designed to ensure Neffie's journey into the afterlife would conclude without strife. She bent over more. Her feet lifted off the ground and she rocked forward, her stomach acting as a lever with the sarcophagus as the fulcrum.

A spell on his thigh included a familiar name—Horus. Not a spell. The text sounded like an affirmation.

We are the Sons of Horus. May Hathor nourish our brother, for whom eternity is denied.

Rick leaned into the sarcophagus beside her. "What've you got?"

She indicated the spell.

As he read the inscription, he tracked the rows of hieroglyphs with his fingertip. Lips compressed into a line, he squinted at the symbols.

"Weird," he said.

Katy touched the resin-soaked bandages. "Pharaohs considered themselves the earthly incarnation of Horus, right?"

"Yes."

"The Meidum stela mentioned the Sons of Horus. They protect Thoth's wisdom."

"And Nefrekeptah was called He Who Knows the Secrets of Thoth." Rick rested his elbows on the sarcophagus. "So the Sons of Horus are, what, a secret society?"

"Why not?"

Theo jerked his head up, tearing his gaze away from the mummy. He frowned, gaze fixed on the ceiling.

"What's taking Tony so long?" he wondered.

"Don't worry," Ethan said. "He climbs slow, that's all."

The night drowned the desert in oil so viscous the night cloyed to his skin, so black nothing save for a smattering of stars infiltrated it. The wind churned the sand up into miniature whirlwinds whose tentacles coiled themselves around anything in their path.

Feet immersed in sand up to his ankles, Bob scratched his arm. The sensation of oil on his skin endured. Intef and his men, five in all, swarmed around him. One man grasped a lamp, a 4x2-inch rectangle no thicker than the jewel case for a CD. The lamp emitted light equivalent to 20 oil lanterns.

A dozen yards away, the remnants of Djoser's pyramid complex hulked.

Since he was the backup plan, why had Intef brought him here?

His mouth went dry, not entirely from the sand blasting into every orifice on his body. If Intef brought him along, the bastard must think the Bergrens had died. Or soon would.

Bob shoved both hands in his pants pockets. He spat out sand.

Intef turned to him. "Is this the correct location, Doctor?"

"Not sure."

"You translated the inscription this morning." Intef took a handful of Bob's shirt and pulled. "Must I prove my power to you?"

"I haven't a clue." *Big fat liar.* "Honestly."

Intef whirled toward his men. "Merka."

The man he'd addressed approached his master. Intef flicked his wrist. Merka produced a device from his pocket, a box with eyeholes inlaid on it. The binoculars were compact as a cell phone.

Intef raised the binoculars to his eyes. Grunted.

He thrust the binoculars at Merka. Bowing, the man took the device and scuttled backward.

Intef lifted his foot, shook the ankle. Bending down, he thumped the heel of his hand against the joint. It cracked.

Bob winced.

Intef straightened.

A realization slapped Bob in the face. "You have false feet."

"Courtesy of your friends, the Bergrens."

"I don't understand."

"The Bergrens inflicted this injury upon me one year ago." Intef snarled, "I shall repay them tenfold."

Lord Intef stomped across the desert, away from the pyramid of Djoser. He snapped his fingers.

His minions hurried after him. Two men, Bob's guards, prodded him in the back. He straggled after the group, succeeded by his sentries.

Perspiration dribbled down the back of his neck, between his shoulder blades. The sweat saturated his shirt. His socks, soaked through, squished inside his shoes. Sand infested his hair like an army of lice, turned his tongue into sandpaper. The sweat pasted sand to his skin. For 15 minutes they schlepped across the plateau, until they arrived at the foot of Sekhemkhet's pyramid. The complex had been abandoned shortly after construction began. Because its summit had never risen above the enclosure wall, even in antiquity, archaeologists nicknamed it the Buried Pyramid.

To the west, lights shimmered.

Intef herded his minions toward the lights. Hazy as phantasms, the lights outlined a perimeter of some sort, perhaps a camp. No one camped at Saqqara. The perimeter must demarcate an excavation.

The lump in Bob's throat congealed into ice—coated with sand.

In five minutes they reached the excavation. A jeep was parked outside the perimeter. No ropes hemmed in the site, just oil lanterns. Near one edge of the perimeter, someone had dug a trench. GPR equipment lay on the ground adjacent to the far perimeter, next to a stack of shovels. Backpacks sagged in the sand nearby.

A man knelt beside the packs with his back to them, unaware he had an audience as he rifled through the contents of one pack.

Intef gestured at Merka, who nodded. Intef's minion crouched down and prowled toward the man.

The stranger froze.

Merka tackled him. The stranger shouted, flailed, kicked at his attacker. Merka clouted him in the jaw. The stranger went limp.

Intef commanded his minions in Kemetian. The ancient Egyptians had called their land Kemet, which seemed an appropriate name for the Planners' language, for they had inspired the ancient Egyptian culture. He took the Bergrens' word on that, since he knew nothing about it himself.

He was learning now. Firsthand.

The other minions swarmed past Intef to Merka. The stranger lay slack on the ground, eyes open but bleary. Merka seized the man's arms and hefted him onto his feet. The stranger buckled. Merka shored him up with one arm.

Intef clamped a hand around Bob's forearm. He dragged Bob alongside him toward the ditch. As they approached, Bob saw the hole in the bottom of the ditch. A shaft tomb.

The stranger had red hair and a tanned complexion. His clothes were dirty, his skin clammy. At his feet, a Polaroid camera had fallen partway out of the backpack he'd been searching. Snapshots from the camera had spilled out onto the sand.

A minion plucked up the camera and photos. He presented them to his master.

Intef perused the photos. He picked one out of the group, holding it toward Bob.

In the photo, Rick Bergren squatted inside the trench, straddling the granite plug that must've blocked the shaft. In the background, Katy Bergren observed.

Intef discarded the photo.

Intef stalked toward the stranger. Their faces inches apart, he locked his reptilian stare on the man.

"Who are you?" Intef demanded.

The man lifted his chin. Gritted his teeth.

Intef grasped the man's chin. He turned the stranger's head side to side. The stranger shook free of Intef's grasp.

Intef chuckled. "I am your master. You shall tell me what I wish to know."

"I have no master."

Intef clenched the man's hair, yanking his scalp. The stranger winced.

"This," Intef said, tugging the man's hair, "means you belong to me."

Confusion contorted the man's features.

Red hair. Katy said the Planners fancied playing gods. No, even Intef wasn't crackers enough to believe…

Yes, actually, he was.

Bob glanced at the trench. A legion of steel-toed ants cavorted in his stomach.

Intef knelt beside the stranger's rucksack. He rummaged through the bag, chucking out a shirt, socks, a spade, a notepad, several pens and pencils. He paused. From the bag's depths, he pulled out a four-inch folded knife.

Rising, Intef flipped open the blade. He circled in front of the stranger.

72

The stranger struggled. Merka pinned the man's arms behind his back.

Intef stroked the knife across the man's throat.

Bob grabbed Intef's arm. "Wait."

A minion slugged Bob in the stomach. Bob doubled over, groaning. He tried to straighten. Pain cut through him. He lifted his head.

Intef stabbed the blade into the man's gut.

The stranger cried out.

Intef tore the knife free.

The man gasped each breath. His face blanched. His legs trembled and he nearly fell, but Merka caught him, forcing him to remain upright. A red stain spread out across his shirt. He clutched his abdomen, but failed to stem the blood.

Intef held the knife down at his side. Blood dripped from its tip.

"Where are the Bergrens?" Intef demanded.

The stranger's jaw quivered. "In th-there."

The man looked at the shaft.

Intef lobbed the knife past Bob. The blade punctured the sand, diving in up to its hilt.

Bob ground his teeth. His jaw muscle twitched.

Intef turned toward the jeep parked outside the site's perimeter.

"The time has come," he said, "to remind the Bergrens of my power."

The quintet of intrepid explorers huddled around the sarcophagus. The stink of sweat permeated the burial chamber. Intrepid or not, these explorers perspired like revelers at a Fourth of July picnic in Death Valley.

Katy extricated a wadded Kleenex from her pocket and swiped it across her forehead. The Kleenex, already damp from previous passes, absorbed less than half the sweat from her brow. She wadded it tighter, stuffing it inside her hip pocket.

The archaeologists had stripped away the wooden coffin's remains, which they'd piled on the floor near the wall. Nefrekeptah himself, dressed in linen bandages, reclined within the stone sarcophagus.

Mummification, plus 3,000 years in a tomb, had transformed the scribe-magician into a skeleton sheathed in beef jerky. Though his eyes bulged behind the lids as if the eyeballs still resided beneath them, the lumps stemmed from the packing the embalmers had stuffed inside the sockets as stand-ins for the eyeballs. Linen lashed his wrists together to hold his arms crossed over his chest. Each finger had been wrapped separately, as had each toe.

Ethan stretched a hand out to touch Nefrekeptah's face, then withdrew it. Theo leaned around his pupil to check out the specimen. He rocked side to side, back and forth, for a panoramic view of the mummy. Yves, bent over the head end of the sarcophagus, appraised the mummy with puckered lips. Rick stood stiff beside the Frenchman with both hands on the sarcophagus.

Beside Rick, Katy propped her elbows on the sarcophagus. She elevated her heels for a better angle on Nefrekeptah. A notion tickled her brain—that he would sit up, groan, and demand to know what the hell all these people were doing in his tomb. Instead he lay inert as the rock around him, yet she felt his spirit observing their exploits with a mixture of curiosity and dismay.

She had to stop hanging out in tombs.

"What should we do with him?" Ethan asked. "We can't let your friends blow him to smithereens."

"They're not our friends," Rick said.

"What did you call them, the Schemers?"

"The Planners."

"Right. We gotta get old Neffie outta here before they show up."

"Neffie?"

His cheeks reddening, Ethan shrugged. "Nefrekeptah's a mouthful to keep saying."

"I like Neffie," Katy said. "And Ethan's right, we have to save the mummy."

Everyone murmured agreement. Once the murmurs had subsided, the quintet lapsed into silence. No one knew how to transport a mummy up the shaft without damaging it.

Boom!

The ground quivered. Limestone powder drizzled down from the ceiling. Overhead, north of the burial chamber, a rumble subsided into a hush.

Ethan whispered, "What was that?"

In unison, Katy and Rick replied, "The Planners."

"How can you tell?"

"Do this long enough," Rick said, "and you learn to trust your gut feelings."

"Do what long enough?"

"Tick off homicidal spacemen."

Katy tisked. "They're not spacemen, honey. You know that."

"Close enough."

Katy tilted her head back. Dust had ceased sprinkling from the ceiling. The Planners must've procured a vehicle, a tank for all she knew, which might account for the rumbling.

Right. Sounded more like they'd instigated a demolition derby.

Tony. He was out there.

Rick tore the .45 from its holster. He started for the door.

Theo blocked his path. "Stay here, find the Book. We'll reconnoiter."

"Reconnoiter?"

"I always wanted to say that."

Rick frowned. "They'll kill you."

"Nah. They're after you." Theo turned toward the doorway. "Besides, I'm so old it's hardly worth the effort."

Theo exited the burial chamber. Yves and Ethan trailed after him.

Rick and Katy followed them out the door into the antechamber. As they passed the table of *shabti*, Katy hesitated. The four-inch-high figures lined up in ranks, an army of servants for the afterlife. All resembled the cartonnage mask of Nefrekeptah.

Except one.

74

Rick, halfway through the opening into the shaft, glanced back at her.

"What are you doing?" he asked.

She held up a hand. "Wait."

A *shabti* near the back featured a face distinct from Nefrekeptah's countenance, the head capped by the double crown reserved for pharaohs, the body enveloped in mummy's bandages. Katy picked up the figurine. The arms were crossed over the chest. In his tiny hands, the man clasped a crook and, instead of the usual flail, a scroll. She tipped the *shabti* to spy its base. Miniature hieroglyphs spelled out a word—Wesir, the ancient Egyptian name for Osiris—inside a cartouche.

A seam split the figurine into halves—front and back. She pried at the seam with her fingernails.

The *shabti* popped apart. The hollow interior encased a scroll.

"It's too quiet up there," Rick said.

Katy shoved the scroll, *shabti* and all, in her pocket. She hurried into the shaft behind Rick, hustling up the rope as he ascended to the midpoint.

A moment later, she flopped onto the sand topside.

Rick hoisted her to her feet, dragging her away from the shaft.

Past the lantern perimeter, fire engulfed the jeep.

Tony slumped against Theo, eyes half closed, his shirt soaked with the same blood that coated his hands. Theo pressed a wadded sock into the wound. Tony trembled, his face pale and damp with sweat. Yves and Ethan knelt beside their colleagues, silent.

Ten feet away, a knife's hilt stuck straight up out of the sand.

Ethan proffered his hand to Rick. "Tony was holding this."

In his palm lay a pocket watch, ticking softly.

Rick took the watch. He flipped it over. His lip twitched.

Katy leaned over to squint at the watch. On its back someone had scored the initials "RB."

"Dad's had that watch since I was a kid," Rick said. "I scratched my initials onto it when I was ten. Thought he'd kill me."

Rick fisted his hand around the watch, clenching his fingers so tight they quivered.

Katy wrapped her hand around his. She said to the archaeologists, "Do you think Tony can make it until we get back with help?"

"I think so," Theo said. "Not much choice, is there?"

"We'll hurry."

Rick stuffed the watch into his pocket. He plucked up his backpack and Katy's, helped her secure hers, then strapped on his own. Theo furnished them with a flashlight, which he'd dug out of his backpack.

They set out across the desert toward the nearest village.

A breeze, blowing through the open windows, ventilated the Land Rover.

Outside the windshield, a quarter mile across the desert, a bonfire devoured an old jeep in the vicinity of an encampment. The flames tickled the darkness. Around the encampment's perimeter, lights wavered. Tiny specters, faintly human in their shape, haunted the site inside the perimeter.

Asru scanned the desert through her binoculars, yet the specters remained indistinct.

Jed and Chin had gone to investigate the encampment in the hopes the Bergrens toiled there. An hour ago Asru had spotted Intef's craft gliding along the western horizon, low enough that few onlookers would notice. The craft had tarried for a moment, dispatching six passengers, then sped away to the northwest. The phantoms at the encampment must be those who had come down from the craft.

If Intef had executed the Bergrens, she would have no one to guide her to her destination. No one who knew the terrain, who understood the environment. She harbored no fears about becoming lost in the desert or expiring from dehydration, for the terrain she traversed was history, its landscape eroded by lies, its atmosphere poisoned by cover-ups. Intef belonged to the corrupted history, subsisted on its venom, exploited his power to contaminate the minds of every being he encountered. He wished to destroy this world—and replace it with one of his own making.

This world did not belong to her, nor she to it. Yet she must protect this world. She had sworn an oath.

She pulled the scarab amulet out of her shirt. With it clinched in her hand, she uttered in her native tongue, "He who is chaos and destruction, you cannot harm me. I know your secret name. I know your mother's name and your father's name. The wings of truth protect me."

She slipped the amulet inside her shirt. Today people prayed to Jesus or Buddha or Allah for protection. She prayed to an ancient power. For no power of the modern world could stop an evil that had existed since the dawn of man, the dawn of Earth. An evil called chaos.

An evil that lived in the beast named Intef.

A metal object nudged her left temple. She gripped the steering wheel in both hands. Without moving her head, she glanced at the man who hunched outside the Land Rover, erect as an obelisk. Clad in black, he held the object to her temple with his gloved hand. A black knit mask swathed his whole head, including his face. More a phantasm than a man, he prodded the cylindrical end of the object against her temple.

The metal felt cool against her skin. She rotated her head. With a thrust of his hand he pushed her head, forcing her to stare through the windshield at the encampment. She watched him out the corner of her eye. The object. A gun—yes, that was it. The ambient light reflected on its metal.

"Who are you?" he asked.

Intensity galvanized his voice as he whispered into her ear. His accent differed from that of the Bergrens.

"A traveler," she replied.

"No one visits Saqqara at night."

"I enjoy communing with the dead under starlight."

"You've been watching the Bergrens."

Her buttocks had grown numb. She wriggled in the seat. "If you wish to kill me, do so. You may inform Intef that death shall not deter me."

He retracted the gun. "Intef?"

She glanced at him. "Who are y—"

He had evaporated into the darkness.

When the visitor had spoken Intef's name, a mixture of surprise and recognition had tinged his voice. A servant of Intef would not speak his master's name in such a manner. The visitor did not serve Intef. Curious.

To the right of the Land Rover, two figures approached.

Jed and Chin boarded the vehicle, slamming the doors shut behind them.

"They found a tomb," Jed informed her. "Intef injured a man. He then caused the explosion and fled. I do not understand his actions."

"It was a message."

Intef considered blood and fear his best weapons. He thought nothing of his fellow human beings, whom he mutilated and murdered, caring only whether their deaths conveyed the appropriate meaning to the message's recipient.

She had received his messages in the past. Their syntax no longer terrified her. She would crush him. No matter the cost.

Her fingers ached. Her fingers, clamped around the amulet, cut their nails into her flesh. She opened her hand.

She no longer possessed the weapons she had once employed to defeat Intef. And she had encumbered her search with the belief she must secrete herself from the world in order to achieve her goal. Intef had ensured she mistrusted and feared the Low Ones. His plan had succeeded. She had let it.

To stop Intef, she required a new weapon. An unexpected ally.

Fear must die. She would kill it.

She started the engine. Shifting the Land Rover into drive, she steered the vehicle toward the lights at the encampment.

"Where are you going?" Chin asked.

"To vanquish fear," she said, "and forge an alliance powerful enough to save us all."

"My lady," said Jed, "the Bergrens possess no such power."

"Pray they do."

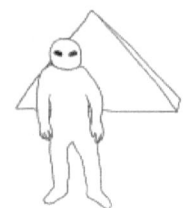

Chapter Six

Past the perimeter of the dig site, headlights bobbled. Rick and Katy charged straight toward the site.

They halted near the lantern-marked boundary.

"The Planners wouldn't come back," Rick said. "They made their point."

Rick glanced back at the archaeologists on the far side of the dig site. Theo motioned for them to skedaddle.

"They want us to go," Katy said.

"I know." Rick turned away from the oncoming headlights. "No more running. No more hiding. This time I face the scumbags, whoever they are."

"And what am I supposed to do, knit a sweater for Neffie?"

He grasped her shoulders, "If I begged, would you hide in the tomb?"

"Not a chance in hell."

"I figured."

The headlights joggled a few hundred yards away.

Rick whisked the Taurus out of her fanny pack. He thrust it into her hand, closed her fingers around the grip. As he pulled out the .45, he pushed her ahead of him toward the shaft entrance where the archaeologists waited.

An engine rumbled, louder each second. The headlights bobbed on the nose of a Land Rover.

The vehicle plowed through the lantern perimeter. The Land Rover parked 20 feet away, angled across the dig site. Two men and women hopped out.

One man looked Asian, the other Mediterranean. The woman had dark hair and eyes, but peaches-and-cream skin like Katy's. She fondled the gold-chain belt around her waist.

The men took up positions flanking her.

The woman looked past Rick, right at Katy.

"We will not harm you," the woman said. "We have come to ask your help."

"Sure you have," Rick said. "Did we win the lottery too?"

"Lottery?"

The Asian man muttered, "It's a joke."

The woman canted her head at Rick, her eyes bright. Her nose, her mouth, they reminded him of someone. He tried to draw out the memory, but it resisted him.

"Who the hell are you?" Rick asked.

"An ally," the woman said.

"Right."

"I can help you defeat Intef." She lifted her chin. "I believe you have met him."

A clearing in the woods. Hairy hominids all around. A snaky, slimy wannabe pharaoh presiding over the scene.

Yeah, he'd met Intef. The bastard had taken his father away, and promptly broken a promise not to attack him and Katy.

"If you know Intef," Rick said, "I don't want to know you."

"He is my enemy as well. Together we can correct a wrong which was perpetrated long ago. We can resurrect the memory of Bakhu."

"Tell me who you are and I'll think about it."

"My name is Asru. Though I will not beg for your help, I do ask for it."

Rick leveled his gun at the newcomers. He felt weird about threatening a woman, especially an unarmed one, even if she was a Planner.

The woman slipped a hand inside her vest. The muscles in her wrist tautened.

Not unarmed after all.

The Mediterranean man took a step toward them.

Rick waggled the .45 at him. "Uh-uh."

Asru raised a hand. She fixed her glare on each of her men in turn. They bowed their heads.

She dropped her hand. "Jed and Chin will not harm you."

Jed mumbled, "Yes, Your Incarnation."

Asru whipped her head toward Jed, glaring hard at him. His cheeks flushed. He stammered sounds that fell short of forming words.

Rick arched an eyebrow at Asru. "What did he call you?"

"I will not ask for your trust," Asru said, "but I request your cooperation."

While she'd shown no weapons, the way she'd slid her hand under her vest suggested she hid one inside it. Jed had wielded no weapons either, but the guy must have one too.

Rick shifted his finger onto the barrel above the trigger. If Asru wanted them dead, she'd had plenty of opportunity to shoot, blow up, hang, or run over them. His right arm still throbbed from whacking the pickaxe into the limestone wall. He cupped his left hand under his right elbow for support. Maybe they should accept her offer. Either way, he wouldn't trust her. He wouldn't trust anyone.

Except Katy.

She'd sidled closer to him, the Taurus clasped in her right hand. The muzzle pointed at the floor.

Asru tipped her head at Katy. "Are you not the one who turned the Revered Ones against Intef?"

The Planners called the hairy hominids the Revered Ones. He hadn't realized Katy turned them against the Planners. He restrained a smile.

"Did I?" Katy said. "Cool."

"I thank you," Asru told her. "The conflict has angered him. Anger is his greatest weakness, for it makes him careless."

Chin checked his watch.

Planners wore watches?

"We should hurry," Chin said.

Asru met Rick's gaze. "Will you join us?"

Rick hooked his finger over the trigger.

Katy holstered the Taurus. She laid a hand on his forearm. "Put the gun down."

"I don't trust them. They could be working for Intef."

"You don't have to trust them." She pressed down on his arm. "Trust me."

He looked at Asru and each of her men in turn before pinpointing his gaze on Katy.

She squeezed his arm gently.

He lowered the gun. Katy had been right to trust Garfield's information about the Washington stela. She'd been right about the directions to Nefrekeptah's tomb. She was usually right, about everything.

Dammit.

He tucked the .45 inside the shoulder holster. "I guess it's a deal."

"We must go," Asru said. "Your friend requires medical attention."

She whispered to her men in a language that sounded like ancient Egyptian. He hadn't heard her words clearly enough to tell for certain, though he felt pretty sure.

The Planners spoke a different language that must've evolved from ancient Egyptian. While they could manage in ancient Egyptian, they rarely used it. They didn't speak to each other in it, for sure.

Jed and Chin marched to the archaeologists. Jed locked his arms under Tony's. Chin grabbed hold of Tony's feet. As one, they lifted him off the ground and carried him to the Land Rover, where they deposited him on the backseat.

Tony moaned. Jed climbed into the backseat, hunkering on the floor. He pressed down on the makeshift dressing Theo had put over the wound.

Asru escorted Yves, Ethan, and Theo to the vehicle. Chin took the wheel. Asru seated herself on the passenger side, leaving the archaeologists to huddle in the back.

Katy started for the Land Rover. Rick clapped a hand on her shoulder.

"How do you know we can trust them?" he asked.

"I don't. It's just a feeling."

"Jed called her Your Incarnation. That's what the ancient Egyptians called their pharaohs."

"Maybe she's a leader among the Planners."

"Intef rules the Planners."

"Maybe she commands a faction of nice Planners."

"Nice Planners"? He snorted. "We're the bread dough they beat down so we don't rise up too high, remember? You said that."

"I know. But they can't all be evil."

"Why not?"

She shrugged and tramped toward the vehicle.

With a bad feeling simmering in his gut, he trotted after her.

Cairo
Monday, October 20

Katy leaned against the doorjamb of the balcony as she gazed over the roofs of the surrounding buildings, across the river to where the pyramids smoldered in the sunrise. A smog bank dispersed the sun's rays into a prism of colors, reds that set the pyramids afire, golds that transformed their pinnacles into precious ornaments, purples that bruised the sky.

The predawn chill caressed her bare arms. She hugged herself, rubbing her arms. Another, deeper chill suffused her flesh. This frost wouldn't succumb to the sunrise. Its touch would stick with her like an unwanted houseguest.

The knife in the sand. Tony's face, white as milk. The blood on his stomach and hands.

After escaping Saqqara, they'd rushed to the hospital in Cairo. Tony remained in serious condition, but the doctors expected him to make a full recovery. Theo, Yves, and Ethan had stayed at the hospital to wait it out together. Katy had wanted to stay too, seeing as Tony's condition was her fault. If she'd found the Book, Intef would never have run into Tony. She shouldn't have let the archaeologists accompany them to Saqqara. She should've, at the very least, ordered them to leave once they'd located the tomb.

Her head ached. She gnawed on her lip.

"It's not your fault," Rick said. "Intef's to blame."

Rick stepped onto the balcony beside her. In one hand he held her jacket, in the other the *shabti* of Osiris. He offered her jacket to her. She slipped her arms into the sleeves. He pulled the jacket over her shoulders. She jammed her hands in the pockets. He gave her the *shabti*.

Bracing himself against the jamb, he linked his arms around her. She rested her head on his chest.

"I wish you'd slept longer," he said.

She yawned. "I'm fine."

"I don't fall for that line anymore."

At two this morning Asru had dropped them off at a hotel near the Giza plateau, on the outskirts of Cairo, in the shadow of the pyramids. She'd sworn to meet them by the Sphinx at nine o'clock. At the hotel they'd rented a room, washed up, and exchanged their dust-ridden, sweaty, smelly clothes for fresh ones. Katy had attempted a nap. It didn't take.

She popped open the *shabti*. The petite scroll reposed inside the figurine, snug and safe as the day its author had stashed it there. A gold thread constrained the scroll. She snapped the thread and unrolled the scroll. The scrap of paper measured about four inches long by three inches wide. The golden paper was fashioned from papyrus, a type of reed, glued together in crosswise strips to create a basket-weave effect.

The paper contained a text written in hieratic, a simplified version of hieroglyphs. Reading hieratic required practice, since the symbols differed from their hieroglyphic counterparts.

She'd neglected her hieratic studies.

"I hope you can read this," she said.

Rick took the scroll. Narrowed his eyes. Hummed tunelessly.

A moment later, he said, "Horus guards the city of Thoth on the threshold of the Domain of Osiris…thirty-eight rivers, seventy rods southwest of his incarnation in the horizon."

"Directions again," she said. "City of Thoth must mean Bakhu. But what's Thoth's incarnation in the horizon?"

Rick fanned himself with the scroll.

Katy looked past his shoulder into the room. A lamp on the beside table drew a circle of radiance inside the hotel room. The light evaporated an arm's length from the balcony.

Footsteps echoed down the alley below.

"Wait a minute," Rick said, squinting at the scroll. "It's not Thoth's incarnation. It's Horus' incarnation in the horizon."

"Which makes much more sense."

"Actually, it does."

He ducked his head down to her level, his cheek flush with hers. Stretching an arm out toward the cityscape, he pointed his index finger at the pyramids.

"Horus' incarnation in the horizon is right there," he said, "next to the pyramids."

"I don't get it."

"The Sphinx. The ancient Egyptians called it Horemakhet—Horus in the horizon."

She wriggled around to face him, snaking her arms around his waist. Balanced on her toes, she planted a kiss smack on his lips.

"You're brilliant," she said.

"Lucky guess, that's all."

"Hardly."

He extricated himself from her and marched across the room to the telephone.

She trailed after him, flopping onto the bed.

He picked up the handset. "We need a faster way to find Bakhu."

"I don't think they have phones in the city of Thoth."

"No…but maybe we can get ourselves some wings."

Giza

The Sphinx towered above Katy, its great paws stretching forth on either side of her. The Dream Stela, a standing stone on which Thutmosis IV had inscribed his tale of the Sphinx speaking to him in a dream, stood between the legs, near the chest. A group of American tourists had congregated a few yards beyond the tip of the left paw.

Rick whistled. "It's taller than I thought."

"The Sphinx or the stela?"

"Both."

Katy checked her watch. Asru was 15 minutes late.

"If she doesn't show," Rick said, "we need a Plan B."

"We've got one plan, period."

"I was afraid of that."

Maybe they shouldn't trust Asru. Yet a force inside her—call it intuition, lunacy, wishful thinking—urged her to trust the mysterious woman who called herself Asru. Katy had no doubts that Asru wasn't her real name. And still she felt compelled to trust the woman.

She shoved her hands in her pockets. Her right hand bumped into a mass in her pocket—the magnesium firestarter her father had given her. She'd forgotten she had it, since she kept it with her always. The rectangle of magnesium had a flint core embedded in one side. Flake off the magnesium, strike the flint to ignite it. Sounded easier than it was.

Horus guards the city of Thoth on the threshold of the Domain of Osiris, 38 rivers, 70 rods southwest of his incarnation in the horizon.

Rick had calculated 38 rivers and 70 rods equated to about 250 miles. The city of Thoth must refer to Bakhu. The Domain of Osiris meant the underworld, where the deceased lived on for eternity in the form of spirits called *akh*s. The last phrase had puzzled her, until Rick reminder her that Ramses II had restored the Sphinx in the form of the god Horemakhet—Horus in the Horizon. Setna had been a son of Ramses.

In the legend, Setna had reburied the Book of Thoth with Nefrekeptah, where he'd found it. Had his father later relocated the Book to prevent his son from succumbing to temptation in the future? Maybe Ramses had been a Son of Horus, like Nefrekeptah. Since pharaohs served as earthly embodiments of Horus anyway, his membership in a secret society that worshiped the god fit right in with his status. It also explained why he refurbished the Sphinx to honor an incarnation of his patron god.

Katy knelt at the base of the Dream Stela. She touched the jagged line that marked where the face had broken away, obliterating the bottom portion of the text. Right before the break, hieroglyphs spelled out "Khaf," which Egyptologists speculated meant the pharaoh Khafra had built the Sphinx. Since they also credited him with erecting the Second Pyramid, the theory satisfied them. Never mind that no text from the Old Kingdom, during which Khafra had reigned, mentioned the Sphinx or its surrounding temples. Never mind the fact that, while exactly zero inscriptions had ever been found that spoke of the Sphinx's construction, archaeologists had found a stela whose text asserted the Sphinx had been ancient when Egyptian civilization began. Never mind that geologists recognized rainfall had caused the erosion on the Sphinx and its enclosure, making the man-headed lion much older than the accepted date. No significant, long-term rain had fallen on Giza for about 10,000 years.

Egyptologists argued that only hunter-gatherers had lived in Egypt back then. Pharaonic culture had obviously created the Sphinx, which meant the statue must date to no earlier than the Old Kingdom.

They had no idea the Planners lived in Egypt 10,000 years or more before the present. Even if they knew, they'd cover it up.

So much of the mainstream version of history didn't fit with the facts. Would whatever she and Rick found in Bakhu prove another chapter needed rewriting? It hardly mattered. The scholars and scientists would never tear a page from their hallowed book of the past.

Katy straightened, turning her back on the Sphinx. Behind the tourists, some locals had gathered to sell jewelry and clothing. One man, taller than the others, stood apart from the group. He carted no items to sell and, as Katy studied him, he studied her in return with hazel eyes that matched the golden undertones in his brown skin.

The face. Those eyes.

She patted Rick's sleeve. "See the tall man standing near the traders?"

"What about him?"

"I think that's Bob Hanover's assistant, Halim."

Taking her hand, Rick piloted her through the throng of tourists toward the man. When they neared him, he spun on his heels. Rick quickened his pace. The man speed-walked alongside the causeway linking the Sphinx and its temples to the Second Pyramid a mile distant. All but the foundation of the causeway had disintegrated. As they hustled after him, Halim upped his pace. Every third step, he glanced back at them, wide-eyed.

They pursued him down the causeway, out of earshot of the tourists.

Katy shouted, "Halim!"

He halted facing them, mouth open. Fear sparkled in his eyes.

Rick and Katy advanced within five yards of him.

He bolted for the pyramid.

Rick sprinted after him. Katy ran as fast as she could but her shorter legs failed to match the men's speed. The morning air was thick with humidity. Sweat streamed over her face, into her open mouth. The salt stung her eyes. She ran faster.

Rick gained on Halim. The Egyptian yanked a knife out from under his robe. He sliced the blade at Rick's torso. Rick tackled Halim. The pair tumbled to the sand.

The knife popped out of Halim's grasp and sailed through the air. Rick, straddling · Halim, pinned the man's arms behind his back.

The knife clattered onto the causeway.

Rick gasped, "We're friends of Bob."

"I know who you are," Halim said.

Katy stopped beside the men. "If you knew, why did you run?"

"Someone told them of our dig at Meidum."

"You mean the Planners." When Halim merely blinked, she explained, "The people who come from a light in the sky."

"Someone told them."

The Planners could monitor every archaeological site in the world, if they wished. But another possibility had presented itself of late.

They had learned about computers—or recruited a Low One who knew about them. A techno-geek disillusioned when his job got outsourced to India, or just a greedy bugger who'd take whatever riches the Planners promised him. Either way, the sap had no clue the Planners would cancel his account, permanently, once they'd emptied his knowledge bank.

She saw no reason to burden Halim with such information.

"No one needed to tell them." She told Rick, "Honey, I think you can let him go now."

Rick released Halim's arms and pushed onto his feet. He pulled a handkerchief from his pocket to swab his forehead.

Halim rolled over onto his back and struggled to his knees. He sat motionless, huffing, for a moment.

When his breathing had calmed, he struggled onto his feet.

"I cannot help you," he said. "Their power is too great."

Halim bolted down the causeway, back toward the Sphinx.

Rick moved to follow.

Katy shook her head. "Let him go. He's scared."

"Can't blame him," Rick said.

From the other direction, a female voice inquired, "Am I so frightening?"

Rick and Katy looked down the causeway behind them, in the direction of the Second Pyramid. Arms slack at her sides, hair billowing around her face, Asru observed them from 30 feet away.

"Not you," Katy said, "It's your friend Intef and his psych-ward pals who scare people."

"You are not frightened of me?"

"No." Katy waved Asru closer. "We need to talk."

Asru jogged across the causeway Since yesterday she'd traded in her skirt for pants. While the barrette remained clipped in her hair, Asru's locks had escaped their confinement. The wind lashed them around her face and fluttered her bangs. Dark crescents had formed under her bloodshot eyes.

Katy surveyed the Giza Plateau. Aside from the tourists at the Sphinx, and a few locals here and there, no one wandered the plateau. Asru had come alone.

"Where are your men?" Katy asked.

"Awaiting our arrival."

Asru waved her arm at the desert behind the Sphinx. A vehicle, tiny at that distance, sat parked in the sand.

Two locals wandered by, heading up the causeway toward the pyramid. The men smiled and nodded as they passed. Katy smiled back.

Hands on his hips, Rick glared at Asru. "You spied on us—bugged our house, broke in to steal stuff—and now you want our trust."

He stepped forward so that his right side blocked Katy, partially, from Asru. Tension converted his muscles into steel cables, his flesh into concrete. Asru countered his glare with a serene expression.

"We mean you no harm," Asru said. "Please believe me."

Katy rubbed her forehead. Though she had no headache, rubbing her forehead gave her an excuse to look away. That feeling inside had strengthened. She knew she ought to distrust Asru, but she couldn't manage it.

Rick glanced at Katy. He frowned. She grasped his hand, intertwining their fingers.

He traded in his glare for puckered lips. To Asru, he said, "I guess we're trusting you."

"Thank you," Asru said.

"We need to get ahead of Intef," Katy said. "Find the Book before he catches up to us."

"Great," Rick said. "How do you suggest we outrun a spaceship?"

Katy opened her mouth to speak.

"Don't say it's not a spaceship."

"I was going to say, we need a faster mode of transportation than a Land Rover."

Rick tramped down the causeway toward the Sphinx, pulling Katy after him, with Asru close behind.

Katy asked Asru, "Just out of curiosity, did your ancestors build the Sphinx?"

"My people built that monument, as well as many of the pyramids you see today."

"The pyramids in Egypt."

Asru smiled. "We played a part in the creation of other pyramids as well."

"You make it sound like you were there."

"Perhaps I was, in another life."

"You believe in reincarnation?"

Asru hesitated. "No."

"What did you mean by another life?"

Asru withdrew a scarab amulet from inside her blouse. She caressed it, gazing across the desert at the horizon, and murmured in ancient Egyptian.

Katy angled her head to listen better. The syntax sounded different than what she'd heard when the hairy hominids and other Planners spoke the old language. The grammar seemed almost archaic. From her studies, she'd learned that syntax had changed somewhat between the oldest version of the language and the later forms. What did it mean for Asru to speak the oldest form?

Both the Planners and the hairy hominids had developed their own distinct languages over the millennia. But the Planners also spoke ancient Egyptian because the hairy hominids understood it. The creatures spoke an intermediate phase of the language, which hinted that they'd last encountered the Egyptian culture during the Middle or New Kingdom. For Asru to speak the archaic version implied that her last contact with the outside world had come during the Old Kingdom—or before.

Which would make her older than any other Planner. Older than the hairy hominids. Older than any living thing on Earth today. Impossible. She must belong to a clan that had separated from the other Planners early on, cutting off all contact with the outside world.

If she had conversed with a hairy hominid in an archaic dialect, the theory would make sense. But Asru had spoken it during a private moment when she believed no one else was listening. Even if she grew up in an offshoot clan, the language of her people should've evolved. Their language should have its own distinctive syntax.

Katy asked Asru, "Who are you?"

Without blinking, or answering, Asru confronted Katy's gaze.

"What do you want?" Katy asked.

"The Book."

"What will you do with it?"

"Read it."

Katy switched to a question the woman might actually answer instead of resorting to the verbal equivalent of the balls-and-cups trick. "Why does Intef want it?"

"He believes it possesses great power, which he can exercise to usurp the throne and rule our people. He will subjugate all people and kill those who rise up against him. We must stop him."

"Usurp the throne? From whom?"

Asru averted her gaze. She dropped her mouth open as if to respond. Her eyes glistened with tears. She clamped her jaw shut and blinked away the tears.

Katy sped up to walk beside Rick. Asru had provided all the answers she cared to give.

As they exited the causeway, they passed a crowd of tourists led by a yammering guide. Katy scanned the crowd. At the rear of the group, a man's gaze intersected hers. A scarf shielded his mouth and nose, draping over his head beneath a canvas hat. The sunlight penetrated the shade cast by the hat's brim, highlighting eyes as deep blue as sapphires.

The man ducked his head.

Katy yanked Rick's hand, stopping both of them. "Rick, it's—"

The man had merged with the crowd, invisible amongst the myriad faces.

"What?" Rick said.

"I thought—I mean, it looked like…for a second I thought I saw Warner."

Rick squeezed her hand. "He's gone, Katy. Intef killed him."

"I know."

He turned and took two steps. Katy didn't move. Rick tugged her hand to impel her onward. She stretched her neck up, peering over the crowd, but saw no sign of the man. He had, most likely, existed as nothing more than a figment of her overstressed mind.

Yeah, that was it.

She let Rick ferry her away from the tourists.

The joint hugged the outskirts of Cairo, southeast of Giza. Katy didn't know what to call it—a bar, a pub, a shack with beer taps. Because she had no clue, she opted for ambiguity. It was a joint.

Whatever its proper designation, they strolled into it at five after nine in the morning. Despite the earliness, three men hunched at the bar sipping drinks. A half dozen others slouched over tables suckling beer bottles. A pair of wayward tourists huddled in the corner examining their beer bottles with suspicion.

Asru and her men had heeded Rick's order to stay outside, despite their protests. Rick had threatened to shoot them if they took one step toward the door. The three of them blended into a crowd like giraffes in a shopping mall. Besides, she and Rick wanted to attract no attention. Five people, two of them women, traipsing into a bar attracted something.

A man at the bar winked at Katy. He slurped his drink and winked again.

She shuffled closer to Rick. "Are you sure Ethan said to meet them *here*?"

"I'm sure. He gave me GPS coordinates."

Rick navigated around the tables to an empty one near the right-hand wall. He pulled out a chair for Katy. She sat down, and he seated himself beside her. Neither Ethan, Yves, nor Theo were in the joint, at the bar or a table. Unless they'd withdrawn to the bathroom.

If the joint had a bathroom.

She'd seen bar such as this back in America. She'd always driven past—and avoided looking back, lest she metamorphose into a pillar of salt.

The man at the bar tipped his glass in her direction. He sneered.

Rick glowered at him. The man raised a fist. Rick half stood.

The man's sneer faltered. He dropped his fist and his drink, turning his back to them.

Rick sat down. He laid a hand on the table, keeping watch on the drunk.

"Let it go," she said.

Rick switched his gaze to her. His glower softened.

She patted his hand. "You're adorable when you act tough."

"Adorable? What's next, sweet and fluffy?"

"No," she said, "you are definitely not fluffy."

He eyed her sideways. "Which means I'm sweet."

Sucking in her lips, she bit down on them. Still the smile threatened to burst free. He'd said the word "sweet" as if it meant "deranged."

Rick rolled his eyes and sighed.

Katy rested her elbows on the table. The legs wobbled. At the tabletop's center, a thin candle squatted inside a shot glass atop a paper napkin. The napkin, candle and all, skated across the table. The candle's flame fluttered. She folded her hands on her lap and leaned back against the chair.

Creak.

The front door swung inward. A gust of wind swirled through the joint.

Katy's hair lashed her face. She blew it away. Rick squinted at the doorway, where sunlight streaming in from outside framed three silhouettes.

"Well if it ain't the Indiana Joneses."

Ethan shut the door. As the backlight gave way to the diffuse lighting inside the joint, Ethan's silhouette resolved into a human being. He grinned at them. At either side of him, Yves and Theo became recognizable too.

Katy motioned for them to come over and sit down.

Theo and Yves dragged chairs from another table. As the chairs scraped across the floorboards, the wood shed splinters.

The archaeologists settled into their chairs. They plopped their backpacks on the floor.

"How's Tony?" Katy asked.

"Conscious and cranky," Ethan said, "which means he's fine."

"He'll be in the hospital a few days," Theo said.

"So what's up?" Ethan asked.

Rick leaned on the table, thumping its short leg into the floor. "Can you really fly?"

"Only when I've got my cape and tights on."

Rick frowned at the kid. Katy poked his thigh. He batted her hand away.

The guy at the bar sneaked a look at her. She bared her teeth at him.

His eyes widened. He bounded off his stool, absconding to a dark corner on the far side of the room.

Fixing his best glare on Ethan, Rick said, "You any good? As a pilot, I mean."

Theo laughed. "You've seen how he drives. He practically flies that jeep."

"But in an airplane," Rick said, "how does he do? Is he safe?"

"He won't kill you. I think."

Ethan raised his hand. "I'm still here, ya know."

Rick sat back. He shot a sideways glance at Katy.

She smiled. He screwed up his mouth.

If Ethan really knew how to fly, and had access to a plane, that solved their problem. They could trust Ethan. She thought. If they had to trust somebody, the kid looked more promising than the Casanova in the corner.

"Got a plane?" Katy asked.

"Yep," Ethan said. Before she could respond, he added, "And it runs and it's safe and I won't crash it, killing us all in a fiery explosion. I haven't caused any fiery explosions in at least six months."

Rick muttered, "That's reassuring."

To Ethan, she said, "How's five hundred dollars sound?"

"Naw, I don't want your money. Where are we going?"

"The western desert. To find the lost city of Bakhu and, hopefully, the Book of Thoth."

"Cool."

Katy tried to hold back the expression of shock that she felt materializing on her face. She'd expected the archaeologists to say the Book was a myth and what kind of research did she do to arrive at such a ludicrous conclusion, before finishing up with a crack about leaving the field work to the real archaeologists. She and Rick had managed to bump into a trio of open-minded scientists. What luck.

"Oh." Ethan whapped Theo's arm. "Show 'em the paper."

Theo dug around inside his backpack. He unearthed a newspaper, which he slapped onto the table in front of Rick, upside-down.

Rick spun the newspaper around. "It's in Arabic."

"Look at the photograph."

The newspaper, folded in half, bared its upper portion to them. In the middle under the headline, a photo captured a cruise ship gliding along at night. A couple stood at the railing, arms around each other, smiling for the camera. The moon glimmered above and to the left of the couple. Behind them, above their heads but under the moon, hung a disk-shaped object. The moonglow washed the craft in luminescence.

Katy couldn't move. Her eyelids refused to blink. Her lungs expanded and contracted, yet she felt breathless.

"That," Ethan said, "is one of dozens of photos showing the UFO. The cruise ship was crossing the Atlantic from Spain to the Caribbean when passengers spotted a huge disk flying past. It flew right over the ship."

Rick asked the question that had caught in Katy's throat. "How huge?"

"The captain estimated its diameter at twice the cruise ship's length."

"Which way was it heading?"

"East-southeast."

"This way." Rick jumped up, toppling his chair. "We have to find Bakhu before Intef's reinforcements arrive."

Katy asked Ethan, "Still think it's an adventure?"

"They attacked my friend. If helping you gets them in trouble, I'm in."

Theo thrummed his fingers on his thighs. Yves murmured a French curse inside a breath. Cursing her for being crazy or cursing the UFO?

Ethan marshaled a smile and stood. "No alien medical exam is gonna scare me away."

An alien exam wasn't the worst that could happen.

But she kept that information to herself.

In the alley between the two buildings, no light infiltrated. The structure to the right housed tenements. The building at the left accommodated the tavern into which the Bergrens had disappeared a few minutes earlier.

Asru waited at the alley's mouth, where she could see when the Bergrens departed the establishment. Chin lolled against the wall of the tenement building opposite her. Jed stood rigid beside her, darting his eyes back and forth to watch the street.

A shiver whispered on her neck, prickling the hairs.

Asru panned her gaze down the street. A block away, inside an alley, a shadow rippled. Scarabs skittered inside her gut. She stepped out of the alley.

"Remain here," she said.

Jed rushed toward her. "Your Incarnation—"

She silenced him with a glance.

He bowed his head. "As you wish."

Asru jogged across the street, veering toward the alley. The shadows masked whatever had moved within that space. She grasped the knife under her vest and crept into the darkness. Her boots crunched on pebbles.

Clothing hung from a rope strung across the alley between windows of the buildings.

The wind blustered. The clothing flapped.

She relaxed. The garments rippled with the wind, apparitions of motion.

Crunch.

The sound arose from beyond the suspended clothing. She slunk toward the garments, pushed aside the robes and shirts, and peeked through the curtain into the murk on the other side.

The alley was vacant. She crossed under the clothing. The robes and shirts fell behind her, closing the curtain.

A man chuckled.

She jerked her head left. Her hair flounced around her face and neck.

He leaned against the building, right foot propped against the wall with the knee bent. His right hand lay on his elevated thigh. The fingers thrummed a rhythm no one else could hear.

The cadence of her heartbeats.

Asru stopped. Her muscles petrified. *Give me strength, Wesir, beholder of my* ka.

Ben's face flashed in her mind. The memory of his touch tingled on her skin. He had believed in her strength. He had declared that she could defeat any foe through the strength of her will and intellect. He had not guessed she would stand before this foe a second time.

She must succeed. A life for a life, the cycle completed.

Then, perhaps, she could rest.

Intef strode across the alley.

Her grip on the knife loosened.

He sauntered two steps closer.

She tore the knife from its sheath.

Intef waggled a finger at her. "Where has your sweetness gone, *neferet*? I recall a time when you held no unkind thoughts, spoke no ill words, opened your door to whatever pitiful creature knocked upon it."

"You were that creature." She backed away. "I learned from my error."

He charged at her. She stabbed the knife at him. He seized her hand, squeezed his fist around it, pressed her flesh into the knife's hilt. Pain coursed through her hand, down into her wrist. She gasped. He pried her fingers apart, plucking the knife from her grasp.

From her pocket she pulled out a pen-sized metal canister.

Stumbling backward, she brandished it at him.

Intef sniggered.

She swung the canister up and punched down the top. Gas, invisible and odorless, spritzed from the canister.

Intef blinked. A grin warped his lips. He grabbed at her arm.

She stumbled backward into the hanging clothes. A robe entangled her arm.

Intef ripped the robe from the rope. He threw it around her torso. As he cinched the robe tight around her, tying it like a straitjacket, she kicked at him. He wound his leg around her calves. His left arm he coiled around her as a restraint.

His nose grazed hers. His breaths washed her in moist warmth.

She writhed and spat at him.

He grabbed her hair in his right hand and wrenched it. Her head snapped back.

She swallowed the cry that welled in her throat. The gas had failed her.

The gas was not to blame. She administered it from too great a distance. The gas had dispersed without entering his nostrils. To work, the gas required a distance of no more than two feet. How could she have forgotten?

Her memory faltered. Next, her sanity would yield to the strain. Though fate had spared her the agony of witnessing her sister's decline, the gods refused to grant her the same fortune during her own decay. The years, the cold, they had atrophied her mind.

No. Fear had robbed her of the capacity for judicious thought. With Intef so near, without Ben to bolster her, she simply lost control. For a moment.

An error she would not duplicate.

Intef murmured in her ear, "I see why you have no friends, Aset. You have grown quite vicious in her your old age."

"My name is Asru."

"I know your true name."

"You cannot have what you desire. I will die first."

"The time for that has passed. My sole desire is that you suffer as I have suffered—through the struggle to live when you should be dead. I shall repay you a hundredfold for poisoning my beloved against me."

He pulled back, releasing her hair.

"Your beloved," she scoffed. "You murdered my husband to take me for yourself. Your wife was your slave, not your beloved."

"She worshiped me."

"She died for her folly."

His face flushed. His jaw quivered.

He stroked the knife against her throat. The metal chilled her skin.

"I found you once, *neferet*," he said, "I will find you again. You cannot hide from me."

He mashed his mouth onto hers. She bit his lip.

Recoiling, he laughed. A droplet of blood beaded on his lip. He daubed it away.

"Next time I will not be so tolerant," he said.

She clenched her jaw. "Next time I will kill you."

As he disentangled his leg from hers, he untied the robe. It fell to the ground behind her. He discarded the knife.

She withdrew the scarab amulet from her blouse. Clasping it, she whispered the incantation that had protected her in life, near death, and resurrection.

Intef's smirk ceded to a look of pity. He shook his head. "She will not follow you."

He strode through the clothes curtain. His footfalls receded into the distance.

Asru slumped down onto her knees. Repressed sobs shuddered through her body. She pounded her fists on the ground.

The knife lay several feet from her. She snatched it up. In her other hand she grasped the gas canister. Pitiful weapons.

Self-pity afforded no defense at all.

If he won the Book, the future was lost. He had gained strength, while she felt hers ebbing away on the tide of her *ka*. She sensed her life force deserting her.

She needed assistance to ward off Intef.

Asru leaped onto her feet. She sheathed the knife, deposited the gas canister in her pocket, and stalked down the alley into the street.

Ethan swerved onto the dirt driveway of the "private airport" where he stored his plane. The "airport," located in the desert five miles southeast of Cairo, occupied a section of land owned by a local artisan who had helped the archaeological threesome reconstruct pottery and other artifacts. Modern pottery, mainly jars and bowls, line up along the porch of the mudbrick house. A metal barrel, scarred by fire, squatted in the front yard. Its lid leaned against the barrel. Theo called the apparatus a kiln, so Katy—lacking for a better word—called it a kiln too.

Behind the house, past a stick fence, a single plane hunkered on a strip of compacted sand that Ethan referred to as "the runway." He waved at the massive airplane.

"There she is," he said, "my little baby."

"Little!" Rick said.

"She's a Douglas DC-3. I call her DC-Threepio." When no one responded, he explained, "Like C-Threepio in *Star Wars*."

Katy and Rick groaned.

Squished into Ethan's jeep, they required five minutes to extricate themselves. Theo had taken the front passenger seat, while Yves and Asru's men jammed themselves into the cargo area behind the backseat. They shared their den with backpacks stuffed with equipment to the point of rupturing. Katy and Asru crammed in on either side of Rick, in the backseat. Theo had insisted upon bringing the GPR equipment too. Yves held that on his lip, inside a cardboard box whose flaps he'd tucked in on themselves.

Katy's legs had fallen asleep. As she dislodged her body from the jeep, with Rick's help, her legs awakened in a rush of blood that prickled her flesh.

Stomping to quell the stinging, she followed the others around the house to the runway.

A ladder under the nose of the DC-3 stretched as tall as two men. While the nose stood high above, the tail sagged low to the ground. Ethan strolled under the wing without ducking, heading for the ladder. Oil smears streaked the wing. The paint, once silver, had faded and peeled. The cargo door at the rear of the plane hung open, as did the main door, which folded down into steps. The aircraft sported six small windows along each side.

Katy pictured the plane shiny, fresh out of the factory. The DC-3 would've looked quite elegant new.

Ethan wrestled the ladder out of the way. One hand stretched over his head to pat the wing, he said, "Ain't she beautiful?"

Katy ambled closer to the plane. The tires were bald. Rust speckled the landing gear.

"She's old," Ethan said, "but reliable. She was a troop transport during the war."

93

"Which war," Katy asked, "the Crusades?"

"World War Two."

Katy glanced at Rick. He shrugged his eyebrows.

Asru gawked at the plane. Her eyes looked on the verge of popping out. Her mouth hung open a bit, the front teeth glinting in the sunlight. She gripped her pack in whitened fingers.

In a hushed tone, she said, "I have never seen such a craft."

Ethan marched over to pat her shoulder. "Don't worry, she looks worse than she feels. Hop on in."

Jed and Chin climbed into the aircraft first. Once they had disappeared, and no shrieks ensued, Rick boarded the DC-3.

Katy's shoelace had come undone. She knelt to tie it. She looked under the plane, out across the desert. Brown, brown, and more brown. Not a living thing in sight.

She finished the double knot.

Out in the desert, a shape stirred.

Frozen, she moved her eyes to look at the shape. Nothing. Brownness everywhere. Must've imagined it.

Yeah. Sure.

Katy boarded the plane with Asru inches behind her.

The floor angled up toward the cockpit. Katy slipped on the gradient. She slapped a hand on the wall to brace herself.

Theo bounded into the plane last. He jogged forward to the cockpit.

The interior was bare. Ribs curved across the ceiling width-wise. Rails stretched down the center of the floor along the plane's length. Straps with ratcheting mechanisms attached to the ribs at intervals. Along each wall a sling seat of canvas, something like a lawn chair, hung secured by each window. Far ahead, through a narrow doorway, she spied Theo in the cockpit. He waved as he parked his butt in the right seat.

Ethan gestured at the rails. "For cargo. Yves and I'll get your stuff and tie it down."

No one moved.

"Take any seat," Ethan said.

As the kid dashed outside to help Yves carry the baggage, Chin dared to select a seat first. He chose the third seat on the left side, lowering his weight onto the sling. He bounced in the seat. It held.

Asru took the seat at his right, while Jed perched in the sling beside her. Rick and Katy chose the seats opposite the Plannerian trio. Katy fumbled under the sling for the seatbelt but found nothing. Rick searched beneath his sling. No seatbelt.

Ethan chucked their packs through the doorway.

Katy said, "Where are the seatbelts?"

"Oh those." Ethan waved a hand dismissively. "I got rid of them. Hardly ever carry passengers and I got sick of hearing the things thumping around back here."

"What do you usually carry?"

"Artifacts. Last year I transported a ten-foot wooden statue of Ramses the Third from Luxor to the Egyptian Museum in Cairo. Usually small stuff in boxes, though."

94

Katy stared past Ethan at Yves, who ambled toward the plane hauling the box of equipment. "Where does Yves sit on these trips?"

Ethan had turned away to heft one end of the box for Yves. Together they hoisted it into the plane and maneuvered it onto the rails. Ethan, slapping the straps across the baggage, ratcheted the straps tight around the box and packs. While Ethan headed for the cockpit, Yves skirted the wall on his way to the door.

"Good luck," Yves said.

He turned to exit the plane.

"You're not coming?" Katy asked.

Halfway out the door, he paused to glance at Ethan in the cockpit. A half-suppressed smile twitched the corners of his mouth. "No."

He climbed down the steps and shut the door.

Ethan, lifting his leg high to step over the pedestal between the seats, climbed out of the cockpit. He trotted back to them, where he stooped in front of Katy and Rick.

He pulled a GPS unit from his pocket. "Tell me where you think the site is and I'll plot a course on the GPS."

He punched buttons on the unit. The LCD screen remained dark. He scrunched his eyebrows, thumped the power button with the heel of his hand. No response.

"Maybe the batteries are dead," Katy offered.

"Batteries?" He flipped the unit over in his hand. "Knew I forgot something."

Tucking the unit back in his pocket, he returned to the cockpit.

Rick fixed his gaze on the back of the kid's head. He exhaled in a growl.

Asru, hands entwined on her lap, scrutinized the floor.

In the cockpit, Ethan fiddled with the radio. He clouted the device with his fist. "Come on, baby, be good for daddy."

"That's it," Rick muttered, half rising, "I'm flying this thing."

Katy pushed him down into his seat. "You don't know how."

"And you think he does?"

She patted his leg.

He leaned close to her. "When we get home, I'm learning to fly."

"Get ready," Ethan called from the cockpit, "here we go."

The engines stuttered like a dragon with a cold. The stuttering built into roaring. The dragon, having spit out the phlegm, had regained his voice.

The plane rolled forward. It jolted over potholes in the runway.

Rick thrust his arm over Katy's abdomen as if he could become the restraint her seat lacked. With his free arm he hung onto his own seat. Across the bay, Asru had shut her eyes. She clutched her seat in both hands. Jed sat straight, hands planted on his knees. Chin slouched in his seat, arms folded over his chest.

They rolled down the runway forever. At least it felt that way. Finally, the tail rose and the floor became level. Katy leaned forward to look through the cockpit, out the windshield. She couldn't see much. But they were definitely in the air.

She shouted to be heard above the engine roar. "Nice takeoff, Ethan."

He twisted around to grin at her. "Yeah, I'm good at takeoffs."

As he turned back to his pilot duties, Katy felt a lump coagulating in her stomach. She tended to notice what people didn't say as much, if not more, than what they did say. *I'm good at takeoffs.*

What about landings?

The DC-3 lifted off the airstrip, its nose reaching for the sky.

On his belly in the sand, clad in desert camouflage, he tracked the aircraft with his gaze. A knit hat shielded his head, its color identical to that of his clothing. He held his body immobile as ice.

No one had spotted him. Of course, they had no reason to look for him.

Thus far his movements had gone undetected, even when circumstances forced him to reveal himself—as in crossing a crowded street behind his quarry. In those conditions, he moved with precision and command. If you presented yourself with confidence, others assumed you belonged.

Before the Bergrens and their entourage had arrived, he'd belly-crawled to the aircraft to plant a GPS transmitter on its belly. He had speculated the young pilot wouldn't notice the transmitter—both because of its tiny size and because the boy wouldn't think to check the plane's belly. If he let them leave without tagging them, he would lose his means of reacquiring them once they'd landed at their destination. And he must reacquire them.

To travel this far and lose them…it was unacceptable.

As the DC-3 soared away from him, he rose into a crouch. His pant leg rode up above the holster on his ankle, which constrained his Glock 9mm pistol. His sock had slumped down during his sojourn in the sand. The holster had worn down a raw spot on his calf, but he paid no attention to the pain as oxygen met the abrasion.

The proprietor of the airstrip had left seconds after the Bergrens arrival. No one remained in the vicinity to see him.

The wind spewed sand in his face, driving it into his mouth and nose. He snorted and spat it out.

The jeep he'd purchased for his voyage sat parked 300 yards down the road, in a depression 50 feet off the dirt track, concealed under a tarp. As he'd expected, no one noticed it.

The DC-3 had headed southwest across the desert. At best speed, his voyage would take five times longer than the Bergrens' trip. He couldn't travel by air, though. They would see and hear an aircraft approaching. His task demanded stealth.

He hiked down the road to the jeep. Removing the tarp, folding it into a square lump, he stashed it in the cargo area behind the backseat. Gas cans sat strapped to the cargo area's walls. A cardboard box, taped shut, rested in the center of the cargo area. The box contained food, water, and ammunition. A backpack, camouflage brown like his clothes, slumped on the passenger seat.

Before they came to Egypt, the Bergrens had first gone to Chicago. The Planners knew nothing about their side trip. He knew they had no choice but to go there, to see, to understand. Yet they understood so little of what they *had* seen.

Once in the driver's seat, he consulted his GPS unit. The DC-3 continued on its southwestern trajectory. He clipped the GPS unit to the sun visor, its LCD screen visible.

He started the jeep's engine, floored the accelerator. The jeep shot out of the depression. The vehicle crashed down on the other side and rocketed onto the dirt road, aimed south. Two miles later, the road curved eastward. He steered the jeep off the track into the desert.

On the GPS unit, a green dot progressed southwestward. A red dot pursued the green one.

The red dot, his jeep, paralleled the DC-3's path.

An hour and half later, 250 miles southwest of Cairo with the Nile far behind them, they neared a clump of cliffs. Katy rotated sideways in her seat and mashed her face against the window. Still she could see little of the cliffs.

"I need to see," she hollered at Ethan.

"Trade places with Theo."

While Theo climbed out of the cockpit, Katy wove her way toward the front of the plane. She held her arms out to steady herself as she walked with knees bent in the hopes she'd gain more stability from a low profile. The DC-3 wasn't as smooth as the Gulfstream jet Warner had lent them. However, if it got them to Bakhu she'd forgive the bumps.

Warner. Her throat constricted. Damn the Planners.

She and Rick still had a chance to save Charlie. If Intef kept his word.

His word carried about as much value as fool's gold.

The Planners had taught her a refrain that echoed in her mind whenever she thought of them or the situation they'd foisted upon her and Rick: *no choice, no choice, no choice.*

In the cockpit she swung her leg high over the center pedestal. Once in the seat, she bent forward to look out the window. Her stomach flip-flopped. The ground seemed far away.

Horus guards the city of Thoth on the threshold of the Domain of Osiris, 38 rivers, 70 rods southwest of his incarnation in the horizon.

She prayed something in the geography would tell her what the directions meant. The text must point to a landmark near the city.

Horus. The falcon-headed god.

The ancient Egyptians had noticed geographical formations that reproduced their sacred symbols. The pharaoh Akhenaten had founded a new capital city at Amarna because the mountains behind the locale resembled the *akhet*, the horizon of the sun. Rulers had also built monuments at Gebel Barkal after noting how a prominence on the cliffs mimicked the rearing cobra pharaohs wore on their crowns.

The people who had settled Bakhu might have chosen a site where a falcon-like outcrop overlooked their city.

Katy scanned the mountains ahead of the plane. No falcons. They needed to fly around the cliffs, in case the falcon guarded the tomb on the other side.

"We have to go over the cliffs," she said.

The DC-3 roared closer to the mountains.

She looked at Ethan. "Did you hear me?"

"Yep."

The mountains towered before the DC-3, which seemed to shrink as the mountains swelled.

"How tall are these mountains?" she asked.

"About a thousand feet."

"We can go over them, right?"

"Sure, we could, but why bother?" He pointed out the windshield. "There's a pass we can go through."

A pass. Katy's gut tightened. Straight ahead, two sheer cliffs bounded a fissure. The fissure revealed a sliver of desert on the far side.

"That's no pass," Katy said, lifting off the seat as she slanted forward, "it's a crack."

"We can make it."

He swerved the plane toward the crack.

Katy flopped back onto her seat. "Please go over the mountains."

"Chill out."

Before she could respond, they glided into the fissure.

The plane jounced. Katy yelped. The cliffs boxed them in with a clearance of no more than ten feet on either side. Katy clutched the edges of her seat. She clamped her jaw shut.

From behind, his voice dampened by the engines' roar, Rick shouted, "What the hell are you doing?"

Ethan whooped.

The fissure narrowed. From wingtip to cliff face they had five feet. A rock formation jutted out of the cliff face. Ethan dove the plane down, ducking it under the formation.

Katy gave up trying to breathe.

The fissure opened. The plane plummeted several feet as they soared out of the cliffs and over the desert. Katy inhaled with a gasp. Below, dunes swept over the ground. Nearer the cliffs, rocks littered the earth. When Ethan banked the plane north, she glimpsed the cliff whose face had formed the northern boundary of the fissure. At its summit, the sandstone tapered into an oval with a ledge protruding from it.

Despite thousands of years of sandblasting by the desert winds, the formation remained as striking today as it must've appeared in ancient times. The beak. The eyehole.

She leaped up. Her head smacked into the ceiling.

"That's it!" she said. "That's Horus."

Where were they?

Bob squinted at the abysmal darkness outside the porthole. Intef had abandoned him in this room, guest quarters of a sort, with instructions that he may explore the vessel so long as he refrained from disturbing the crew. A bed hugged the wall in the rear corner. The beige walls had no decoration. The beige sheets had no decoration. The beige carpet, however, had gold threads sprinkled throughout.

Intef had switched from calling the contraption a craft to calling it a vessel. Perhaps he thought the term vessel, which sounded less alien than craft, would relax Bob. He was wrong. The tension in Bob had tripled. He felt, atop his head, the weight of every pyramid ever constructed on Earth. If he moved too quickly, the weight might tumble down around him to bury him alive. If he held still too long it would crush him.

The vessel had hovered over the Western Desert, near Saqqara, while Intef traveled into Cairo in a car his men had commandeered from some tourist—no doubt an bystander innocent enough to have no knowledge of Planners or ancient UFOs or men named Intef who fancied themselves pharaohs. Whether Intef's men had killed the tourist, Bob didn't know. He hoped Intef had let them live, if only to avoid the commotion mangled bodies tended to inspire.

Perhaps an hour ago—he'd lost all concept of time, since Intef had confiscated his watch—the vessel had picked up Intef and his minions outside Cairo. Afterward, the ship had embarked on a journey that ended with a descent whose swiftness thrust Bob's stomach into his throat.

He must get out, wander through the "vessel," familiarize himself with its layout. He had to do something. Anything. He'd lain dormant, morally and physically, far too long.

The man at Saqqara. Intef had stabbed him. Did the man survive?

Bob shut his eyes. If the man died, he had caused it. By his inaction. His fear. He should've—

What?

He stomped toward the door. It swooshed open before him. In the corridor, he swerved right. The walls were beige, of course, though marked with red scripts reminiscent of hieratic. They must represent the evolved form of hieratic, just as the Planners' spoken language represented the evolved form of ancient Egyptian. They must use an evolved form of hieroglyphic as well. He might find that interesting if not for one fact.

He was trapped in a vessel with murderers intent on quashing humanity.

For hours ideas had swirled through his mind. He could sabotage the vessel—if he knew how it worked, which he did not. He could kill Intef—but another murderer would assume his place. He could scream for help next time they set foot on land—but who would hear him and, if someone heard, how could they help? He'd realized an hour ago that he had no hope of stopping the Planners unless he accomplished one of two feats.

Learn the workings of their vessel—or find an ally among them.

Both impossible. No, he must believe he could do it. The power of the mind was immense. If he believed he could accomplish such feats, he might well achieve them. Since he could waste no time on learning the vessel's intricacies, he must seek out an ally. Choose and recruit a collaborator from a collection of psychotics.

Bloody hell.

He turned to a door. It swished open and he tromped into a galley. Men in polo shirts and cotton slacks consumed meals alongside men in jumpsuits fashioned from a rubber-like material. Women ate at tables separated from the men's by metal railing. In the back, a buffet offered a variety of foods. Behind the buffet, cooks prepared the cuisine.

No one looked at him.

Oil lanterns lit the room. He walked closer to the nearest lantern. The flame wavered, yet its color and brightness were constant. He held his hand near the flame. No heat. He ran his hand through the flame. No pain. No scorching.

Back in the corridor, as the door shut behind him, he meandered past doors marked in the Kemetian script. He stopped before one door and stared at the script emblazoned across it at eye level. His eyes lost focus. He blinked, rubbed his eyes, studied the script. Symbols popped out at him, similar to though different from the ancient hieratic. He picked out partial words, enough to jumpstart his curiosity without enabling him to translate the message.

Exploring the corridor as it curved ever leftward, he passed double doors marked in the Kemetian script with a large hand imprinted on the door above the text. A hand with fingers straight, palm out. The gesture for stop, he would've said if he'd been anywhere else. Whatever its exact meaning, the gesture conveyed importance.

He stepped toward the doors. They parted for him. He ambled into the room.

Control panels along three walls housed computer displays, flashing lights, keyboards, buttons, switches, innumerable gadgets whose purpose eluded him. Men sat at stations along the control panels. Here a man typed on a keyboard, gaze intent on the screen. There a man tapped buttons, causing equipment to bleat. One man stood in the center of the room, hands linked behind his back, facing away from Bob. If Intef was the captain, this man must be the first mate.

A large screen high on the back wall displayed video of strange creatures swimming about in artificial light. Screens on the other walls showed the pyramids at Giza, the Saqqara necropolis, the desert, and a log house in the woods. The videos all peered down on the scenes from an angle.

Bob sneaked closer to the screen displaying the log house video. Pine trees towered over the little cabin. A man tramped in front of the house, across a field toward the woods. The man swiveled his torso to glance in the direction of the camera.

Not a man. The hairy creature possessed a humanlike face, save for the hair cloaking it, with no neck and enormous shoulders. Like an ape, the being had to turn his torso to look back because the high shoulders and lack of a neck prevented turning the head. The creature looked away. Arms swinging, he galumphed into the woods.

Bob staggered toward the screen. His hip smacked into the console. He stumbled forward, grabbed a chair. The chair clattered into the console. He hobbled backward toward the doors.

The first mate spun around. He scowled at Bob.

"Hello," Bob said.

The first mate shouted at him in Kemetian.

Behind Bob, the doors hissed apart. A hand clapped down on his shoulder. The fingers dug into his flesh. He grimaced.

Intef strolled around in front of him. With a flick of his hand, Intef dismissed the first mate, who whirled on his heels to face the main screen.

"So," Intef said to Bob, "you have begun exploring the vessel. What do you think of our command center?"

"How can you see all this?"

"We have surveillance drones in the skies over much of the planet. They are invisible to your primitive detection systems."

Surveillance drones. Naturally. The Planners would have creepy little buggers flitting about in the skies, allowing them to spy on the rest of humanity from a detached distance.

Bob hooked a thumb at the screens. "Where is that log house?"

"Michigan. The United States."

"I know where Michigan is. It's the Bergrens' house, isn't it?"

"Very astute, Doctor."

"What about those swimming creatures? Where are they?"

Intef clamped his hand on Bob's shoulder again. "You have many questions. It is a good sign, but I have no time for answers. I will be unavailable for some hours. Behave while I am gone, Doctor."

"Where are you going?"

He knocked the floor with the heel of his false foot. "Repairs."

"Re—"

A creature not unlike those on the video screen thrashed its tail inside Bob's gut. Repairs. Perhaps he didn't want to know.

Unfortunately, Intef told him.

"It has taken one year," Intef said, "for the physicians to repair the burns on my legs and grow the replacements. At last all is ready. Soon I will be whole once more."

Grow the replacements. The very phrase propelled Bob's gorge high in his throat. He gulped it down.

He should've kept to excavating workmen's houses at Deir el-Medina. Never found anomalous evidence there. Never had reason to doubt the accepted chronology for human history. Never ran the risk of getting kidnapped by ancient Egyptians and having to listen as their leader described his foot replacement surgery.

He was too old for this.

Intef released his grip on Bob's shoulder. "We have time, Doctor, before the Bergrens discover Bakhu."

"And the Book of Thoth."

"Yes."

"What if Katy and Rick find the Book while you're recuperating and hide it?"

"Another vessel has traveled to Egypt in our stead. They will keep watch."

Intef brought a palm-sized device out of his pocket. The gadget resembled the palm computers Low Ones used. Intef proffered the device to him.

"We call them scrolls," Intef explained.

Bob took the scroll device. Its face was a screen, like an LCD. A wire connected the device to a small pen clipped onto its side.

"Return to your quarters," Intef said. "I will send someone to teach you the scroll's operation. It is connected to our main processor, so you will have access to all the texts the Bergrens have discovered thus far. Verify the translations."

"Aye, captain."

"Lord would be more appropriate."

Bob envisioned himself genuflecting before Lord Intef. The creature in his gut electrified. He straightened, raised his chin. To hell with Intef.

Ancient Egyptian mythology had no hell.

To the Devourer with him then.

Intef impelled Bob toward the door. "Come, I will provide one answer before I go."

Bob shadowed him outside, down the curving corridor, to a doorway marked with the Kemetian script. Rather than an image of a hand, the entrance bore, above the text, a box that surrounded an eye.

The door whooshed open.

Intef said, "The viewing room."

They entered the room, forsaking the brightness of the corridor for the murk of a chamber lit by the false oil lamps. A sofa encircled a round pedestal capped by a statue of Maat, goddess of truth, justice, and universal order. Her feather, the symbol of the goddess and the concepts she embodied, projected from her headband. In the traditional striding-forth pose, she faced a rectangular panel inset in the left wall. More sofas abutted the walls on the right and at the rear. Along the wall that included the door, tables supported bowls of smoldering incense. The lamplight flickered across paintings that covered the wall from floor to ceiling. Texts composed in Kemetian hieroglyphs accompanied the paintings.

Bob shuffled deeper into the room. He turned in a circle as he moved closer to the statue of Maat. The paintings portrayed the people in three dimensions through a combination of raised relief and painting techniques. The figures wore the ancient garb—linen kilts and robes, pectorals and armbands, sandals—yet they gazed outward with lifelike eyes that seemed to question his presence. They knelt before shrines, eyes closed. They smiled and danced while a woman plucked a sistrum, an ancient instrument similar to a small harp with bells attached to its strings. On the left wall, a man laid his hand on the head of a hairy creature.

The creature bowed its head, arms slack.

"This," Intef said, striding to the panel in the rear wall, "is the window to our world."

He swiped a hand down the wall beside the panel.

Deep within the wall, a mechanism hummed. The panel inched open, exposing a blackness beyond the confines of the ship.

When the panel had finished opening, the humming ceased. A glow commenced outside the window, intensifying as lights brightened from nothing into imitation sunlight. In the rays frolicked creatures identical to the beasts he had seen in the command center.

They swam, swirled, floated, dove. The light glinted off eyes, scales, white skin that gleamed in the light.

Bob collapsed onto the sofa. Under the protection of Maat, he watched the creatures that inhabited the ocean's deepest reaches cavort in their native habitat. He watched from his new home. The bottom of the ocean.

"Dear God," he said.

"You should thank me, Doctor." Intef smiled at the scene outside the window. "You are among the fortunate few who have seen this world first-hand."

The weight of the pyramids threatened to crush him. Now the weight of the ocean settled on him as well, and he'd be damn fortunate if he could keep from sinking into the earth's core.

"Where are we?" Bob asked.

"East of the Mid-Atlantic Ridge. Your scientists call it the abyssal plain."

Bob wiped sweat from his forehead.

Intef chuckled. "Feeling claustrophobic, Doctor?"

"Hot, that's all."

Intef sauntered out of the viewing room. The doors, as they swished shut behind him, cut off the laughter. But it echoed in Bob's mind.

Outside, an eel-like creature gaped its maw at him.

The Western Desert
250 miles southwest of Cairo

"I'll take us in for a low pass," Ethan said. "See if there's a place to land."

Katy tilted sideways to look out the window at her right. The desert, far below a few minutes earlier, zoomed closer as Ethan swooped the DC-3 down for a low pass. The plane plunged lower. And lower.

The ground rushed up at them. Katy gulped in a lump of air.

They leveled off at 50 feet. The ground felt so close she expected her feet to brush the sand. The DC-3 bounced and lurched. The turbulence jostled her eyeballs, and her brain. Katy stared out the window, transfixed by the landscape whirring past. The dunes gave way to flatter ground where the sand looked denser.

"This'll do," Ethan said.

He turned the plane to circle around for the landing. The DC-3 pitched upward. Katy was thrown back into her seat. From the cargo area, Rick shouted a curse. Asru yelped. Katy peeked backward to see Asru clambering back onto her seat while Rick staggered in a half crouch toward his seat. Jed, firmly in his own sling, pulled Asru onto hers. Chin buttressed himself between the wall and floor, hands on the wall and his sling, feet flat on the floor.

The DC-3 banked westward, wrenching Katy sideways. She faced the front. As Ethan settled the plane's nose down, rolling the wings level, they soared past a patch where four small dunes humped on the ground.

The dunes shuddered.

Katy blinked. She craned her neck to look back at the dunes. They looked as she had first seen them. The size of armchairs. Oblong. Motionless. Either she had imagined the movement or the wind had buffeted them. The plane's speed must've produced the illusion of movement below.

Sure, that was it. She watched out the windshield.

The plane descended. Down, down, down. Though she watched the ground, nothing stirred. Ethan pushed down a lever between the seats. From the underside of the plane, metal grated. He depressed a second lever. The grinding multiplied, joined by a squealing.

Thunk.

"Don't worry," Ethan told her. "Just the wheels and the flaps lowering."

The wheels skipped on the earth. Katy bounced in her seat. She braced her hands against the instrument panel.

Bump, bump, bump. Her teeth clacked together.

The tail dropped down as their speed reduced and the roar of the engines cut back to a rumbling. The plane slanted toward the sky, though the wheels remained on the ground.

Chunk. The plane fishtailed. The force tossed her against the side window. From the rear of the plane, bumps and crashes resounded. Voices shouted.

"Whoops," Ethan said. "Wheel hit a soft patch."

The DC-3 straightened and slowed. She contorted her body around to glance through the cockpit doorway into the back. Asru, breathing hard, huddled on the floor clutching her seat. Her dark hair had fallen over her face. Chin had managed to hold onto his seat, but Jed lay prostrate on his belly atop their baggage. He pushed onto his knees, palpated his scalp, then scuttled to Asru.

Rick stooped on all fours further back, ten feet from the nearest seat. He scrunched his face at Katy. She smiled, waggling her fingers at him. He gathered his lips into a pucker. While he got onto his feet and stomped back to his sling, she unscrewed her torso to look ahead again. Ethan eased the plane to a stop. He shut off the engines.

The kid grinned at her. "My best landing yet."

The midday sun burned on their backs as they collected their backpacks and the GPR equipment. The backpacks got heaped into a pile at the foot of the steps that led out of the DC-3. The cardboard box that had protected the GPR equipment wound up on the sand ten feet away, upended and empty. The GPR antenna stood propped against the steps, with the digital control unit balanced midway up the steps.

Silent as the dead, Asru and her men loitered under the plane's nose. Ethan, Theo, and Rick conferred about starting points for the hunt. A city lost for thousands of years would've vanished—mudbrick buildings disintegrated, stone structures collapsed, sand filled in the cavities. GPR might reveal those cavities, but they needed a place to start. The plateau on which they found themselves stretched for miles and miles on the north and south sides. To the west, low mountains rimmed the plateau. To the east, the cliffs they'd negotiated earlier fringed the region. Northeast of their makeshift airstrip, the plateau sloped up toward the cliffs. Directly east of them, however, the earth was level.

Rick had said in Egyptian mythology Bakhu was a mountain range on the western *akhet*, the horizon that served as the doorway to the kingdom of the dead.

The hieroglyph that symbolized the *akhet* comprised two mountains with the sun cradled between them. The sun rose over the *akhet* in the east, and set through it in the west.

In ancient times, the land east of the Nile had functioned as the precinct of the living—the temples were erected there. The lands west of the river, though, became the domain of the dead. Pharaohs built their mortuary temples on the western side. Tombs riddled the deserts west of the Nile. Bakhu had sat in the Western Desert, smack inside the death district. The falcon prominence indicated the city had lain on the western side of the cliffs, where the sun would set over it each night.

Ethan had set the plane down roughly an eighth of a mile from the cliffs. Katy turned toward the mountains, sheltering her eyes from the sun with her hand. The sunlight painted the jagged, steep cliffs in hues of honey gold and orange. The peaks soared high above her head. She trundled backward.

Behind the jagged outcrops hid rounder summits, their crests barely visible.

She backed up further.

The summits nosed higher above their neighbors.

She stumbled over a rock. Steadied herself. Backed away further, further…

There. She halted.

Twin mountains. A valley scooped out between them. When the sun rose through that valley, the summits would look just like the *akhet* hieroglyph.

Katy raced past the DC-3, past the archaeologists and Rick and Asru's clan, straight toward the cliffs below the *akhet* valley.

Rick took off after her. "Katy, wait!"

She ran, ran, ran.

Behind her, Rick's footfalls pounded. Other footsteps joined his. The clamor of boots on sand and pebbles resounded in her wake. She kept running.

"Where's she going?" Ethan hollered.

"Who the hell knows?" Rick replied.

Ahead, maybe 50 feet from the cliffs, sand had amassed into a mound three feet high. Katy sprinted for the mound. Pebbles crunched under her boots.

The earth caved in beneath her.

She plummeted downward into darkness. *Whump.* Her feet struck bottom. Her knees crumpled, and her buttocks hit the ground. The breath burst from her.

Sand drizzled down on her. Dust, roused from the floor, settled around her.

Coughing, she looked up. Light siphoned through the hole she'd punched in the plateau. A figure leaned over the hole to peer down at her.

"Katy?" Rick called.

She cleared her throat. "I'm here."

"Are you okay?"

She pushed up onto her knees. The ground listed. She grabbed for a wall. Her fingers met air. The floor pitched. She slapped her hands on the floor for support, flattening out her fingers.

Her fingertips found empty space. She bent her fingers. They closed over an edge.

The light from above afforded little illumination by the time it sifted down to her. The murk obscured her surroundings. Without leaning or moving her upper body, she probed the spaces around her with her fingers.

Air, air, rock. Air, air, air, rock.

Her stomach flip-flopped. Oh no.

She gazed up at Rick. "Got a slight problem."

A pause. Then he asked, "What?"

"I'm sitting on top of an unstable column."

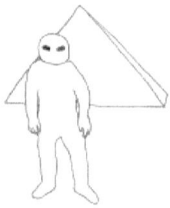

CHAPTER SEVEN

"Ethan's getting the ropes," Rick said. "Just hold on."

Katy grasped the edges of the column's capital. Why had she run? She saw the *akhet* valley, knew Bakhu must lie somewhere in its vicinity, had to find it. The force that drove her to recklessness had overpowered her reason—again.

Great excuse. *I couldn't help it.* No wonder Rick got so mad at her.

She could help it. She must help it. Stop herself before the force conquered her. Fight it. Yet each time the force goaded her into casting off reason, she made a discovery. The Washington stela. Bakhu.

Maybe the force was more than her inner demon tormenting her. Maybe it was…

Fate.

Oh Rick would love that.

"Katy?"

Rick's voice echoed down the chasm.

"Still here." She sighed. "Still stuck."

"Here comes Ethan."

Shadows blocked the light. Suddenly, she felt cold.

The light returned, wan as before.

"Okay," Rick said, "we're lowering the rope."

Katy looked up at the hole. The rope snaked down toward her, the opposite of a cobra rising from a basket.

Sand sprinkled onto her face. She sneezed.

The column rocked.

She froze. Her breath congealed in her lungs. Her pulse hammered in her head. Moving only her eyes, she searched the blackness for a handhold or a ledge or *anything*.

The column swayed left, right, left, right.

Something tickled her ear.

She jerked. The rope spanked her in the face.

The column rocked forward as it skewed left.

Crap.

She flailed for the rope. Her fingers grazed it.

The column toppled.

She clawed at the rope. Her fingers missed it. She sailed down after the column.

Boom.

Dust plumed out of the hole into Rick's face. Hacking, eyes watering, he struggled to see down into the gulf. Below, pattering subsided into a hush deeper than the chasm.

Jesus.

He hauled up the rope.

"Tie the ropes together," he barked at Ethan. "And somebody get me a flashlight."

The kid obeyed. Theo scurried back to the DC-3, where they'd left the backpacks. Asru hissed a command at her men in their language. Chin and Jed helped Ethan knot the ropes into a chain.

Theo cantered back to the group with his backpack looped over one shoulder and a cordless spotlight under his arm. Wheezing, he handed Rick the spotlight.

In between gasps, he said, "Five million candlepower. We use it to scope out tombs before we go in."

"Thanks," Rick said.

He leaned over the hole. No sound broke the silence below.

He aimed the spotlight down into the void.

Its beam lit the cavity beneath him, a 40-foot-wide columned hall that extended northward away from him into blackness and ended five feet south of the hole, underneath where he stooped. Several columns had tumbled over, while others had cracked in two. Before they'd fallen, the tops of the columns must've stood ten feet below the hole—and at least 50 feet above the floor.

The column directly under the hole had tipped over, catching halfway down the right-hand wall. Partway down the column, Katy lay sprawled on her belly.

His chest constricted. His mouth went dry.

Theo, rummaging through his backpack, unearthed a tent stake. Rick hammered the stake into the ground and lashed the rope onto it. He lobbed the other end of the rope into the pit. Seconds elapsed.

Splat.

Rick shined the spotlight into the hole. The rope had hit the column above Katy's head.

Theo exhumed a smaller flashlight from his bag. He gave it to Rick.

After securing the flashlight to his belt, Rick took the rope in both hands.

He jumped over the edge.

Thump! His boots struck stone. The column wobbled. He threw his arms out for balance. The column steadied itself. He switched on the flashlight.

Katy lay eight feet down the column. Her eyes were closed.

In a crouch, he waddled toward her.

She opened her eyes, lifted her head, and looked at him.

"Hi," she said.

"Hi."

She pushed up onto all fours. Blinked slowly. Swiveled her head left and right.

Swallowing, she said, "I was hoping I'd dreamed this."

"No such luck."

He touched a scrape on her chin. She winced.

Her hair had spilled out of the elastic band she'd used to tie it back. Her sleeve had torn. Dirt streaked her face and clothes. Otherwise, she looked unscathed.

He let out the breath trapped in his chest.

"How do you feel?" he asked.

"Okay, considering I just fell…" She glanced up at the hole 30 feet above. "A long ways."

"The column broke your fall."

She massaged her jaw. "Yeah."

Pulling her into his arms, he kissed her cheek. She hugged him. Her arms tightened into steel bars around his chest. He gasped.

Katy loosened her grip. "Sorry."

The rope retreated up toward the ceiling.

Rick craned his neck back. A figure hovered over the hole.

"Sending down the spotlight," Theo called.

A moment later, the rope descended to them with the spotlight knotted onto it. The spotlight touched down behind Rick. He let go of Katy to retrieve it.

He swept the light around the chamber. The cylindrical column of limestone had a girth of seven feet, though toward the top—where carvings of papyrus stalks ringed the capital—it tapered down to three feet. Hieroglyphs covered every inch of its surface area. The top layer had crumbled off the raised inscriptions on the walls and columns, flaking the paint away with the stone. The symbols were recognizable as hieroglyphs, but translating them would be tricky. Not that he had the time to translate what must amount to thousands of pages of text.

At the far end of the hall end, some 80 feet distant, a gateway accessed another chamber or chambers.

Katy stood up. "Wow."

Rick turned off the spotlight.

She shuffled around and took two steps, gingerly, down the column.

He seized her arm. "Wait."

Half turning, she gave him an innocent look. "What?"

"Before we move an inch, I want to talk about this running off business."

"The mountains looked like the *akhet* symbol. I knew we were close to Bakhu."

"And that explains the running off how?"

"Um…" She looked down, chewing her bottom lip. "I just had to run. It wanted me to."

"It?"

She raised her head and fixed her eyes on his. The irises twinkled with green fire.

"Fate," she said.

He stared at her. His mouth fell open. He closed it, gritted his teeth.

The gleam in her eyes mirrored the fire in her spirit, a glow nothing could squelch. He wouldn't want to stifle her even if he could. But he wished to hell she'd learn to temper the fire a little.

"Fate," he said. "You have got to be kidding me."

"Every time I get the urge to run off, I wind up discovering something important. How do you explain that?"

"I—well…it…"

He threw his hands up.

She smiled that knowing smile he hated—because it meant she'd won the argument. She knew it. He knew it. And, apparently, fate knew it.

How could he compete with fate?

Katy laid a hand on his cheek. "You don't have to, honey."

Don't have to what, he almost said. Of course, he knew. She'd read his mind again.

Shit.

Katy inched down the column. It rocked. She froze.

Rick knelt to pat the column.

"Nice and solid," he assured her. "Want me to go first?"

She nodded.

As he squeezed around her, she said, "Not exactly the intrepid explorer, am I?"

"Finally got some common sense." He flashed a sour smile at her. "I won't complain."

When he'd scrambled a few yards down the column, Katy padded after him. As they tottered past the halfway mark, with the floor in sight at last, a report resonated behind them. The column teetered.

Katy glanced over her shoulder.

Asru was traipsing down the column as if she had spent a lifetime performing in a high-wire act. When she'd caught up with them, Asru greeted them with a smile that hinted at secrets the woman withheld from them. Probably for their own good, or so Asru would claim.

The three of them headed down the column in silence. At the bottom they leaped the seven feet from the column to the floor. Rick clicked on the spotlight.

They had descended into a columned hall similar to the hall at Karnak. Like Karnak, this hall had once been roofed. The weight of sand built up over thousands of years had collapsed most of the roof, littering the floor with limestone monoliths, the largest of which towered six inches over Katy's head. Debris from fallen columns had scattered throughout the hall. A handful of columns remained upright—the rest had either split in two, with one half on the floor, or tipped over onto their sides. None but the one she'd ridden down had lodged against the wall.

Specks of color clung to portions of the rear walls, memories of the temple's grandeur.

For it was a temple. In the north wall, battered by the collapse, stood the 20-foot-tall, 15-foot-wide pylon, the gateway to the inner temple. On the sides of the pylon, flanking the opening, rose two carved figures of a pharaoh. The cartouches that would've contained his name had disintegrated or been smashed out of the wall, along with most of the text. The pharaoh wore the scarf-like headdress seen on the Sphinx, with the heads of a serpent and a vulture protruding from the front. In each carving, he raised one hand toward the gateway.

Across the pylon's top, hieroglyphs carved into the limestone blocks spelled out the words "The House of Thoth of Bakhu."

"We found it," she said.

"You found it," Rick said.

His voice had taken on a sourness that matched the smile he'd given her a moment earlier. She should've kept her revelation about fate to herself. The male mind abhorred mystery. A problem to solve, that's what a man needed, preferably a machine to fix. Though Rick didn't excel at fixing machines, he held onto the male mindset.

You'd think after meeting hairy hominids and Planners and encountering weirdness of every variety he'd adjust.

Nope.

The pylons, situated at the pit's edge, supported the roof for the rest of the temple. Beyond the pylon, the inner sanctuary awaited.

Rick, flashlight in hand, clomped through the gateway.

The room was dark, yet even in the gloom its immensity awed. Their footsteps echoed off the walls. The flashlight met emptiness as it groped for a surface off of which its light could reflect. Katy's foot bumped an obstruction.

She tugged Rick's sleeve. He pointed the light at her feet.

A human head rested by its cheek against her boot.

Its body lay several feet away. The desert's aridity had mummified both. The face, withered by desiccation, gawked at her in an expression of shock and agony. The eyeballs had shriveled, leaving the lids sunken. The hair clung to the scalp. The lips, which had curled back further in an exaggeration of the final cry for mercy, revealed teeth clamped shut within the mouth.

On the body the skin had tanned into leather, stretched over the bones without fat or water to pad them. The fingernails were glossy. The clothing, a linen tunic, shrouded the mummy down to its ankles. Dirt stained the fabric.

Katy crouched beside the body. Not dirt. Blood.

Ancient blood—the blood of Bakhu—shed to protect the Book of Thoth. Protect it from what, or whom?

Rick turned on the spotlight. Twilight became day.

A dozen feet away lay another mummy, its head intact. Katy scuttled toward it. Face-down, the man lay with arms outstretched above his head. His hands clawed at the floor. The nail of his left middle finger clung to the cuticle by one corner. Katy blew at the area around his hand, clearing the sand. Several of the man's fingernails rested in the channels he'd gouged from the earthen floor.

The man wore a kilt and sandals. His head was shaven. He must've worked as a priest in the temple.

A gouge disappeared under his shoulder. She flipped him over onto his back. His mouth hung open in a frozen scream, the teeth brown and chipped. His nose had collapsed. Though his eyeballs had long ago rotted away, the empty sockets gaped at her.

The dry conditions had desiccated his body. The process of mummification, natural or artificial, could've caused the mouth to fall open. She knew that. Besides, she knew nothing about the circumstances of his death. Yet his expression seemed to capture his final moment like a snapshot.

Nobody had recovered the bodies from the temple. Either they'd all committed crimes that their relatives deemed worthy of eternal damnation, or...

No one was left to bury them.

Where he'd lain before she moved him, gouges formed symbols. He'd scratched hieroglyphs into the dirt and hidden them with his own body.

She traced the symbols with her fingertip. "The Spirits of the Dead have risen."

Rick looked first at Katy, then at the mummies. Noticing the hieroglyphs, he bent down beside her.

"The same message Garfield left us," he said.

"Who are the Spirits of the Dead?" Katy wondered.

"Mythical gods who ruled—"

"Long before the pharaohs, I know. Whoever killed this guy was no myth."

Katy picked up the mummy's arm. She ought to put him back where she'd found him. Somehow it felt wrong to disturb him, despite the fact he rested for eternity on his stomach, in a forgotten temple, with the agony of his death petrified on his face. She took hold of his torso, rolling him onto his side.

His left arm snapped off. She picked up the arm. The hand was fisted around a leather pouch from which a string dangled. An amulet pouch. The ancient Egyptians had believed in magic, so they devised ways of taking it with them wherever they went. Aside from amulet pendants, they also carried little pouches that held scraps of paper with spells written on them. The pouches hung on strings around their necks, much like the amulet pendants. The practice served as a poor man's substitute for the expensive pendants molded from gold and precious gems.

Katy pried the pouch from the mummy's fist. His knuckles shattered. The fingers tumbled to the floor. So much for putting him back the way she'd found him.

"Sorry," she whispered.

"What?" Rick said.

"Nothing."

A string bound the pouch. She unfastened it and opened the pouch. Inside snuggled a folded scrap of papyrus paper. She removed the paper, unfolding it. A corner had been torn off the scrap.

Beneath a hieratic spell composed in one hand, a second author had scribbled several symbols in his—or her—own handwriting. The additional glyphs were in red, instead of black, further separating them from the spell.

She touched the symbols. The crusty ink had darkened into maroon. Ink didn't get crusty. The blank ink in which the spell was written had not become crusty. She scraped at the maroon hieroglyphs. Flakes detached from them.

Not ink. But surely not…blood?

"Here," she said, relinquishing the paper to Rick.

He looked over the text. "First part's a protection spell. The second part's a name—Isesi."

"His name." Katy gazed into the face of Isesi. "Someone added it to the amulet spell, to restore his name to him in death give him a fighting chance of entering the afterlife."

"Why'd they leave him here?"

Asru hopped over the first mummy. "Do not dwell on this. History cannot be undone, but injustices can be rectified. For that reason, we must find the Book."

"What injustice?" Katy asked.

At Isesi's mummy, Asru halted and grasped her amulet. Eyes shut, she murmured.

Rick crossed the chamber to a smaller pylon. A wood plank barred the gate's doors. Rick slid his hands under the plank, hoisting it out of the slot, and hurled the board aside. The plank whacked down on top of the first mummy. Dust puffed up from the remains.

The doors creaked, parting a sliver.

With both hands Rick pushed on the doors. They swung inward. Flashlight in hand, Rick walked across the threshold. Katy and Asru stole into the inner sanctuary behind him.

Sconces pinned oil lamps to the walls. The lamps consisted of metal bowls that had once brimmed with oil. A floating wick would've burned in the bowl. Now the bowls sat empty, their oil evaporated or spilled out centuries ago, the wicks missing.

Inside the sanctuary time felt stationary. Stuck in the Old Kingdom, when priests had last bathed and anointed the god's image by lamplight. Sacred law forbade anyone else to enter the sanctuary or look upon the statue of the god. When the priests carried the statue outside during processions, they would transport it inside the shrine.

At the back of the room, on the altar, a pile of ashes strewn with charred papyrus stalks replaced the god's bark, a boat constructed from woven papyrus stalks which had supported the shrine. Stone blocks the size of human heads had been smashed out of the altar. The wooden shrine lay in shards, its doors flung to opposite sides of the room. Judging from the size of the shards, the shrine had stood about eight feet tall.

The statue was missing.

Katy kicked a stone block from her path. Time had battered the temple, for sure, yet the destruction done to the sanctuary conflicted with the notion time had wreaked the damage. She glanced up. Though cracked, the ceiling was intact.

Rick rooted around behind the altar.

Katy tiptoed through the rubble. Punting a stone aside, she uncovered an axe. The weapon of the temple's destruction? Since the axe had no blood on it, at least she could rule out its having served as the instrument of a killer's wrath.

Rick hrumphed. He straightened, shook his head.

Katy meandered around the altar.

A statue, split in two lengthwise, slanted face-down against the altar's backside. One half poised atop the other, offset a smidgeon. Katy knelt beside the statue. At first she'd thought the axe-wielder had attacked the statue, rending it in two. But hinges on one side connected the halves. The statue acted as a container.

She gripped the open edge and pulled.

The hinges squealed.

Rick hurdled over the altar to Katy. "Don't—"

The rear half tilted upward. The hinges broke. The rear half clanged onto the floor.

"—open that," he finished.

The statue enclosed a mummy. Linen bandaged the body, which rested on its belly since the statue had ended up face-down against the altar. The mummy's arms draped down his side.

A third hand stuck out between his right elbow and his abdomen.

Rick flipped the bandaged mummy over, depositing it on the statue's rear half. Inside the top half lay a second mummy, unbandaged, stuffed into the cavity with one arm bent behind his back, his right ankle crooked under the left. His hand was fisted, the fingers closed around a piece of paper. Katy tugged the paper. It slid free. Unlike Isesi's amulet spell, this paper was not folded. Its edge was ragged, torn from a larger piece.

Torn from Isesi's amulet spell.

The same person who had scribbled Isesi's name in blood on his amulet spell had also written two hieratic symbols on this paper.

Rick looked at the scrap in her hand. "Akhmose."

"Another name."

"Someone wanted to spare these guys the humiliation of dying without their names."

"But why spare only two? What about the other bodies?"

From the doorway, Asru said, "She did not know their names."

As one, Katy and Rick turned their gazes on Asru.

The woman looked at each of them in turn.

"You know what happened here," Katy said. "Tell us."

For half a minute Asru loitered in the doorway, head down, her eyes unfocused as if concentrating on a sight within her memory.

She tilted her chin up, focusing on Katy. Her eyes seemed to glow like the crystals the ancient Egyptians had used for eyes in statues. They had painted the backs of the crystals so that the eyes possessed a glow that eerily mimicked life. That glow, an ethereal light from beyond, had infiltrated Asru's eyes.

114

"The tale begins," Asru said, "after the death of pharaoh Pepi the Second, when drought and starvation had devastated the nation. The Old Kingdom had fallen. The wars for kingship had ripped the Two Lands asunder."

She strolled into the sanctuary. "In that time of chaos lived a woman called Merytamen."

Bakhu
Second month of growing, day 15, year 2 in the time of strife
Circa 2183 BC

The dust storm swirled around her. Merytamen staggered down the street in the wind's embrace, blinded by the dust scorching her face.

Screams echoed from the direction of the temple. As she hastened onward through the storm, people collided with her. In the instant each glanced at her—wide-eyed, pale, the skin hanging limp over their bones—her stomach lurched. She hugged herself. *Keep moving.*

Her home resided beyond the temple. The chaos, whatever its cause, had initiated at the temple. She should choose another route, but in the storm she couldn't tell one path from another. She knew this street led home. She dared not attempt another.

Her sandals slapped on the earth. Across the street, a figure stumbled toward her.

The wind abated for a heartbeat. She saw his face, his shaven head. He was a priest. In his hand he clutched a scroll.

A dark shape lunged at him from behind. He twitched. His eyes widened, his mouth dropped open, he cried out. His fingers slackened. He dropped the scroll.

It twirled across the street, borne on the wind, toward Merytamen.

The priest collapsed. Though his eyes remained open, his *ka* had left him.

The scroll reeled into her foot. She grabbed it. The papyrus, wound tightly inside a gold thread, fit within her circled fingers.

The assailant surged toward her.

The scroll clasped to her chest, she fled.

Footfalls pounded behind her. Close. She pushed her legs to move faster, though her breaths stabbed pangs through her chest and her muscles screamed. The dust stung her eyes, burned her throat.

Ahead, lightning exploded. The temple.

Flames, crackling at the rear of the temple, licked at the dust that roiled outside.

Surely the assailant would abandon his pursuit of her if she sought shelter in the temple, whose holy walls constrained a battle. She raced toward the hammering-thrashing-blasting that emanated from within the Temple of Djehuty. She must find sanctuary there. The great god would protect her.

Lightning coruscated so near she winced. The hairs on her arms, neck, and scalp bristled.

She veered right through the outer pylon into the columned hall. Though the clamor in the temple drowned out the footfalls of the assailant, she sensed he had gone. She ducked behind a column. Panting, she risked a glimpse around the column.

The storm obscured the figures who fled past the temple.

Merytamen shuffled across the antechamber. The light from the oil lamps fluttered as if moths danced around their flames. Nothing stirred inside the chamber. The two men who lay on the floor moved no more.

The first she came upon halfway between the middle and inner pylons, a few strides from the sanctuary doors. None but priests entered the sanctuary. The man sprawled on the floor, face up, was no priest. He wore the sash of a royal guard. His chest was blackened. Had someone rubbed coal upon his breast? When she stooped to look, she knew it was not coal. His flesh had burned.

His eyes gaped at her. His final expression of agony had frozen on his features. She eased his eyelids closed.

The second man she discovered on his stomach near the inner pylon. He was Isesi, one of the priests who tended the temple. He held one arm outstretched above his head, the fingers trapped in the ridges he had dug in the floor. Blood, having dribbled from the corner of his mouth, congealed on his chin.

Merytamen rose, the scroll in her hands.

A ticking issued from the sanctuary. A wedge of light escaped through the gap between the doors. Beyond the doorway, a creature grunted.

She tiptoed toward the doors. Bent forward, she peered through the gap.

The altar had been hacked into rubble. The shrine had fallen to the floor in pieces. The god's boat floated atop the altar, askew as if riding a turbulent river.

A red-haired man picked up pebbles from the ruins of the altar, casting them aside. The altar's doors leaned against the god's bark. The man heaved the doors away.

A golden statue lay on the floor at his feet, split open to reveal its hollow interior. In that space, once held upright by the statue, slumped a mummy. Steam curled upward from the linen-wrapped body. Its arms, secured by the bandages, crossed over its chest.

The red-haired man kicked the mummy. The body shifted and gave under the pressure, as if its flesh remained malleable.

Merytamen had seen a mummy once, when her brothers had broken into a crypt believing they would find great treasure within it. Instead they had found a shriveled, desiccated mummy, its bandages stained brown, the spells written on its wrappings blurred. Too fearful to search the mummy's wrappings for amulets, the siblings had abandoned the crypt.

This mummy looked robust. Alive.

The red-haired man knelt behind the ruined altar. She heard the scraping of his hands sorting through the rubble.

He leaped upright. A frown deformed his mouth, narrowed his eyes, tightened his jaw. His fists trembled. The tremors bled into his arms, up into his shoulders, wobbling his head. His entire body shuddered. His kilt quivered. She might've thought him frightened, had she not seen the muscles constricting across his bare shoulders and chest.

Her tongue, already parched, hardened into a rock. She clutched the scroll until her knuckles throbbed. Her fingers crushed the papyrus. The paper crackled.

The red-haired man stiffened. He cocked his head.

Merytamen scurried behind the door.

From inside the sanctuary, footfalls crunched.

The door swung outward, pinning her between it and the wall. She flattened her body against the wall, held her breath, and waited. A shadow elongated across the antechamber from the doorway.

The red-haired man strolled out of the sanctuary. Leaning to the side until a sliver of her face, including her left eye, cleared the door, she watched him inspect the bodies. He lifted Isesi's head. A sneer spread across his face.

He mashed the priest's face into the floor.

Outside, the lightning and thunder had ceased. The wind churned the dust into cyclones that keened like wild animals.

The red-haired man wandered out of the antechamber, through the hall, out the temple's main pylon.

Merytamen hurried into the sanctuary. Reaching the mummy, she bent down to touch its wrappings. They chilled her fingers. The vapor rising from the body was cold. She pushed her finger into the mummy's abdomen. The flesh gave.

Flesh. On a *mummy*.

She slipped the scroll under one arm. Carefully, she unwound the bandages from the mummy's head. Something hissed nearby. Having uncovered his scalp, and the cinnamon hair that swathed it, she paused. The hissing came at regular yet protracted intervals. She glanced at the mummy's chest.

It rose and sank in rhythm with the hissing. The chest quivered at each inhalation.

Her heart thudded. Her hands trembled. Biting into her lip, she lowered her head until her ear came within a hair's breadth of the mummy's nose. His breath whispered over her ear.

She jerked backward. Her heart hammered against her chest. Darkness encroached on her vision. One hand on her chest, she breathed slowly. While the darkness receded, her heart refused to calm.

Her teeth chattered—from the cold that leaked from the statue's interior, yes, but also from the coldness that grew inside her with each breath the mummy took. Her hands shook as she grasped the linen and resumed unfolding it. The bandages lifted from his eyes. His nose. His mouth.

He moaned.

Merytamen dropped the linen.

His skin was white, the lips blue. His eyes jiggled behind the lids. He moaned once more, and parted his eyelids. Reddened eyes met her gaze.

In a voice brittle and hushed, he said, "Where am I?"

Her voice trembled in unison with her hands. "The Temple of Djehuty in Bakhu."

He let out a cough that resembled laughter. His breathing coarsened into wheezing.

"Who are you?" she asked.

He struggled to curve his lips up in a smile but faltered. "I am Djehuty."

The front half of the statue rested face-up an arm's length away. Merytamen looked at the statue's face, then the man's. She looked again.

"You *are* Djehuty," she whispered. "You are the god."

"No god." He squinted at his surroundings. "What has happened?"

"A red-haired man destroyed the sanctuary."

"Red…" Djehuty fixed his bloody gaze upon her. "He must not take the Book."

She touched the scroll under her arm. A priest had died protecting the scroll. A man had pursued her when she took it. People did such things when an object carried great import.

"I have the Book," she said.

"How…"

He coughed. The sound was harsh, dry.

"Do not worry," she assured him. "The Book is safe."

He fought to move his arms. The bandages restrained him. When she reached for the linen to finish unwrapping him, he shook his head. The movement wracked coughs through his body.

"I must help you," she said.

"You must go," he croaked. "Take the Book where no one can find it. Do this or all is lost."

She surveyed the ruins around her. "He destroyed the temple for this book."

"He will destroy you and all of Kemet for the Book."

The storm wailed beyond the temple walls. Its howls veiled the cries of her people.

"Leave," urged Djehuty.

The Book of Djehuty. She had heard tell of it, of a book that contained all the wisdom of the great god. She had believed it a myth.

She had also believed none but a priest could ever see the gods. Their images remained in closed shrines in the sanctuaries within temples, where none but priests entered. During the festival processions, the priests carried the shrines in barks made of papyrus reeds. Yet the shrines remained closed, the gods unseen.

A god lay ill at her feet. Seen, touched, heard. She had broken the greatest law of her land.

"Please forgive me," she said. "I did not intend to violate the sacred space."

"Those are your laws, not ours." He coughed, his eyes watering. "Leave before he returns. Defend the Book as you would your own child."

She hesitated.

"Leave at once," he rasped. "Or die without your name."

Merytamen scampered through the sanctuary doors into the antechamber. She tripped over the priest's body, falling onto her knees beside him.

Die without your name.

Others would come for the priest's remains. They would embalm him and bury his mummy in a tomb suitable for a priest of Djehuty. His name would live on for eternity. Wouldn't it?

Whatever power besieged the city today, it cared not whether its victims died nameless, their souls cursed to languish in oblivion. If anyone survived the onslaught…if she survived…

Bakhu would not survive. Her home, the place of her birth—the besiegers would raze it. The sandstorm entomb the ruins.

And the bodies of all who died within the city.

The rope from a necklace drooped down Isesi's back. Merytamen wrenched the rope from his neck. An amulet pouch was sewn onto the necklace. She opened the pouch, pulling out the papyrus tucked inside it. The papyrus contained a spell to protect his soul, but the text failed to name him.

She dipped her fingernail into the priest's blood. With the tip of her nail, she wrote Isesi's name on the papyrus.

Footsteps resounded in the columned hall, each step louder than the previous.

The pouch and papyrus in her fist, she darted behind the sanctuary door.

The red-haired man stomped into the antechamber. He carted a dead priest over his shoulder. Blood sheathed the dead man's back, trickled onto the red-haired man's arms and chest. He disregarded the blood, though, as he carried the priest into the sanctuary. When the man passed by the door, Merytamen glimpsed the dead priest's face. Akhmose, brother of Isesi.

Thumping and scraping ensued.

A moment later, the red-haired man emerged from the sanctuary. A moment after that, he had gone.

Merytamen tore a corner from the papyrus. The rest she stuffed inside the amulet pouch. On her knees beside the priest Isesi, she placed the pouch in his palm and closed the fingers around it. Dipping her fingernail in his blood once more, she inscribed Akhmose's name on the fragment she'd ripped from Isesi's amulet.

In the sanctuary, the statue and Djehuty himself had disappeared. She ran inside the sacred room, around the altar. The red-haired man had propped the statue against the altar, shutting the case without latching it. A bandage hung out through the slit. Merytamen heaved the statue's front open. Djehuty lay atop the dead priest, as lifeless as his devotee. One of the priest's hands was bent behind his back, the other clamped at his side.

She inserted the papyrus fragment into his clamped hand.

Thunder detonated outside. The temple walls shook.

Merytamen spun and bolted through the pylon, across the antechamber and the outer hall, under the outer pylon, and out of the temple.

Through the dust she ran. Her eyes watered and stung. The dust scoured her throat, coated her tongue. She stumbled into an old man who had fallen to his knees. Grasping his arm, the scroll clutched in her free hand, she guided the man toward the doorway to a shop. She pushed him through the doorway, shutting the door behind him, and raced through the storm.

The dust clouds rippled to the ground, and the air cleared. Her home, a mudbrick structure no larger than the sanctuary of the temple, materialized before her.

A vortex of sand whorled toward her. She burst through the door into the kitchen.

The door banged shut after her. She sagged against the wood. As she shut her eyes, she released the breath she had withheld for fear of ingesting sand.

"I was certain the storm had taken you."

She looked at her husband. Nakht hunched near the bed. Dust flecked his hair while his face and arms had reddened from the scouring of the wind. Her own arms felt sore when she touched them.

Tears brimmed in her eyes. She sniffled.

Nakht rushed to embrace her. "What is wrong?"

She sobbed. The tears flooded down her cheeks. Nakht enfolded her in his arms, stroked her hair, murmured words to soothe her. She held the scroll pressed between them.

"I went to the temple." She gazed up at him. "I entered the sanctuary."

His face paled behind the ruddiness.

She told him the tale.

"We must take the Book to the vizier," he said. "He will know what to do."

"The vizier is in Mennefer, ten days' journey from here."

"We must leave immediately."

Screams broke through the howling of the wind. Merytamen shivered. Nakht held her firmly against him.

He cradled her chin in his hand. "We must go together. This is no longer our home."

"You cannot mean that."

Thunder roared. The walls shivered. Bits of mudbrick plopped onto the floor.

"Meryt," Nakht said, "Bakhu is dying. We cannot save it. We must leave and take the Book with us. The great god asked you to defend it as you would your own child. We must honor that request."

He kissed her.

She gripped his hand in her own. He shoved the door open.

Together, they charged into the storm.

Mennefer
Second month of growing, day 27

The vizier's residence lay west of the royal palace, a white walled fortress at the center of the town. A pair of sentries posted at either side of the main doors guarded the vizier's residence. Merytamen waited across the street with Nakht, in a path between two houses where shadows masked their presence.

Since the king's death, a struggle for power had taken hold of the Two Lands. One man would claim the throne only to have another assassinate him. The cycle, which had repeated for over a year, showed no signs of ending. Until a strong leader arose to claim the throne, Kemet would live inside a storm even after the winds had died.

Her stomach grumbled. Food had been scarce along the unknown paths they'd forged through the desert.

120

Nakht stepped forward.

Merytamen grasped his arm. "The sentries will take you."

"We must try."

He pulled her out of the shadows and across the street. At the vizier's residence, they halted. The sentries examined them without emotion.

"We must see the vizier," Nakht announced.

The sentries exchanged sneers. One said, "No one sees the vizier, peasant."

Merytamen felt Nakht tense his body. She squeezed his hand.

"We have a book which may interest him," Nakht said.

He nodded at Merytamen. She produced the scroll from under her robes.

Nakht said, "It is the great Book of Djehuty."

The sentries sniggered.

Merytamen unfastened the gold thread. She rolled out a portion of the scroll to expose the opening lines. This she held toward the sentries for their perusal.

The sentry who had spoken gnawed his lower lip. He glanced at Merytamen and Nakht before turning to his companion. The second sentry shrugged.

The first sentry rapped on the door. Footfalls reverberated inside the vizier's manor. The door swung inward a hand's width. A tanned face stared out at them, green eyes wide, auburn hair falling over the girl's features.

The sentry gestured at Merytamen and Nakht. "My lady, these two must see your father."

The girl scuttled backward, swinging the door open with her. Nakht and Merytamen walked into the house. The girl, perhaps 15 years past her birth, shut the door. She escorted them down a corridor, through a doorway into a shrine room. The altar bordered the rear wall, the wooden shrine atop it closed and latched. Incense smoldered in bowls. Oil lamps affixed to the walls lapped at the dimness with wavelets of light. At the altar, hands linked behind his back, head bowed, knelt the vizier Kagemni.

"Father," the girl murmured. "A man and woman have come to see you."

Kagemni pushed onto his feet, turning toward them. "You may go, daughter."

When the girl had left, Kagemni waved his guests closer. Hand in hand Merytamen and Nakht approached the vizier who had served King Pepi before his death, who had earned more power and respect than any other in Kemet, the one man from whom all claimants to the throne sought approval. Thus far Kagemni had withheld that approval from all. If he did not grant approval soon, he would meet the tip of a dagger.

"Why have you sought me?" Kagemni asked.

Merytamen presented the scroll to him. "I found this in the Temple of Djehuty at Bakhu."

Kagemni accepted the scroll. As he read the opening lines, his eyebrows arched upward. Rolling the scroll, he knotted the gold thread around it.

"Who gave you this book?" he asked.

Merytamen paused. "The great god himself. Djehuty of Bakhu."

"Are—are you certain?"

"Yes, he was swaddled as a mummy yet alive. He spoke to me."

"Truly?" The vizier chuckled. "It is as he said. I did not believe it."

"Of whom do you speak?"

A shadow in the corner resolved into the figure of a man. His face surfaced from the darkness as he advanced into the lamplight. The flames cast writhing serpents of light upon his red hair.

"So," the red-haired man said, "you are the one who unwrapped him."

The red-haired man smiled. Merytamen wrung her husband's hand.

"I thank you," said the red-haired man. "I have been searching for dear Djehuty's book since before you were born."

He will destroy you and all of Kemet for the Book.

She nudged Nakht. He pried his hand free of hers and patted her arm.

The red-haired man tapped the scroll on his palm. "Kill them."

Kagemni's smile faltered. "But, Your Incarnation—"

"Do it!"

Nakht dove at the red-haired man. He pummeled his fists into the man's chest and face. The scroll bounced across the floor. Merytamen snatched up the Book. Kagemni backed into the shrine. Its doors rattled.

The red-haired man threw Nakht into the wall. Hot oil spattered from a lamp onto the floor.

Nakht crumpled against the wall.

The red-haired man saw the scroll in Merytamen's hands. He stormed toward her. She whirled to run, but his hands clinched around her neck. She clawed at him and beat him with the scroll. He shook her, squeezing harder. The dimness within the room darkened further. She kicked at him. Though he cried out, his hold on her throat strengthened. The room grew darker. Ringing in her ears deafened her.

His hands constricted. She gurgled.

A light pulsated. It filled the room with each flash, blinding her even as her vision darkened. The red-haired man released her throat. She collapsed to her knees, gasping.

Kagemni muttered a prayer.

The red-haired man scowled at the doorway. "The Book is mine."

Merytamen looked at the doorway. Two men, one dark-haired and tanned like many of her people, the other resembling the foreigners who occasionally tried to invade Two Lands. If they were attempting another invasion, they might succeed.

The strangers wielded small boxes like weapons.

The red-haired man clenched his fists.

The strangers, stepping aside, aimed their boxes at the red-haired man. A woman swept through the doorway with her robes swishing around her. The gold pectoral that draped over her chest bounced and jingled. Armlets glittered in the lamplight. Her sandals were clean, polished. A golden cobra with jeweled eyes reared from the diadem that wreathed her head.

The woman halted at the room's center. She gestured at Merytamen. "Rise."

The scroll in her grasp, Merytamen obeyed. "Who are you?"

"You may call me Nitiqret. I have come to reunify the Two Lands."

"You will be pharaoh?"

"Yes." Eying the red-haired man, Nitiqret curled her lip. "My husband will torment your people no more."

The men who had preceded the woman marched across the chamber to the red-haired man. Each gripped one of his arms. The foreign man brought another box from his robes, into which he mumbled.

Lightning flashed. The three men vanished.

Merytamen dashed to her husband. When she caressed his hair, Nakht opened his eyes. His gaze, though bleary, settled on her face.

"You must give me the Book," Nitiqret said. "The Sons of Heru have sworn their lives to protect the Book. They shall not fail me."

Nitiqret drew nearer to Merytamen.

Nakht whispered, "Do as the great god would want. Only you know his wishes."

Merytamen ran her finger over the papyrus. Djehuty had asked her to protect it, and she had nearly lost the Book to the red-haired man. She had trusted Kagemni. A pure soul would have recognized the vizier's deceit.

She surrendered the scroll to Nitiqret.

The woman bent down beside Merytamen to touch her cheek. "You are safe, daughter, do not worry. When the Two Lands are reunited, all will be well."

Nitiqret glided toward the doorway amid the flutter of her robes.

Merytamen called after her. "Who is the red-haired man?"

Nitiqret paused in the doorway.

Without looking back, she said, "He is chaos."

Bakhu
Present day

Katy averted her gaze from the mummies crammed into the statue. She avoided thinking about how they'd died, but Technicolor movies complete with surround sound unreeled in her mind.

Murder. Destruction. Chaos.

An average day for the Planners.

"How do you know this story?" she asked Asru.

"Jed shared it with me."

"How does he know it?"

"The men of his family belong to a secret brotherhood called the Sons of Heru—the Sons of Horus, to use your terms. The tale has been passed down for hundreds of generations among them."

Rick grasped Katy's elbow. He tugged, compelling her to move.

She shook off his hand.

He sighed. "Please step away from the rotting corpses."

"They're everywhere. I can't avoid them all."

"Give it a try."

Asru observed them with amusement, like a mother watching her children tease each other. Katy tried to ignore the woman, to forget the questions that buzzed around her mind. Didn't work.

Rick grasped both her shoulders and pushed.

Katy feigned irritation. She let Rick propel her around the altar toward the doorway.

Asru stifled a smile.

Katy stopped beside the woman. "If Nitiqret reunified Egypt, how come I've never heard of her?"

"Actually," Rick said, "Egyptologists know a woman named Nitiqret ruled during the First Intermediate Period. We don't know much about her or any other pharaoh from that period, though, because hardly any records survived."

Katy made a face at him, this time not feigned. Understanding he'd disrupted her interrogation of Asru with facts, he shut up.

"Well?" Katy said to Asru.

"Nitiqret quickly took control of the Two Lands," Asru said. "She deployed troops to all regions faster than anyone believed possible, through the use of our airborne craft. The people believed she used magic to transport her troops, and the tales the soldiers told—of sun chariots that carried them to battle—only solidified this belief. They declared Nitiqret a goddess incarnate."

"I'm sure she worked hard to dispel that myth."

Asru stared at her.

Katy didn't flinch from the woman's gaze. If Asru wanted to intimidate her, she'd have to do more than stare.

"What about the Book?" Katy asked.

"The Sons of Horus secreted it away," Asru said.

"And the red-haired man?"

"He suffered the *mut ankh*."

Mennefer
Fourth month of inundation, day 2, year 1 of Nitiqret
c. 2183 BC

The great doors parted with a whoosh as the two priests heaved them apart. Beyond the doors, the throne room of the royal palace gleamed in multi-colored splendor. The inscriptions on the wall bore paint no more than a week dried. The gold throne reflected the light from the oil lamps and the rays of the sun that filtered through windows high in the walls.

On the throne perched Nitiqret, savior of the Two Lands, the double crown on her head. Lips upturned in a partial smile, she assessed the subjects who milled around her. Priests whispered incantations to protect her from harm while the vizier Kagemni murmured praise to the new pharaoh.

Merytamen hesitated in the doorway. She had never before entered the royal palace, never believed she might stand in the doorway to the throne room. Her heart pattered in her chest like that of a falcon. If Heru saw fit to allow her into the royal residence, she would not disappoint the god by cowering in the doorway.

She took two steps into the room.

Nitiqret raised a hand. The bracelets encircling her wrist chinked. All voices silenced.

"Come forward, daughter," said Nitiqret.

Merytamen straightened her shoulders, lifted her chin. She strode toward the throne as if she had quite often approached the pharaoh after being escorted to the palace by royal guards. She smoothed the linen of her plain tunic, eyeing the pharaoh's pleated robe, gold armlets and pectoral inlaid with turquoise, reed sandals, and cosmetics. The black outlining her eyes fanned outward from the corners. Her wig draped over her shoulders in straight, smooth locks that shimmered in the light.

Barefoot, wearing what little cosmetics she had scrounged from her home, Merytamen fingered the chestnut locks that fell in waves over her shoulders. Nakht had wanted to buy her a wig, like all ladies of the court wore, yet with his work in the fields stopped they could scarcely pay for the food that sustained them. Until the time of strife ended, until the gods replenished the rains, she must satisfy her vanity with the amulet she wore around her neck. The amulet pouch held a protection spell written on papyrus, folded to the size of a scarab. It dangled from a string around her neck. Nakht had traded his sandals for the amulet.

As she neared the throne, she clutched the pouch.

"You are wondering," Nitiqret said, "why I have summoned you."

Merytamen could not move to nod her head.

"I wish to reward your bravery."

"I was not brave," Merytamen said. "The god bade me take the scroll. I merely obeyed."

"Many others would have fled. You saved the Two Lands by your bravery in spiriting the scroll to safety."

Nitiqret waved a hand. Kagemni trotted to the throne, offering the small scroll in his hands to the pharaoh. She snatched it from him.

The vizier bowed his head.

Nitiqret frowned. "I have decided to absolve Kagemni, for I need an experienced vizier. He did not realize, after all, whom he had aided when he conspired with my husband."

"Your husband?" Merytamen cringed as the words leapt from her tongue.

"It was long ago." Nitiqret tipped the scroll toward Merytamen. "This document appoints you and your husband as First God's Servants of Amen at Waset. We leave for the temple city this day."

Merytamen took the scroll. The papyrus felt cool in her hands, and she caressed the bands of the reed that formed the paper. For a peasant to become god's servant, that was rare. For a peasant to journey with the pharaoh, that was unimaginable.

"You wish that I travel with you?" Merytamen asked, certain the pharaoh would smite her for imagining she deserved such an honor. Surely she had misunderstood Nitiqret's words.

"Yes," Nitiqret said, "I thought you should witness my husband's punishment."

"What will you do with him?"

"He must live." Nitiqret shut her eyes, digging her fingers into the throne. "Ra forbade us to kill our own. Therefore my husband must remain alive yet immobilized, so that he may harm none. I shall deal with him at the necropolis of Abedju, on the journey to Waset."

The pharaoh called to her servant, a round woman with the eyes of a falcon and the face of a hippopotamus. The servant carried a bundle of clothes to Merytamen. Atop the clothes lay jewelry—a pectoral of gold, lapis lazuli, and alabaster that depicted a winged scarab; bracelets of gold and silver; a belt of leather inlaid with rubies, emeralds, and turquoise; and a beaded headband. Under the jewelry, a black wig spread its locks over the linen robe.

"A First God's Servant does not wear rags," Nitiqret said, "especially to a burial ceremony. I also have clothes for your husband."

"I do not understand."

"You will." Nitiqret rose from the throne. Settling a hand on Merytamen's shoulder the pharaoh propelled her toward the doorway. "I have made a tomb for my husband at Abedju."

"Tombs are for the dead."

Nitiqret smiled. "Not every tomb is for the dead, and not every mummy has lost his *ka*."

The necropolis of Abedju
Fourth month of inundation, day 6

In the depths of night, the procession shuffled past the burials of kings and noblemen, the mortuary temples erected by pharaohs in honor of their gods and themselves.

Night had descended upon the desert as they disembarked from the boat. The vizier Kagemni, Merytamen, Nakht, four priests, and the pharaoh's two sentries inched across the necropolis slower than the scarab beetles pushed their dung balls. Alone at the front of the procession, Nitiqret led them onward.

The priests carried the golden statue that contained the body of Nitiqret's husband. Nakht and the sentries bore torches whose flames lapped at the night.

The night had taken on a chill. The breeze wafted the chill over Merytamen's arms and shoulders, bared by the robe the pharaoh had provided. She shivered. Behind her, Nakht's breathing hissed. He stroked her left forearm. She touched his hand. He wore new clothes as well, provided by the pharaoh, fitting the position he would soon acquire at the Temple of Amen in Waset.

The Temple of Amen. She would become god's servant on her first visit to the god's abode.

Her new sandals slipped. She careened into the sentry in front of her. He helped her onto her feet. She muttered a thank you.

"Stop," Nitiqret commanded.

The procession halted. The pharaoh had turned toward her subjects. The breeze ruffled her robes as the torchlight kissed her creamy skin, imbuing it with ruddy tones. Nitiqret stood at the brink of a precipice, on the perimeter of a pit at least ten cubits long by eight cubits wide. Shadows disguised its depth. On the far side, a mound of earth flanked the pit. From beneath the mound, a great cloth draped down into the pit.

The sentries assumed positions at either end of the pit, with its length between them.

Nitiqret signaled the priests. The foursome lugged the statue to the pit's rim.

"Come, daughter," Nitiqret called.

Merytamen glanced around the procession. No other women had accompanied them.

Nitiqret crooked a finger at her. "You, Merytamen. Come."

Merytamen's cheeks flushed. She hurried to Nitiqret's side.

The pharaoh nodded to her sentries. With the priests' aid, they secured ropes around the statue. As they lowered it into the pit, Nitiqret bowed her head and joined her hands over her belly.

Flies buzzed in Merytamen's ears. She swatted at them to find they did not exist. The buzzing came from within her. Realizing she had stopped breathing, she inhaled. The buzzing receded.

The statue thumped down onto the pit's floor. The priests cast their ropes into the pit.

Nitiqret gazed into the pit. Tears etched rivulets down her cheeks.

The red-haired man—Nitiqret's husband—was gone...though not dead. So said Nitiqret.

What had the pharaoh meant when she said not every mummy had lost his *ka*? Becoming a mummy required dying. The *ka* vacated the body at death.

Merytamen rubbed her arms, but the chill endured. She had first seen death at Bakhu. She prayed to see it no more.

Bakhu...the name slit swords through her soul. She had wanted to return. Nakht forbade it. Bakhu is dead, he had told her, and the living cannot venture to the land of the dead. Yet this night they traveled to the city of the dead to bury a man who lived.

Nitiqret daubed tears from her eyes. To the statue at the pit's bottom, she said, "My husband, you have angered your father and betrayed your brothers. You murdered and stole from your own people. For these crimes, you must suffer the *mut ankh*."

The pharaoh outstretched a hand over the pit. "Sleep, my husband, that we may live."

The sentries marched behind the earthen mound. They grasped the corners of the great cloth, dragging it toward the pit. As they pulled, the cloth poured its load of earth into the pit. The statue submerged beneath the sand.

"Your Incarnation," Merytamen said, "may I know one secret?"

"Ask it."

"With what name were you born?"

The pharaoh smiled. She leaned close to Merytamen, her lips brushing the ear of the god's servant.

She whispered, "Nebthut."

Bakhu
Present day

Rick pulled her into the antechamber, past the mummies, toward the pylon. His hand had tightened into a vise around hers. The air in the antechamber smelled dank, stale, like a basement after the sump pump broke.

Asru jogged to catch up with them. The woman knew a lot about events that transpired over 4,000 years ago. She was a Planner, which might explain her knowledge—except the Planners knew nothing of ancient history. They had kidnapped Charlie because they needed him to teach them. Yet Asru seemed intimately acquainted with ancient history. Listening to the story, Katy wondered how anyone alive today could speak with such confidence about the events of the First Intermediate Period.

How did Asru know?

She could ask that question later. First, she had some questions about the story.

In her best imitation of a mule, she stopped dead 15 feet from the pylon. Rick pulled her hand. She dug her heels into the earthen floor. He dropped her hand, spun toward her, and planted both hands on his hips.

She mouthed, "Wait."

He rolled his eyes.

Katy said to Asru, "Nitiqret's real name was Nebthut, the ancient Egyptian version of Nephthys. Are you saying Nitiqret was the goddess Nephthys?"

"Yes," Asru said.

"So the Djehuty you mentioned was the god Thoth."

Rick huffed. "Nephthys ruled Egypt as pharaoh. And Thoth was alive in a statue at Bakhu. Who was the red-haired man?"

That smile revisited Asru's face.

"Let me guess," Rick said. "He was Nephthys' husband, so he must be Setesh—a.k.a. Seth, the god of chaos. We're supposed to believe he's buried at Abydos. And you know this...how?"

"The Sons of Horus hid the Book for Nephthys. They have continued to protect it, moving it as necessary to defend the secret. That is why I have needed your help."

Rick clenched his jaw tight. Through his teeth, he snarled, "Look, lady, I want to know *how you know.*"

Katy settled a hand on his chest. "Calm down, sweetie."

"I'll calm down after she tells us the truth."

Asru sighed. The exhalation deflated her shoulders. "I cannot. If I explained, you would not believe."

Katy raised her eyebrows at Rick. He said nothing.

"Explain anyway," Katy said.

"As you wish." Asru sidestepped the mummy of the palace guard. "Thoth had been preserved in a state of minimal life. Several of the Spirits of the Dead were preserved in this manner."

Katy thought back to the description of Thoth. Cold air rising from him. Blue lips.

"They were frozen," Katy said. "Cryogenic suspended animation."

"We called it *mut ankh*, the living death. Theoretically, one could survive forever in such a state. Thoth died because he was removed from his sarcophagus too abruptly."

"Why was he in a statue?"

"Each of the Spirits had been buried inside a statue at a secret location. The gold formed a shell around an interior composed of a special alloy. The metal resisted cold and confined the gaseous compound that preserved the body. Only Horus and his sons knew where the statues were hidden. Thoth and Setesh were entombed together, along with Nephthys, who had asked to be buried with her husband. Later, long after Horus had died…"

Asru closed her eyes. She let out a ragged breath.

Opening her eyes, she said, "Tomb robbers happened upon the tomb of Thoth, Setesh, and Nephthys. They fled with one of the statues, which they took back to their home in Bakhu. It became the centerpiece of the Temple of Thoth."

Thoth had survived inside his statue for thousands of years. He'd become an idol inside a temple, worshiped by followers who had no clue their "god" was right in front of them. Frozen. A Thothsicle.

Creepy.

"My people," Asru continued, "discovered the looted tomb before the robbers could return to steal the other statues. They transferred Nephthys and Setesh onto one of our airborne vessels, where they remained in *mut ankh* for many centuries."

"Until…"

"Until the Old Kingdom collapsed."

Asru drew the scarab out from inside her blouse, into her hand. Palm up, fingers extended, she considered the amulet as if it might speak to her. Maybe she thought it did.

"For thousands of years," Asru said, "a powerful elite has maintained control of my people. They view your kind as Low Ones, vile enemies who must be crushed. The Sons of Horus see you as our brethren. They wage a constant yet secret battle against the elite, never daring to reveal themselves or the breadth of their support within the masses. Intef and his progeny maintain control because of their ruthlessness and guile."

"What happened when the Old Kingdom fell?"

"The Sons of Horus saw the chaos in the Two Lands. They believed only the original Spirits of the Dead could save the country. With a choice between Nephthys and Setesh, they chose to resurrect Nephthys."

"Who woke up Seth?" Katy asked.

Asru folded her fingers over the amulet. "Two thousand years of *mut ankh* had weakened Nephthys' memory. She remembered her love for Setesh but not his anger, his treachery, his evil. Naturally, she felt very alone after her resurrection, like an artifact in a museum. She needed companionship from another Spirit, someone who understood her situation."

"She revived him," Katy said.

"He immediately went in search of the Book. That is how he came to be in Bakhu. That is why he ravaged the town."

"That's where Merytamen met him."

Katy let the conversation end. Something in the way Asru had talked about Nephthys bothered her. Maybe it was Asru's tone of voice when she said Nephthys felt alone after her people revived her. She'd sounded sad.

Asru knew more than she should. More than she could. She knew everything except where to find the Book.

Maybe she didn't know so much after all.

"What happened to Nephthys—Nitiqret?" Katy asked.

"After one year," Asru said, "she was assassinated."

Asru looked over her shoulder, through the sanctuary doors, at the altar. Her eyes glistened. Tears?

The Spirits of the Dead had lived. The gods had ruled Egypt deep in prehistory, before scholars accepted that civilization began, during a time Egyptologists dismissed as myth. She'd known the Planners inspired the culture of ancient Egypt. She'd known they gave their language to the ancient Egyptians. She'd known the Egyptians, awed by the Planners' advanced technology, came to worship them as gods.

The Washington stela claimed humans had developed on another planet. The Planners had lived on Earth for countless millennia. They possessed the technology necessary for interplanetary travel, yet they stuck to Earth, despite their hatred for the Low Ones.

Rock art around the world depicted the Planners and their craft. From ice-age Europe to Dreamtime Australia, from ancient Egypt to prehistoric North America, people had known of the strange craft that haunted the heavens and the enemy who flew them. Ancient depictions of the Planners' craft looked identical to the flying saucers they jetted around in today.

But they couldn't be identical. They had to change, to evolve.

Or not.

"Your technology," Katy said to Asru, "has it evolved over the years? Has it progressed, advanced, changed somehow?"

"In small ways, it has. But the bulk of it remains unchanged."

"Why?"

"We did not invent it. Our technology was the gift of Amen-Ra."

"Amen-Ra wasn't a real person, a Planner like Nephthys or Setesh?"

Asru shook her head. She twirled the amulet on its gold chain. Symbols on the backside flashed in and out of view.

Katy nabbed the amulet. She flipped it over to expose the inscription on its back.

The gold had been pounded down to create raised hieroglyphs, four of them. The circle symbol for day or sun, the rounded bar that represented sand, the scooped-out glyph for mountain, and a pyramid symbol. The sand symbol lay flat. The mountain and pyramid symbols were tipped on their sides. The four hieroglyphs lined up horizontally across the amulet, from wingtip to wingtip on the scarab.

"What's this mean?" Katy asked.

"I do not know," Asru answered. "Those symbols are the most ancient and sacred to my people. The Sons of Horus revere them most of all."

Katy skimmed her fingertips over the hieroglyphs. Anything sacred to the Planners must serve as a key to either opening the door to the true history of humanity or turning on a weapon that would blow up the planet.

Probably the latter.

Katy let go of the amulet. It flopped onto Asru's chest.

Either way, she needed to know.

The Book of Thoth would tell her. It must.

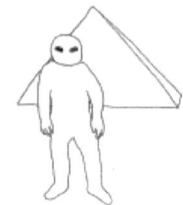

Chapter Eight

Abyssal Plain
Atlantic Ocean

Maat watched the sea monsters flit about outside the window. Her serene expression persevered despite the bizarre beasts who romped in the faux sunlight emitted by the ship. Beyond the window, creatures whose names Bob had learned a few hours ago whirled, glided, and snapped their tails. The umbrellamouth gulper opened its maw as if to swallow him. Tubeworms swayed in the currents. Sea spiders skittered to and fro.

Bob, unlike Maat, oscillated between resignation and anger. While at first he'd found fear the predominant emotion, lately the fear had dissipated into a residue of discomfort.

He had left the observation room three times. Always he found his way back to this room to stare out the window, shoulders slumped, eyes grainy. The landscape outside the vessel could not have seemed more alien if Intef had flown him to Jupiter. He had the strangest sensation of not belonging here. Humans had no place among creatures called umbrellamouth gulpers.

He didn't want to know what they gulped.

Occasionally he glimpsed a large shape darting by at the rim of the vessel's lights. A giant squid? Did they live this deep in the ocean? What other monstrosities inhabited these depths?

Rhetorical questions. He hoped.

Behind him, the doors whooshed open.

Without looking, he said, "Greetings, Lord Intef. So sorry, but I haven't looked at the damn scroll yet."

He waggled the scroll device over his head.

An American voice said, "Frigging computers."

Bob swiveled his torso to glance back at the man who stood near the doorway. He was Bob's age. His gray hair, cropped short, morphed into a beard. He stood about Bob's height, dressed in blue jeans, a flannel shirt, and hiking boots. His blue eyes twinkled in the half light.

The man rocked back on his heels. "You must be Hanover."

"You don't sound or look like one of them."

"I'm not like them. I'm more like you, I suppose."

"They kidnapped you?"

"In a way. I sort of volunteered for it."

The man crossed the room and sat down next to Bob. He looked at the creatures frolicking outside as if watching chimps at the zoo.

Bob felt strangely happy. To see a man his own age, also a hostage of Intef, lessened the anxiety. The granite mountain pressing down on his head seemed to shrink a little.

The man clapped him on the shoulder. "I think you know my son."

"I rather doubt it."

"Rick Bergren."

"Oh." Bob hesitated. "Yes, I do know him."

"I'm Charlie Bergren." The man grabbed Bob's hand, shaking it. "Pleased to meet you."

Words failed him. Dr. Charles Bergren had vanished a year ago. Would the Planners keep him for a year? Longer?

They wouldn't release him. He knew that. He would spend the remainder of his days on this vessel—or the remainder of his hours.

"You must know Katy too," Charlie said.

"Katy Bergren recruited me into the Human Origins Project. Right now I can't say I'm feeling grateful." He looked away from Charlie. "Sorry, I didn't mean that."

"Sure you did, but I understand the senti—" Charlie blinked. "They're married?"

"You didn't know?"

"I've been out of the loop for awhile." Charlie grinned. "Married."

Chuckling, he slapped Bob's shoulder.

His grin faded. His shoulders sank, and he hunched forward. "Intef swore I'd get to visit Rick and Katy. Hasn't let me off this ship in a year. But he still expects me to keep my end of the bargain."

"What bargain?"

"I agreed to go with him, teach him about our history, if he left Katy and Rick alone. Couple weeks later, I found out he'd tried to kill them. Intef didn't know I knew." A bitter smile tainted his features. "I taught him history all right, just not the kind he expected."

"What kind is that?"

"Freshman Hogwash."

Bob stared at Charlie. His expression must've matched the blankness in his mind.

Charlie squeezed Bob's shoulder. "I lied, Doctor. Like a good academic, I snowed him with the best claptrap he'd ever heard."

"I see."

"Awhile back he found it. Threw me in the poky—solitary confinement, for three months straight."

"Good lord. He's let you out then?"

"Nope, I escaped. Getting to know this ship pretty well, and its security measures. The more complicated technology becomes, the simpler it gets to muck it up." Charlie leaned toward Bob to whisper, "I poured milk on the control panel for the door. Thing shorted out, I pushed the door open, and then I skedaddled."

Bob felt light, as if the weight of the ocean had lifted from his head. Butterflies fluttered in his gut. If Charlie could short out a door panel, together they might wreak a bit of havoc on Lord Intef's vessel. They might even stop the bastard before he before he destroyed the world with whatever he expected to find in the Book of Thoth.

"Doctor Bergren," Bob said, "would you be amenable to kicking Intef's ass?"

"Hell, yes. What did you have in mind?"

"Not sure yet."

He had an ally. At last. Now they needed a plan. A bloody good one.

The doors shooshed apart. Intef sauntered into the room.

"I see the doctors have met." He slithered toward them. "How naughty of you, Doctor Bergren, to leave your quarters without permission."

Charlie snorted. "There some reason for this little heart-to-heart, or did you just miss us?"

"Watch."

Intef took up a position alongside the sofa. Hands clasped behind his back, he gazed out the window. For the first time Bob noticed the motion of his ankles had become fluid. He couldn't help staring at the man's feet.

Intef lifted his pant leg. He wiggled his ankle. "As you say, good as new."

No scars. Feeling an umbrellamouth gulper flopping in his gut, Bob switched his attention to the window.

The vessel shuddered. An upward surge thrust Bob's feet into the floor. He held onto the sofa. Charlie slouched back against the sofa, arms slack.

"Here we go again," Charlie said.

The vessel's exterior lights petered out. A rush of bubbles eclipsed the view through the window. Amid the bubbles, two shapes writhed.

Charlie bolted upright, eyes wide. Bob repressed a gasp.

The men clawed at their throats, flailed in the water, eyes bulging. After a moment they ceased fighting. Their bodies drifted away from the vessel.

An umbrellamouth gulper yawned at the camera.

Bob gulped down his gorge. His jaw trembled. His fingers ached.

He pried them away from the sofa. Indentations lingered where he'd gripped the cushion. The ship rose.

A wave of dizziness crested through him. He ducked his head between his knees.

"Why?" Charlie demanded.

"They conspired against me," Intef explained. "They pledged their loyalty to *her*. Jed and Chin shall suffer a worse fate, for they deserted me to go with her. Now they conspire with the Bergrens."

"Not everyone worships you, eh?"

Bob lifted his head. A rift amongst the Planners?

The ship broke through the swells on the ocean's surface. Foam splashed across the window. As the vessel climbed higher, it whizzed eastward across the Atlantic. Toward Africa. Toward Egypt.

Bob pushed up off the sofa, struggling to his feet. In spite of what he'd said when he mistook Charlie for Intef, he had verified the Bergrens' translation of the text they'd found at Saqqara. Katy and Rick translated it correctly, of course. He expected nothing less from them. Although they lacked degrees in archaeology or linguistics, they understood the ancient language of Kemet better than most Egyptologists.

He had no intention of telling Intef that. He did wonder about something, though.

How did Intef know the Bergrens had found a clue at Saqqara? How did he acquire both the hieratic text and their translation? Intef had abandoned Saqqara after making his statement in blood and fire.

Intef sniggered. "Feeling impotent, Doctor?"

Bob stared straight into Intef's eyes. "No."

He would kill the bastard. He would kill himself and everyone on this vessel if necessary. They must never reach Egypt. Never.

He looked at Charlie, rolling his eyes toward Intef. He sliced his index finger across his throat.

Charlie nodded.

Bakhu

Rick turned to leave the antechamber. He motioned for Asru to exit first, and she complied.

Katy glanced back at the mummies of those who'd died protecting the Book. Isesi had scrawled a message with his fingernails as the life leeched out of him. The message must carry great import, or else why bother?

A dying man wouldn't bother, unless his message conveyed a clue. Since he'd died defending the Book of Thoth, his message must concern that tome.

The Spirits of the Dead have risen.

Okay, she knew from Asru the Spirits of the Dead were the Planners who'd ruled Egypt thousands of years ago. Asru's tale about Merytamen had involved several characters upon whom the ancient Egyptians had based their gods and goddesses.

"Let's go," Rick said.

"Hang on."

Mentally, she tallied the names, equating them with the Greek names by which most people knew the ancient Egyptian gods. Djehuty, Nebthut, Heru, and Setesh were Thoth, Nephthys, Horus, and Seth. The four Planners' names equated to four gods—members of the Ennead, a group of nine gods the ancient Egyptians had venerated as supremely important within their pantheon. Atum, the creator god, headed the Ennead. Could they all have been Planners?

Why not?

The marital couples Osiris and Isis, Geb and Nut, and Shu and Tefnut rounded out the Ennead. If she arranged the names by family relationship, in chronological order, she had a family tree of Planners. To sort that out, she needed more than her mental table.

Kneeling, she brought out her pocket knife and scratched out the genealogy on the dirt floor.

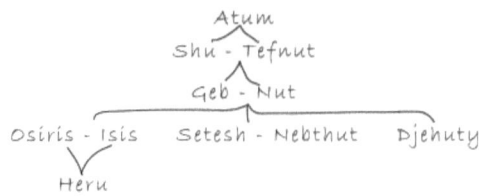

A Plannerian genealogy was interesting, but hardly useful. Asru said the Planners had preserved Thoth, Nephthys, and Seth in *mut ankh*, suspended animation. The rest of the Spirits of the Dead had, well, died.

Wait. Asru had said "several" of the Spirits had been cryogenically frozen. Thoth and Seth had been buried together...how had Asru phrased it? *Along with Nephthys, who had asked to be buried with her husband.* The phrasing implied other Spirits of the Dead had been entombed in the *mut ankh* as well, though buried elsewhere.

Katy stood. "Asru, how many Spirits of the Dead were condemned to *mut ankh*?"

"Five," Asru replied from beyond the doorway.

"Which others?"

Asru's voice became a whisper. "Wesir and Aset."

"Osiris and Isis."

Katy met Rick at the doorway. On the other side, Asru hunched her shoulders.

"Why?" Katy asked. "Why did the Planners freeze their own people?"

Asru looked toward the hole in the ceiling, at the far end of the columned hall. A river of sunlight streamed through the puncture, cascading down the upended columns onto the floor.

Rick followed Katy through the doorway, into the columned hall.

"Time is short," Asru said. "We must go."

Rick shook his head. "We have no idea where to look next."

The Planners had sentenced Osiris and Isis to *mut ankh* along with their kin.

Osiris. The *shabti* from Neffie's tomb. It had safeguarded the scroll whose text instructed them to head southwest from Giza. But the figurine's underside had been inscribed with a cartouche.

Osiris' royal seal.

The Planners had entombed the Spirits of the Dead, their own people, in secret locations. *Entombed.*

"I know where to look," Katy said.

Rick and Asru looked at her.

Their gazes stacked lead weights on her shoulders. If she was wrong...

She wasn't. Instinct and—possibly—fate had not disappointed her so far.

"The tomb of Osiris," she said.

Rick furrowed his eyebrows. He puckered his mouth, hands on his hips.

"Of course," he said. "Imsety's grave in Washington had a stela shaped like the hieroglyphs for Osiris' name. Imsety was Horus' son."

"Osiris' grandson."

"Yep. I guess the secret society called the Sons of Horus started with the *real* sons of Horus."

Asru dabbed the corners of her eyes with her thumb. Tears pooled in her eyes. She dipped her head down and to the side, hiding behind her long hair.

"But where's the tomb?" Rick asked.

"It must be close by," Katy said.

"What makes you say that?"

"Because," she said, opening her arms wide, "this town, Bakhu, is a city of the dead. It lies in the western desert, west of the *akhet* mountains, smack in Osiris country."

"Bakhu was the City of Thoth."

"Yes, they worshiped Thoth here during a later period. But its placement symbolizes a connection to Osiris."

Although he relaxed his brow, his mouth stayed bunched. He screwed the corner of his mouth up, as if fighting off a smile.

"You said the Bakhu of mythology was a mountain range in the western horizon, the doorway to kingdom of the dead." She raised her outspread arms toward the ceiling. "This is the city of Osiris."

Rick surveyed the hall. His pursed lips gave in to the smile.

He scooped her up in his arms and kissed her. When he finally set her down, she jogged to the column they'd used as a bridge to reach the floor earlier.

Asru had already mounted the column. She faced away from them, head bowed, as she sought the right footing for her ascent. She sniffled.

"You okay?" Katy called to her.

Asru said nothing. Arms out for balance, she scaled the column.

Rick boosted Katy up onto the column. Once she'd crawled out of the way, he hoisted himself onto the pillar. By the time they reached the summit, Asru had shimmied up the rope to within a few feet of the opening. As she wriggled through the hole, Katy grabbed hold of the rope and dragged her body up toward the hole.

A moment later, she plunked down in the sand on her buttocks.

Asru crouched an arm's length from her. As Rick bounded out of the hole, the population of topside Bakhu increased to three.

Ethan, Theo, Jed, and Chin had vanished.

A storm of bootprints, impressed deep into the sand, evidenced a struggle. The two archaeologists had ditched their backpacks and left the GPR equipment on the sand.

No blood. Good sign.

In a crouch, Katy tiptoed around the mess of prints. The skirmish had involved at least five people—she made out five distinct patterns from boot soles—but most likely more had taken part. The bad guys could've worn boots with similar soles.

Some of the bootprints overlaid other tracks. She paused where the prints from a large pair of boots were superimposed over another track. The bottom track appeared smooth. Sand preserved tracks poorly, though, and often collapsed in on itself, obscuring the outlines. The bootprints from the skirmish remained legible because of their freshness. The smooth prints probably stemmed from earlier movements, when Rick and the gang had rushed to save her.

The assumption made sense. It fit the evidence. Yet a thought tickled her brain.

The tracks are too big.

Of course, she couldn't determine the size of the bottom tracks with any accuracy. The later prints obliterated them, leaving nothing but traces.

The tracks established a trail that meandered from the hole toward the cliffs 50 feet away. Katy withdrew the Taurus from her fanny pack. Rick, the .45 in his fist, took the lead as they chased the track. Asru tagged along, a dozen feet behind them.

The cliffs vaulted 100 feet above their heads. The tracks led into a cleft in the mountains, beyond whose five-foot-wide entrance the rock walls narrowed into a natural passageway three feet in breadth. They skulked down the passageway. The rock corridor curved left 45 degrees, then right at 30 degrees. The floor sloped down at a steep grade, leveling again after a few yards. Rock outcrops jutted into the passageway. They sidestepped the protrusions.

The walls spread apart into an oval space 30 feet long by 15 feet wide. Rick halted. He raised his arm in front of Katy to stop her.

A small fire smoldered near the cleft's rear wall. The smoke dissipated as it curled upward out of the cleft. Boot impressions circled the fire and angled toward the entrance.

Pushed against the rock face, half hidden by shadows, sat four ammunition canisters.

Grabbing Katy's elbow, Rick spun her around and shoved her ahead of him down the passageway. She crashed into Asru. They tripped over each other's feet, both losing their balance. Rick caught Katy before she hit the ground. Asru thrust an arm out to the wall to arrest her fall.

"What is it?" Asru asked.

"Sh," Rick hissed.

A figure clad in camouflage leaped out from behind an outcropping. The man jabbed an automatic rifle at them. He shouted in Arabic.

The man tilted his head back to peer at them over his nose. His rifle had a sight mounted on top, a pistol grip underneath augmenting the rifle butt, and a curved magazine extending down and out from the stock. It was an AK-47.

The man sputtered in Arabic.

Though she recognized the language, Katy couldn't understand it. If she'd had more time, she might've learned some Arabic before coming to Egypt.

Four men jumped down from ledges above the passageway. She hadn't even noticed the ledges until now. The men aimed their AK-47s at Katy, Rick, and Asru.

Another pair of men armed with their own AK-47s appeared from fissures inside the oval cleft. The seven men surrounded their prey like jackals who smelled a fresh kill. The undersized army nonetheless outnumbered their captives more than two to one.

Asru had produced a knife from under her vest.

Katy glanced at her Taurus. Six rounds. She had two speed-loaders in her fanny pack, which upped her ammo to 12 rounds. She doubted these guys would wait while she got out the speed-loaders.

Six rounds. Seven men with AK-47s. Rick's .45 had seven rounds. If their captors stood still while she and Rick shot them, they might prevail. She kinda doubted the men would, no matter how nicely she asked.

The first man, apparently their commander, bellowed at Rick.

Through clenched teeth, Rick muttered, "Anybody have a clue what he's saying?"

"What language does he speak?" Asru asked.

"I'll take that as a no."

Katy said, "They don't look like Planners."

"Islamic militants," Rick said. " I'd guess we stumbled onto their hideout."

The commander barked at them. He waved the muzzle of his AK-47 at Rick's gun. He repeated his demand.

Rick tossed the .45 at the man.

One of the other men picked it up. The commander indicated Katy's Taurus. She lobbed it the underling who'd retrieved Rick's .45. The Taurus smacked into his shin.

The underling yelled at her. He snatched up the gun. Rushing at Katy, he threatened to clout her with the Taurus.

Rick slugged the man in the gut.

The commander aimed his AK-47 at Rick.

Grinding his teeth, Rick backed off from the man.

The underling spat at Katy.

The commander scolded his underling in a spittle-spritzing tirade. The underling stuffed Katy's gun inside his waistband, ripped the knife from Asru's hand, and retreated behind his commander.

Satisfied, the soldiers herded them into the cleft. There the ragtag army lined them up against the left wall, arms straight at their sides, to let the commander inspect them. The underling who'd taken their weapons dumped his load on the ground, across the fire opposite them. Hands joined behind his back, his AK-47 slung over one shoulder, he paced the length of the wall. With each circuit past them, he fixed his gaze on each of them in turn. His pupils had dilated so widely in the dimness of the cleft that his dark brown irises turned into Saturn-like rings. His black hair, about two inches long, frizzed around his head in crimps. Stubble peppered his cheeks and chin.

On his fifth circuit past Asru, he paused before her. He targeted his gaze on hers. She returned his stare without flinching or blinking. He spoke to her.

She said nothing, moved nothing.

He swung his right hand up as if to strike her. He stopped just short of her face. His jaw trembling, he hovered his hand in midair.

Asru remained still, calm.

The commander seized a lock of her hair and yanked it. Asru gasped. Tears welled in her eyes. The commander released her. She resumed her composure, despite the tears that trickled down her cheeks.

Outside the cleft's entrance, boots crunched.

The men jerked their rifles toward the entrance.

A man stumbled through the opening, panting, dressed like his comrades. The men hooked their rifles over their shoulders. Chattering in Arabic, the newcomer dropped onto his knees before his commander.

Blood oozed from gashes on his face and neck, dribbled down his arm from puncture wounds on his right hand. His shirt was torn, the knees of his pants smeared with dirt. Beneath the blood and dirt, a pallor drained the color from his face. His whole body quivered.

As he babbled, the man waved his arm at the passageway.

The commander kicked the newcomer. The man bent over into an upright fetal position. He whimpered in Arabic.

The commander raised his arm to strike the man.

The newcomer stuck out his hand, palm up, offering something to his leader.

The commander took the offering between his thumb and forefinger. He held it up for his comrades to see.

Long, tan hairs.

What the hell?

The hairs twanged a memory in her mind. She strained to hear the note it sounded.

Oh God. The mounds she'd seen move during Ethan's landing. She'd dismissed the movement as a figment of her imagination, caused by the plane's speed.

The mounds had been living creatures. Hairy hominids.

Captured by militants in hairy hominid territory.

The news just kept getting better.

Hunkered behind a rock formation, he observed the scene playing out 15 feet below him in the crevasse. The commander paraded the hairs before his men.

The soldiers snickered.

The injured man looked at his comrades. Eyes wide, he whined, "Monsters, I saw monsters."

The foreigner hiding above the crevasse slipped a hand over the grip of his Glock. Quietly, he popped it out of the holster. Resting his finger flat on the barrel above the trigger, ready to snap it over the trigger if necessary, he listened to the soldiers conferring in Arabic below him. Excitement elevated both the pitch and volume of their voices. Fortunately, Arabic was one of the seven languages in which he had become fluent.

His five-hour trip across the desert had gotten him to this place only moments ago. He'd parked the jeep behind a sand dune, a quarter mile from the hole in the ground out of which the Bergrens and their new friend had emerged. They'd not noticed him. As he shadowed them toward the crevasse, he'd hugged the cliff face so that its protrusions concealed him.

Below him, the commandos' laughter subsided.

"Omar," the commander chortled, "believes in great, hairy monsters."

The amusement on the commander's face hardened into a scowl.

He leveled his AK-47 at Omar. "I cannot suffer such ignorance."

He fired. Bullets sprayed across Omar's chest. The man fell down dead.

"What of the infidels?" a soldier asked, gesturing at the trio lined up against the rock face.

Katy and Rick Bergren, along with a strange woman, sought eye contact with the soldiers rather than shying from it. Admirable. But that sort of bravery would get them killed. Better they should fall on their knees in prayer to Allah.

The commander studied the trio. He cocked his head to one side.

The foreigner observing from above curled his finger around the Glock's trigger.

Easing his arm across the top of the boulder, he trained his Glock on the commander. Although he preferred to remain anonymous, if the soldiers attacked their prisoners, he would have to act. Katy and Rick must live. No one else could find the Book—and the Book must be found.

Visually, he searched the cliffs across from his position for commandos. Thirty feet off the ground, caves ringed the crevasse in which the militants had made their camp. The cave mouths gaped black as voids in outer space. He saw no more commandos. Unless some had holed up in the caves, the soldiers had all joined their leader in the crevasse.

Red glinted in one of the caves.

He scanned the cliffs around the crevasse's perimeter again. In a cave near the crevasse's back wall, twin stars burned red.

A second pair winked on beside the first. And another. And another.

In other caves, red stars appeared.

Not stars. No, he had seen the red pinpoints before. He knew what they signified.

Below, the commander aimed his AK-47 at Katy's face. "This one dies first."

Rick hurled himself between Katy and the commander.

A shot exploded.

Rick jerked. Katy grabbed him, expecting him to collapse onto her, yet he stayed on his feet.

She leaned sideways to look around him. The commander lay sprawled on his back on the ground. Blood soaked his chest. His hand still gripped the rifle, his finger tensed over the trigger.

The Taurus, Rick's .45, and Asru's dagger sat on the ground across the fire from them. She could make it to the weapons in two seconds, tops.

She took a step.

Rick thrust his arm in front of her. "Don't move."

"Our guns are over there."

"Their guns are right here."

Every soldier had directed his weapon at them.

Shots boomed above their heads. Two more soldiers fell.

A soldier shouted a phrase that ended with "Allah." The men fired, spewing bullets around the cleft. Shots ricocheted off the walls as the soldiers rained ammo up, down, everywhere. Their cries resonated through the cleft. Gunshots detonated overhead.

Asru dropped onto her belly on the ground. She shielded her head with her arms.

Rick slithered away from Katy toward their guns. The dirt erupted inches from his head. A soldier had frog-hopped halfway across the cleft after Rick. He aimed his gun for another shot.

Katy grabbed a rock. She hurled it at the soldier's head.

He ducked sideways. The rock smacked into the dirt.

A shot from above grazed the soldier's head. He scuttled backward.

The soldiers clustered at the cleft entrance, directing their volleys up at the cliffs.

Shots boomed from above. One soldier dropped to his knees cradling his shooting arm. Another slapped a hand over his thigh. The blood seeped out between his fingers.

Rick scooped up the guns. In a crouch he hurried back to Katy and gave her the Taurus.

The soldier who'd seized command gesticulated while he barked orders at the others. The army swarmed across the cleft.

Katy fired the Taurus. Her shot ricocheted off the wall near a soldier's shoulder.

Flame burst from Rick's .45 as he fired at the soldiers.

Gunfire exploded, chattered, ricocheted, splintered rock. Another soldier doubled over with a red stain spreading down his arm from his shoulder.

A final burst of gunfire rat-a-tatted.

Four soldiers gathered at the entrance, three coddling wounds.

Overhead, a growl resonated.

The soldiers jerked their heads up, in the direction of the sound. They lifted their AK-47s, pointing the muzzles at a hole in the cliffs 30 feet above the cleft.

A chorus of voices snarled down from around every side of the cleft.

The soldiers bolted for the cleft's entrance. In five seconds they had evacuated the area.

Katy and Rick looked up at the dark spaces from which the growls originated. Caves.

Asru slowly rose to her feet.

"Rick," Katy said, "if these militant guys kidnapped Theo, Ethan, and Asru's buddies, what'd they do with them?"

He panned his head left and right, back and forward. "Um..."

The footprints.

The mess of tracks in the sand where Theo and the boys had brawled with the commandos. Or had they? Certainly, they'd tussled with someone. But if the soldiers had abducted Theo and the others, why hadn't they exploited that advantage? The soldiers had wanted something from Katy, Rick, and Asru, something they failed to communicate because they couldn't speak English and their captives spoke no Arabic.

But Theo knew Arabic. If he'd been held hostage by the soldiers, he would've talked to them in their language. Theo could have acted as an intermediary for the soldiers. So why had the militants not used the leverage they had?

Because they had no leverage. Someone else kidnapped Theo, Ethan, Chin, and Jed.

The footprints were too big.

Katy gazed up at the caves. Red eyes glared down at her. Growls reverberated from the caves.

"The hairy hominids have them," Katy said.

"Oh great," Rick said.

Pebbles tumbled off the cliffs, onto the ground at the cleft entrance.

Rick swung his .45 toward the entrance.

A man leaped down from behind an outcropping eight feet above the ground. He whumped down inside the entrance.

The man wore tan camouflage clothes with a matching ski mask, pulled down over his face. He grasped a Glock 9mm handgun in his right hand.

Rick held the .45 on the man. "Drop the gun."

The stranger rolled the ski mask up, off of his face, turning it into a knit cap. His blue eyes twinkled in the filtered sunlight.

"You jerk," Katy said, "how long have you been following us?"

Warner smirked. "I'm sure you know the answer."

Rick dropped his arm, aiming the .45 at the dirt. "The whole damn time."

Warner nodded.

Katy ran to Warner, threw her arms around him, and smacked a kiss on his cheek.

"Watch it there," Rick said. "That's my wife your fondling."

Warner blushed. As she let go of him, he fiddled with his cap, a great excuse to hide his face behind his arm.

"We thought you died," Katy scolded.

Grabbing a handful of Warner's shirt, Katy dragged him across the cleft to Rick.

"Someone wanted me dead. Giving him what he wanted seemed the best way to stay alive."

"You mean Intef."

"Who else?" Warner scratched his head under the cap. "I had discovered a weakness that might break him. He knew this."

"How did you know?"

"Shortly before my...demise, I met with an informant who had knowledge of the Planners. He claimed he could tell me about the Book of Thoth, but instead he questioned me about it. Through him, I learned of Intef's weakness."

Weakness. Discovered. Informant. The words bounced around Katy's brain until she thought her skull would crack. In that instant, all became clear.

"J," she said. "The person you met at the museum the night before the plane crash. That was Asru's buddy Jed."

Rick frowned at her. "Where'd you get that?"

"The entry in Warner's journal," she explained. "He was planning to meet J at the museum after closing, to talk about Thoth."

"You know German—and you deduced J's identity. Very clever."

"You're talking to a genius," Rick said.

Now Katy blushed. She hunched her shoulders, averting her eyes.

"Not that I don't enjoy the flattery festival," Katy said, "but we need to find our friends."

In the cleft's center, Asru stood with arms slack at her sides, head tilted up, gaze on the caves.

The red eyes had disappeared. The hairy hominids must've retreated into their caves.

Rick slapped a hand on the cleft wall, staring up the rock's face. The cliffs rose a sheer 20 feet to the level of the outcroppings where the soldiers and Warner had hidden. Ten more feet separated the caves from the outcroppings.

"Can't climb it," Rick said.

"Warner," Katy said, "how'd you get up there?"

"A path on the outer face. But it doesn't go to the caves."

"It leads to the ledge of outcrops."

"That's correct."

"Well, it's only ten feet from the ledge to the caves. We can make that."

Rick groaned. "We usually means me."

"Warner will help you." She smiled sweetly at Warner. "Won't you?"

Warner sighed out a groan.

"We have to save them," she said.

The men exchanged pained glances. Remembering the time hairy hominids had held them captive, no doubt. Rick had gotten himself whacked in the head by a hairy hominid. Warner had the sense not to tick off the colossal beasts. Usually. Of course, Rick had ticked them off on purpose to gain entry into the hominid caves so he could "rescue" her. How arriving unconscious, dumped at her feet by an angry hominid, constituted a rescue baffled her to this day.

It was the thought that counted, she supposed.

Sometimes adages made no sense whatsoever.

"Take us to the path," Rick said. "After we pick up our stuff."

The afternoon sun seared their backs as they collected their backpacks and equipment. Most of it, including the GPR, they piled near the hole—the doorway to Bakhu. Rick hefted his backpack onto his shoulders, snapping the waist strap into place, and plucked the pickax from the ground.

Katy raised her eyebrows at him. Her gaze darted from his face to the axe and back again.

A pickaxe only worked as a weapon at close range. It would do him no good against a hairy hominid unless he got nice and cuddly with the monster. He knew that.

A year ago, when they'd packed up for their trip into the woods in search of his father, he'd spotted a knife in Katy's backpack. He'd told her if the bad guys got that close, they were in trouble. The same applied to the pickaxe.

If he wanted a damn pickaxe, he'd take one.

"Bring it then," Katy said. "But I think bullets are more useful."

"I've got ammo in the pack."

Katy popped out the Taurus' cylinder. She dropped bullets into the empty chambers.

She looked up at him through her bangs. "You didn't freak out when I read your mind."

"I'm getting used to it." He tossed the pickaxe into his left hand. "Or else I'm getting used to having the heebie-jeebies."

Katy's backpack rested on the ground near her feet. She dug a water bottle out of the main compartment and strapped it onto her waistband with a Velcro strip. Mashing her hat onto her head, she donned her sunglasses.

He hadn't gotten used to her mind reading. If she bought his story, well, he wouldn't complain. Her knowing his thoughts bothered him less than the notion she'd latched onto now—that fate had led her to the Washington stela, Nefrekeptah's tomb, Bakhu, and anything else she stumbled over in her flights of recklessness.

Fate was bunk.

Katy holstered the Taurus inside her fanny pack.

Warner led the procession toward the cliffs. Asru followed him, Katy followed her, and Rick slogged through the loam behind and to the left of Katy. Her hat shaded her face. The shade concealed her expression. Not that he expected to glean anything from her face. She could bluff the best poker players on the planet into betting their fortunes on her winning hand.

Her hair spilled down her back like chestnut waves over a waterfall. By her ear, a short lock curled into a spiral.

She glanced at him. "Why are you staring at me?"

"This fate crap—"

"It's not crap."

"You can't honestly believe some cosmic force is guiding you."

"Why not?"

"Don't get mystical on me, Katy."

She smiled. "I've always been mystical, honey. I used to hunt hairy hominids and UFOs."

"That's not mystical."

"Mystical, paranormal. Same thing."

He gave up. They walked in silence behind Warner and Asru.

At the cliffs, Warner swerved right away from the cleft into which the militants had herded them.

If they clashed with hairy hominids, they'd need plenty of firepower. Katy had her Taurus, with the two speed loaders. Warner had his Glock, somewhere on his person, though Rick couldn't see it. Warner without his Glock was like Thor without his hammer.

Yeah, he could picture Warner as a Norse god hurling thunderbolts.

Too bad Warner couldn't *actually* hurl thunderbolts at the bad guys.

Rick stared at the back of Warner's head. Last year Warner had been the bad guy, or so they'd thought. He'd tried to bribe them and, when that failed, he'd threatened them with "fates worse than death" in order to coerce them into keeping the truth of the hairy hominids' existence secret. Today he protected them. Today they trusted him.

Life was weird. Or else he'd gone crazy.

He must be bonkers to trust not one Planner, but three of them. Until last week, he'd worried mainly about keeping Katy from jumping head-first into snake pits, bonfires, and other hazards with whose lethal properties she seemed unacquainted.

No, she was acquainted all right. She just didn't care. If she thought "the truth" lay at the bottom of the pit or the middle of the fire, she'd hop right in.

She'd never risk anyone else's life. But her own…

The worst part was her hunches always proved right. Whether fate or coincidence or her own intelligence directed her to the goal, she succeeded. Always.

He hated it.

Once they rescued Theo, Ethan, and Asru's lackeys, they still had to find the tomb of Osiris. With a Planner in tow.

Make that three Planners.

Christ. He *must* be insane.

Warner turned into a cleft.

Katy glanced over her shoulder at the sky, so blue, so empty, except for Ra. The god, in his day form of the sun in the sky, traced an arc overhead. At night he sank into the *duat* for his nightly journey through the domain of the dead. The domain of Osiris.

No longer a myth, Osiris rested for eternity in the mountains of Bakhu, a real town also steeped in mythology. The lord of the dead awaited his resurrection.

If Setesh and Nebthut could survive in *mut ankh* for millennia, a chance existed that Osiris—Wesir—had endured the cryogenic suspension too. Before too long, she might look into the face of a god.

Not a god. A Planner.

What was a god, if not someone who lived for thousands of years and inspired legends? What was magic if not technology advanced far beyond that of the modern world?

Myth. Truth. Fate. The barriers between realms, once solid as steel, disintegrated around her.

What destiny had brought her here, to this place of myth and magic? She sensed a connection between her fate and that of Bakhu. The longer she spent in Bakhu, the stronger the sensation grew. What the connection meant, how it had formed, she didn't know. She knew only that she must find Wesir before Intef. She must find the Book. In its pages, Djehuty had recorded the means by which she would destroy the Planners forever. She hoped.

Rick tugged her hand.

She blinked at him.

"Coming?" he asked.

Asru and Warner had entered the cleft. As she let Rick pull her into the rift in the limestone mountain, Katy felt certain the cleft would transport them into the *duat*. It didn't.

The cleft sloped upward into the cliffs.

Rick cupped his hand under her elbow. "I've been thinking about the messages Garfield and Isesi left."

"The Spirits of the Dead have risen."

"That's the one. We know the Spirits of the Dead are freeze-dried Planners."

Katy hopped over a skull-sized rock. "So?"

"Garfield was telling us he saw one of them near our house. The only Planners around those parts were Asru and her bodyguards."

"You think she's a freeze-dried Planner."

"I think she used to be—until her descendants woke her up."

A sensation tingled through her brain, like a thought that almost surfaced. The legend of Setna stated that the Book of Thoth waited in his hideaway for the Day of Awakening to come, when Osiris would return from the *duat* to reclaim his throne. Asru said Intef desired the Book because it offered him the power he needed to usurp the throne.

From whom, Katy had asked her. The woman had neglected to answer.

From Osiris. Like an explosion in reverse, the fragments of the mystery snapped back together to reconstruct the whole. The whole what? Not enough pieces had been restored for her to know. Not yet anyhow. But the reconstruction had begun.

"Think about it," Rick said. "Asru knows a heck of a lot about events that happened four thousand years ago."

"You think she's Nephthys."

"Makes sense."

"She said Nephthys died."

"Oh gee, you don't think the nice lady would lie to us."

The cleft decanted them onto a ledge fronted by prominences. The ledge's width varied from three feet near the cleft entrance down to less than two feet behind the prominences.

Warner squeezed around an outcrop. He stopped under a cave, tilting his head back to squint up at its maw four feet over his head.

"I'll give you a boost," Rick said.

Linking his hands into a stirrup, he crouched beside Warner. The German settled his foot into Rick's hands.

Katy slipped the water bottle from its holder. She sipped from it.

A chill flash-froze her. She glanced around. Nothing. She looked up at the cave mouth. Red eyes. One pair.

Two. Three. In neighboring caves, a galaxy of red eyes appeared.

Katy shuffled backward toward the cleft entrance. "Forget it. We'll find another way in."

Warner, his foot in Rick's hands, hesitated. Rick questioned her with his expression.

She gestured at the caves.

The men glanced at the openings. Warner yanked his foot out of Rick's hands. Rick jumped up.

They ran into the cleft, careening through its zigzags and out the exit onto the desert. Ahead of Katy, Rick skidded to a halt. She collided with him. Around his shoulder, she saw what had stopped him.

A hairy hominid, his coat the color of sand, hulked before them.

Six plumes of sand burst up around them. The sand poured off the fair-haired hominids' backs and shoulders. As the creatures shook themselves, sand sprayed onto the dunes.

The hairy hominids surrounded them.

Rick and Warner grabbed for their guns. Katy tore open the fanny pack, shoving her hand inside to grasp the Taurus.

The creatures rushed at them. One threw his arms around Rick's arms and chest, hoisting him off his feet. The creature's arms encircled Rick and his pack. Shouting, Rick flailed his legs. Though the creature winced at each blow, he held his grip.

A second creature seized Warner. Clutched in the hairy arms, his feet dangling 18 inches off the ground, he gasped for air.

Four others bared their teeth at Katy and Asru. Growls reverberated through their chests. Their hair undulated as they waved their arms in a beckoning gesture.

Katy pulled the Taurus partway out.

The creature nearest her barked. He grunted at his comrade who restrained Rick in mid-air. The creature squeezed his arms. Rick cried out.

Katy let the Taurus fall back into the pack. She raised her hands, palms out.

Asru imitated her gesture.

The creature holding Rick eased his grip.

The hominid next to Katy took hold of the fanny pack's strap and ripped it from her waist. She staggered sideways.

The beast shrieked. She grimaced. The sound, a cross between a scream and a lion's roar, deafened her no matter how many times she heard it. The scream always sliced a shiver through her too.

The creature fixed his gaze on hers like twin lasers locked onto a target. He wriggled his nostrils. A bare spot covered the cut-off cone of his cranium. A wide, pale scar slashed across the bald patch. Another bare patch on his shoulder hosted a smaller scar. The aftermath of hairy hominid infighting?

The last two creatures stomped forward. They carried lengths of rope wound into donuts which they had looped over their shoulders. The duo parted—one headed for Warner's captor, the other for Rick's. The creature restraining Rick dropped him. When Rick's feet hit the sand, his knees buckled. He sank down on his heels, panting. The creature grabbed Rick's wrists and yanked them behind his back.

The rope-bearer lashed Rick's wrists together. As the creature cinched the rope tighter, Rick grimaced. The beast cut the rope with his teeth. He used the remainder to bind Rick's feet together, leaving enough leeway for him to walk.

The creatures with Warner bound him identically.

The scarred creature grunted at Katy. He grabbed at her hair.

She ducked away. He honked.

Rick's captor smacked him in the head. Rick glared at the creature.

The scarred male reached for her hair again. She resisted the urge to punch his hand, kick his groin, nab the Taurus from his other hand, and shoot him in the head.

He fingered a lock of her hair, grunting softly. He touched a fingertip to the skin under her left eye.

"*Wadjat*," he muttered.

"The Eye of Horus? That's a brown eye. Mine are green."

He furrowed his heavy brow at her.

In ancient Egyptian, she said, "I am not Horus."

"Mother of Horus," he replied in the same language.

"No."

He twirled a lock of her hair around his finger. "Aset. *Neteret a'a*."

"I give up," she said in English. "Do all hairy monsters think I'm Isis?"

Asru said, "Do you not wish to be a goddess?"

"I do not."

The scarred male turned to his comrades. He delivered a series of grunts that, in hairy hominid land, functioned as an oration. A round of ahs murmured all around her. Several creatures pointed at her. One bowed his head.

The hairy hominids ushered them away from the cleft, northward along the cliffs. The scarred creature led the way while Katy tailed him with his comrade poking her in the small of her back if she paused, tripped, or uttered a sound. Behind Katy's guard, Asru ambled in front of another creature. The creatures who had bound Rick and Warner forced the men to hobble side-by-side before them, inches behind Asru's guard.

The last creature trailed several yards behind the procession. He glanced over his shoulder every minute or two. Twice he let out apelike cries that spurred his comrades to quicken their pace.

The sun had dunked low in the sky. Within a few hours, Ra would descend into the *duat* for his nightly excursion through the perilous depths of the netherworld.

The creatures steered them into a fissure similar to, though smaller than, the one through which Ethan had flown the DC-3. The cliffs rose around them 500 feet high. At its mouth the fissure stretched 50 feet across. It narrowed to 20 feet as they progressed deeper inside it.

Ten minutes elapsed. The fissure widened into an oval area about 80 feet wide, 150 feet long. Overhead, the fissure walls slanted toward each other until a sliver of sky remained visible. When Katy raised her hand at arm's length over her head, her index finger blocked the sliver of sky.

Her guard prodded her. She shuffled into the opening. At the farthest end of the oval, a rock pillar obstructed the exit. The pillar towered at least 90 feet high, its base ten feet square, tapering up the pillar's height. Shadows shrouded the pillar's zenith.

A mound of ashes and charcoal slumped in the center of the oval area. Hand-sized stones, their sides sharpened into blades, lay stacked against the north wall. The hairy hominids had brought their captives to their camp.

The creatures halted the procession. Katy tipped her head backward to scan the height of the pillar. The rock had crumbled away in places. Dirt, which encrusted much of the pillar, obscured the symbols and figures carved onto its surface in sunk relief.

More than a pillar, the monolith was an obelisk akin to those found in Egypt proper. Pharaohs erected them as monuments to their own glory. Who had erected this obelisk, here in a remote region rarely visited even today?

The creatures shoved Rick and Warner onto the ground. They coerced the men into kneeling at the fissure's southern wall, halfway between the entrance and the obelisk, with their backs to the wall. The creatures snapped the straps on Rick and Warner's backpacks. They tore the bags free of the men's shoulders and jettisoned them. The packs plopped down in the sand by the obelisk. One creature snatched Warner's cap from his head.

The throng gasped.

The scarred creature scuttled toward Katy. She had dubbed him Neb, the ancient Egyptian word for lord or ruler, because he seemed to command his brethren. His eyes shimmered as brown as melted caramel. He narrowed his eyes at her. When he halted in front of her, nostrils wriggling, he spoke to her in the ancient language. His speech was halting, like a toddler's. He employed the archaic syntax associated with the oldest form of the language, rather than the intermediate phase that Garfield and his tribesmen spoke.

She couldn't go on calling the language ancient Egyptian. The Planners had spoken the language millennia before Egyptian civilization existed. Like the later Egyptians, the Planners had referred to their country by several names, among them Kemet. Fine, she'd call the language Kemetian.

Neb jabbed a finger toward Warner. "Priest."

Katy opened her mouth. She clamped it shut. Warner was bald, so naturally the creatures thought him a priest. In ancient Egypt, priests had shaven their heads. The creatures had also confused her with Isis. Maybe she could use their confusion to her benefit.

"He is my priest," she told Neb. "The other is my guard."

Neb pointed at Asru.

"She is..." Katy queried her brain for an answer. "My sister."

"Nephthys?"

"Yes."

Neb clumped toward Asru, squinting at her. Asru aimed a faint smile at him. Neb raised his index finger before her eyes. A growl rumbled in his chest like a volcano awakening inside him.

He stamped back to Katy. His eyes glimmered red.

Katy matched his glower—minus the red glow.

Neb jerked his head back to glare down his nose at her. "Brown eyes. Not Nephthys."

From behind her, Rick said, "Careful, Katy."

She glanced back at him. He arched an eyebrow. She curved her tight lips into a smile. He sighed.

She returned her attention to Neb.

"Free us," she said, "or I will use my magic to punish you."

Neb looked at Asru, Warner, Rick, and finally Katy. With a grunt, he waved at his comrades and stalked toward the entrance to the camp. The creatures congregated around him.

Katy trotted to Rick.

"Is threatening them such a good idea?" he said.

"Got a better one?"

"I'm thinking."

She tugged on the ropes that bound his wrists. "These ropes are made from some kind of plant fiber. Where'd they find plants in the desert? They must be nomadic, traveling to more fertile areas to gather food and supplies."

"Fascinating." He squirmed. "What if they demand proof of your magic?"

"I'll wing it."

"How?"

"Try to have a little faith, honey."

"In what?" He let his head fall back against the wall. "Let me guess. Fate."

She patted his cheek.

He screwed up his mouth.

She looked at their backpacks lumped atop one another near the obelisk. Their guns rested on the backpacks. Her knife—the skinning blade she carried on every hunt, whether for hairy hominids or ancient books—was inside her pack. The creatures conversed in a circle near the entrance. Some stood with their backs to her, while others faced her. None looked at her, though.

Katy lowered onto hands and knees. She scrambled toward the packs.

A creature shrieked.

She froze.

Neb snarled at her.

She retreated to Rick, where she sat up on her knees. The creatures resumed their conversation.

Warner leaned forward. "Those rocks piled over there. They look like the handaxes the Michigan creatures use."

Three pairs of human eyes focused on the handaxes amassed 80 feet away, adjacent to the northern wall. Asru, seated 15 feet from them in the open, tracked their gazes toward the handaxes.

"Those monsters cut the ropes with their teeth," Rick said. "Maybe we can chew through them."

"The creatures also toss megaliths like footballs," Warner said.

Rick slumped against the wall. "You're right, it's stupid."

Katy drummed her fingers on the dirt.

Rick stared at the obelisk. Warner observed the creatures.

The hairy hominids grunted, mumbled, and gesticulated at each other.

"You wish to cut something?" Asru asked.

"You just grasped that?" Katy said.

Asru lifted the left side of her vest. She patted her knife, snug in its sheath.

Katy glanced at the creatures. "Roll it to me. Quietly."

Slipping her hand over the knife's grip, Asru let go of her vest. As the vest flapped down, she withdrew the knife.

Neb barked.

Asru froze.

Waving his arms at his comrades, Neb muttered to them. His attention remained on the other creatures.

Asru set the knife on the dirt with the blade facing her. She pushed it toward Katy. The knife skittered two feet.

Grabbing the knife, Asru laid it on her palm. "The earth is uneven. The knife will not slide."

Katy chewed the inside of her lip. Damn.

Asru sat up. "I have thought of an idea."

Asru threw the knife at her. The dagger smacked into the earth between her and Rick, its blade lodged in the dirt, the handle pointing toward the skies.

Katy pulled the knife out. "Thanks."

She sliced Rick's bindings. He took the knife and freed Warner.

The creatures marched into the center of the camp.

Katy whispered, "Pretend you're still tied up."

Rick and Warner left the ropes draped around their ankles. They clasped their hands behind their backs. Rick held the knife behind him.

Katy stood. She must make it to the backpacks.

Neb lumbered one step toward her. He shook his head.

"Free us," she said, "or suffer my wrath."

He grunted at one of his comrades. The creature, a dark-eyed male, hustled around the obelisk where he vanished into the shadows. Seconds later, he trotted back to Neb carrying an object in his hand. He presented the object to Neb. Neb held the object toward her.

It was a statue, gold, 18 inches tall. The paint colored portions of the gold, vivid as the day thousands of years ago when an artist had applied it.

Neb gestured for her to come closer.

Rick sat forward.

She waggled a finger at him.

He held still.

She walked to the creatures.

Neb cradled the statue in both hands. He lowered his hands for her to examine the statue while keeping it far enough from her that she had no chance of stealing it. The statue depicted Isis, wearing cow horns with the sun disk nestled between them. In her left hand she grasped an *ankh*. Her right arm she crooked over her chest, the hand fisted. She wore a white gown, its fabric knotted between her breasts. A wide necklace consisting of a dozen strands interconnected by beads of carnelian and lapis lazuli draped around her neck. Her chestnut hair tumbled over her shoulders, while a gold diadem—a headband-like crown—ringed her head. A cobra reared from the diadem, centered above her eyes. The eyes had been painted to mimic life, the irises delineated from the pupil, the color vivid.

Katy stumbled closer. Neb growled.

She backed off.

"What is it?" Rick asked.

"The eyes," she said. "They're green."

Neb tipped the statue toward her. He whispered, "Aset."

In a chorus of asynchronous whispers, the creatures echoed, "Aset."

The face did resemble hers. Not an exact duplicate, for sure, but close enough to make her stomach flip-flop.

"*Tiu*," she said. In Kemetian, the word meant "yes."

Neb shambled backward away from her. He tripped over Asru's feet. The statue popped out of his grasp, plunked onto the ground at Katy's feet. Neb bolted for the obelisk.

The other creatures fled to the northern wall. There they huddled in a throng. Eyes bulging, skin pale beneath the hair, they muttered to each other.

At the obelisk, Neb knelt facing it. He clawed dirt from its surface.

Their backpacks were heaped a yard from Neb's feet.

Katy crept toward the obelisk. She paused several yards from Neb. As the creature scraped at the dirt, he revealed inscriptions—hieroglyphs etched into the rock. Neb cleared a section that extended three feet up from the base. At the top of the section, above the text, an image showed Isis swallowing an *ankh*. Beside her stood Nephthys, her sister goddess, breaking an *ankh* with her hands. Both goddesses squashed scarabs beneath their feet. The god Horus lay behind them, supine on the ground. His falcon head had been severed from his human neck.

Swallowing the symbol of life. Squashing the symbol of regeneration and protection. Murdering the god of kingship. This was not good.

Neb rose to his full height. Whirling on Katy, he stabbed a finger in the air a hair's breadth from her left eye. In Kemetian, he grunted, "Bringer of death."

Katy laid a finger on his and pushed his hand away.

He roared at her. His breath blasted her face.

Katy flung herself at the backpacks. She scooped the guns up in her arms, hugging them to her chest, and ran back to Rick. He and Warner sprang to their feet. Rick chucked Asru's knife to her. Katy tossed Rick the .45 and Warner the Glock. The Taurus she gripped in her hands.

Neb screamed.

The creatures grabbed handaxes from the pile. As one, they charged at the humans.

Neb lunged at Asru.

Katy fired at him. Asru scrambled out of the way. Neb hit the ground on his side, rolled over, and jumped onto his feet. Blood spurted from a wound on his thigh.

Asru gored his side with the knife. As she ripped the blade out, he twisted toward her. She rammed the knife deep into his gut. The creature fell to his knees. He toppled forward, face-down in the sand.

Rick and Warner fired at the other creatures. Two collapsed.

Neb roared. He dove at Katy.

She fired.

Rick seized her arm, dragging her toward him.

Neb collided with the rock wall. He grabbed at her, snagged her sleeve, pulled.

She lost hold of the Taurus. It tumbled to the ground.

Neb jerked her sleeve. Rick swung the .45 toward Neb. Another creature tackled him. As Rick hit the ground with a hairy hominid on top of him, Neb threw his free arm at Katy's legs. His fist closed around her left ankle.

She booted him in the jaw. Her toe jammed into the soft flesh beneath his chin. His hold loosened. She kicked him again. His hand slipped from her ankle. She grabbed the Taurus.

A gunshot exploded behind her.

She spun around. Rick shoved a dead creature off of him.

Asru shouted. Warner fired.

A creature crumpled at her feet, one arm outstretched, his fingers loose around her ankle. She shook off the creature's hand.

Neb mewled.

Rick trained the .45 on the creature's head.

"Wait," Katy said. She laid a hand on the gun. "He might be able to help us."

Rick uncurled his finger from the trigger, though he kept the muzzle lined up on Neb.

"What are you thinking?" he said.

"Not sure. You hold him while I read those inscriptions."

"Go."

Warner helped Asru up off the ground. She sheathed the knife under her vest.

Katy jogged to the obelisk. She knelt before the inscriptions. For several minutes she pored over the hieroglyphs and the image of Isis and Nephthys. When she walked back to Rick, she felt lines tightening across her forehead and around her eyes.

"The hieroglyphs," she said, "talk about the tomb of Osiris. I'm guessing the Planners erected the obelisk when they buried Osiris, and installed the hairy hominids as the tomb's protectors. The inscription's deteriorated, but the part I can read warns the creatures that Isis wants to find the tomb to get the Book of Thoth. If she gets the Book, it says, she will destroy all life in the universe."

"Why would the Planners demonize Isis? One of their own."

"I don't know."

Rick said to Warner, "Watch this guy for a minute."

Warner assumed Rick's position in front of Neb. He leveled his Glock at the creature.

Katy followed Rick back to the obelisk. He brushed his fingers across the hieroglyphs.

"Look," he said, indicating the fourth line, where the text began its tirade against Isis.

The symbols were messy, hard to read. She'd struggled to make them out. The hieroglyphs sat against a backdrop of hairline fractures.

"Stone's cracked," she said.

"No." He traced the cracks with his fingers. "See? They're hieroglyphs. The inscription's been altered."

He was right. As he outlined the shapes for her, she recognized what they were. Rewrites.

Rick raked a hand through his hair. "No wonder the creatures wanted to kill us."

"There is an upside."

"Which is?"

"Neb must know where Theo and the boys are."

She crouched in front of Neb, who lay with his back propped against the wall. Blood matted on his leg and head, dribbled into his eyes. He breathed in gasps.

"Where are our friends?" she asked in Kemetian, pointing at the obelisk.

He wheezed.

"Where?" she demanded.

"Inside."

"Inside what?"

The creature shut his eyes.

Katy nudged him with her foot. He opened his eyes just enough to see her.

"Where are our friends?" she repeated.

He tried to growl. His lips fluttered, but the sound came out as a whimper.

"Tell me," she said.

He exhaled in a growl. His body slackened.

She stood.

Rick lowered the .45.

Neb was dead.

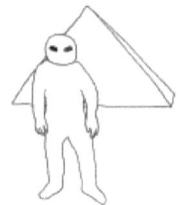

CHAPTER NINE

Neb's body lay sprawled against the fissure wall.

Katy shoved the Taurus inside her waistband. She searched the cliffs above their heads for caves. None there.

Rick holstered the .45.

"Neb said they're inside," she said. "Inside caves, I thought, but I don't see any."

"Must be an entrance around here," Rick said.

He wandered behind the obelisk.

Katy ambled to the monolith, to the inscription Neb had uncovered. Squatting, she picked at the encrustations above the cleared section. Globs broke off in her hand. As she dumped them on the ground, she scratched more dirt away to expose fragments of hieroglyphs. She clawed at the dirt. Chunks broke away, plummeting onto the sand, shattering when they hit.

Footsteps crunched behind her. She twisted around. Warner clomped from hairy hominid corpse to hairy hominid corpse. Asru tagged along behind him. Once he'd inspected the whole grisly assortment, he tromped into the center of the camp. He frowned.

He asked Katy, "How many creatures detained us?"

"Six," she answered.

"How many bodies do you count?"

As she surveyed the corpses, she tallied them in her head. "Five."

She jumped up.

Warner swung the Glock up in front of him. "One of them is hiding."

Rick poked his head out from behind the obelisk. "I found it."

"We've got a problem." She pulled the Taurus out of her waistband. "One got away."

Rick hurried to her, yanking the .45 from its holster, as Warner and Asru met them at the obelisk. Weapons raised, Rick and Warner dropped into half crouches. Asru slid a hand inside her vest to grasp the knife's handle.

"Wait here," Rick said.

He signaled for Warner to follow him. Together, they slunk across the camp toward the entrance. Halfway to the opening, the men separated. Each sidled along the wall on either side of the entrance, heading for the opening. They halted alongside the entrance. Rick tilted his head. Opened his mouth. Listening.

Katy did the same.

Silence.

Her heart pitter-pattered in her chest. She felt Asru clutch her elbow.

"Grrf."

The sound resonated from beyond the cleft entrance. Warner inched around the corner into the shadows within the entrance.

Through the opening, deep inside the shadows, a creature growled.

Thump.

Warner hollered.

A shape sailed through the opening. Warner hit the ground halfway across the camp.

A hairy blur sprinted through the entrance. The creature slapped a hand on Rick's chest and propelled him backward. Rick's feet lifted off the ground. He smacked into the northern wall.

The creature barreled across the camp.

Dazed, Warner aimed the Glock at the hominid. He pulled the trigger but gun kicked back. The shot swerved into the rock wall.

The hominid seized Warner's shirt, pitching him aside. Warner thudded onto the ground on his side, rolled, and slammed into the wall.

The creature stormed toward Katy and Asru.

Katy fired the Taurus at his head.

The beast ducked sideways. The shot hit the wall by the entrance. Shards splintered off the rock.

She fired again, again, again.

The hominid dodged side to side. Two rounds struck him. Blood streamed down his neck and shoulder. She fired twice. He shied sideways. The bullets grazed his head.

She pulled the trigger. Click. Empty.

The creature bellowed. He surged toward her.

Boom!

The hominid froze. He crumpled.

Across the camp, Rick slumped onto his knees with the .45 in his right hand. He lowered the gun at his side.

Katy ran to him. He pushed up onto his feet.

"You okay?" she asked.

"Yeah." He rubbed his jaw. "Getting tossed around by Bigfoot isn't as much fun as it sounds like."

Katy led Rick back to the obelisk. She retrieved her fanny pack, reloaded the Taurus' cylinder, and tucked the revolver into its holster. Hairy hominids got ticked when humans infringed on their territory. She glanced over her shoulder at the corpses that littered the camp. They got downright nasty when humans killed their brethren.

Rick rooted through his backpack until he found the flashlight. "I found a way into the caves. Behind the obelisk."

Katy bypassed the obelisk. The footsteps of Rick, Warner, and Asru shooshed after her. Rick edged past her into an area where the rock walls converged to close the oval cleft, curving over it into a rock canopy ten feet high. The grotto swallowed the light from the late-afternoon sun.

Rick switched on the flashlight. Its beam cleaved the darkness inside the grotto, straight back to a portal in the rear wall. Through the portal, a void.

The gateway to the netherworld.

They trudged through the grotto into the portal.

And into a hollow the size of a walk-in closet. No doors opened into other chambers or corridors. On the wall directly in front of them, notches cut into the wall at regular intervals resembled steps. Round indentations the size of hairy hominid hands paralleled the notches.

Rick shined the light up the wall, following the steps. They extended straight up from the floor into darkness. Eight feet off the floor, the wall sloped into a gradual incline. If they made it up the first eight feet, the going would get easier.

A hair fell over her eyes. She blew it away.

Eight feet. It seemed like a mile.

Rick handed her the flashlight. Placing his toes in a notch at knee level, his fingers in the oversize handholds, he pulled his body up off the floor.

And tumbled back down. He landed flat on his butt.

"Get the ropes out of my backpack," he told Warner.

Then he shoved his toes into the notch, his hands into the handholds, and thrust his body off the floor. This time he held on.

Warner jogged out of the grotto, around the obelisk.

Rick climbed three feet up the steps. His left foot slipped.

Katy grasped his heel and pushed his foot back onto the step.

"Thanks," he said.

"Maybe we should look for another way in," she said.

"No time." He bent his head back to look up at the ascent ahead of him. "They're not hominids. They're hairy mutant spiders."

He scaled the remainder of the eight feet, to the point where the wall sloped. He paused.

Warner dashed back into the hollow. A wad of ropes, still tied together into a single line, overflowed his arms.

"Toss me an end," Rick said.

Unraveling the mess, Warner lobbed an end to Rick, who caught it. Rick tied the rope onto his belt.

He resumed his ascent up the wall. His pace increased as the slope's angle moderated from 90 degrees to 85, 80, 75. In a minute, the shadows had consumed him, though his movements reverberated a scritching-scraping noise down the shaft.

The rope writhed up the shaft in his wake.

She aimed the flashlight over her head. Its light dispersed before touching the shaft's end. The beam kissed the soles of Rick's boots as he ascended higher into the mountain, though soon even his feet had risen out of sight.

The rope ceased climbing. It jiggled, flapped, and danced. As the rope stilled, Rick's voice echoed down the shaft, distant as a phone call from the moon.

"Hold the rope for support," he said. "And come on up."

Katy hooked the flashlight onto her waistband. She took hold of the rope, using it to haul herself up the first eight feet, then holding it like a handrail for the remainder of the ascent. The flashlight, which pointed up, rattled as she climbed. Its beam slashed back and forth across the shaft, a lighthouse beacon gone mad.

The beam flashed across Rick's face. He leaned over a precipice 15 feet above her.

When she'd climbed to within an arm's length of the precipice, Rick reached over the edge to grab her hands. He heaved her over the rim onto a flat earthen floor. As he lifted her onto her feet, he swiped the flashlight from her waistband.

He clicked the light off.

Torches lit the corridor, each fastened to the wall by a sconce hewn from the rock itself. Rick had knotted the rope around the sconce closest to the precipice.

The creatures had assembled each torch from a tree branch split at one end to create a slot. Into the slot they wedged a length of bark, folded several times. The flame burned from the bark's tip, bathing the passage in amber light. The hairy hominids in Michigan made similar torches, although they fashioned theirs from birch bark. These torches were made from a wood she didn't recognize.

Rick bent over the precipice to help Asru over the edge. A moment later the crown of Warner's cap-covered head popped above the precipice. Rick reached for Warner's arm, but the older man batted his hand away. Warner dragged himself over the rim, onto the floor.

They ventured down the corridor.

Firelight flickered ten feet ahead, from inside a doorway on the left-hand side of the corridor. The fire crackled inside a chamber.

Rick motioned for Katy to fall back. Instead, she brought out the Taurus.

A shadow blotted out the firelight.

Rick stopped. He stuck his arm out in front of Katy to halt her.

A hairy hominid trod out of the chamber into the corridor. Gray streaked her sandy hair. She rotated her torso and head together, looking at the humans. Her hairy breasts swung like pendulums.

She sniffed.

"Aset?" she queried. *"Neteret a'a?"*

"*Tiu*," Katy responded.

Rick shot her a sidelong glance. She shrugged.

In Kemetian, she asked the creature where they could find Theo, Ethan, Jed, and Chin. She had to call the men "the humans whom your brothers captured."

The hominid crinkled her nose. She grunted.

Rick aped her vocalization.

She canted her head at him and uttered a noise that sounded like "huh?"

"Careful," Katy said. "For all you know you're asking for her hand in marriage."

Rick jerked his toward Katy. His eyes widened.

"I was kidding," she said.

He relaxed. "Not funny."

The hominid grunted twice. She waved her arm as if beckoning them to follow.

Rick gestured for her to lead the way.

The creature galumphed down the corridor. They trotted after her. Glancing backward to verify that they followed, she upped her pace to what—for a hairy hominid—amounted to a brisk walk.

The humans galloped after her.

She guided them around a corner, down a corridor past darkened chambers, around another corner, and through a curving passageway that dead-ended at a slab door. They had encountered slab doors in the hominid caves in Michigan. The doors consisted of rectangular monoliths set into the walls to block doorways. Like other slab doors, this one protruded from the wall a few inches.

The creature grasped the slab's side. She pulled.

Stone grated against stone. The slab door inched open.

Light swamped the chamber beyond.

Ethan, Theo, Jed, and Chin squinted at the light. Ethan shielded his eyes with his arm. The men sat on the floor of a small chamber, surrounded by stacks of handaxes and wood blocks.

Scrambling to their feet, the men fled the chamber.

"You guys okay?" Rick asked.

"Bumps and bruises," Ethan said. "We'll live."

The hairy hominid, head bowed, took refuge behind the slab door.

Rick pointed at the creature. "She doesn't think Isis is evil."

"Guess not," Katy said.

"Why? Her buddies wanted to kill you because they think you're Isis."

Katy posed the question to the hairy hominid.

The creature looked up at her. "Sons of Horus."

"The Sons of Horus fear Isis?"

The hominid stared at her.

Katy repeated the phrase in Kemetian.

The creature nodded. "Sacred room. For Aset."

Sacred room. Katy gazed into the chamber. Garfield had taken her into a sacred room in the Michigan caves, where she and Rick had found hieroglyphic texts that explained the relationship between the hairy hominids and the Planners, as well as introducing them to the pharaoh Imsety. Katy walked toward the doorway.

Rick grabbed her arm. She hesitated. He pushed past her, entering the chamber. Once inside, he turned on the flashlight.

Katy followed him in.

The flashlight illuminated hieroglyphic inscriptions on the back wall.

Crouching at the wall, Rick read the text. He said, "It talks about how the Sons of Horus erected the obelisk as a memorial to Osiris. They were forbidden to mark the location of his tomb, and faced a death sentence if they revealed that information to anyone. They found a loophole in the decree, though. They put up the obelisk near the tomb but away from it and they got the hairy hominids to defend both the obelisk and the tomb."

He skimmed his fingers over the vertical registers. "Doesn't say where the tomb is."

He spun on his heels to examine the right-hand wall. Someone had scored hieratic symbols into the rock, divided into two segments by a six-inch gap. Hieratic had been used for everyday purposes, while hieroglyphic was reserved for functions deemed of supreme importance, such as religious texts or stela inscriptions. For the author to have written in hieratic meant either he'd had no time for plotting out hieroglyphs, or he'd considered the text unimportant. Since he'd chosen the "sacred room" as the canvas for his text, he must've thought it vital.

A crack half an inch wide fractured the wall three feet from the junction with the rear wall. Right of the fault, smaller cracks splintered the wall in a lacework pattern.

Katy stooped beside Rick. "Can you read it?"

"I've got the gist of it," he said. "Tells how many years later, the Sons of Horus returned with the sacred Book of Thoth. They asked the great god Osiris to take it into the *duat*, where those who would abuse its power can't reach it. They altered the inscription to scare off anybody who might try to find the tomb."

"Does it say when this happened?"

"Sometime during the reign of Ramses the Second." Rick stuck his finger into the crack. "Text breaks off."

Katy sagged her shoulders. Perfect. An earthquake had probably ravaged the sacred room centuries ago.

Rick skimmed his finger along the lines of symbols below the six-inch gap. "There's more. In Year Five of Merenptah, the pharaoh's warriors came in search of the Book."

"Merenptah. He was a son of Ramses."

"Right. Says they needed the Book's power to ward off a powerful enemy."

Katy thought back to the books and magazines about ancient Egypt that she'd read over the past year. She'd read about Egypt before but, since meeting the Planners, boning up on ancient Egyptian history had seemed prudent. Now a tidbit came back to her.

In Year Five of his reign, Merenptah had waged war against invaders known as the Sea Peoples, who had united with the Libyans in an attempt to overthrow Egypt. In the end, Merenptah's forces trounced the enemy. Although the Sea Peoples would launch other incursions during the reigns of future pharaohs, particularly Ramses III, Merenptah had subdued them for the remainder of his reign.

Had the Book of Thoth facilitated that victory?

"I know what you're thinking," Rick said, "but it says their mission failed. The hairy hominids were afraid the warriors would wake up Isis, so they killed all of the warriors except one. They kept him as a hostage, in case Merenptah sent more warriors to finish the mission. While they waited, he scribbled this account of the incident."

"Wonder what happened to him."

"The last line explains." Rick tapped the hieratic symbols. He recited, "One season has passed, and still my brothers have not come for me. I am to die when next Ra emerges from the *duat*, as an offering to placate the great god Osiris."

The morning after he wrote the account, the creatures had sacrificed him. Nice.

The Sons of Horus had demonized Aset, the mother of their patron god, to frighten away anyone who dared to hunt for the tomb. After the Setna fiasco, they must've felt they had no choice. Their act, born of desperation, had triggered a chain reaction that over the span of millennia had provoked the hairy hominids to fear Aset so much they'd kill anyone who sought the Book or who happened to look a little bit like the "evil" goddess. The Sons of Horus couldn't have known the outcome of their ruse, yet the consequences had brought about countless deaths.

Had they learned their lesson?

Asru had said nobody outside the Sons of Horus knew the location of the tombs where they'd interred the Spirits of the Dead within their statue-like coffins. A Son of Horus must've told Merenptah where to find the Book.

"Does the text mention how Merenptah's warriors found this place?" Katy asked.

"Somebody clued them in." Rick puffed on the wall, clearing dust from the inscription. "The Followers of Seth."

Asru leaned through the doorway. "They are the elite who control my people."

"Great," Katy said.

"Apparently," Rick said, "the Followers of Seth came down in a chariot of light. They told Merenptah the Book had the power to stop the invaders, and they suggested where he should look for it."

"They let Merenptah's soldiers do the work for them."

"Do the dying for them. Typical Planners." He glanced at Asru. "No offense."

"Do not worry," Asru said. "For the Planners to whom you refer are the scourge of my people."

Katy rocked back on her heels. Over 12,000 years ago, Horus had buried his parents and several other relatives in cryogenic suspension, inside tombs the location of which no one else knew. He'd confided the locations to his four sons—Imsety, Duamutef, Hapi, and Qebhsenuf—and entrusted them with guarding the secret of both the tombs' locations and the Book's existence. They passed down the knowledge, and the responsibility, to their children, who passed it down to their children, and so on until the present day. The ranks of the brotherhood known as the Sons of Horus must've grown over the years as each generation produced heirs. How large had their numbers grown?

Asru knew. She knew a heck of a lot, which she refused to share.

By a strange coincidence, Imsety had been the pharaoh in power when a volcanic cataclysm forced the Planners underground—undersea, actually. He'd installed the hairy hominids in caves to ensure their survival. The Low Ones he'd abandoned.

Earlier in his reign, the Low Ones had rebelled against Imsety and the Planners, who used them as slaves to build temples and pyramids. Imsety had quashed the rebellion by slaughtering tens of thousands of Low Ones.

Katy stood up. "The Sons of Horus are just as evil as the Followers of Seth."

Asru stomped toward Katy. She hissed, "Do not call them evil."

The woman's face had flushed. Her lips quivered. Her hands, clenched at her sides, rippled tremors up her arms.

"They turned the creatures against Isis," Katy said.

"They committed an error. That does not make my people evil."

"Your pal Imsety," Katy said, "murdered thousands of *my* people."

"He would *not*."

"Oh yes he would."

Asru's expression had heated up to the boiling point. The flush threatened to burn itself into her features.

Katy's gut simmered. An outburst rose in her gullet. She swallowed it.

And then she recounted the story of Imsety's atrocities, as recorded on the walls of the sacred room in the Michigan hominid caves.

Asru shut her eyes. She clasped the amulet in her hand, whispering to herself. She let out a long breath. The exhalation eased the tension in her.

She met Katy's gaze. "Imsety did not perpetrate the acts of which you speak."

"Imsety thinks he did."

"Do not a handful of your people rewrite your history for their own nefarious purposes?"

Rick settled a hand on Katy's shoulder. "She's got a point."

Katy looked up at him. He shrugged his eyebrows, tipping his head to the side. He wasn't saying he believed Asru. But if they wanted the truth, or at least a morsel of it, they had to acknowledge that she made a valid point.

The impulse to trust Asru nagged at her, like a voice murmuring in her ear, too soft for her to make out the words.

Asru slipped a hand into her pocket. She pulled out a stone, black basalt incised with hieroglyphs.

Imsety's headstone.

Asru flipped the stone between her fingers.

Maybe Asru had brainwashed her. Someone had gassed her to steal the headstone. Asru possessed the headstone, which meant she or her lackeys had gassed Katy to get it.

They could've killed her. Instead, they knocked her out in a painless, nonviolent manner.

"Why'd you steal that?" Katy asked.

"To bring me closer to Imsety." She closed her fist around the stone. "The Followers of Seth wrote the text of which you speak. They had deposed Imsety because he wished to emancipate the Low Ones. He incited the rebellion. He died with the slaves, at the hands of Seth's progeny."

She sniffled. Tears streamed down her cheeks, over her lips, onto her chin. The beads dribbled from her chin onto her chest, speckling her blouse. A single tear dripped onto her amulet.

"Imsety was a fair and wise king," Asru said. "The Followers of Seth desired to slander his reputation. They had already turned the Revered Ones against your people. After Imsety's treason, they created the sacred room to tell their version of the story, to destroy Imsety's memory."

"But his brother, his successor to the throne, buried him."

"Duamutef rallied forces loyal to Imsety. He recaptured the throne, for a time."

"How long?"

"A matter of months. When the catastrophe was imminent, he offered the Low Ones shelter amongst our kind. Seth's followers murdered him."

Duamutef had buried his brother in Washington, far from his homeland. Why? She asked Asru.

"By order of Ra," Asru said, "anyone who knew the location of the Book of Thoth must die without his name. His soul must never reach the *duat*, for there he might divulge the secret unwittingly."

So, while Duamutef had buried his brother without his name, he'd equipped the tomb with a stela carved to resemble the hieroglyphs for the name of Osiris, their grandfather, as a hint to his true name. Perhaps Duamutef felt that such a clue would give Imsety at least a shot at entering the afterlife. Why, then, had Duamutef added the headstone?

Someone else must've placed it on the grave. Someone who thought the stela lacked the power to ensure Imsety's soul achieved eternal life.

"Who put the headstone on Imsety's grave?" Katy asked.

"It is believed," Asru said, "that Duamutef stole back into the crypt after the priests and mourners had left. Imsety was cursed to die without his name, but Duamutef saw to it that he did not."

"I suppose you know all this because Jed told you."

"Indeed."

Imsety and Duamutef, the original Sons of Horus, had protected the Book and its secrets. For their service, they were condemned to die nameless, forever shut out of the afterlife. Duamutef had guaranteed his brother's soul could live on for eternity. Perhaps Hapi and Qebhsenuf had done the same for him, in a tomb concealed within hairy hominid caves elsewhere on Earth.

The Sons of Horus had continued as a secret society, with members including pharaohs' sons. The message on Nefrekeptah's bandages—*We are the Sons of Horus*—hinted that he had belonged to the society. But he'd misused the Book. Whether magically, as the legend said, or simply by stealing it for his own glory or even for the Planners mattered little. He'd died without his name, like all the Sons of Horus, though no one had rescued his soul by secreting his name into his tomb. His punishment for abusing the knowledge with which he was entrusted?

"If the Book of Thoth is so top secret," Katy said, "how come Duamutef summarized its content on Imsety's stela?"

Asru chewed her lip. "I do not know. He must have felt the Book was in danger, and reproducing its knowledge on the stela served as a means of preserving that knowledge for the future."

Or perhaps Duamutef had wanted someone to find the stela, eventually. Nephthys had erected the Meidum stela to preserve the memory of Bakhu and the sacrifice its people made to protect the Book. She must've wanted someone, sometime, to uncover the stela and realize what it meant. To follow the directions she'd given to the Book's location. To share the Book's wisdom with the rest of the world.

One problem. The Sons of Horus kept shifting the Book around. To protect it, sure, but their intentions didn't mitigate the effect. No one knew where to find the Book today.

Whatever knowledge the Book of Thoth, it must rank as the most valuable and powerful information ever written down on paper. Generations of Planners had conspired to hide the Book. Hundreds, perhaps thousands, of people had died to secure the secret of the Book's location. Men risked their very souls to assure the Book's safety.

"We have to find the Book," Katy said. "We have to find it now."

50 miles northeast of Bakhu

Gloom saturated the chamber.

Lamps flickered their artificial flames on the walls. On a table sat a large bowl, filled with water. Ancient symbols decorated its exterior and interior, glyphs from a language Djehuty had stolen from his own kind so he might impart it to the Low Ones, the parasites who infested the land that had once belonged the Planners. Gods should never confer their wisdom upon lower creatures, especially those as vile as the Low Ones.

He dunked his cupped hands into the water. Ducking his head as he lifted his hands, he sipped the water. Tainted with the oils from the clothing of Bob Hanover—a Low One with whom he had been forced to consort and lay hands upon—the water tasted salty, bitter. He gulped it down and dunked his hands for another mouthful.

Once he obtained the Book, its contents would grant him the power to cleanse the Earth of the Low Ones. The parasites would infest Kemet no more.

The vessel had descended over the western desert as it advanced on the ruins of Bakhu, submerged under an ocean of sand. The blood of Bakhu had once guaranteed the security of Djehuty's book. Before the night crested at its midpoint, he would grasp the Book in his hands. The knowledge of the ancestors, the wisdom of Amen-Ra and the great Atum himself, would course through his body, imbuing him with a power greater than any the world had beheld since the First House of Man fell.

The power of those who had inhabited the First House. The power of his ancestors.

Long ago, Aset had warned him the Book contained no physical or magical power. Its potency stemmed from the knowledge it sustained on its papyrus. Why then had their people, since before recorded memory, referred to their written language as the Words of the Gods? If the words retained no power, why name them thus?

Aset had lied. She feared the Book's force.

He harbored no such fears, for he *was* fear. It lived in him. He nourished it.

Soon the vessel would arrive at Bakhu. He wished to purify his body, as well as his mind and soul, before he engaged the Bergrens in battle. They had brought him to the Book. That they aided him unwittingly, and that the woman who called herself Asru also aided him without knowing, pleased him all the more—though the pleasure he gained from the deception would seem trifling compared to the bliss of eradicating the Low Ones. He would test his might on the Bergrens, without the Book's benefit. Their usefulness had expired.

Purifying himself required time, a commodity of which he possessed a boundless supply. He had already lived an eternity. A few additional minutes mattered none—to him. For the Bergrens, the clock counted down the final seconds of their lives. Tick, tick, tick. Though the clocks he knew had no ticking mechanism, he liked the sound, therefore he conjured it in his mind. So quaint. So feral.

Tick, tick, tick. The heartbeat of a desiccated being.

On the voyage to Egypt, he had observed the sunset and sensed a kinship with the daystar. Ra had claimed the sun for himself, as a symbol of his light and benevolence. He failed to comprehend the death inherent in the sun. Its rays stimulated diseases in the flesh, charred the skin, siphoned from the body the lifeblood of every living thing—water. During eclipses, the sun's power could blind onlookers. When the star finally self-destructed, it would engulf the Earth and obliterate every creature that lived upon the planet.

In the sunset, he had foreseen his future. The sun, its heart pierced by the horizon, had bled across the sky. Clouds had flowed away from the sun as streamers of blood.

The blood-red hues had been an omen. The sun belonged to him.

The doors parted. Guards shoved Bob Hanover inside, propelled him across the chamber to the table. They forced him onto his knees. The table came up to his nose. Genuflecting before his god, Bob gazed across the table, over the water bowl.

Intef smiled at him. "I thought you should witness my rebirth."

"You're dying then?"

Intef chuckled. "The impending death is not mine."

Bob's face blanched.

"Nor yours," Intef said. "You may yet prove useful."

"I won't help you find the Book."

"You are correct. For the Bergrens have led me to it."

"Don't see how I'll be useful then. Might as well kill me."

Intef shook his head. He clucked his tongue. "You should not be so willing to die, Doctor. For you are about to embark on a great journey. Together, you and I will resurrect the power of the gods and initiate the day of reckoning."

"No thanks. Sounds too Armageddon-ish for me."

"You will aid me, Doctor. Whether you wish to or not."

Bob set his jaw. The color had returned to his face, and a fury glinted in his eyes.

"I have asked for your help." Intef rested his hands on either side of the bowl. "I will not ask again. If you refuse me, I shall use other means to obtain what I seek."

"Good luck," Bob muttered. "Charlie won't tell you either."

"You misunderstand, Doctor. I will use other means on *you*."

Bob's expression faltered. He darted his eyes from Intef to the doorway and back to Intef. As he stared at the lamplight reflected on the water in the bowl, he ran his tongue across his lower lip.

Intef removed his shirt, dropping it on the floor beside him, and bent over the bowl. He immersed his head in the water. The liquid cooled his face and scalp. As he rubbed his hands through his hair, he imagined microscopic creatures nipping at him, sampling his blood, screeching in agony at the taste, for he had drawn the forces of chaos around him as a robe. Protection against whatever or whoever attempted to harm him. Yes, allying oneself with chaos had its advantages.

Maat had its uses. Righteousness often did. But chaos possessed the ultimate power.

When he withdrew his head from the water, he straightened. A dark slick had formed atop the water where he had rinsed his hair. The color pooled outward across the waters.

Intef threw his head back. Water splattered around him. He swiped his hands over his face, raked them through his hair.

Bob Hanover gasped.

A smile tightened Intef's face. He fixed his gaze on the water. Wavelets transformed his reflection into a living thing, a creature that writhed amid the waters, ready to strike at the first beast that lowered its lips to drink. His image, mimicked by the water, sneered back at him, one corner of the mouth upturned. His hair glistened the color of fresh blood.

The color of chaos.

Intef touched a fingertip to the water. His reflection rippled.

"I have shed my mask, Aset," he said. "Will you now shed yours?"

The cliffs near Bakhu

Rick crouched at the obelisk, focused on the inscriptions Katy had cleaned off before the wayward hominid attacked them.

Katy observed from a few feet away. The hairy hominid who'd taken them to Theo and the boys, and shown them the sacred room, lingered behind the obelisk in view of Katy. Without an invitation, the creature had opted to follow them outside. Katy had decided to call the female Beset, after the ancient Egyptian goddess. While Beset had been a dwarf, the goddess' hairy appearance made her a good match for the hominid.

Warner and Asru sat on the ground near the entrance to the camp. Asru had her legs folded under her, hands clasped on her lap. Warner, seated with knees bent before him, shook his head as she said something to him. Jed stood behind Asru, stiff as the obelisk. He scanned the camp every few seconds.

Chin huddled along the southern wall in the shade of the overhangs. Bent forward, head down, he tinkered with an object in his hand.

Theo slumped against the northern wall, not far from Warner and Asru. His eyes were closed, his arms limp at his sides. His mouth had fallen open. Ethan reclined beside him, also asleep.

The sliver of sky that showed above them had darkened to navy blue. The first star twinkled in the waning daylight.

Rick tapped the obelisk about a foot above the Isis/Nephthys inscription. His finger underlined a series of four hieroglyphs, larger than the rest and set apart on their own line. Katy had seen them once before, on the back of Asru's amulet. They were the symbols for sun, sand, mountain, and pyramid. The scribe who created the obelisk inscriptions had aligned the four symbols in a manner unlike any inscription she knew of from ancient Egypt or from the Planners repertoire. Both the Egyptians and the Planners arranged their hieroglyphs in an orderly layout that maximized space while maintaining an aesthetic sensibility.

On the obelisk, the symbols had been laid out in a horizontal line, with the mountain and pyramid symbols on their sides, perpendicular to each other. Just like Asru's amulet—with one exception. Here the scribe had appended two extra glyphs, the symbols for star and sky, onto the series.

She had seen those symbols before too. On Imsety's stela in Washington. The symbols' arrangement stirred a memory, one that refused to let her capture it. The layout had meaning. She'd seen something, somewhere, similar to the hieroglyph grouping.

Behind the obelisk, Beset grunted.

Katy looked at the spot where the creature had hunkered. Beset was gone. Noises came from behind the obelisk.

Rick wiped dirt from the hieroglyphs. "You thought the symbols on Imsety's headstone had to do with another planet."

"Yeah…" Katy peered around the obelisk. "The symbols were right after the phrase First House of Man."

Beset grunted, snorted, huffed. Sand spewed out from behind the obelisk.

"I don't understand the other symbols," Rick said. "No matter how you interpret it, the text doesn't make a lick of sense."

"Mm."

"The best translation I can get is the foreign sun mountain pyramid. Or the sun desert mountain pyramid. Or maybe the sun island of the pyramid mountain."

Katy trotted behind the obelisk.

Beset stooped facing the obelisk. She pawed at the sand, excavating a hole already two feet deep and three feet in diameter. The hominid hugged a wooden box under one arm. Double doors, suited to a Barbie doll, sealed the box's front. Four legs carved to resemble lion's paws would've supported the box if it sat on the ground. At two feet tall and one foot wide, the box fit the Isis statue Neb had shown her.

Not a box. A shrine.

Beset stopped pawing. She set the box inside the hole.

"What are you doing?" Katy asked.

The creature jumped. She gaped at Katy, eyes wide, then bowed her head so low her chin bumped into her chest. Her grunts formed Kemetian words.

"Forgive me," Beset beseeched.

"For what?" Katy asked.

"They stole." She jabbed a finger at the shrine. "From your husband."

"My husband...?"

Katy glanced at Rick, who remained fixated on the strange inscription. Unless he'd sneaked off when she wasn't looking, found the shrine somewhere, and sneaked back without telling her what he'd done...Beset didn't mean Rick.

The creatures mistook her for Isis. In the myths, Isis was married to Osiris.

Thanks to the well-intentioned but boneheaded Sons of Horus, the creatures feared Isis. The obelisk depicted her as a demon who devoured life, squashed it under her feet. Yet the shrine hinted at worship. The ancient Egyptians had worshiped evil deities—like Setesh, god of chaos. But when the creatures had believed her to be Isis, they tried to kill her. She'd sensed no reverence or desire to placate the evil goddess. They simply feared her. To the point of violence.

Katy chewed the inside of her lip. The creatures hadn't crafted a shrine to Isis. If they'd stolen the shrine from Osiris, that must mean they'd pinched it from his tomb.

Her heart revved like a racecar's engine. She asked Beset, "They stole the shrine from Osiris' tomb?"

The hominid nodded.

Maybe the Sons of Horus weren't such boneheads after all. Their ploy had guaranteed the tomb's security. No human being could get past a hairy hominid without serious firepower.

Katy glanced at Asru and Warner. Why couldn't Asru find the tomb on her own? Why couldn't Intef? The Planners should know their own history better than her and Rick, mere Low Ones.

Wait a minute. Asru had said the Sons of Horus knew the tomb's location *and* the Book's location. Jed was a Son of Horus.

Katy marched across the camp toward Asru. Hands on hips, she locked her gaze on the woman.

"If Jed's a Son of Horus," Katy said, "how come he can't tell you where the tomb and the Book are?"

Asru and Jed exchanged looks. Asru nodded. Jed tipped his head to her.

Lifting his chin, he met Katy's stare. "That knowledge has been lost."

"How?"

"The Sons of Horus have operated in secret since the burials of the Spirits of the Dead. We have no secure means of communicating with each other. The Sons who last moved the Book died before they could pass on this knowledge."

"What about the tomb?"

"Only Horus and his sons knew its location. They neglected to pass on the knowledge."

"You mean only Horus and his actual, biological sons knew the tomb's whereabouts."

"Yes."

Asru got to her feet, brushing sand from her clothes. Warner stood as well.

Rick approached from the direction of the obelisk.

Katy folded her arms over her chest. "That's why Jed met with Warner to ask him about the Book. He thought we knew where to find it, and Warner might tell him."

Intef had taken the Meidum stela, the one whose blank cover had hidden an inscribed core, but left the other stela. He hadn't known the inscribed stela originally had a covering, so he never guessed that the second might also hide an inscription. It didn't, which was irrelevant. The point was, Intef hadn't known to look at the second stela. Asru had needed to send Jed to question Warner in hopes of finding the Book of Thoth. Intef threatened Katy and Rick into searching for it on his behalf. Now Asru had joined with Katy and Rick to recover the Book.

Hmm.

Katy said, "You did such a good job covering up the Book's location that you accidentally erased your own history."

"Correct," Asru said.

"Brilliant."

"Expunging all records that mention the Book or the Spirits of the Dead seemed wise at the time. My people have long suffered from short-sightedness. "

"No kidding."

Two more stars had appeared overhead. Asru scowled at the new stars. A muscle in her jaw tensed.

Katy walked to the obelisk. Above the Isis inscription, and the strange symbols she thought referred to another planet, ghosts of hieroglyphs haunted the stone. She clawed at the dirt encrusted on them. When she had found the start of the text, she backed away to read the hieroglyphs.

Rick stood behind her. He gazed at the inscriptions over her shoulder.

"It's the original inscription," he said.

Katy read the inscription out loud. "We, the Planners, seal this place for eternity in the name of Osiris-Khentiamentu, lord of the Two Lands. None may disturb his rest until the Day of Awakening, when the Spirits of the Dead shall arise to reclaim their kingdom. Those who desecrate his tomb shall suffer the wrath of...I think it says Amen-Ra, but the text is worn away."

Rick blew on the symbols. Sand evacuated the reliefs, though the segment about Amen-Ra remained hard to discern. After that text, a line introduced the sun-sand-mountain-pyramid group.

Katy read it. "His family lived in the First House of Man, home of Atum."

"The creator god," Rick said. "Some legends say Atum led the Ennead, the group of nine gods who were the Spirits of the Dead."

Rick settled his hands on her shoulders. With her index finger she traced the outline of the Isis figure. The paint had long since disintegrated. The statue had green eyes. An aberration? Or had this inscription also depicted Isis with green eyes? What did it matter?

The eyes. They meant something.

A light pulsed overhead. Katy glanced up at the sliver of sky visible above them. A light, bigger and brighter than the North Star or Venus, floated along the length of the sliver heading west. Halfway across the cleft, the craft paused. It swelled bigger and bigger, descending on the mountain.

The craft blotted out half the sky. Katy shielded her eyes with her hand. Static electricity tingled over her body. The craft inflated to block the entire sliver and more. Her scalp prickled as the hairs raised. Her eyes hurt. She looked at Rick.

He was looking at her.

Ethan and Theo had roused. They squinted up at the craft, winced, averted their eyes. They leaped up and scurried across the camp to the others.

Warner, Asru, and Jed braved the brilliance to watch the craft drift away from the cleft. As the craft disappeared over the mountain, its light lingered behind it, casting a sickly glow on the cleft and the cliffs above.

"How did they find us?" Katy wondered.

Rick asked Warner, "How did *you* find us?"

"I placed a G-P-S transmitter on your plane."

"Think the Planners could've tapped into it?"

"No," Asru said, "Intef views your technology the way you view the stone tools the Revered Ones create. He would not deign to use it."

At the southern wall, Chin pocketed the object he'd fiddled with earlier.

"What's he got?" Katy said.

Rick strode to Chin. He grasped the man's shirt and hauled him off the ground, depositing him on his feet. Rick held onto Chin's shirt. His free hand he shoved into Chin's pocket. He yanked out the object, a device the size of a hand-held electronic organizer. A thin cord fastened a pen-like object to the device's side.

"What is this?" Rick asked.

Chin shrugged.

Rick shook him. "What is it?"

Chin smirked at him.

Rick threw him backward into the wall. Chin's head smacked into the limestone. Rick switched the device to his left hand. With Chin pinned under his left arm, he whipped out his .45 and jammed the muzzle into Chin's cheek.

"I won't ask again," Rick said. "What is this thing?"

Asru said, "We call them scrolls. They are portable computers, connected to the main processor on their home vessel."

"Which means this one's plugged into Intef's ship."

Chin smiled—a foul, arrogant expression that warped his entire face, narrowed his eyes to slits, and bared a mouthful of teeth that glistened like the fangs of a wolf.

"My lord has arrived," Chin said.

Rick wrapped his finger around the trigger. He clenched his jaw. Through his teeth, he snarled, "You bastard."

"The tomb's nearby," Chin said. "We don't need you anymore. My lord will take the Book and claim the throne that should've been his to start with."

"Like hell he will."

Chin sniggered. "You can't stop a god."

Rick hurled Chin across the camp. The traitor landed face-down in ashes of the fire, where red-hot coals still smoldered.

Chin shouted. He rolled away from the fire. His left sleeve smoked. Clutching his left arm, he clambered onto his knees.

Rick slipped the scroll device into his shirt pocket.

Asru tore her knife from its sheath. She stalked to Chin, thrust the knife lengthwise against his throat. Her voice roughened into a hoarse whisper.

"You have betrayed me," she said.

"*You* betrayed *him*," Chin answered.

Asru's hand trembled as she held the knife on his flesh. The blade nicked his skin. Blood trickled down his neck.

Rick walked back to Katy. The .45 he kept in his hand, leveled at Chin.

"He's not a Planner, is he?" Rick said. "He's a Low One, like us."

"He is," Asru said.

Katy arched her eyebrows at Rick. "How'd you know?"

"He wears a watch. He talks like us and he knew what the lottery was."

Of course. The Planners needed Low Ones to help them navigate the modern world. Chin must've forged the email from Warner that enticed them to Mackinaw City. He showed the Planners how to make a phone call—he likely provided them with a cell phone too—so they could call her up and threaten to kill Charlie if she and Rick didn't find the Book for them. Chin must've also hacked into the Warner Industries server—to search for information, no doubt. He'd sent the email instructing her to turn on the TV, to see the news flash about Warner's jet crashing, and the subsequent email ordering her to find the Book.

The son of a bitch had ratted them out.

Warner pointed at Chin. "What do we do with him?"

Rick tightened his finger around the .45's trigger. "Shoot him."

Katy glanced at the obelisk. Beset cowered behind it, her face surfacing from the shadows as she peeked out at the humans.

She laid a hand on Rick's arm. "He's not worth it. Besides, I have a better idea."

"Better how?"

"Beset can take care of him."

"Who's Beset?"

Katy waved at the hairy hominid. The creature lumbered out from behind the obelisk. When she'd reached Katy, the creature ducked her head.

In Kemetian, Katy instructed Beset to hide Chin until informed otherwise.

Beset glanced up at Katy. Her lumpy brow furrowed.

"Guard him," Katy said. "He is an enemy of Amen-Ra."

The creature grunted agreement.

Beset grabbed Chin's arms and plucked him off the ground. His feet dangled in the air. He kicked her in the knee, pounded his fists against her chest. She punched him in the side of the head.

He passed out.

The hominid slung him over her shoulder with his head upside-down behind her, both his arms and his legs restrained under one of her arms.

She started toward the obelisk.

Katy stopped her with a shout. Beset swiveled her head and torso to look back at Katy. "Where is Osiris' tomb?" Katy asked.

"North," Beset grunted. "Passage goes east."

Beset carted her prisoner behind the obelisk, into the grotto, out of sight. Her footfalls muted into silence.

A passage goes east. Beset must've meant another fissure, like the one through which they'd reached the hominid camp.

Katy surveyed their clan. Two archaeologists, a couple Planners and Warner.

Rick led the group into the fissure. A few minutes later, they exited onto the plateau.

Stars sprinkled the sky around the half moon, which sunk toward the western horizon. A wind swirled sand into mini whirlwinds as it keened across the plateau.

No glowing craft.

"Where'd they go?" Katy said.

"Nowhere," Asru said. "We cannot see the craft, yet you may be certain it lingers nearby."

"Invisible?"

"Camouflaged."

Nothing hovered in the sky save for stars. Without the light pollution from a city, the sky sparkled with so many stars that it resembled a blanket knit from diamonds.

Across the plateau, 30 degrees above the horizon, the stars wavered.

Her eyes must've gone blurry. She blinked.

Nope. Her eyesight was fine.

In a circular patch of the sky about as long as her thumb when held at arm's length, the stars were distorted. Nobody would notice the distortion unless they really looked. She wouldn't have noticed, if Asru hadn't mentioned camouflage.

The craft hovered over the plateau. Watching. Waiting.

Katy held her index finger over the distortion. "There it is. Intef's ship."

Rick leaned in front of her to squint down her arm's length. "Where?"

"Where my fingertip is. The ship's camouflage distorts the stars. See it?"

"Yeah."

Katy dropped her arm.

"Right." Rick straightened. "Ethan and Theo, head back to the plane."

The men bobbed their heads a degree, their gazes pinned on the distortion in the sky.

"Warner and Asru should go with them," Katy said.

"Good idea," Rick said.

"No," Warner said. "You need backup."

"Please go with them," Katy said. "At least that way some of us survive to keep fighting."

Warner clenched his jaw, wringing the words through his teeth. "Intef murdered four innocent people when he tried to kill me. I will not cower under a rock."

"The crash wasn't your fault."

He exhaled through his nose. She could almost see the steam roiling from his nostrils.

"The pilot and copilot were old friends," he said. "The other two were archaeologists. I'd loaned my plane to them so they could fly to a conference in Toronto. I had planned to fly to Michigan, to see you. When I cancelled the trip to meet with Jed, I let the archaeologists take my place on the plane. Apparently, Intef was unaware of the change. I didn't realize Intef wanted to kill me until I heard the jet had crashed. If I had known..."

"You would've stopped the plane from taking off."

He rubbed his hands as if cleansing blood from them. She could think of platitudes appropriate to the situation—it's not your fault, you couldn't have known. None of them would alleviate his guilt. She knew about guilt. It wouldn't wash off, no matter how hard you scrubbed.

Warner must know that. He would try anyway.

In his position, she would've tried too.

Rick turned on the flashlight. The beam, aimed at the ground, backlit the clan of would-be warriors, five Low Ones and two Planners, who had banded together as humanity's sole defense against Intef and his ilk.

Warriors. Humanity's defense.

God help humanity.

Warner gazed across the plateau, toward the distortion that heralded Intef's ship. When he looked at Katy again, she swore his eyes glistened as if tears had formed in them. Since Warner crying would happen right after NASA admitted the moon really was green cheese, she must've mistaken a reflection for dewiness.

Sure, and the UFO sighted over the Mackinac Bridge four days earlier had been swamp gas surrounding a weather balloon while a temperature inversion layer refracted Venus.

In the flashlight's glow, Rick checked the GPS. The unit bleeped.

"We'd better escort them to the plane," Rick said. "In case our militant friends arrange a welcoming party."

"Or the hairy hominids," Katy reminded him.

"Yeah. Them too."

The craft hovered a distance away. Intef would wait until they found the tomb before making his move. She thought. She hoped.

He would. She knew it. He needed them to find the tomb for him. He knew nothing about the hairy hominids who guarded the vicinity, and how they worshiped him. He knew nothing about the obelisk.

Unless Chin had told him.

Dammit.

Before they breached a 12,000-year-old tomb in search of a 12,000-year-old Book with a crazy ufonaut on their butts, they needed a few more answers. Questions and answers demanded time.

Right now, she had none to spare.

They'd jump into the void blindfolded. Again. Whatever awaited them at the bottom— snakes, scorpions, a carpet of knife-sharp stakes—they would deal with later.

At least she had one less mystery to solve. The man in camouflage she'd seen fleeing their cabin in Michigan. The fact that Warner had forsaken his Glock, leaving it in an open suitcase in his home. The glimpse of movement she'd caught outside Warner's home. The man she'd seen at Giza who looked like Warner.

The man had been Warner, of course. He'd left his Glock in the open suitcase because they'd interrupted his packing.

Katy thumped her fist into Warner's arm. "You jerk. You saw us at your house, didn't you? Then you followed us to Egypt."

"I did."

Asru rotated her head in slow motion toward Warner. Her lips parted.

"It was you," Asru said, "at Saqqara. You threatened me."

"I didn't threaten you," Warner said.

"You held your weapon to my head."

"I thought you were working for Intef. I apologize."

The clan lapsed into silence.

Rick held the GPS unit over his head in his right hand. With his left index finger, he traced paths in the sky.

"What the heck are you doing?" Katy asked.

"I can't keep the flashlight on, somebody might see it. So I'm comparing the GPS data to the stars to plot our route to the plane."

"Oh." She pecked a kiss on his cheek. "Very clever."

He mumbled, "Yeah, whatever, thanks."

Rick clipped the GPS unit onto his belt and switched off the flashlight. He set off across the plateau with the others behind him.

Bob thrummed his fingers on his kneecap. Beyond the observation window, desert stretched across a plateau between mountain ranges. The western mountains hunkered behind the vessel, though he glimpsed their northern and southern extremities as they curved around the plateau. Five miles to the east, cliffs bounded the plateau. From behind the vessel, moonlight dimmed by thin clouds smeared its paleness over the desert.

He shifted on the bench, clacking his teeth together in a drumbeat. Near the window, Charlie hunched with hands in his pockets.

"We have to do something," Bob said.

"Don't think milk in the control panel will work this time."

Bob pictured the command center. The workstations, the monitors, the chairs, the men. He had counted at most three men, plus the first mate. Four men. With a weapon, he and Charlie might capture the command center.

He had no weapon. He had no clue where the Planners kept them. Besides, what would they do once they took control of the command center?

"Do you know how to fly this vessel?" Bob asked.

"Nope."

Charlie shambled to the bench, dropped onto it. The bench wobbled.

Bob leaped up. He paced the width of the room. The lamplight projected shadows that nipped at his heels.

He let his shoulders sag. "We're buggered, aren't we?"

"Looks like."

"There must be a way..."

Charlie rubbed his beard. He gazed at the panel that concealed the observation window. Bob heard the seconds tick past on his watch. One. Two. Three. Four.

"Still got that scroll thingamajig?" Charlie asked.

"Intef took it back."

"Damn."

Bob paced past the window. The clouds must've departed westward, for the moonlight shone clean on the plateau. The pallid blush gleamed on an object on the far side of the plateau, a short distance from the cliffs. The object was elongated, taller at one end, tapered at the shorter end. The moonlight flashed off glass.

An airplane.

"Dear God," Bob said. "They're out there."

Slanted forward, Charlie squinted out the window. "Who?"

"Rick and Katy." Bob twirled around, putting his back to the window. "We can't sit here like a couple of old fools."

Clearing his throat, standing erect with hands fisted, Charlie stalked across the room to the doorway. The doors parted for him. Bob hurried after him as he entered the corridor, turned left, and stomped onward.

When he caught up with Charlie, he asked, "You have an idea?"

"Nope."

"I see. We're getting exercise so we'll be fit for the afterlife."

"Didn't know Brits could be sarcastic."

"We're supposed to be gloomy and dour, aren't we? Sorry to disappoint."

"Nah, it's refreshing after two years cooped up with the Planners. My whole family is sarcastic, I miss it."

"At least I've made you feel at home then."

They rounded a curve.

The lights went out. A second later the lights came on again at half strength, while red lights blinked overhead.

Charlie stopped. Bob halted beside him.

"Red alert," Charlie said.

"The Planners call it that?" Bob asked.

"No, it's my term. I love *Star Trek*."

Behind them, footsteps clapped. Soon the owner of the feet would round the bend.

"Got an idea," Charlie said.

He shoved Bob into the wall and flattened his own body against it beside Bob. Nearest the bend, Charlie stared in the direction of the footsteps.

Louder. Closer. Clap, clap, clap.

Charlie tensed his body.

Bob hugged the wall, his back spine sandwiched to it.

Clap, clap.

The red strobes cast a shadow from around the bend. The footsteps silenced. The shadow stood motionless, animated only by the blinking lights.

Bob held his breath.

Clap, clap. The shadow traveled across the corridor, onto the wall.

A man sauntered around the bend.

Charlie kicked him in the gut. The man clutched his stomach. Charlie chopped his hand into the back of the man's head. The man grabbed at Charlie's legs.

Bob punted him under the jaw. The man let out a muffled cry.

Charlie slugged him in the jowl. The man slumped down onto the floor. Hand trembling, he grasped Bob's ankle. Charlie booted him in the back.

The man went limp. His eyes closed.

Bob's heart pummeled his chest. His pulse throbbed inside his head. Breathing hard, he glanced around the corridor. No one in sight.

Charlie straddled the unconscious man. He probed the man's pockets.

As his heartbeat slowed, Bob sucked in a deep breath. He released it gradually.

"Felt good, didn't it?" Charlie said.

"Yes…seems wrong to enjoy it."

"The scumbags deserve it." Charlie tapped the man's cheek. "This one's good buddies with old Intef."

The guilt that wrenched his gut moderated a bit. Any chum of Intef's must've butchered dozens of people. Perhaps hundreds.

Besides, they hadn't killed the man. He would wake up with a ghastly headache, but he would survive. Unlike the innocents he and his lord had exterminated.

Charlie raised his hand high. In it he grasped a scroll device.

He tossed it to Bob. "Give it a shot."

"What should I do?" Bob powered up the device. "A scroll can't control the ship."

"No, but it can send and receive messages."

"Katy and Rick don't have a scroll."

Charlie straightened, stepping away from the unconscious man. He scratched his beard. He held up a finger, as if pointing at a light bulb that had popped on over his head.

"Katy and Rick don't have one," Charlie said, "but the men who went with Asru might."

"Asru? Who the bloody hell is Asru?"

Charlie dismissed the question with a wave of his hand. "Long story. She hates Intef, so she might be an ally for us. Jed and Chin went with her."

"Jed and…I heard Intef cursing them for deserting him to go with a woman. He said now they're conspiring with the Bergrens."

A smile split Charlie's beard in two. He slapped Bob's shoulder.

Bob focused on the scroll. Its menus and commands were in Kemetian—a hieroglyphic variant rather than the hieratic version he'd encountered on the doors. The Planners must've considered the scrolls more important, of higher rank, than the control panels on the doors.

Fascinating, but thoroughly unhelpful. He wiped the thought from his mind and focused on the little screen. Unhooking the pen from the device's side, he tapped it on the screen to select commands. He chose a phrase he thought meant "communications." Instead he got an inventory of suggestions for prayers Intef's subjects could offer to him. How thoughtful of Intef.

"Hurry it up," Charlie said.

"I'm trying."

Another page, labeled "scrolls," provided a directory of books in the ship's library. Intef maintained a library. Bizarre. Bob would've thought the man preferred his subjects remain ignorant. Of course, the existence of a library didn't mean Intef allowed everyone to access the books.

"Oh for crying out loud," Charlie muttered. "I could've sent a message by carrier pigeon faster than this."

A menu titled "choices" gave him options for displaying the results of commands. He clicked on the final option, "word aspect." The device offered him a choice between divine and low. He picked low. A list of languages spoken by the humans other than the Planners filled the screen. He tapped English.

The Kemetian symbols morphed into English words.

Divine and Low. Divine signified Kemetian, the language of the Planners, who considered themselves gods. Low meant the languages of the Low Ones.

Bob chose a command identified as "transmission agents." A list of names spilled down the screen: Usermaatra, son of Ramose; Sataset, daughter of Neithhotep; Senenmut, son of Waenra. Jed must be short for Djed-something. He found dozens of names beginning with Djed, from Djedkara to Djedmaatesankh. Since the latter was a feminine name, he ruled it out. Still, he had more chance of producing a pigeon from his pocket than of locating Asru's Jed amongst the multitude of Djed names enumerated in the list. He kept scanning through the names, though, since he had nothing else to do.

The names unreeled down the screen. He glimpsed an odd name, a very un-Egyptian and therefore un-Plannerian moniker. He slid the pen up the screen, rolling back the list to the strange name. There it was.

Djasen Tjin.

He'd never seen such a name in any text from Ancient Egypt. The Planners might've devised their own names, since their language had evolved over the millennia. Yet, from perusing the list, he gathered they favored old-style names. Intef and Asru both had archaic names. Merka, Djed, and other Planners he'd met also called themselves by ancient names.

Like its ancient counterpart, Kemetian employed no vowels—the letters he interpreted as vowels, based on the Egyptological method for translating hieroglyphs, represented sounds which had no direct counterpart in English. Because Kemetian ignored the vowels, native speakers might have trouble translating a modern name into the language.

Djasen Tjin might represent a modern name, mangled to fit Kemetian syntax. The consonant *tj* was pronounced "ch." As for the first name, *dj* was vocalized as "j" and no one knew for certain how the "a" would've been pronounced. Jasen. Chin.

Jason Chin. Could he be the same Chin who'd accompanied Asru?

He selected the name. The screen emptied. At the top, the word "connected" appeared. The name Nu, probably belonging to the man who lay unconscious on the floor, blinked at him on the next line.

"I'm in," Bob said. "What should I say?"

"Gimme that."

Charlie took the scroll. Grasping the pen, he scribbled a message.

The clan slogged past the hole into which Katy had fallen, the gateway to Bakhu.

Katy shuddered. The Meidum stela had listed 148 names of people who died at Bakhu when Intef besieged the town. Their bodies must lie elsewhere within the ruins, interred by the itinerant sands of the desert. They had stumbled over a handful of the dead. The rest must lie undisturbed, unknown, though not without their names. Thanks to Nitiqret—Nephthys—Bakhu's dead had reclaimed their names, in a way, via the Meidum stela. Perhaps her actions had spared their souls from eternal limbo.

Up ahead, the DC-3 squatted like a troll under an invisible bridge. The moonlight glinted off its windows, bleached its fuselage an ethereal white.

A dozen feet from the plane, they stopped. Rick faced the archaeologists.

"Get out of here," he ordered. "And take them with you."

He waved at Asru and Jed.

"Nobody's leaving," Ethan said.

"We'll wait for you," Theo affirmed.

Rick stared at the silhouettes of the archaeologists. Katy watched his silhouette. Though the moon sparked off his eyes when he moved his head, its glow surrendered to the shadows around his face. Yet she knew exactly which look he was giving the archaeologists. Lips twisted halfway between a frown and a weary smile. Head angled down. Gazing up at them through his eyelashes.

He'd given her the same look so often she knew every wrinkle it creased across his face.

"Jed will remain with them," Asru said.

"My lady?" Jed said.

"You know Intef's ways," she said. "You can safeguard them."

Rick grumbled. "Protected by a Planner. That's comforting."

"We'll be fine," Theo said.

Katy grasped Rick's arm. She squeezed a little. He turned his head toward her, and the moonglow reflected on the whites of his eyes.

"What makes you think we can trust her and Jed?" Rick asked.

"Intuition."

She practically heard the cogs spinning in his head as he strove to think of a challenge to her assertion. He craved logic, stability, order amid the chaos, even after all they'd seen and done together. He would've made a great ancient Egyptian. They had cherished harmony and justice, a cosmic order they called *maat*, above all else. The pharaoh's job description encompassed the task of maintaining *maat*.

Rick should've been a pharaoh.

She hoped he wasn't reading her mind right now, because the last thing she needed was a husband who knew she'd compared him to a pharaoh. If he knew that, the male ego he'd managed to restrain so far would balloon to the size of the Goodyear blimp.

Ethan opened the DC-3's main door. He and Theo shepherded Jed up the steps into the aircraft. Jed halted a few feet inside the doorway. He spun around, pulled a box weapon from his pocket, and stared out the doorway at the desert.

The boys had a sentry. Whether they wanted one or not.

Rick pushed Asru toward the steps. "Stay here."

"I must go with you," she said.

"Forget it. We've got enough trouble without you tagging along."

Her voice hardened. "I must go."

Katy marched closer to Asru. A foot separated them.

She met Asru's gaze head-on. "Why *must* you go?"

"I…"

Asru ducked her head, cradling her forehead against her palm. When she spoke again, her voice sounded fragile and brittle as ice.

"I simply must," she said. "Please do not ask for an explanation. You would not believe it."

"Try me."

A gale sucked dust into the air. The chill of night had draped over the desert, depositing shadows and demons, demons in the shadows, shadows that were demons. Who knew what hid in the desert night. Katy rubbed her arms. Her fingers felt cold already.

Rick's shirt beeped. He pulled out the scroll device. It beeped again, the sound reminiscent of a hawk's cry with electronic undertones.

Rick turned on the flashlight, aimed it at the scroll, and squinted at the device's display. He said, "What the…"

Katy leaned over to read the screen.

> *NU:*   *Who's there?*

Under the question, the name "Chin" blinked.

"Answer," Katy said.

"Are you crazy?" Rick said. "What if it's Intef?"

"He could kill us with his razor-sharp wit."

Rick unclipped the pen-like object from the scroll. With it, he wrote a response on the screen.

> *CHIN:*   *You first.*
> *NU:*   *Friends of Asru. Are you Chin?*
> *CHIN:*   *No.*
> *NU:*   *Who are you?*
> *CHIN:*   *The guy who's about to kick your asses straight back to the pyramid age.*

"Good move," Katy said. "Tick him off before we even find out what he wants."

> *NU:*   *Rick?*
> *CHIN:*   *Who's asking?*
> *NU:*   *Your father.*

Katy looked at Rick. He scrunched his eyebrows at her. A Planner could be tricking them. To what end, she had less than an inkling. Impersonating Charlie seemed fruitless, since the Planners had located them already and sped to the neighborhood in their glowing vessel.

On the screen, a new message appeared.

> *NU:*   *Congrats on your nuptials. At least you didn't wait until Hell completely froze over before proposing.*

"It's him," Rick said.

> *CHIN:*   *We need time. Can you help?*
> *NU:*   *Is Asru with you?*
> *CHIN:*   *Yes.*
> *NU:*   *Ask her how we can take down the ship.*

Rick aimed the flashlight at Asru's face. "Dad wants to know how he can disable Intef's ship."

Asru shrugged, shaking her head. "I am not familiar with its workings."

"Remind me again why I let you tag along."

CHIN:	*She's no help.*
NU:	*We'll figure something out.*
CHIN:	*Be careful.*
NU:	*Won't do anything Katy wouldn't do.*

Rick shot a look at her.

She assumed her most innocent expression.

He sighed.

NU:	*Gotta go. Take care of yourselves.*

The screen went blank.

Katy zipped her jacket, plunged her hands into the pockets. The chill clung to her flesh.

The moon had sunk halfway below the horizon. To the west, above the mountains opposite Bakhu, the distortion rippled. A glow started around its circumference, radiating inward until the light consumed the distortion. The orb bloated into a sphere of light so large it blotted out the moon's vestiges and obscured the stars across half the sky.

"Rick," Katy said.

She nodded at the sky beyond the DC-3.

He stuffed the scroll in his pocket.

The orb drifted across the plateau. Running lights blinked around its equator. Behind the shield of light that cloaked the craft, she noticed a sheen. The orb was metallic.

The craft floated closer.

The hairs all over her body prickled. Static electricity tingled over her.

Rick said, "Run."

The orb pulsed. It loomed as large as ten moons, though brighter.

They ran. Past the hole Katy had punched in the desert floor. Toward the cliffs.

Katy tripped. Her feet flipped out from under her. She hit the sand face-first, knocking the breath out of her.

Asru stumbled over Katy's legs. She sailed forward in mid-air and belly-flopped onto the ground five feet away. Her head struck a rock. A silver pen, ejected from her breast pocket, skittered across the sand.

The craft soared over their heads about 100 feet up, right above them. Its light drew a circle in the sand around them. The circle pursued them across the plateau.

Asru lay motionless, her head raised, eyes half shut. Blood oozed from a gash on her forehead.

The craft descended. The circle expanded. 500 feet.

Warner scooped Asru up and threw her over his shoulder. Clasping her legs to his chest, he sprinted out of the lighted circle.

Rick boosted Katy off the ground. He dropped her on her feet, snaring the silver pen Asru had lost.

They raced after Warner.

The circle of light chased them.

The floor shifted. Bob staggered, caught himself. The ship had started moving.

Bob chose commands on the scroll device. Wrong. Backtracking, he picked different commands. Five times he repeated the action, until finally a useful document appeared on the screen.

A map of the ship's corridors and rooms.

"Got anything?" Charlie asked.

The map described a room on the lower level as "heart of the god's chariot."

A literal translation of the Kemetian. Sounded like an engine room to him. Another room sounded like the armory.

Bob sprinted down the corridor, around a corner, down another corridor. He rounded a bend and crossed under an archway into another corridor that dead-ended at a set of double doors. He punched keys on the control panel.

A mechanism hissed. The doors parted to reveal a small chamber. A lift.

Charlie regarded the lift with pursed lips. "Where's the elevator go?"

Bob trudged inside. "Down."

"Good enough for me."

Charlie stepped into the lift. The doors hissed shut.

The control panel featured four buttons. From what he'd gathered from the scroll device, the buttons represented the three levels of the ship plus an emergency stop switch. The scroll seemed to show them on the middle level, with the engine room and armory below them. He pressed the bottom button.

The lift transitioned into movement without a stutter. As its speed increased, Bob felt his feet rise off the floor. An illusion, he hoped. He grabbed for a handrail but the lift had none. Backing into the corner, he slapped both hands on the wall to shore up his body.

Charlie chuckled. "First time's a surprise. You start to like it once you get over the vomiting."

The mention of vomiting thrust Bob's gorge high in his throat. He choked it down. A wave of vertigo engulfed him, and he wedged his body into the corner.

Panting, he said, "Thought you didn't know where the lift went."

"The what?"

"The li—the elevator."

"I've never been in this one. The ship has several."

The lift slowed. As smoothly as the descent had begun, it ended. The doors slid apart.

Charlie took a step toward the doors.

Bob gulped in air. His flesh felt pliable, like clay packed into the corner. He pried his left leg free, followed by his right, and finally peeled his arms away from the wall. He tottered out of the lift into a corridor. The emergency lights winked off, on, off, on. Sweat chilled his skin.

"Don't die," Charlie said. "They'll mummify you."

Bob pictured Intef jamming a metal rod up his nostril, rupturing the bone, and swishing the rod about in his skull to liquefy his brains.

Mopping the sweat from his face, Bob squared his shoulders and raised his chin.

Charlie patted his shoulder. "How's about we go save the world? Our little part of it, anyhow."

"You're on."

Down the corridor they went. At an intersection identical to the one they had exited on the upper level, they hesitated. Voices echoed from around the corner. Two men conversing in Kemetian.

Charlie poked his head around the corner. He pulled back.

"Sentries," he whispered.

They must get past the sentries. The map showed one route to the armory.

The corridor in which the men conferred.

A distraction might furnish them the chance they needed. How did one distract Planners?

They were people, nothing more than men. *Think*.

Bob walked into the intersection.

The men cut off their discussion. They turned their heads to look at him. One man smirked. His companion whisked out a box weapon.

Bob raised his hands, palms out. He ambled past the corner into the adjoining corridor.

Peripherally, he saw Charlie shake his head.

The smirking sentry produced his box weapon. The duo advanced on Bob. The corner, and Bob's body, impeded their view of the intersecting corridor—and Charlie.

"You are Doctor Hanover," the smirker said. "Lord Intef commanded you to stay in the observation room."

Bob swabbed his brow with the back of his hand. Luckily, the cold sweat from the ride on the lift had yet to evaporate. He wiped his hand on his pants.

"Where's the infirmary?" Bob gasped. "I—I'm not feeling well. Must be the excitement, what with the lights flashing and the ship speeding away."

The men each had a device strapped onto their biceps. The contraptions resembled scaled-down versions of the MP3 players youngsters wore, due to the necessity of listening to music every conscious moment of their lives.

The smirker touched the device on his arm. He chattered in Kemetian.

Intef something something Hanover...prisoner...something him.

"My lord requests your presence," said the smirker, "in the control room."

"Today doesn't work for me," Bob said. "Perhaps I could pencil him in next week."

"I will render you unconscious if I must, and drag you by your nose."

"My nose?"

The smirker…smirked. His companion scowled. Both targeted their box weapons on him.

Bob rubbed his chest. He coughed. Hugging his left arm, he bent forward.

The sentries stared at him. Faces blank. Weapons aimed.

Bob bellowed. He doubled over, buckled his knees. As the sentries rushed toward him, he collapsed onto the floor. He let his mouth drop open. Eyes closed to a slit, he went limp.

The smirker holstered his weapon. He stooped over Bob.

The other sentry crouched beside his chum. They babbled to each other in Kemetian.

They worried about Intef. His anger. Bob suspected his death by natural causes would rob Intef of the chance to kill him. The sentries must worry they'd suffer their god's wrath for allowing their prisoner to expire without Intef's permission.

The smirker jerked. His eyes widened. He reached for his box weapon, but a boot whacked him in the jaw. He lurched backward. In his place stood Charlie.

The other sentry swung his box weapon toward Charlie.

Bob bit the man's hand. The sentry howled. He dropped the weapon. Charlie kicked him in the throat, square in the Adam's apple.

Gurgling, the man flailed for his weapon. Bob snatched it up. The sentry floundered onto his feet. Charlie kneed the man in the groin. The sentry passed out.

An alarm honked.

"Damn," Charlie said. "They must have cameras."

"Why didn't they sound the alarm when we jumped the first chap? The one we robbed of his scroll device?"

"Who the hell cares."

"Quite right." Hopping up, Bob said, "Armory's this way."

He loped down the corridor to a door marked with a red hand. The Kemetian hieratic under the hand included a word that, while spelled differently, resembled the ancient Egyptian word for spear. The door refused to open for him. Bob hit the biggest button on the control panel. The door whooshed open.

The door shut behind them.

The room housed racks of weapons. Rows of the little boxes that shot fire covered the right wall from floor to ceiling. The left wall accommodated weapons that looked like oversized handguns, save for the gritty texture of the metal and the shape of the weapons, gnarled like the twisty straws children loved. On the back wall, a clear-fronted cabinet protected one weapon larger than the others, the size of a bazooka—from what he'd seen of similar weapons in Rambo films. It was no bazooka, however. Its silver patina glistened in the half light. Its barrel was rocket-shaped, while its grip was long and sculpted to fit a hand. No, not *a* hand. Two hands.

Bob looked at the box weapon in his hand. "I haven't a clue how to use this."

He flipped the box over. Colored dots distinguished the two buttons set flush with the body of the weapon. One sported a red dot, the other blue.

"Push the blue button," Charlie said.

"You know how to fire it?"

"No, but red buttons usually do bad things—like overload reactors or make your computer go loopy. I'd pick blue."

"Brilliant logic."

Bob closed his fingers around the weapon. Its metal chilled his skin. Gradually, though, the warmth of his skin overcame the metal's chill. Would he succumb to bloodlust as easily as the metal had succumbed to his body heat? He had already reveled in the satisfaction of clobbering three men.

He must stop Intef and his minions. Whatever that entailed.

"If you feel like pushing the red button," Charlie said, "warn me so I can run."

Pocketing the box weapon, Bob trotted to the rear wall. Inside the glass—or whatever Martian material composed the divider—the bazooka-like weapon sat upright, angled away from him, seated in a holder molded to fit its shape. The clear-fronted case had no control panel, no buttons or levers, nothing that suggested how to open it. Bob waved his hand in front of the case. Perhaps a voice command—

The panel clicked and popped open.

Bob grabbed the weapon. It had a trigger, similar to a rifle's. He threw the weapon to Charlie.

Charlie caught it. He held the weapon in both hands, testing its weight.

"Think you can shoot it?" Bob asked.

"How hard can it be?"

Bob retrieved the box weapon from his pocket. "On to the engine room. Quickly."

Charlie brandished his weapon crosswise over his chest. "Old farts to the rescue."

Old farts? For the first time in years he felt invigorated, useful, *young.*

The door swished open for them, and they ran out into the corridor. The alarm honked, the lights flashed. Bob veered right, recalling the map in his mind. The corridor dead-ended at a doorway.

He skidded to a stop. The door was marked with the Eye of Horus and a heart symbol.

Bob tapped the control panel. The mechanism bleated. The door stayed shut.

Charlie glanced at the weapon in his hands. "Stand back, pard'ner. We're going in the old-fashioned way."

"By knocking?"

"You could call it that."

Charlie slipped two fingers around the weapon's trigger. Holding the contraption in both hands, he hefted it onto his shoulder.

Bob shuffled backward. When he hit the wall, he tucked the box weapon in his pocket and slapped his hands over his ears.

Charlie backed away from the door. He pulled the trigger.

The air between Charlie and the door rippled. The door exploded inward. The concussion threw Charlie backward into the wall. His head smacked into it first, followed by his back and shoulders. The bazooka weapon popped out of his hands, clattering onto the floor.

Inside the engine room, men shouted.

The weapon had spewed no fire to match the lightning the box weapons expelled.

Springing onto his feet, Charlie nabbed the weapon from the floor. "Nice."

"Hardly the word I would've chosen."

From inside the engine room, lightning burst. Bob ducked.

The shot struck the wall. The stench of burned plastic permeated the corridor as the wall smoked.

Charlie fired his weapon. The men inside the engine room flew backward into the wall. Chairs crashed into their bodies, pinning them to the wall for a second, until they slid down onto the floor. The chairs clanged down around them.

The alarm. The lights. The smoking wall.

Bob and Charlie ran through the doorway into the engine room. As Charlie cleared the doorway, a man leaped out from behind a partition, reeled toward Charlie, and swung his box weapon up at Charlie's head. Bob leveled his box at the man's shoulder. He punched the blue button.

The man grunted and fell.

Fire erupted to the left.

Bob whirled toward the flash. Charlie leaped off the floor. Near where he had lain, the wall was scorched. The shooter, using a chair as a shield, took aim at Charlie.

Bob shot him in the shoulder. The man screamed, jerked, crumpled onto his knees. Bob fired again. The man wilted.

"Thanks," Charlie said.

"You're welcome."

Charlie spun on his heels to face the left wall. "Back to business."

The left wall consisted of shiny panels, smoky like tinted glass. Behind the din of the alarm, Bob detected a humming that emanated from behind the panels.

Charlie buttressed his weapon against his shoulder, spread his feet apart, and planted his soles flat on the floor.

Bob covered his ears.

The panels shattered. Fire exploded behind it. Secondary explosions rumbled and boomed deep inside the vessel, beyond the wall. The vessel trembled.

In the corridor, distant yet drawing nearer, footfalls pounded.

Charlie snuggled up to the wall left of the door. Bob cuddled with the right wall. Weapons raised, they listened.

"Lock the door," Charlie said.

"How?"

"You know their language."

"Barely."

Bob studied the control panel. It had four buttons, identical in size and shape, each stamped with a Kemetian glyph. He chose one. As his finger grazed the button, he yanked his hand away.

"Guess," Charlie said.

The footfalls of an army thudded down the corridor. Louder. Nearer.

"I can't be sure of their meanings," Bob said. "If I choose the wrong one—"

"Jesus, take a guess."

The footfalls stopped right outside the door.

Bob slammed his hand down on a button. An apparatus inside the door chunked.

The control panel bleeped. Outside, someone banged on the keypad. The control panel reproached them with another bleep.

Explosions boomed in the vessel's bowels, behind the engine room. The vessel rocked. Bob stumbled sideways, dropped the box weapon.

The floor fell away from his feet. He plunged after it, hitting bottom on his buttocks.

Charlie, prone on the floor, pushed onto his elbows. "Uh oh."

The bazooka weapon lay on the floor near Bob. He grabbed for it.

"Forget it," Charlie said. "We've got bigger problems."

Charlie hurried toward two chairs which sat along a table that protruded from the wall. Computer monitors blinked atop the table. The chairs were bolted into the floor.

In the corridor, voices shouted. Fists beat on the door.

Whump. A body rammed the door.

The floor listed. The walls and floor quivered.

Flopping into one of the chairs, Charlie located a strap tucked into a slot in the back of the chair. He secured the strap across his lap. One end of the strap had a locking clamp, which he clipped onto a hook mounted under the seat.

Bam! The men outside rammed the door again.

"Better strap in," Charlie said.

Bob jumped into the chair next to Charlie's. He found the strap and fastened it.

The trembling in the walls and floor escalated. Bob's teeth chattered. His eyeballs jiggled. His bones vibrated.

"Why must we strap in?" Bob asked.

Boom. The vessel pitched sideways.

"This ship's a sphere," Charlie said. "It's gonna roll."

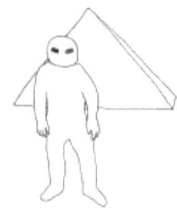

Chapter Ten

Thunder grumbled overhead.

Fleeing across the desert with the craft's light whizzing after her, Katy glanced back. The craft had slowed. Its lighting had failed, except for the ring of white bulbs around its equator. The lights sputtered. One bulb blew out, then another.

The craft teetered.

Rick grabbed her wrist and pulled her faster.

She squinted at the darkness before them. The desert lurked around them in the guise of shadows. The light from the craft faded until the night swallowed it.

An explosion detonated behind them. Fire flared above and to the rear. Rick threw Katy onto the ground, hurling himself on top of her. Ahead of them, Warner grunted.

A boom cracked the air. The earth shivered as sand drizzled down on their backs.

Rick scrambled onto his knees. Katy pushed into a sitting position. They both looked to the area from which the boom had issued.

Eight hundred feet away, flames shed living shadows on the metallic sphere that rocked at the end of a long scar it had gouged in the sand. In the firelight, smoke spiraled toward the heavens.

"You okay?" Rick asked.

"Better than Intef, I'm sure," she said.

"Let's hope he broke his neck."

Rick switched on the flashlight. The backwash of the beam lit his face.

A streak darkened his cheek. Katy touched it. The blood slicked her fingers.

Her heart skipped. "You're hurt."

"A scratch," he said. "I'll live."

A few yards away, Warner knelt beside Asru. Despite her head injury, she'd propped herself up on her elbows. She blinked slowly, as if washing grit from her eyes.

A hint of a slur thickened her voice. "*Maat* is on our side."

"Excuse me?" Katy said.

"*Maat* has provided us an opportunity. We may yet prevail."

"Right. Universal harmony wrecked Intef's ship."

Asru struggled onto her knees. With Warner's help, she stood.

"The modern conception of *maat* is flawed," she said, her voice stronger, clearer. "You fail to grasp the extent of the force we call *maat*. It runs through every living thing. It inhabits the landscape. It drives the universe and creates life. *Maat* is everything."

Rick snorted. "She's seen *Star Wars* too many times."

"I couldn't care less," Katy said, "whether Intef's ship crashed because of *maat* or because scarabs crapped in the warp drive."

"Maybe it was Dad and Bob," Rick said.

Katy nailed her gaze on Asru. "Who *are* you?"

Asru smiled that all-knowing, damn-annoying smile. "My birth name was Aset."

"Isis."

Rick rolled his eyes. "What, now she's a goddess?"

"No, honey," Katy said, "she's human. The ancient Egyptians elevated her to a goddess."

Rick let out a sigh heavy enough to blow Intef's ship clear across the plateau. "I miss the hairy hominids. Figuring out what they are was easy compared to this."

Katy asked, "So, Aset, how old are you anyway?"

"I was born in the year you call ten thousand one hundred and forty-five B-C."

10,145 BC. That made her…

"More than twelve thousand years old," Rick said. "Gee, you don't look a day over ten thousand."

Katy said nothing. Though she felt Rick watching her, she avoided looking at him. His frown, his narrowed eyes, his crinkled forehead would insinuate doubt into her mind. She had a feeling she needed to believe in Asru—in what the woman claimed to be—if she wanted to stay alive. If she listened to his rationalizations, she'd start to doubt.

Start to doubt? When had she slid into believing?

Slid she had. The intuition she had about trusting Asru served as the stimulus for the need to believe. Slowly, inexorably, like sap dribbling down a tree, she had sunk into belief. When it happened, why and how, she couldn't recall. She ought not believe.

Yet she did.

She looked at Rick. He frowned, narrowed his eyes, crinkled his forehead.

Don't believe her. She heard him speak, though he'd sealed his lips.

Katy averted her attention to Asru. "Why do you want the Book?"

"To prevent Intef from acquiring it."

"You're not telling us everything."

Asru's expression darkened. She scrutinized the hem of her vest. "The tomb of Wesir is my true goal. I must find it before…"

"What?"

"Before it is too late."

Katy folded her arms over her chest, tilted her head to the side. "You said Wesir. The ancient name for Osiris."

Asru jerked her head up, eyes wide.

Katy said, "You Planners use the old names, huh?"

Asru slumped her shoulders. She closed her eyes for a second. "We do."

Rick placed a hand on Katy's back. He nudged her with his index finger. She prodded his foot with her toe. She'd believe Asru if she felt like it, regardless of his skepticism.

"Before we do anything," Rick said, "we better check out the ship. See how badly hurt Intef and his buddies are."

Katy glanced back at the wreckage. Smoke. Flames. Bodies? If Intef had died, she might celebrate. But the others? Certainly, his cohorts deserved no sympathy and they had caused their own suffering. Yet she lacked the hardness to wish them all dead or relish in their anguish. They had obeyed Intef's orders—abducting both Charlie and Bob, killing innocent people, destroying whole civilizations to cover up their own existence. She should hate them.

As she watched the flames whither around the craft, the finger of empathy plucked at her heart. Fire. Pain. Men and women dying.

Murderers.

"Leave them," she said. The frost in her voice made her wince, and she added, "They're in no condition to chase us."

"We have to know for sure."

"Why?"

He hesitated. "Dad's in that ship."

Oh God. She'd forgotten about Charlie.

Rick grabbed the .45 from its holster, ejecting the clip to inspect his ammo. "Warner, you're with me. Katy and Asru stay put."

Asru shook her head frantically. Her hair lashed her face. "No, please, we have no time. The tomb—"

With heel of his hand, Rick shoved the clip back into place. "Look, lady, you're not in charge."

"We must—"

Rick pulled the silver pen out of his pocket. He bolted his blue eyes, intense as propane flames, onto Asru's face. "I think this belongs to you."

Asru moved her lips, worked her jaw, but her vocal chords failed to generate sound. She reached for the pen. He clamped his hand around the object. She retracted her hand.

"What is it?" Rick asked. "I'm pretty sure it's not a pen."

"The canister discharges an undetectable gas which renders the victim unconscious."

He twirled the gas canister between his fingers. "You used it on Katy."

"Yes," Asru said. "I—I am sorry."

Rick plunked the canister back in his pocket. "Think I'll keep this. In case you get any ideas."

Rick stashed the .45 in its holster. His backpack he unhooked, letting it drop off his shoulders onto the ground.

Warner checked the clip on his Glock. Satisfied, he snapped the clip back into place and dug his tan knit cap out of his backpack. He pulled it down over his bare head.

"I will not stay put," Katy said.

"We check out the ship, you babysit Her Incarnation. That's the plan."

"Screw the plan," Katy said. "I'm going with you."

"Stay here." Rick grasped her upper arms and bored his gaze into hers. "Please."

Mute and still, she refused to look away. He maintained his hold.

Warner, arms straight at his sides, opened and closed his hands as if wringing water from a rag.

Head down, Asru excavated the sand with the toe of her boot.

"Well?" Rick said.

Katy slumped her shoulders. "Fine, I'll stay. Though I'd like to point out how not safe I am sitting in the desert in the dark."

Rick unzipped Katy's fanny pack, removing the Taurus, and zipped it shut again. He took her right hand, placed the Taurus' grip in her palm, the barrel aimed toward the ground, and curled her fingers around the grip.

"You know what to do." He kissed her forehead. "We won't be long."

Sliding his watch off his wrist, he handed it to her. The watch was gold, with hieroglyphs engraved on the underside. It would create shine, reflected light that could give away his position—which he knew.

He turned away from her.

She grabbed his shirt. "If you're not back in ten minutes, I'm coming after you."

"Make it twenty."

He strode away from her.

"Ten," she said.

In two steps he closed the distance between them. Taking her face in his hands, he bend his head down until their noses touched. His thumbs stroked her cheeks.

He pressed his lips to hers, holding the kiss for a long moment.

When he pulled away, he said, "Twenty minutes."

"Okay."

Warner bent down into a half squat and waddled into the darkness. Rick hustled after him in the same posture. They scuttled toward the fireball that doubled as the corpse of Intef's ship. Soon even their silhouettes merged with the night.

Intef's ship had run aground 800 feet northwest of the cliffs, at an diagonal to the path they'd carved out as they fled from the vessel. In the daylight, she'd noted a hillock sloped down from the cliffs in that vicinity. Intef's ship must've hit on the incline and scored the long gouge when it rolled downhill.

Katy clasped Rick's watch in her left hand, the Taurus in her right.

Across the plateau, the bonfire flicked its blistering tongues at the stars.

Crackle. Whoosh.

His head lolled to the left, the same direction his body listed. The seatbelt dug into his abdomen. The restraint battled against gravity to bind him in the chair, which had rotated leftward enough to triple the pressure against his gut. One arm dangled in the air while the other draped across his stomach. His head throbbed. Fluid dribbled into the corner of his mouth.

Bob licked at it. Blood.

He lifted his left arm to explore his forehead, temples, and scalp with his fingers. On the right side of his head, several inches above the ear, he found a cut. Neither deep nor serious, the wound still bled like a burst tick. He shifted his right arm. Pain lanced through his shoulder.

A voice moaned to his left. No, below him. The left *was* below him. He stretched his arm down toward the sound. Hair bristled against his fingertips. A chin bone. Charlie's beard.

Bob croaked, "You all right?"

Aside from the flames that sizzled beyond the wall they'd destroyed, the room was dark. Smoke clogged the room. No wonder his voice had gone hoarse. Suddenly he recognized the tang of smoke in his mouth, the stink of it percolating through his nose into his lungs. The smoke stung his eyes, eliciting tears. He coughed.

Charlie's cough answered his.

"I'm alive," Charlie said, "if that's what you mean by all right."

"Can you get out of your chair?"

"Think so. Let me try."

Charlie's jeans scritched against the chair's upholstery. Click. Thump.

"Ouch!" Charlie grunted. "How'd that damn table get on the floor?"

"The ship landed sideways."

"I know, that was a joke."

"Not terribly amusing under the circumstances."

The huffing of Charlie's breaths and the thumping of his hands and feet painted a portrait of the man climbing up the floor, which had become the wall, to Bob's chair, which had turned into a chandelier. Charlie pushed the chair until it swiveled left. Bob sagged forward, wrenching his shoulder. He bit back a cry.

"Brace your feet against the other chair," Charlie said. "And hang on."

Bob propped his soles on the back of the other chair. He gripped the seat of his.

Charlie fumbled with the seatbelt latch. It clicked open. The belt released.

Bob slumped down, kneeling on the other chair. Charlie grasped his arm. As they inched away from the chairs, Bob slid his feet off the seat onto the wall. He was wrong. They hadn't landed sideways, not entirely. The ship rested off-kilter, not precisely sideways yet nowhere near right-side-up. The angle permitted them to lean against the wall and crawl up it like spiders, edging toward the doorway above.

Once they'd pried the door open, they climbed into the corridor where the emergency lights flickered and pulsed, no longer in unison. They traveled at a tilt in a strange gait in between a spider and a human being. They hiked sideways up the corridor, walking their hands along the wall as they shuffled their feet along the floor. Of course the floor was actually the wall and vice versa, but Bob struggled to keep those thoughts from his mind. He would go insane trying to sort out the details.

Tendrils of smoke wafted down the corridor from a section where fire crackled, invisible behind the smokey curtain.

No voices. No moans, no cries for help, no shouts. Had anyone else survived?

Deep within him the thought transmuted into a wish. *Please let them all have died.*

Bob bit down on his lip. The pain drowned out the thought.

The smoke thickened. He might've convinced himself it was London fog, that he'd been transported home via some gadget from *Star Trek* whose name Charlie would know. When the smoke tickled his nose, burned his throat, and congealed into slime in his lungs, his hacking erased the fantasy.

The air grew sweltering. Sweat trickled down Bob's face. When they neared a doorway, the heat smothered him. As he climbed through the threshold, the heat seeped through his shoes to blister his feet.

He bit into his lip. Blood trickled into his mouth.

Onward they traveled.

The smoke thinned. Light glowed ahead, at first the size of a flashlight beam. The glow enlarged and brightened as they drew closer. The wan light sputtered through a hatch in the ceiling, which currently served as a window in the wall.

Charlie halted a few feet from the hatch. It was oval, wide enough for one man to pass through it. The light outside quavered like firelight.

Grasping the hatch's lip, Charlie hauled his body halfway through the opening. After a pause he swung his legs through and slid away from the hatch. He thrust his hand back through the opening to Bob.

He clutched Charlie's hand. With his free hand he seized the hatch's lip. When Charlie pulled up, he pushed his feet off the floor. Soaring through the hatch, he flopped onto his buttocks on the lip and swung his legs out of the hole.

They perched on the skin of the vessel. Its hull sloped away from them on all sides. Four sets of footholds, with matching handholds, led away from the hatch in opposite directions, like spokes on a wheel. The Planners must've recognized the possibility their spheres might crash-land on their sides or tops, so they included provisions for such a scenario. They'd created ladders.

The light stemmed from a fire 100 feet away. Its flames lashed up from an inferno that seethed deep inside the ship.

Bob scanned the desert. No lights. No landmarks, aside from the mountains. The moon had forsaken its post shortly after the sun absconded, relinquishing the plateau to the night. Though a battalion of stars glittered, their iridescence lacked the strength to banish the murk.

The firelight flickered across the sand around the craft. No one lurked on the ground.

A feeling shivered through him, one he had not felt in quite a long time. For a moment he mistook it for a chill induced by the night air which, even in the desert, became nippy. Yet the feeling was no chill. The shiver resulted from hope.

Charlie scrambled onto the ladder that led downward. The ship's tilt meant the ladder curved down at a 45-degree angle to the hatch.

Bob hurried after him.

Minutes later they touched down on the desert floor. The shiver quaked through him again, stronger this time. Free. They were *free*.

Charlie trotted away from the ship. Bob hustled after him.

A hand locked down on Bob's shoulder. The owner of the hand jerked him to a stop. A voice snarled behind him.

"No, Doctor," Intef said, "you are not free of me yet."

In the shadows up ahead, Charlie cursed.

Intef clinched Bob's wrists, twisted them behind his back. He wrenched Bob backward into him. Intef's lips skimmed Bob's ear, his breath puffing humid warmth into it.

"Did you think you could kill me so easily?" Intef growled. He closed a hand around Bob's throat with a hint of the pressure he could exert. "Gods do not die at the hands of mortals, Doctor."

He constricted his hand. Bob gasped.

"Gods live," Intef said. "Forever."

Night. Like an overcoat she wore it, and like an overcoat it draped heavily over her shoulders.

Seated cross-legged, Katy laid the Taurus on her lap. She rested her hand on the grip to feel the comfort of the metal, the smoothness of the barrel, the texture of the grip, in hopes the sensation would unravel the knots in her gut. Of course it didn't.

The air had assumed a chill. While a fire could allay the chill and the anxiety, somewhat, they lit no fire. If they started a fire, might as well shoot off flares too.

The wind had subsided. The hissing nearby stemmed from Aset's breathing. The hissing closer to her betrayed her own breaths, dampened by the thumping of her heart and the gushing of blood through her veins. She gripped Rick's watch tighter. The band dug into her flesh. She crammed the watch in her pocket. No fire, no shine.

"May we speak?" Aset asked.

Her voice, disembodied by the darkness, seemed to drift up from the Domain of Osiris, through the nine gates of the underworld, to exit the *duat* at this very point on the Earth. The voice of death. The voice of resurrection and eternal life.

The voice of *maat*.

Aset's tone escalated a fraction of a pitch. "Are you there?"

"Calm down." Katy lodged her left hand on the ground to prop herself against it. "If you want to talk, I've got a few questions you can answer. Otherwise, shut up."

"Ask them."

"Why are you looking for the tomb of Osiris?"

"To reclaim my life."

Katy strained to see Aset. The night, however, refused to draw back its cloak.

"What does that mean?" Katy asked.

"Wesir is my husband. Nebthut was my sister. I learned of her death upon my awakening. Wesir is all I have left, I must find him."

Aset, Wesir, Setesh, Nebthut, Djehuty.

Isis, Osiris, Seth, Nephthys, Thoth. Freeze-dried Planners, as Rick had phrased it, all sentenced to lose their lives without an execution, without pain, without dying. How did Intef fit into the picture? Aset had despised him enough to stage a coup—a failed coup, yes, but at least she'd tried.

"When were you awakened?" Katy asked.

"One year ago."

"Who woke you up?"

"Jed and the other Sons of Horus. They believed I could help them defeat Intef."

Around the time Intef had tried to kill her and Rick, and had succeeded in kidnapping Charlie, the Sons of Horus awakened Aset. Why would they choose her to defeat Intef?

He who protected Thoth's wisdom lies in this tomb far from his birthplace where the Condemned One may never find him.

The statement came from the Washington stela, which stood in Imsety's tomb. The Meidum stela declared the "wrath of the Condemned One" had spilled the "blood of Bakhu." Damn, if only Rick hadn't taken off to explore the wreckage of Intef's ship. He would remember who the Condemned One was.

She knew his identity too. In a mental cubbyhole she'd stored the information. Over the past year, her interest in ancient history had zeroed in on ancient Egypt. She'd convinced herself the change had sprung from their encounter with Intef and his goons, yet deep down she knew another source had stimulated her curiosity, magnifying it into a near obsession. She'd learned the language swifter than a Concorde flew from New York to London.

Forget it. She needed to concentrate on Aset and Intef. Their relationship.

"Who is Intef?" Katy asked.

"Chaos," Aset said.

He is chaos.

Aset had used the phrase when she recounted the story of Nebthut's reawakening after the fall of the Old Kingdom. The Condemned One. Nebthut had been married to Setesh, a red-haired man who had inspired the god of chaos in Egyptian mythology. The red-haired man had destroyed the Temple of Thoth at Bakhu. Setesh had suffered the *mut ankh*.

"Intef is Setesh," Katy said.

"Yes." Aset made a noise that almost turned into laughter. "I knew you would deduce his identity. You are quite clever."

The woman sounded...proud.

Aset laid a hand on Katy's knee. Her hand felt cold, even through Katy's jeans.

Her voice low and forceful, Aset said, "We must find Wesir's tomb. Time flows away from us faster each moment."

"Life is a cycle," Katy said, repeating an axiom from ancient Egypt. "What's the rush?"

"The cycle is long. If we wait for the time to arrive again, it will be too late to stop Setesh. We must find Osiris without delay."

Katy shoved Aset's hand from her knee. "I don't sneak around desecrating tombs behind my husband's back. When he gets here, we'll look for the tomb."

Aset's breathing wavered. She sniffled.

Crying? Katy frowned at the area where she thought Aset sat. How could she trust a woman who refused to tell the truth the whole truth? Aset sprinkled fragments of truth throughout her speech, yet she withheld the balance. No trust without truth, that was Katy's motto—since about five seconds ago.

Aset blew her nose.

The sympathy ploy would not work. Until Rick came back, she'd make no decisions based on Aset's counsel. The woman had brainwashed her. Probably. Or else the thread that tethered her mind to the earth had snapped. She floated into the stratosphere, a helium balloon caught in the jet stream.

Where the hell was Rick?

Katy consulted her watch, a digital model that neither ticked nor emitted shine. She punched the button that lit up the watch's face. Rick and Warner had departed nine minutes ago.

Katy glanced at the wreckage of Intef's craft. The flames had died down to a burning more akin to candlelight than a bonfire. The smoke coiling into the sky had thinned. Rick and Warner must've reached the crash site by now. What if Intef had survived?

She had taught Rick about tracking, as much as she knew, and Warner knew more than either of them. They would stay hidden. They would make it back.

They had to.

"I apologize," Aset murmured. "I should not ask you to be disloyal. Please forgive me."

"I might, if you start explaining."

Katy counted ten heartbeats before Aset spoke. When she did, her voice had grown weary and thin.

"What do you wish to know?" she asked.

"What happened between you and Intef—I mean Setesh?"

"It is—what do you say?—a long story."

"Seems like we've got time."

"As you wish." Aset inhaled deeply, releasing the breath ounce by ounce. "Setesh had coveted me since before my marriage to Wesir. He wed my sister because he believed I would grow jealous and abandon Wesir for him. When this did not happen, resentment took root in his soul. When our son was born, Setesh's anger increased tenfold. It boiled inside him like water inside a covered pot."

"If you knew, why didn't you banish him or something?"

"I failed to recognize the depth of his hatred. Setesh is my husband's brother. We prefer to see the goodness in our kinsmen."

"We meaning your people."

"No, humanity."

Aset sniffed. Katy saw the silhouette of her arm move toward her face. Seconds later, her arm fell to her side once more.

"Years passed," Aset said, "until, finally, the lid burst from the pot."

Waset, capital of Kemet
Day 32 of harvest, year 31 of Wesir
10,106 BC

She woke with a start. Fists banged on the door to the library. Her heart thundered inside her chest, synchronized with the cadence of the fists. The door rattled at each concussion as if her heartbeat transmitted through the air to clatter the wood.

Aset reclined on her side atop the bench, her left elbow mashed into the cushion beneath her. The papyrus scrolls she had spread out on the floor around the bench jostled in a breeze that wafted through the window. She laid a hand on her chest. Her heart thudded against it.

At the window, the curtains unfurled in the breeze. Outside, sandals clapped on the stone walkway that led into the palace. Voices mumbled.

A scroll reeled into the bench's leg. It tapped against the lion's paw that formed the bench's foot. The breeze fluttered the lamps, installed in gold sconces, that lit the room.

A man shouted at her to open the door.

Aset leaped off the bench. Her robes whirling around her, she rushed for the door. She fumbled with the latch. Her fingers trembled. She grasped the latch at last and unhooked it.

The guard burst through the door before she could open it. The man's face glistened red in the half light. Sweat drenched his clothing. He spoke between gasps.

"Your Incarnation," he said, "you must come. The king, he—he—"

"Take me to him."

The guard sprinted down the corridor. She chased after him. Her bare feet slapped on the alabaster floor, while all else within the palace remained quiet. The footfalls and voices from outside had silenced. The guard veered left down the corridor to the pharaoh's bed chamber. Four guards congregated in the corridor. Faces ashen, they whispered to the vizier Geb.

The guards blocked her entrance to the chamber.

She tried to push past them. A guard clinched her arm. His fingers stabbed into her flesh. She shook her arm yet he held firm.

"Release me," she demanded.

Geb clasped her free arm. "Daughter, please. Do not enter the chamber."

She looked at the guard's hand, which encircled her right forearm. Red smeared his fingers.

Her vision blurred.

"I must see him, Father," she said.

Geb shut his eyes. He released her. The guard, freeing her arm, stepped aside. Blood streaked her arm where his hand had gripped her.

She bolted into the chamber. At the bedside, she froze. A sob caught in her throat.

Wesir lay sprawled on the bed, arms stretched to the sides as if embracing the afterlife, eyes wide. Dark bruises ringed his neck. Blood poured out around a knife that protruded from his chest.

Her knife. She stored it in a drawer within the table beside the bed.

On the bedside table, a false wick burned within a reproduction of a bowl-shaped oil lamp. The lamp shed serpents of light onto his skin, emulating a true flame. Reflections of the glow shimmered in his eyes. She knelt on the bed beside him.

The blood soaked the sheets, which covered him to his waist. Stripping the sheet away, she took hold of the knife's hilt. The blade shifted within his flesh.

Her stomach heaved. She choked back the gorge. Her hand firm around the hilt, she drew out the knife. Blood dripped from its tip onto her thigh.

She cast the knife onto the table. Blood splattered across the wood surface, over the lamp, and onto the wall.

Her jaw quivered. She pressed her finger into the flesh of his neck, three fingers' widths below the jaw. For ten beats of her own heart she waited for his to throb against her finger. No hint of life. She pressed her finger deeper into his neck. His blood no longer pulsed through his body.

A hand lighted on her shoulder.

She jumped. Her father gazed down at her. The corners of his lips curved down into furrows that cleaved his chin.

"You have your son," he said. "Wesir lives on in Heru."

He squeezed her shoulder.

Wesir's eyes gaped at nothingness, his expression trapped in the moment of death.

No. His *ka* had not left his body. She sensed him in the room, watching.

Waiting for her to act.

She had heard tales of the great medicines Amen-Ra had possessed. He could heal the sickest man, the story professed, and he could even heal the dead, providing only a brief time had elapsed since their hearts had ceased beating. She should place no faith in rumors. She needed truth.

Perhaps...

"Fetch my cousin Djehuty," she said.

"You require the services of Anpu, not Djehuty."

Leaping off the bed, she whirled on her father. Her face flushed hot as fire. Her body stiffened.

"Wesir needs no embalmer," she said. "Bring me Djehuty."

Her father wrung his hand around his scarab amulet, suspended on a necklace. "Why do you wish to see Djehuty?"

"He knows the old ways. If Wesir can be saved, Djehuty will know."

"I cannot allow this, Aset. Resurrecting the dead is forbidden."

Her lips quivered. She clenched a handful of the linen sheet. Her knuckles paled.

"My *ka* is bound to his," she said. "If he dies, I die."

Her father pulled her into his embrace, stroking her hair. She stood stiff, erect. He pulled her head down to rest on her chest.

"You shall live," Geb whispered into her ear. "Wesir would wish it."

She resisted the impulse to shove her father away, grasp Wesir's arms, and drag his body out of the palace to the temple where Djehuty conducted rituals.

Body? He had not died. She could not let him. From the side of her eye, she glimpsed Wesir's face.

She tightened her fist around the sheet. Her fingers ached. Tears welled in her eyes. She blinked them away.

Leveling her shoulders, elevating her chin, she backed away from her father.

Outside, the guards awaited instruction. They pledged their lives to protect the pharaoh yet, if she called upon them to transport him to the temple, would they side with her father? Would they shun her, forsaking their king?

She knew the answer. Geb would instruct the sentries to thwart her if she attempted to leave the bed chamber. He would warn them she planned to resurrect the dead. Superstition reigned among her people, a relic of the time eons ago when Amen-Ra had granted them his power. The sentries would fear what she intended and, as an extension, fear her as well.

The time for restoring Wesir had yet to pass. With each rap of her heart, though, she felt the moment receding from her.

A tear trickled down her cheek. Her father wiped his thumb against her face, rubbing out the tear.

She clasped Wesir's hand. His skin felt cold.

"I will stay," she said, "until the servants of Anpu come for him."

"I shall give orders that no one must disturb you."

Geb exited the chamber. The guards shut the door behind him. Through the door, she heard her father muttering orders to the men.

Footfalls retreated.

The breeze flapped the curtains that screened the balcony.

She bounded off the bed and trotted to the doorway. Her ear she placed against the door. A guard coughed.

Her father had promised to leave her in peace. He had said nothing of leaving her unguarded.

She huddled at the door for a moment. Listening.

Unlatching the door, she swung it open and strode into the corridor.

The two guards glanced at her. Their eyes widened, though they kept silent.

"Fetch me a bench," she said. "That I may sit near the pharaoh to mourn him."

The guards nodded. They hurried down the corridor.

When the slapping of their sandals faded, she rushed back into the chamber. At the bed, she hesitated. The knife lay on the table, its blade caked with blood.

She grabbed Wesir's arms and pulled. Pangs shot across her shoulders. She pulled harder. He slid across the bed toward her.

Gasping, she released his arm.

"You require assistance."

Aset jerked her head to look at the doorway. A figure blocked the opening.

Setesh moved away from the door. From behind him, Djehuty hurried out of the corridor into the chamber.

"We have come to aid you," Setesh said.

She backed away a step.

Djehuty approached her. "Please, Aset, we wish to help you. Word has spread throughout the palace and the village. They say the pharaoh was assaulted. I see the rumor is true."

She glanced at Setesh. A coldness infiltrated her.

"And you?" she asked Setesh.

"If my brother can be revived," he said, "then I must try to save him."

The lamplight glistened on Setesh's hair. His head seemed to glow within a halo of carnelian-red fire.

She searched Djehuty's face. "Is there hope?"

"Yes, but we must take him to the temple without delay."

Setesh took Wesir's arms as Djehuty grasped his ankles. Together the men hoisted him off the bed, lugging him toward the doorway.

Aset ran out of the chamber before them. Setesh and Djehuty carried Wesir behind her.

She escorted them down the walkway, across the courtyard, through the pylons that flanked the gateway to the palace complex. The villagers slept in their houses, while those in the palace had retired to their chambers. The moon had set, drenching the night in a darkness deep as a well. She tore across the village toward the temple, barefooted, her robes swishing around her, hair whipping her face. Behind her, Djehuty and Setesh grunted under their load.

The torches burning at the gates of the great temple guided her toward the sanctuary. The walls of the sacred complex glowed white in the darkness, a phantasm of hope. Despite the stones that cut her feet, she hastened her pace. They flew past the pylons, across the courtyard, through smaller pylons into the great hall. The columns soared high above her head, their capitals shrouded by shadows. Setesh and Djehuty panted behind her.

She glanced back. They lagged several paces behind her. Their footsteps clacked on the limestone floor, reverberating through the temple.

Ahead, a pair of wooden doors secured the inner sanctuary.

Aset halted at the doors. The men set Wesir on the floor.

Two priests wandered out of the darkness between the columns.

The high priest Imnefer regarded her without emotion. In a hushed voice, he said, "Your Incarnation, how may we serve you?"

"I must take the pharaoh into the sanctuary."

"Only you may enter with him."

"You see no one else. I came alone."

He bowed his head. "As you wish."

Imnefer glanced at Wesir.

He directed his cinnamon eyes at her. "The pharaoh's *ka* has left his body. I shall instruct the servants of Anpu to begin preparations immediately."

"No. He has not left us yet."

She tried to push past him. The priest barred her path with his arm.

"I shall call for Anpu," he said. "But you may not violate the god's chamber."

"I can heal Wesir if you allow me into the sanctuary."

The priests exchanged glances. Imnefer held his position, his stance rigid. The other priest retreated into the shadows.

"You cannot," said Imnefer. "Reviving the dead is forbidden."

Her words sliced the air like ice daggers. "Step aside—or I shall move you myself."

Imnefer retreated into the shadows between the columns.

Aset unlatched the doors to the inner sanctuary. She thrust the doors inward.

The hinges creaked as the doors came to rest against the walls. Inside the sanctuary, torches lit the space. The shrine, a wooden box as tall as a man, stood at the rear of the room, balanced atop a dais. The shrine's doors were closed, the latch secured. Along the right-hand wall, a table held offerings of food, wine, and beer.

She marched into the sanctuary. Setesh and Djehuty dragged Wesir into the room, where they set him down near the shrine.

Djehuty gestured at the shrine. "The tools you require are inside the shrine. You will find instructions for the rite within the book."

"Book?"

"I have been chronicling the ancient knowledge, from texts I discovered hidden throughout this land and others."

"Our fathers' father, the great Ra, forbade us to know the ancient secrets."

"Yes." Djehuty bit his lower lip. "But knowledge should not be secreted away. It must be understood, employed, and advanced—a sentiment I believe you share, Aset."

"I do." She kissed his cheek. "Go now. I must perform the rite alone."

"Look for the ritual to heal a mortal wound first."

Djehuty hastened out of the room. His footsteps resounded through the great hall. As the clamor diminished, Setesh shut the doors to the inner sanctuary. He sauntered to her.

He fixed his eyes on hers. A sneer deformed his lips.

Clinching her upper arms, he said, "The time has come."

"Yes, I must perform the spell. You should leave, for I alone risk this peril."

"No." He drew her close to him, their faces separated by the scantest gap. "Aset, the time has come to let him go."

He bent his head down until their his forehead touched hers. His breaths whispered over her. He enveloped her in his arms, his skin hot against hers, and lowered his mouth toward her lips.

She wriggled out of his embrace, recoiling from him.

"Let Wesir's *ka* leave him," Setesh said. "I will become pharaoh and you shall rule beside me. We have both wanted this, *neferet*."

"Do not call me that." She stumbled backward. "You are my husband's brother. How can you say such things?"

"I speak the truth."

He reached for her arm. She darted away from him.

Setesh curled his lip up, exposing his teeth. His eyes, dark as chaos, mirrored the wavering light of the torches.

"If you care for Wesir," she said, "you will leave me to do what must be done."

Setesh took a step toward her.

She straightened. From the offering table, she grabbed a wine jar.

He chuckled. "What will you do, *neferet*, drown me?"

She poured the wine onto the floor. As she clasped the jar in both hands, she raised it before her at chest level.

Setesh smirked.

She tensed her body.

"Do not worry," Setesh said. "I see my feelings are not returned. I will no longer bother you."

He stalked toward the doors.

She lowered the jar a fraction.

He swung the doors wide. "Perform your ritual. I pray you succeed."

Through the doors he sauntered, into the great hall. He closed the doors, and she headed toward the shrine. Unlocking the doors, she swung them apart.

A gold statue of Amen-Ra, the supreme god, stood inside the shrine. Ram's horns adorned his head. Implements lay scattered around his feet—the tools of which Djehuty had spoken. In his arms, Amen-Ra cradled a thick scroll.

Aset removed the scroll from his arms. Thicker than her arm, the scroll weighted down her hand with more mass than a sack full of granite. A gold band secured the papyrus. She unfastened the band and rolled out the scroll.

The headings, written in red ink, delineated sections. As she unfurled the book with her right hand, she rolled the other end of the papyrus into a new scroll with her left hand. She perused the headings, searching the text for the rite she needed.

There! The heading proclaimed, "To heal a mortal wound." Beneath the title, the page contained instructions.

Obtain the blue jar which houses the invisible servants who cannot die, for they have never lived.

Invisible servants? She rifled through the implements in the shrine. Behind the statue's feet, she found a blue jar. The text instructed her to pour the contents of the jar into the wound. Next she must awaken the invisible servants by waving the silver wand over the wound while compressing the wand with her fingers.

She located the silver wand, a stick thin as a papyrus reed and shorter than her hand.

At Wesir's side, she knelt with the jar and the wand. She removed the jar's stopper, held the jar over his wound, and tipped it. A clear gel spilled from the jar. When the gel had filled the wound, she replaced the stopper and set the jar down beside her.

She took the wand in her hand. Compressing it between her thumb and forefinger, she waved the wand over Wesir's wound. A beam of light, hair-thin, shone down into the wound. The wand hummed. Its pitch rose and fell, almost musically, above a low buzzing.

Her hand tingled. She swept the beam back and forth across the wound.

The gel bubbled. Deep inside the gash, tissues sewed themselves together.

Beyond the doors, footsteps echoed through the great hall.

The tingling spread into her wrist. Her hand grew numb. She wrapped her other hand around it to keep her fingers from losing their grip on the wand.

The tissues just under Wesir's skin knit into one another. As the tingling infected her arm, Wesir's skin stitched back together.

The beam shut off. The humming and buzzing quieted.

Voices. Outside the doors.

She searched the scroll, letting it roll out across the floor unrestrained.

Someone rapped on the doors.

"Come out at once," a voice commanded.

The scroll unreeled before her. A heading rolled out past her.

She slapped her hands on the scroll to halt its movement. The heading said, "To reanimate a heart which has ceased beating."

If the heart has not beat for more than three hours, the text warned, *the ritual shall fail.*

Three hours. She could not know how many hours had elapsed before Wesir's guards had discovered him. His assailant must have attacked him in silence, while he slept. His skin felt cold. Did the chill signify a long delay?

The rite must succeed. She had to attempt it.

Fists pounded on the doors.

Aset dragged the offering table to the doors. The legs scraped against the floor, squealing. She wedged the table against the doors.

Back to the book.

Find the moonstone and place it over the heart.

To the shrine she ran. Stooped over, sweating and panting, she rummaged through the implements. What was a moonstone? She had heard of no such mineral.

She tossed out a leather bag. Objects inside it clinked when it struck the floor. Under where the bag had sat she saw a round, flat device larger than her hand. Its luster mimicked polished stone. When she touched it, however, the warmth of her skin suffused the material. The surface felt soft, though it did not give under pressure. The stone-like object gleamed white as the moon, with pink and lavender streaked through it.

Bang! The men outside butted the door.

Back to Wesir she raced, falling onto her knees at his side. She placed the moonstone on his chest, over the spot where the heart resided.

Bang! The doors splintered. The table legs screeched on the floor. The table jounced toward her a finger's length.

Press down upon the moonstone, the book commanded, *and maintain the pressure.*

She laid her palm on the device. It warmed from her touch. She leaned on the moonstone with all her weight.

The device clicked.

Wesir's body jerked.

Bam! The table flew across the room toward her. She ducked her head and prepared for the impact.

The table sailed past her. Its leg struck her back. She gritted her teeth to stifle a cry.

Wesir's chest heaved.

The table collided with the shrine.

Wesir breathed.

The doors shattered. Guards stormed into the sanctuary.

Aset thrust her fingertip into Wesir's neck. His blood throbbed against her finger.

Outside, the high priest Imnefer shouted, "None but the god's servants and pharaoh may enter the sanctuary. Halt before Amen-Ra unleashes his wrath on us all!"

Wesir moaned. His eyelids parted.

A guard grabbed Aset's arms, twisting them behind her back, and towed her away from Wesir. Another guard kicked debris from the doorway.

Aset fought against the guard. Her arms ached from his grip.

Wesir turned his head. His gaze focused on her face.

Tears streamed down her cheeks. She choked back a sob. Through the haze of tears, she watched her husband sit up and rub his neck. The moonstone slid off his chest onto the floor. The second guard took Wesir's arms, urging him onto his feet.

Imnefer scampered through the doorway into the sanctuary. He fell onto his knees, head bowed. "Amen-Ra forgive us."

Aset wrenched an arm free. She jabbed a finger in the air at the priest. "You told them. How does the great god look upon men who cower in the shadows, finding strength only to betray the pharaoh's wife? You *should* beg Amen-Ra's forgiveness, and Wesir's as well."

"I did not tell them," Imnefer said.

"*Neferet,*" Wesir murmured, his voice hoarse, "he tells the truth. If you look upon his face, you shall see it."

She met her husband's gaze. His eyes, blue as lapis lazuli, focused on hers. The constriction in her throat relaxed. She stopped struggling with the guard.

A shadow broadened over Wesir. She looked at the doorway, where a figure obstructed the glow from the torches outside. The man strolled into the sanctuary, into the light.

Setesh smiled at her. "Yes, *neferet,* do not blame the pitiful priest for my betrayal."

He had spat the word *neferet* at her. Poison from the stinger of a scorpion.

She opened her mouth. No sound emerged.

"I watched," Setesh said with mock dismay, "as you and Djehuty carried the pharaoh here. I knew what you intended. As a good subject of Amen-Ra, I could not let such blasphemy go unpunished."

Wesir fisted his hands at his sides. "Aset has committed no crime. She saved me."

"She used forbidden magic. Even the pharaoh's wife may not violate the laws of Kemet."

"Magic," Aset scoffed. "I used ancient medical instruments to resurrect him."

Setesh glanced at the five guards who waited outside the sanctuary. A chuckle rumbled in his throat.

"Who shall they believe?" Setesh said. He poked the moonstone with his toe. "The evidence of your blasphemy surrounds us. If these are medical tools, why have we not seen them before?"

Imnefer picked up the moonstone. His face blanched. "It is magic."

The two guards inside the chamber hauled Aset through the doorway into the great hall. As she passed Setesh, she spat at him.

He wiped the spittle from his face. A sneer arched his lips.

The guards shepherded her out of the temple.

Bakhu
Present day

The fire inside Intef's vessel had weakened. A handful of flames flicked their tails through breaches in the craft's hull, but the conflagration had lost its energy. Smoke wisped into the heavens, dispersed by the wind into clouds that fanned out across the stars.

Katy risked hitting the illumination button on her watch. Rick and Warner had left 13 minutes ago. In seven minutes she'd run for the ship, shoot any Planners who got in her way, and find Rick. Seven minutes. It felt like seven years.

Make that 7,000 years.

Suddenly, she knew how Rick felt every time she took off after a hairy hominid or an *akhet* mountain or whatever notion had possessed her at the time. Whether fate spurred her into recklessness mattered little. Actually, it didn't matter one damn bit. Until last year, the abandon with which she'd sought the truth had affected nobody but her. When Rick had trekked into the woods with her to search for Charlie, they'd shared the risk. Faced the danger together.

She'd nearly gotten them both killed.

Not her fault, Rick would say. Intef bore the responsibility for that fiasco.

Setesh. Intef's real name was Setesh. And Asru was Aset, queen of the Planners.

"Why'd they call you Your Incarnation?" Katy asked. "That's a title for pharaohs."

"I had ruled as pharaoh when Wesir embarked on a mission to befriend the Low Ones around the world. Although I relinquished my co-regency upon his return, my people continued to honor me as they would a pharaoh."

Another parallel with the myths. The legend of Isis and Osiris explained how Osiris had traveled the world forming alliances with other cultures. During his absence, Isis had acted as pharaoh.

Befriending the Low Ones. Setesh must've loved that.

If she believed Aset's story, the Book of Thoth contained information about technology more advanced than what the Planners had.

"I don't get it," Katy said. "Why did Amen-Ra forbid you to know these ancient secrets?"

"He did not."

"You said he did."

"No, I did not."

Katy ground her teeth. A pressure inside her head seemed about to burst through her skull. She half expected steam to whistle out her ears.

"You told me," Katy said slowly, "that Djehuty told you Amen-Ra forbade your people to study the ancient secrets."

"My father's father, the great Ra, decreed it."

"I thought Ra and Amen-Ra were the same person."

"No. Ra was a man. Amen-Ra is a god."

"Oh for crying out loud." Katy planted her elbows on her knees and dropped her head onto her palms. "Can't you people name your kids after animals or flowers or something?"

Ra was a man, Aset's grandfather. Okay, great. How did knowing it help?

It didn't.

The Planners had erased their own history, she knew that. If Thoth—Djehuty—had discovered caches of documents hidden around the world, he could've restored the lost knowledge to his people. Instead, he chose to record what he found in his book.

Katy lifted her head. "If Djehuty believed knowledge shouldn't be suppressed, why didn't he tell everyone what he'd found out?"

"He must have feared doing so would incite panic."

The same excuse many ufologists ascribed to the US government, to explain why they covered up the truth about UFOs. The reasoning rang false in that instance, and it had the same discordant tone in this case too. Djehuty's people had advanced technology already. Why would learning about more advanced technology panic them?

Maybe the truth about the technology involved another, darker truth.

Invisible servants. The Book had instructed Aset to use invisible servants to heal Wesir's wound. Servants who can't die because they never lived. What kind of servants had never lived?

Maybe it was magic. No…what had she read? An article, in a science magazine. About future technology. The possibilities. Robots, spaceships, and the like.

Robots. Servants who never lived? Possibly. What about the invisible part? Something could become technically invisible if it was too small for the naked eye to see. Tiny robots.

Nanotechnology.

No wonder Ra had wanted to keep his "brethren" from finding out about it. If someone like Setesh got a hold of nanotechnology, or another technology just as advanced, he could…

Destroy the world. Or at least kill off everyone he deemed unworthy of life.

Rick get back here.

She had time. She'd promised to give him 20 minutes.

And she needed to know one more thing before she confronted Setesh.

"Tell me," Katy said, "how did you, Wesir, and others end up in *mut ankh*?"

"Do you remember, when I told you of Nebthut's awakening, how she could not put Setesh to death?"

"You said Ra forbid you to kill your own kind."

"Precisely."

Waset
Day 33 of harvest, year 31 of Wesir
10,106 BC

The guards ushered Aset and Wesir into the throne room of the palace. They passed through the curtain of jewels crafted from strings of emerald, diamond, and sapphire that dangled from the ceiling to the floor. Beyond the curtain, the golden throne hunkered atop a tiered dais. In the throne slouched Geb.

A black wig covered his bald head. He wore a kilt of linen embroidered with gold threads. An amulet hung around his neck, the gold inlaid with lapis lazuli in the shape of a scarab. An arm band, also of gold, had his name engraved into its surface.

The guards halted Wesir and Aset at the base of the dais.

Scuffling erupted behind them. Aset turned.

Guards shoved Setesh through the curtain of jewels. They herded him toward the dais, stopping him an arm's length from Wesir. Aset peered around her husband at Setesh.

Three paces behind Setesh's guards, another pair of guards escorted a prisoner into the chamber. Djehuty walked to the dais. His guards held their cupped hands under his elbows but had no need of impelling him. Djehuty stopped beside Aset.

She had witnessed the expression he now wore on one previous occasion—at their grandfather's funeral.

The guards had assembled them in a row before the vizier. Aset looked at her father. He remained silent, shoulders hunched, head in his hand.

"Father," she said.

He held up a hand.

After a moment, Geb rose. "I have been chosen to oversee the proceedings and pass sentence on those judged guilty of crimes against Kemet and its people. The pharaoh has informed me of the identity of his attacker."

Geb raised an arm. He uncurled a finger to indicate Setesh.

"You," Geb said, "attempted to murder the king, your own brother."

"He lies," Setesh snarled, "to protect Aset. She stabbed him, for she is jealous of Wesir's power. You saw how she blasphemed the gods by performing forbidden rites inside the sanctuary. Did you not find her knife lodged in his chest?"

"How did you know Wesir was murdered with Aset's knife?"

Setesh pinched his lips, squinted at the wall. He aimed a half-suppressed sneer at Geb.

"I saw the knife," he said, "when I entered the pharaoh's chamber."

"You swore to me you had not entered the pharaoh's chamber."

Setesh's face flushed. His upper lip quivered.

"Will you not admit your crimes?" Geb asked. "And beg absolution from the gods?"

Setesh clenched his jaw. "I did nothing."

Geb tramped back to the throne. Though he remained standing, he rested a hand on the throne's back. Bowing his head, he rubbed his eyes.

The vizier lifted his head. He straightened his posture and turned to the prisoners.

"I have decided," he said.

"Father," Aset said, "why must Wesir be judged with us? He committed no crime."

"The people fear him—what he may have become through your use of forbidden magic. He can no longer rule as king. He can no longer live among his people without inciting fear and panic."

"I used no magic. You cannot yield to superstition."

"We are a superstitious people, you know that as well as I. The people believe he has returned as a demon born of dark magic. Even Anpu himself, overseer of the embalmers, refuses to stand in the same room with Wesir."

"You cannot believe I have committed a sacrilege."

Geb averted his gaze to the throne. He caressed the gold.

When he spoke again, he looked past her. "I do not know."

Her voice abandoned her. She shuffled closer to Wesir. He slipped his hand over hers. She entwined her fingers with his.

Geb rolled his shoulders back. He shut his eyes for a heartbeat, then looked upon them without emotion, nodding at each as he spoke their names.

He said, "Wesir, lord of the Two Lands, king of Upper and Lower Egypt. Aset, Great Royal Wife, high priestess of Amen at Karnak. Setesh, brother of the king, overseer of the armies. And Djehuty, overseer of priests at Karnak and Mennefer, overseer of scribes, protector of knowledge. We have come to pass judgment on you."

The guards backed away from their charges.

"You have angered the gods," Geb said, "violated the sanctity of the temple, and used forbidden magic."

Setesh grunted. "You speak of Aset's crimes, not mine."

"You have all acted against *maat*—except Wesir, who lay near death. By the will of the gods, he should have passed into the afterlife. His renewed life is itself a blasphemy and a danger to our nation."

"Release me," Setesh growled.

"Silence!" Geb concentrated on the curtain of jewels behind them. "Aset used forbidden magic. Djehuty both aided her and disregarded Ra's decree concerning the ancient knowledge. But you, Setesh, attempted to murder the pharaoh."

Setesh ground his teeth. Djehuty lowered his head, hands interlocked before him.

Aset grasped Wesir's hand tighter. He winced. She loosened her grip and edged closer to him.

Geb let his shoulders sag. "Aset is my daughter. Djehuty is the son of my sister. Setesh and Wesir I treated as sons. Ra forbade us to kill our own, even those who committed the most heinous of crimes. I cannot bear to see you imprisoned, though by law I must punish you."

Aset swallowed. The lump had embedded itself in her throat.

"Therefore," Geb said, "as vizier of Kemet, I pronounce this sentence. You will endure *mut ankh* from this day forward, your coffins buried in separate tombs the location of which no man or woman shall know. Those who take part in the burial rites shall vow never to reveal the locations."

Geb waved at the guards. They stepped forward to reclaim their charges.

Setesh bared his teeth at Geb. "You will not do this to me."

"It is already done."

Setesh lunged at Geb. The guards seized him. He flailed, gnashed his teeth, howled. One guard slammed him to the floor, while the second yanked his arms behind his back. The guards tied his hands with a rope. They bound his feet as well, allowing him leeway to walk.

The guards hefted him onto his feet. They shoved him. Face red, breaths gasping from him, Setesh hobbled forward.

Wesir tightened his grip on Aset's hand. He asked, "Who shall rule the Two Lands?"

"Your son," Geb said, "Heru."

"We shall go peacefully."

Djehuty nodded.

Aset felt her heart beating fast as a falcon's inside her chest. Her face had grown numb, her vision blotchy. She stretched her free hand toward her father. He grazed his fingertips against hers, his face pinched. His eyes glistened.

He dropped his hand. As he walked closer to Aset, he removed the scarab amulet from his neck. With one hand he lowered the necklace over her head, while with the other he lifted her hair out of the way. The amulet draped down her chest.

"This will protect you," he said.

The guards hurried them out of the throne room. Setesh fought and screamed, kicked and flailed, yet the guards subdued him. As they dragged him down the corridor, he spat curses at them.

The guards took them to a wooden structure nestled against the temple walls. A painting above the doorway identified the structure as "the house of Anpu's servants, gateway to the *duat*."

The embalmers' workshop.

A guard knocked on the double doors. The doors swung inward to reveal a darkness penetrated only by a pair of torches on either side of the chamber. A shaven-headed man waved for them to enter. Two guards propelled Setesh toward the doors.

"Wait!" a woman cried.

Aset twisted around to glance behind her. From across the meadow where the palace's walls shimmered white in the moonlight, Nebthut ran toward the workshop. She stopped between Aset and Setesh. Dried tears streaked her cheeks from her eyes to her chin. New tears rolled down her cheeks in the tracks of the old.

Nebthut flung herself at Setesh's feet. Sobs shook her body. A guard thrust his hands under her arms and hoisted her onto her feet. She clawed at his face.

"Stop," she wailed, "let me near my husband."

The guard released her, yet remained behind her. She threw her arms around Setesh's neck and kissed his cheeks, his mouth, his hand.

He jerked his hand away.

She took his face in her hands. "Husband, please, take me with you."

Aset pulled Nebthut toward her. "No."

"There is no other way for me."

"He stabbed Wesir," Aset said. "He wanted my husband dead so he might have me for himself. He has betrayed you."

"No." Nebthut yanked her arm from Aset's grip. "You lie."

Aset flinched as if her sister had struck her.

From the doorway, the embalmer asked, "Shall I prepare another coffin?"

"Yes," said Nebthut.

The guards shoved Setesh through the doors into the workshop.

The embalmer closed the doors.

Nebthut crumpled onto her knees. Her body trembled.

Aset laid a hand on her sister's shoulder.

Nebthut shrugged off Aset's hand.

Aset's lip trembled. She bit down on it. While *mut ankh* would remove them from this life, their *ka*s would remain with them, unable to find peace, trapped in the twilight between this world and the *duat*. They would live, yet their lives would end.

Setesh screamed. "I will rise again! You will suffer for this, all of you!"

Clattering issued from the workshop. Men grunted.

A hush ensued.

Form inside the workshop arose a hissing. Thunk.

The doors opened. The guards escorted Djehuty into the workshop. The doors shut. Hiss. Thunk.

The doors swung inward. The guards motioned for Wesir to enter the workshop.

Nebthut staggered into the doorway in front of Wesir.

The embalmer laid a hand upon her chest. He eased her backward. "Your coffin is not ready."

The guards urged Wesir forward. Releasing Aset's hand, he strode through the doorway.

Aset grabbed his hand. He touched her cheek, squeezed her hand, and walked into the workshop. The guards clapped the doors shut.

Hiss. Thunk.

Tears burned her eyes. She squeezed her eyelids shut. The tears leaked out, flowing down her cheeks.

The doors parted. The guards waved her inside. She walked through the doorway into the gloom. A wedge of sunlight streamed in through the doorway.

The guard shut the door. The sunlight receded into the darkness.

Three coffins, shaped as men, hewn from gold and inlaid with jewels, leaned against the far wall. The coffins bore faces sculpted into the gold, crystals seated within the eye sockets painted as eyes. A cartouche on the nearest coffin contained the name of Wesir. Hieroglyphs on the other coffins identified them as those of Djehuty and Setesh.

A fourth coffin rested on a table. The lid lay face-up on the earthen floor at the head of the table. The crystal eyes were green. The cartouche spelled out "Aset." Her hands trembled. She clasped them over her belly.

The embalmers gathered around the table. A set of stairs led onto the table.

Two embalmers approached on either side. They held rolls of linen. A third embalmer circled in front of her. He carried a bowl filled with a viscous liquid.

The two unrolled their linen. One wrapped her right arm, while the other began with her left. When they reached her shoulders, they tore the linen. Dipping their fingers in the liquid, they glued the linen in place.

They wrapped each of her fingers separately. They encased her legs and feet in the linen while each toe they wrapped individually. After they had sealed the linen sections with the glue, they wound the linen about her waist, her abdomen, her chest, and her neck.

The embalmers stopped.

Her hair was tucked inside the neck wrappings. The hairs pulled on her scalp. The linen around her chest pressed against her at each breath. A wave of dizziness crashed over her. She listed.

The embalmers steadied her.

A man emerged from the darkness at the rear of the room. Anpu, his jackal-head mask tucked under his arm, bowed his head to her.

"Please, Your Incarnation," he said. "step into the coffin. I promise you will feel nothing."

She glanced sideways at the other coffins. "Setesh cried out."

"He struggled."

The embalmers grasped her elbows in their hands. They exerted a slight pressure, encouraging her to move toward the table.

She mounted the stairs.

An embalmer climbed the stairs after her. Once she had settled into the coffin, he took her hands and crossed them over her chest. With a length of linen, he tied them together.

He tiptoed backward down the stairs.

Anpu bent over the coffin and returned her gaze with an expression whose serenity conceded only to a hint of a frown. With two fingers he touched her forehead. Oil slicked his fingers. Skimming his fingers down her nose, over her lips, and across her chin onto her chest, he anointed her. An attendant handed him the *pesesh-kef*. He touched the forked instrument to her mouth.

Aset shivered. She had watched as Anpu touched the *pesesh-kef* to the mouth of her grandfather's mummy at his funeral 12 years earlier. He had lain wrapped in bandages, his *ka* gone from his body.

Unable to move her head, she turned her eyes to examine her own wrappings. The lump in her throat hardened.

Anubis slipped a hand under her head. As he lifted her head, an embalmer handed him a roll of linen. He wrapped it around her face, covering her chin. Her mouth. Her nose. Her breaths penetrated the linen one last time as Anubis wound the fabric over her nostrils again. He covered the bridge of her nose.

Her heart pounded against her chest. She inhaled, struggling to breathe through the bandages. Her ears rang.

Anubis placed a hand flat on her forehead.

"Do not resist," he said. "You will harm yourself."

He wound the linen over her eyes. Darkness enveloped her. She sucked at the air. The linen hindered her breaths. Her chest heaved against the wrappings. Her chest ached. Tears stung her eyes, soaked the linen.

She felt Anubis wrap the crown of her head, tear the linen.

"May Amen-Ra watch over you," he said.

Footsteps shuffled. The embalmers had hefted the coffin lid off the floor.

Hissing erupted around her. A fog colder than ice enshrouded her. She shuddered from head to toe. Her teeth chattered. She squeezed her eyes shut. The hissing faded.

Her muscles relaxed. She could no longer feel her limbs, or incite them to move. Thoughts evaded her. A weariness akin to sleep tugged at her mind, beckoning her downward.

As the lid thunked into place, she succumbed.

213

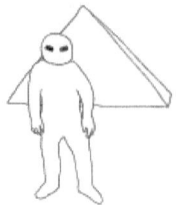

Chapter Eleven

Katy rubbed her arms, suddenly cold. Finished with her story, Aset lapsed into silence.

"They froze you," Katy said, "buried you in a tomb, and left you there for eternity. Nice."

"My father felt he had no choice," Aset said.

"He could've exiled you. Or put you in jail for awhile."

"I cannot question his decision. At first, when they awakened me from *mut ankh*, I blamed my father. I soon realized he chose as best he was able, and nothing I think or feel can change the past."

"Guess you're right."

"I lay every crumb of fault at Setesh's feet."

The chill gone, Katy pushed onto her knees with the Taurus in her right hand. Setesh was evil, but not invincible. However powerful he had become, he still possessed the weaknesses every human suffered. His body had grown no stronger. He thought himself a god, yet he lacked omnipotence.

Until he found the Book of Thoth. If he got his hands on the invisible servants or another, equally advanced technology…

Goodbye, world.

Katy bit her lip. Time dribbled away from them like water from a cracked pot.

Find the tomb. Get the Book. Save the world. At what cost? If Setesh hadn't killed Charlie and Bob yet, he soon would. If he discovered Rick and Warner sneaking around by his ship, he'd kill them too.

Her chest tightened. Acid frothed in her gut.

She checked her watch. Rick's 20 minutes were up.

"I'm going after them," she said.

"How will you find them?" Aset asked.

"Don't worry about that. You stay here."

Something jingled. Aset took hold of Katy's hand and slipped an object into her palm.

"Take this," Aset said. "It has seen me through death and rebirth."

Katy wrapped her fingers around the object. The scarab amulet on its chain.

"Thank you," Katy said.

She fastened the amulet around her neck.

How would she find Rick? She could head for the embers of the craft, but she'd have no way to pinpoint his location in the dark. She had no night vision scope. No GPS unit with buddy tracking. Those technologies had aided her last year, on their search for Charlie. The night vision scope had broken a month ago, and they'd had no time to think about replacing it. She'd forgotten her GPS unit on their Gulfstream jet, which sat parked at Cairo International Airport.

No way to find him.

Wrong. She had a way to find him. She'd argued with Rick about it for the past year. He insisted it wasn't real, despite its record of 100% accuracy. Of course, she had never employed it for this purpose.

Could mind reading act like GPS?

With no options available, she might as well try it.

Katy shut her eyes. A hand on each thigh, with the Taurus in her right hand, she breathed in and out, concentrating on the rhythm of her breathing. She emptied her thoughts.

The sound of her breathing fused with the whooshing of the wind. Her fingers slackened. The gun slid down her thigh, plopped onto the sand.

A feeling. A thought. A voice she could almost hear.

Northwest.

She stuffed the Taurus inside the fanny pack. On hands and knees she snuck across the desert on a northwest trajectory.

The ship towered 200 yards above the ground, stuck inside the groove it had scored into the ground. The globe-shaped craft had rolled down the slope at the base of the cliffs until a sand dune caught it. Like a living thing, the craft had belched out the fires and gulped in the darkness.

Dual ridges marked out the path the craft had carved in the sand. Rick lay on his belly near the top of the northern ridge. He peeked over the crest at the crash site 60 yards downhill. Warner had slithered up the ridge alongside him.

In a voice one notch above nothing, Rick said, "Closer."

"No," Warner said.

A light flashed at the base of the ridge. Rick stiffened.

Voices murmured below. Figures blacker than the night moved off to the right. The light enlarged into a cone that engulfed the figures in gaslight. Not gaslight, though, something like gaslight. A tall man dressed in khaki pants and shirt hoisted a lantern above his head to light the path ahead for his master. No flame flickered within the lantern. Instead a constant, sulfurous glow radiated from it.

Intef strode out from behind the tall man. He followed the path his underling had demarcated with the light.

People morphed from the shadow of the craft into a procession behind Intef. After the third man had passed him, the tall man holding the lantern joined the procession. A second lantern-bearer disunited with the shadows. Dozens of men, interspersed with a handful of women, materialized from the craft's shadow. Every third or fourth person carried a lantern. At the rear of the single-file procession, two men trudged between a pair of guards.

Hands tied behind his back, Bob Hanover clomped through the sand. Behind the Egyptologist, also bound, a gray-haired man with a beard plodded in the procession's wake.

"Dad," Rick whispered. "He's alive."

"We must go," Warner said.

"What? We have to rescue them."

Below them, the procession filed away from the craft, toward the northwest.

Rick backed down the ridge. He rose onto all fours.

Warner grasped his elbow. "We must not alert anyone to our presence."

Rick shook off Warner's hand. "Stop arguing and help me figure out how to rescue them."

Warner's sigh fizzed like air escaping a just-opened tomb.

Rick scrabbled along the ridge in the direction the procession had taken. Since their lanterns acted as beacons, trailing them proved simple—not much of a test for his tracking skills. Intef was either stupid or arrogant.

Arrogant, Rick decided. Although he despised the wannabe god, he knew Intef was never stupid. Impatient, sure. Ruthless, of course. But never ever stupid.

The procession halted. Intef gesticulated as he addressed his people, the general deploying his soldiers for an ambush.

Seven men, including Bob and Dad, detached from the group. They congregated around Intef. The remainder of the throng trooped out across the desert on a northwesterly course. What the hell?

Rick dropped onto his belly. Warner did the same a few inches to his left. They lay as still as cougars observing deer.

To their northwest, Intef's procession disappeared into the desert one by one. Straight down the groove, Intef and his cronies chatted. One man carted a metal container similar to a suitcase. Another man held a Plannerian flashlight, a rectangle the size of a cell phone that threw off a beam equivalent to a five-million-candlepower spotlight. Intef didn't worry much about being spotted.

Planners never did.

The men looked unarmed. Since the Planners used pager-size weapons that fit into any pocket, looking unarmed meant nothing.

Easing the .45 out of its holster into his hand, curling his finger over the trigger without touching it, Rick leaned crawled along the ridge with Warner behind him. The pinnacle hid them from Intef's view. Halfway down the slope, he paused to listen. A breeze rustled the air. Underneath it, voices. He tilted his head toward the sound, opening his mouth a crack. Couldn't make out the words.

He crept closer, closer, always with the ridge between him and the Planners. The light from a Plannerian flashlight flared across the summit of the ridge. The voices got louder. They chatted in Kemetian, a language Rick knew about as well as he knew German. He recognized the language, but understood not one syllable of it.

Intef and his minions set off up the hill, on the path gouged out by their craft, to a spot 50 feet from the wrecked spaceship. Rick slunk closer to the gang. They'd gathered 50 feet from the ridge. The man with the spotlight lingered behind the others where his beam lit the whole crew. The man with the suitcase unlocked the container, flipping up the lid. From inside the case he brought out little devices, which he distributed to his comrades. Each device looked like a pair of granny glasses cut in half, with an earpiece notched to conform to the ear's shape. The lens was tinted. The men clipped the devices onto their ears.

The two guards kept Bob and Dad away from the group, less than 30 feet from the ridge.

Rick peeked over the ridge.

"Shall we make a break for it?" Bob asked.

"How?" Dad asked. "Flap our arms and fly away?"

"Would you care to formulate a plan?"

Their captors, positioned at either side of them, paid no attention to their conversation. Maybe the guards didn't understand English. Maybe Intef had convinced them he was a god, and nothing the professors did could stop him.

Dad worked his jaw as if trying to dislodge a bone chip from between his teeth. Bob rolled his shoulders forward and back.

The spotlight swept toward Rick. He ducked behind the ridge.

The light curved away from him. He sneaked a look over the crest.

A man stepped in front of the light. A silhouette in backlight, he swaggered toward Dad and Bob.

"Where'd your worshipers go?" Dad asked.

Intef moved out of the light. He paced back and forth in front of the professors. Dressed in beige slacks and shirt with leather loafers, his black hair ruffled, he looked like a businessman whose car had broken down in the desert. It didn't seem right. He should wear all black. His arms should be tattooed with cobras, his tongue pierced, his face leathery and sallow.

A scowl cinched tight the muscles in Intef's jowl and around his eyes, pleating his skin. He ground his teeth.

"At first," Intef said, "your actions amused me. When you stole weapons, I ignored it. But when you sabotage my vessel, I cannot ignore it. And the result of your treachery does *not* amuse me."

Dad feigned a sniffle. "Stop, I think I'm gonna cry."

Jesus, Dad. Rick stared at the back of his father's head. He tried to shoot a telepathic ray of sense into the old coot's brain. Dad had spent more time with Katy than he had, since he'd known her for two years before the Planners took him. Part of Katy must've rubbed off on him.

Great.

A breath blasted from Intef's nose, inflating his nostrils. He stalked toward Dad.

Rick raised the .45. He set its barrel on the ridge, the muzzle aimed at Intef's head.

The pseudo-god stabbed a finger at Dad's face. His fingertip knocked into Dad's nose.

"You," he growled. "You are the source of this treachery. I have abided your insults and your deceit too long. You will trouble me no more."

Intef pulled a knife from his pocket—a curved blade used for skinning.

"Hey," Dad said, "that's mine."

Intef turned the knife side to side. The spotlight glinted off it.

"I confiscated this," Intef said, "when you first boarded my vessel one year ago. You attempted to murder me with it. How fitting that you should die by it tonight."

Rick glanced at his father's gray head. Dad had tried to kill Intef with a knife last year. Here he thought his father had given himself up to the Planners without a fight. Should've known better.

"Go on and kill us," Bob said. "You've lost your mother ship. We've beaten you."

The pseudo-god sniggered. "You are mistaken on both counts, Doctor."

Bob glanced at Dad, who scrunched his face.

"I intend to kill only Doctor Bergren." Intef raised the knife to Dad's throat. "And that was not my mother ship."

The flying saucer seen by people on a cruise. A huge craft bigger than the cruise ship. Intef had dispatched a second vessel to Egypt as a contingency plan. Leave it to the scumsucker to have a backup.

Intef gestured at the northwestern horizon.

A distortion warped the stars a few degrees above the horizon. As Rick watched, the distortion enlarged. The craft was coming closer.

Aw crap.

Rick looked at Warner. He was gone.

"Kill him," Bob said, "and I won't help you."

Intef shrugged. "Then you will die as well."

Something tickled Rick's ankle. He wiggled his foot.

The thing hissed.

He glanced down at his foot.

A snake bared its fangs at him. He shoved his toe under the snake and kicked it away.

On the other side of the ridge, Intef froze. He cocked his head toward Rick.

Lowering the knife, Intef muttered to the flashlight-bearer. The man doused his light.

Darkness blinded Rick. He blinked, squinted, blinked again. His eyes needed more than a few seconds to adjust. Damn.

Shoosh. The sound had come from behind.

Rick flipped around, the .45 in front of him.

The spotlight winked on. Its beam poured over the ridge onto the four men who surrounded him, each training a box weapon at him.

Rick kept the .45 raised. He tensed his finger over the trigger.

From over the ridge, Intef's voice resounded. "Drop your weapon—or watch your father die."

Rick leveled the .45 at the man directly in front of him. "You'll kill him anyway."

"True. If you discard your weapon, I will spare him great pain by killing him quickly."

"You're a real humanitarian."

A shot boomed. The spotlight imploded into darkness.

Rick fired. A shadow ahead of him, Intef's goon, crumpled. He rolled sideways as a shot burst from a box weapon to his left.

The shot struck the sand. The smell of hot caramel wafted over him.

He aimed for the source of the shot and fired. The man grunted. Whump, he hit the ground. Fire burst. Rick rolled down the hill on a diagonal. The shot missed it, scorching sand.

Flashes exploded after him. Bam, bam, bam, the fireballs punched into the ground.

Boom. Boom.

Men cried out.

Rick stopped rolling. He listened.

Footsteps. Coming from where Intef and his gang had amassed.

Intef barked orders at his men. Box weapons fired. A volley of fireballs sprayed across the hillside.

Boom! A tiny light, like a firefly, winked to his right. Rick barreled toward the flash.

He tripped over Warner's foot, flopped face-first into the sand. Warner grabbed his arm, yanking him upright. They bolted up the hill parallel to the ridge. Past the ridge, voices shouted and feet thumped from the direction of Intef's gang. Rick pumped his legs harder.

Boots thwumped behind them, on this side of the ridge.

They ran faster. Rick's foot got stuck in the sand. He lurched forward, stumbled onto his knees, thrust a hand out to stop the fall. His palm slipped on the ground, wrenching his wrist. He crashed onto his belly. The .45 reeled across the sand.

Lightning cracked the air.

Sand erupted inches from his feet. Burnt caramel. Snorting out the smell, blinking away the starbursts in his vision, he pushed up with both hands. Pain seared his right arm. He grit his teeth and vaulted onto his feet.

With his left hand, he swiped the .45 from the ground.

Boots pounded closer behind them. Warner shoved him. They careened over the ridge.

Lightning. Hot caramel.

Grunts just behind him.

They scrambled up the slope inside the smoothed-out path.

The ground sloped up steeper. He skidded, tottered sideways, straightened. As he ran up the hill, his chest twanged at each breath. The air felt like it had thickened into jelly. He glanced toward Warner.

The Planners fired another shot. The fireball flared daylight over the hillside.

Warner was gone.

A gunshot exploded. Flame sparked up ahead.

Katy.

He tossed the .45 from his left hand to his right. Pain tore through his wrist and up his arm to his elbow. Jaw clenched, he gripped the gun.

A hand nabbed his jacket. An instant later the man's body slammed into him from behind. The .45 flew out of his hand. With the man attached to his back like a huge parasite, one arm latched around his neck, Rick tumbled onto the ground. They rolled downhill, entangled. The man's fingernails dug into Rick's throat, jabbed his windpipe.

They stopped rolling. Rick landed on his back, the man underneath him. He slammed his elbow into the man's side. His attacker grunted. The man flung an arm around Rick's neck and squeezed. Gasping and gurgling, Rick drove his elbow backward again, again. He jammed the heel of his hand under the man's chin and pushed.

With a muffled cry, the man let go.

Rick jumped to his feet. He spun around, kicked the man in the face. His attacker slumped.

A silhouette beside him swung the .45 up at his temple.

The man said, "Do not move."

He shouted in Kemetian.

Figures scrambled up the slope to them. Rick recognized Intef's voice before he saw the slimebag approach from the side.

Intef tipped his head at Rick. "Shoot him."

A shot thundered.

The man holding the .45 collapsed. As the gun slipped from the man's hand, Rick nabbed it. He fired at Intef.

Intef lunged sideways.

Pain blazed through Rick's arm. He glanced in the direction where the shot had come from. The ambient light outlined a figure. He sprinted toward the apparition.

Intef shouted. Men hurried after Rick.

More shots chased Intef's men back to their lord. The shots had come from a different direction. God, he hoped it was Warner.

Intef bellowed at his men.

Rick looked back. The Planners were retreating to their crashed ship.

Panting, Rick collapsed onto his knees a few feet from his savior. His eyes had adjusted to the dark enough for him to see the face of his savior, the most beautiful woman he had ever seen.

Shoving her Taurus into its holster, Katy threw her arms around him.

When she pulled back, moonlight glimmered on her face.

Moonlight?

Rick glanced over his shoulder.

A luminous, disk-shaped craft glided toward them.

Tuesday, October 21

Merka skated down the craft's side with a sack slung over one shoulder and a hand on the railing. He leaped the last ten feet onto the ground. Ka-whump. Merka dashed to his master.

From within the sack he produced three hand lamps. Merka dispersed the lamps amongst the men.

Setesh surveyed his army. Rick Bergren had eliminated two of his men. Gunfire from an unknown source had killed a third and wounded a fourth. The injured man hunched near his god, cradling his right arm. Blood soaked his shirt over his right shoulder. Another man had allowed Rick Bergren to beat him. A large bruise purpled his face. The men who guarded Bob Hanvoer and Charles Bergren had both suffered minor wounds from gunfire. The bullets had nicked their skin, nothing more.

Merka switched on his lamp.

By the clock of the Low Ones, midnight had arrived.

The second vessel hovered above the eastern cliffs awaiting his orders. For now, he had none to give. He must discover where the Bergrens had gone, for they had located the Book. He felt certain of it. Although they had escaped him once, their flight could not save them. Nothing could.

He had believed the throne of Kemet belonged to him. His brother had usurped it from him, and he intended to take it back. However, the voices of the gods whispered a new goal into his ear now. A being of his power deserved the title King of the Gods, a rank he would soon claim. Once he had the Book, his power would increase tenfold, enabling him to seize the throne that truly belonged to him.

The throne of the gods.

Setesh flicked his wrist. The men guarding Hanover and Bergren forced the professors onto their knees before their god.

A tingling infused and buoyed him, like a wind lifting a falcon higher and higher into the sky. The power of his destiny coursed through him.

"They've gone for the Book," Bob said. "They'll find it first and use its power to destroy you."

"Only a god can comprehend the Book's power."

"Thoth was a god then?"

Setesh clenched his jaw. The muscles spasmed. He wrung the words through his teeth. "Djehuty was not a god. He stole the knowledge of Amen-Ra. I am the true descendant of the great god. The knowledge in Djehuty's book belongs to *me*."

Bob looked squarely into Setesh's eyes. He crooked his mouth into a partial smile.

"Sounds to me," Bob said, "as if Djehuty's got the power. How all-powerful can you be when you can't even find a bloody book?"

Bergren chortled. "He has to browbeat old farts to feel like a god."

Setesh's jaw trembled. His voice grew hoarse. "Silence!"

"Why?" Bergren said. "You'll kill us anyhow. Might as well go out laughing."

The professors exchanged a look. They laughed, softly at first. Their chuckling escalated into cackling. Snorting between guffaws, the professors wiped their watering eyes.

Setesh fisted his hands. The nails broke the skin. Blood oozed down his fingers, dribbling onto the sand at his feet.

He had let Bob Hanover and Charles Bergren live. He had tolerated their escape attempts, their sabotage of his first ship, their sarcasm, and their insolence. Their pitiful rebellions had amused him. No more. He would keep the promise he had made before Rick Bergren distracted him.

Setesh loosened his fists. Every god needed a sacrifice. For weaklings such as Amen-Ra, offerings of wine and food sufficed. For one as mighty as Setesh, no sacrifice as trivial as wine would do. He required an offering of blood.

Blood of the Low Ones.

"My lord!" Merka said. He stabbed a finger in the air.

Setesh visually traced a line out from the man's finger toward the rim of the corridor his vessel had created in the hillside. A pair of red eyes observed them.

In the old language, Setesh beckoned the creature.

The creature rose to full height, twice the stature of a man. The animal approached. Kneeling before Setesh, head bowed, the creature gazed up at his god through thick eyelashes.

"You recognize me?" Setesh asked in the archaic language.

"Yes," the creature grunted. "Setesh. Our god."

"Indeed." He indicated the professors with a sweep of his arm. "These two have conspired against me. You have met their brethren, have you not? Two women and two men, one a priest?"

The creature nodded.

Setesh extracted a lightning box from his pocket. He offered the weapon to the creature. The animal accepted it. He crinkled his nose.

"It is a weapon," Setesh said. "Press the blue button to fire. Do you understand?"

"Weapon. Kill."

"Excellent. You will use the weapon to kill their brethren."

The creature grunted. His head jerked up and down twice.

"Go," Setesh said. "Do not fail me."

The beast leapt up. As he fled into the night, toward the cliffs, a dust cloud pursued him. Setesh faced the professors. He smiled.

Hanover and Bergren had stopped laughing. As Setesh brought the knife out of his pocket, he prowled toward Charles Bergren.

"You," he said, "shall trouble me no more."

Overhead, silver flecked the obsidian sky. Katy had seen starry skies before, but none had seemed so cold, so alien. Setesh's flying saucer had flown over the cliffs, stopping there, and turned off its lights. A wisp of a cloud obscured Orion's Belt. According to scholars, the ancient Egyptians had seen Orion as the embodiment of Osiris. All the gods lived in the heavens as immortal stars.

Osiris watched over them tonight.

Bring us to you.

He wasn't listening, of course. Wesir slept inside a refrigerated sarcophagus, unaware of the furor outside his tomb.

She marched alongside Rick toward the base of the cliffs with Warner and Aset behind them. Beset had told her the tomb lay north, in a passage that angled east. The creature must've meant north of the fissure where they'd found the obelisk.

Rick had shut off the flashlight. Anything that brightened their path also alerted onlookers to their whereabouts. Ambient light guided them. Her eyes had acclimated to the gloom, allowing her to perceive the contours of the cliffs, the silhouettes of Rick and Warner and Aset.

At the cliffs, they swerved north toward the fissure. At its mouth, Rick hesitated.

"Head north," Katy said.

"Got a creepy feeling all of a sudden."

"You just now got a creepy feeling?"

Katy hustled past him, hopped over a rock, and jogged northward. Back to the southwest, a dim glow marked the spot to which Setesh and his men had retreated. Plotting their next assault, no doubt.

Rick sprinted to catch up with her.

A patch of shadow within the cliff face suggested a fissure lay several yards ahead. She slowed as they neared it. The fissure was too narrow for a person to enter.

She resumed her northward course.

Rick glanced at the distant light from the Plannerian camp. "What's Intef up to?"

"Setesh."

"Fine, what's Setesh up to? Hanging around by his ship. I don't like it."

"I don't like anything he does."

Aset's voice arose from the gloom behind them. "He needs you to find the tomb for him."

Rick stopped. He pivoted on his heels to gaze back at the glow from Setesh's gang. Despite the cloak of darkness around him, she knew he'd crinkled his forehead. Squashed his lips together. Hunched his shoulders.

"You did your best," she said.

"Setesh is going to kill them both."

She stroked his arm. "They're tough old coots. I wouldn't count them out yet."

"I guess..."

Katy grasped his hand and shepherded him north along the cliffs.

Rick's creepy feeling infected her, percolating through her veins. The hairy hominids guarded the area around Wesir's tomb. They might also protect the tomb itself. They'd broken into the tomb to steal a statue of Aset and who knew what else. If Beset had informed her kin of their quest for the tomb, they'd have big trouble.

Beset wouldn't tell. Unlike the other creatures, she revered Aset as a benevolent goddess. She'd keep their secret, and guard Chin until told otherwise.

She would.

Clouds raced across the moon. Slivers of darkness cleaved the moonglow. A breeze kicked up around them as they passed another fissure, this one wide enough for a person. The cleft angled off to the southeast, though, and Beset had said the passage went east. The creature knew the cardinal directions, so Katy had to assume Beset understood the difference between east and southeast.

The breeze tickled Katy's face. She brushed hairs away from her eyes.

An odor settled over her. Decayed flesh mixed with rotten eggs.

Goosebumps prickled her skin. She stopped, muscles tense.

Rick stiffened his hand around hers.

"You smell it too," she said.

"How can anyone miss it?" He released her hand, pulling the .45 out of its holster. "Only a hairy hominid stinks that bad."

Behind them, a ka-chunk signaled Warner had chambered a round into his Glock.

Katy grabbed the Taurus.

Rick unzipped her fanny pack, groping inside it. When he'd found what he needed, he retracted his hand and zipped the pack shut. Seconds later he clicked on the flashlight. The red filter, designed to preserve night vision, dyed the beam crimson. Rick scanned the flashlight left and right as he rotated in a circle. The beam flashed on Aset, Warner, the cliffs. The light stretched across the desert until it lost its cohesion, scattering into the darkness. No hairy hominids. No life whatsoever, aside from the four of them.

The stench descended over her again.

Descended.

She snapped her head back. The stench drifted down on the wind from above their heads.

"Up there," she whispered. "Shine the light straight up."

Rick swept the flashlight past her face and up the cliff. Rock, rock, more rock.

The light dove into a recess. Rick focused the beam on that hole. The light penetrated maybe a foot into the recess, beyond which anything could've hidden.

Anything. Like an eight-foot-tall, hairy monster with a body odor stronger than a skunk's.

Rick shifted the light left. It struck rock, then another recess. Skimming the light over the cliff face, he discovered two more recesses.

"The caves," Katy said.

"Damn, they're like ants," Rick said. "They're everywhere."

"Kill the light."

He shut off the flashlight.

"Eh-eh-eh."

Her skin tingled. The hair on her head bristled. The sound had come from overhead. She tilted her head back to gaze up at the caves.

Twin pinpoints of red hovered in the first cave. A second pair appeared beside them. And a third.

In the next cave over, two pairs of eyes shimmered red.

Four pairs flickered in the third cave. Five in the fourth.

Growls echoed down the cliffs.

Together, she and Rick backed away from the cliff.

"We must run," Aset said.

"Run where?" Katy asked. "There's no place to—"

Rick switched on the flashlight. It splashed red light over the cliff, a coating of blood spattered on the rock. The blood-red glow flooded into the fissure.

A place to hide.

A fissure little wider than her body. Not her first choice for an escape route. She couldn't remember the last time she'd had a choice.

A creature shrieked.

He leaped out of the cave and sailed downward at them in slow motion. His feet thudded into the sand, ejecting dirt from the craters of his footprints. The wind captured the dust, cast it at them. Coughing, Katy stumbled backward. The creature lunged at Rick.

He dropped the flashlight. Its beam slashed across the cliff.

The hairy hominid clutched Rick's neck. Rick shoved the .45 into its gut and fired.

The creature howled. Blood trickled over Rick's hand. He thrust the creature away from him. The hominid fell onto its buttocks moaning.

Three creatures soared out of the caves.

When they had landed, another pair descended from the cliffs.

Two stampeded after Warner. He fired at them.

One creature charged toward Aset. She yanked out her knife. As she launched herself at the creature, she threw her arms around its neck, driving the knife into its flesh. The creature linked its arms around her torso and squeezed. Aset gasped. Her fingers opened. The creature hurled her at the cliff.

Her back hit the rock. She slumped forward.

The creature tore the knife from its neck.

Two hominids rushed at Katy. She shot at them. Boom, boom, boom. They kept coming. Boom, boom.

Hairy hominids seemed to pour from the caves. They swarmed around Rick and Warner. Aset got up, but a trio of creatures surrounded her.

Katy fired again. *Click*. Out of ammo. Rick had the ammo in his backpack. She couldn't see him through the swarm of creatures.

One of the creatures snarled. He sprang the last few yards to her, landing in a puff of sand inches from her. The creature nabbed at her neck. She darted sideways, tripped, floundered. Her hip smacked into the ground first. Her elbow banged into a rock as her legs twisted under her.

Two creatures whirled on her.

"Rick!" she yelled.

Everywhere, creatures shrieked.

Rick shouted. Gunfire exploded.

The two creatures barreled toward her.

She rolled away, jumped up, seized a hand-sized rock, and fled in the direction where she'd last seen Rick. Creatures grabbed at her as she sped past them. Stubby fingers clawed her flesh. She punched them, kicked them, walloped them with the rock, belted them with the Taurus.

Breaking through a cluster of creatures, she spotted Rick. He lay sprawled on the ground, the .45 in his hands. A creature straddled him.

Motionless, arms limp at his sides, the hominid gaped at his captive. Blood dribbled down the creature's chest.

Rick pulled the trigger. Click.

The creature collapsed onto him.

Rick had shouldered the creature off of himself by the time she slid to a stop beside him.

The creatures formed a ring around them. Fifteen feet separated them from the beasts on all sides.

Rick got up. A wide scrape reddened his forehead. Blood seeped from scratches on his cheeks and hands.

Warner and Aset had vanished amongst the creatures.

Katy dropped the rock. It thwumped onto the sand.

Breathing hard, Rick appraised the creatures.

"Where's your backpack?" she asked.

"I don't know." He rubbed his shoulder. "One of them ripped it away from me."

"No ammo then."

"We can't fight them hand-to-hand."

Katy withdrew the scarab amulet from inside her shirt. She closed her hand around it.

The creatures growled. Dozens of eyes burned redder than the flashlight beam that lit them from behind.

A chill rippled through her.

As one, the creatures stomped two steps toward them. The growling built into snarling. Some creatures bared their teeth, while others clenched their fists at their sides.

Katy holstered the Taurus. It was useless without ammo.

Rick stuffed the .45 inside its holster.

The creatures hushed. They swayed side to side, their gazes fixed on the humans.

Rick started to step in front of Katy, then ducked behind her. Turning his head left and right, he grasped her forearms. With a sigh, he moved up beside her. He slid his arm around her shoulders.

"They're everywhere," she said.

"I noticed."

226

Katy glanced up at the cliffs. Pairs of red eyes dotted the cave entrances. She retrieved the rock from the ground.

The creatures shrieked.

They stormed toward Katy and Rick.

Setesh's reflection glimmered on the knife's blade.

On his knees, Bob watched Setesh saunter toward Charlie.

The Plannerian flashlights immersed them bluish-white light. The guards posted behind Bob and Charlie rested their hands on the men's shoulders. The hands of Bob's guard felt like steel bars clamped on his bones.

"You can't really think you're a god," Bob said.

"I do not think," said Intef. "I am Setesh, lord of chaos. The Low Ones worshiped me, as they should, yet over time they began to believe I was a mere myth. Even when they resurrected me, to save them when their country had collapsed, they did not truly believe in my power."

Charlie said, "They awakened Nephthys to save them, not you. She was dumb enough to thaw you out."

Setesh whisked the knife under Charlie's chin. He held the blade against his neck, flush with the underside of his chin.

"Who told you of that?" Setesh demanded.

Charlie swallowed. His Adam's apple bulged against the knife. "A little birdie."

"The Sons of Horus." Setesh tipped the knife up into the soft flesh under Charlie's chin. "Jed told you, I am sure."

Charlie told Bob, "The Planners put him in suspended animation for thousands of years. I think it's made him even more bonkers than he must've been to start with."

"Dear God."

"Don't say that too loud, he might think you're worshiping him."

"I will find your precious friends soon enough," Setesh said. "And you shall help me."

"Like hell," Charlie said.

"Not you, professor."

Bob shook his head. "I won't be your minion either."

Setesh pressed the knife into Charlie's flesh. Charlie grimaced.

The pseudo-god said, "Did I give the impression that you had a choice?"

Bob glanced at the knife, Charlie's face. His gut tightened as if the serpent Apophis had coiled around his innards.

"Go ahead," Charlie said. "I'm ready to die."

Bob muttered, "I've heard about your martyr complex. This isn't the time."

"I'm trying to save your ass."

"Don't bother."

"You can still save the world, Doctor."

Bob gritted his teeth. He'd heard about Charlie's obstinacy too. He'd also experienced it first-hand. This time he could not allow Charlie to sacrifice himself for the greater good, or any lesser goods.

"You're an imbecile," Bob told Setesh. "Do you honestly believe you're a god? Are you really that daft?"

Setesh centered his gaze on Bob. He narrowed his eyes.

"The blood of a stupid old man won't help," Bob continued. "What you need is a lobotomy. You don't know what a lobotomy is, do you? How smart can you be if you needed a Low One to teach you about our world?"

Charlie scrunched his forehead. He whispered, "What are you doing?"

Out the corner of his mouth, Bob muttered, "Saving *your* ass."

Lines etched across Setesh's features, wrinkles induced by the scowl that poisoned his expression. Setesh ground his teeth. The sound reached Bob's ears as a soft grumble.

Bob started to speak but clamped his jaw shut. He had said enough.

The lines smoothed from Setesh's features. He chuckled.

A chill flash-froze Bob.

"A commendable effort, Doctor," Setesh said. "But you fail."

Setesh flicked his hand. The guard grasped Charlie's arms.

Bob rushed at the guard who restrained Charlie. He pummeled the guard's back with his fists. The other guard slugged Bob in the gut. He sagged onto his knees. Gasping, he clutched his abdomen.

The second guard pulled him away. He restrained Bob's arms with his steel hands.

Setesh grasped Charlie's hair and jerked his head back, exposing his neck.

Charlie spat at him. Through clenched teeth, he said, "My son will send you to hell."

"There is no hell," Setesh said, "only the *duat*, which I will soon rule. Along with the rest of the universe."

Setesh raised the knife over Charlie. He let go of Charlie's head.

Bob bit down on his tongue. The tang of blood filled his mouth.

Setesh stabbed the knife into Charlie's heart.

Bob gnashed his teeth so hard pangs shot through his jaw.

Charlie fell forward. He hit the ground on his face, head turned toward Bob. His eyes stared without seeing.

Setesh smiled.

A creature grabbed for Katy. Rick shoved her backward as he jumped between her and the creature. The beast chucked him aside.

The creature caught her wrist. She punched him in the gut. He released her arm but seized her under her arms. She kneed him in the groin, booted his thigh. He hoisted her off the ground, raising his arms high over his head. Her feet dangled four feet above the earth.

Rick tackled the creature.

Katy flailed her legs at the beast's chest. She thumped her fists on the crown of his skull.

The creature bellowed.

The throng grunted a chorus of "eh-eh-eh."

The creature shook her.

Rick beat the creature with a rock. One of his brethren separated from the throng. The second creature dropped onto his knees and grasped Rick's ankles. He yanked Rick's feet out from under him.

The first creature shook Katy harder. She slammed her fist into the creature's skull. His grip loosened. She wedged her feet against his chest and pushed. He stumbled backward a step, losing his hold on her. She hit the ground on her buttocks. Pains stabbed through her hips, down into her thighs, up into her low back.

The second creature ran in a circle dragging Rick by his feet.

Katy scrambled onto her feet.

The creature threw Rick in the air. The beast caught Rick by his neck and throttled him.

Katy leaped onto the creature's back, cinching her arms around his head. She jabbed her fingernails into his eyes. The hominid howled. He let go of Rick to claw at her.

Rick landed on the ground in a lump.

Another creature thundered toward them.

A gunshot detonated nearby.

The approaching creature jerked. Blood poured from a wound in his shoulder. He veered toward the cliffs left of Katy.

Still on the other creature's back, she hung on as the hominid twirled around in an effort to reach her. Her hand slipped down. The creature bit her finger.

She jumped off the hairy carousel. The momentum pitched her past Rick, where she struck the ground on her knees.

Boom!

Katy twirled on her knees toward the gunshot. Warner huddled inside the cleft.

The creature with the shoulder wound now sported a bloody temple. The hominid seized Warner's gun hand and heaved him out of the cleft, spinning him across the sand toward Rick. The creature lost his grip on the Glock. Warner careened past Rick and Katy, fell, rolled several feet. The gun popped out of his hand. It plopped into the sand by Katy's foot.

She grabbed the Glock.

The creature who'd dragged Rick snarled at Katy.

She fired the gun.

The hominid thudded onto the ground spread-eagled on his belly.

Katy bounded onto her feet. The gun raised before her, she turned in a circle.

Prostrate at the creature's feet, Rick blinked. He palpated the back of his head.

"Leave," she commanded the creatures. "Do you wish to battle the great Aset?"

The hairy hominids stared at her. A dozen lumpy brows furrowed.

She bared her teeth at them and growled.

The creatures stumbled backward. Their eyes bulged.

Katy snarled, hissed, roared. She aimed the Glock at the nearest creature's foot and fired.

Sand spewed up around the creature's toes.

In her best imitation of the hairy hominids, she shrieked.

The creatures fled.

Rick propped himself up on his elbows. Eyes bleary, he squinted at the fleeing hominids.

Katy knelt beside him. The creature she'd shot lay dead a few feet away.

Rick groaned, massaging his neck. "I hate Bigfoot."

"Oh honey, they're not all evil. Like people, there are good ones and there are bad ones."

"Why do we always meet the bad ones?"

"Lucky I guess."

He struggled onto his knees. Running a hand through his hair, he said, "What the hell were you doing?"

"I don't know what you mean."

"The screaming and growling. For a second I thought you'd lost your mind."

She looked at the dead creature. "I had to scare them. Didn't have enough ammo to take out all of them."

They stood. The scarab amulet bounced around her neck.

Rick fingered the amulet. "When did you get this?"

"Aset gave it to me."

Rick trotted to the flashlight, which he snatched off the ground. He shined it at the area where Aset had collapsed.

She was gone.

Katy and Rick ran to the spot. Crescent marks, dented deep into the earth, evidenced where boot heels had dug into the ground. Scuff marks on the cliff and ground showed where the struggle had occurred. The earth hosted a mishmash of hominid footprints, bootprints, scuffs, and scrapes. Drag marks drew parallel lines away from the area. Katy spotted a half-moon mark, impressed lightly in the sand, wider than Rick's bootprint. The mark of a hairy hominid's heel. Along the base of the cliffs, in a swathe three feet wide, the sands compacted into a structure too dense for holding prints. Rocks as large as human skulls speckled the swathe.

Warner shambled toward them. "Where is Aset?"

"They took her," Katy said.

The creature had walked where he knew the ground concealed his footprints. Yet he had dragged Aset, which left visible marks. Maybe he walked in the compacted earth by habit, to camouflage his prints as he went about his business each day, rather than for this occasion in particular.

Katy handed Warner his Glock. She tracked the drag marks for a dozen yards until they disappeared. Rick aimed the flashlight at the spot that had drawn her attention.

She spied an outline near the base of the cliff. The oblong imprint delved an inch or more into the sand. She straddled the imprint. Bent low, the tip of her nose brushing the ground, she studied the print. At the end nearest the cliff, she made out the outlines of toes. Behind the toes, the push-off mound rose then sank into the rear of the print. The footprint displayed no arch.

A hairy hominid had stepped here.

230

Holding still, Katy swept her gaze in widening arcs away from the print. An arm's length away, she glimpsed a second print. As she visually traced the line of travel backward from the prints, she found an impression near where the drag marks ended. The impression, while faint, showed the distinct characteristics of a hairy hominid footprint.

Stooped over the first print she'd found, Katy sniffed. As she pulled back from the print, she saw a thin, dark line in the sand a few inches away. A hair. She plucked up the strand.

A long, black hair.

Katy straightened. "At least one creature was here. He dragged Aset to this spot. The print smells recent."

"What's that?" Rick asked.

He gestured toward the cliff face, at hip height. A streak of dirt marred the rock.

Katy bent near the streak. She sniffed. Recent. Probably. While freshly exposed dirt smelled different, she'd never tested whether dirt freshly smeared off a hairy hominid's sole smelled different as well. Since the footprint was recent, the smear must be recent too.

Rick tilted his head back to stare up the face of the cliff. Katy did the same.

He aimed the flashlight up the cliff.

The light unveiled a cave.

Once the creature brought his prisoner here, he ascended the cliff with Aset. The creature's buddies must've waited in the cave for him with a rope on standby. Maybe they had rope ladders. Hell, maybe they had caves equipped with retractable titanium ladders. The Planners had built caves for the hominids in other locations. They might've built the caves for these creatures too.

The entrance through which they'd breached the caves earlier had been equipped with no ladder. The shaft had stairs carved into the wall, though. Here she saw no steps.

The creature had probably tied Aset to the rope his brethren lowered for him. They had hoisted her into the cave. Afterward, the creature shimmied up the rope himself.

Rick asked, "What makes you think they took Aset?"

She held up the hair. "This belongs to Aset."

Rick lowered the flashlight's beam. Darkness draped over the cave.

The flashlight's beam, while it painted Katy's hand red, lacked the strength to color the hair she held between her thumb and forefinger. The strand retained its follicle. She raised the hair close to her face.

"This is strange," she said. "The hair's lighter at the root."

"So?"

"She dyed her hair."

Katy lifted the hair so the light struck it dead-on, reddening the quarter inch of chestnut color near the follicle.

"Look," Warner said.

They trotted back to the spot where Aset had fallen earlier. Warner crouched over the mess of tracks. He held up his hand, grasping something between his thumb and forefinger.

Katy bent down to examine the item. It was paper-thin disk of clear material, with a brown ring in its center.

"A contact lens," Katy said. "A colored contact lens."

"I don't get it," Rick said. "Why would she dye her hair and wear tinted contacts?"

"To disguise herself."

"But why?"

Katy took the contact lens from Warner. In one hand she held the lens, and in the other the hair.

Aset had disguised her appearance. Though she might've done so to fool Setesh, he had known her true identity from the start. Tomb paintings and other artwork portrayed the ancient Egyptians as dark-haired, dark-eyed people. Maybe Aset thought she had to fit the stereotype in order for Katy and Rick to believe her story about being a Planner named Aset, whose life served as the basis for the myth of Isis and Osiris.

The ancient Egyptians had worn wigs which concealed their hair color. At least two pharaohs, Seti I and his son Ramses II, had red hair. Katy and Rick no longer believed the dogma about ancient Egypt, and they already knew the ancient Egyptians had based their myths on the Planners, all of which predisposed them to believing Aset's story. She had no need of conforming to a stereotype to win their support.

"Wait a minute," Rick said. "I didn't think about it at the time, but when I saw Setesh down at the crash site, his hair was red."

"He had black hair before," Katy said.

Warner stood. "Last year, he was bald."

"Yeah," Katy said, "but he shaved his head to make us think he was ancient Egyptian."

Setesh had concealed his hair color. Aset had masked hers too, along with her eye color. Both of them were ancient Planners who'd languished in *mut ankh* for over 12,000 years.

"Until now," Katy said, "they didn't want us to know their true identities. If we'd known Intef had red hair, we might've guessed he's Setesh. Same goes for Aset."

Rick frowned. "Okay, that makes sense for Setesh. But Aset told us who she is. Why not confess she's really a brunette with green eye—"

He turned his head, slowly, toward Katy.

She looked into eyes. And she knew what he thought.

The creatures mistook her for Aset. The statuette of Aset the creatures had found in Wesir's tomb resembled her. Resembled them both.

Katy released the hair. It floated away on a breeze.

The guards dumped Charlie's body over the ridge.

Bob got to his feet. His knees quivered. His stomach knotted.

Charlie's body. Why had he thought of his friend that way?

Friend. Until this moment, his only real friend had been Halim. He'd let Setesh murder a good man. How could he tell Rick? How could he explain his failure to save Charlie?

He'd tried to intervene. Tried. Bob huffed out a sour laugh. Knowing he'd tried might assuage his guilt, but it did nothing for Charlie, Rick, or Katy.

Over the ridge, he glimpsed Charlie's body. He'd wound up on his side with his left cheek pressed into the sand, his torso twisted, arms askew. His eyes remained open. The blood had coagulated into a huge scab around the knife, which still protruded from his chest. His face was ashen, his lips pale with a hint of blue.

The guards had bound Bob's hands behind his back and shackled his feet. The material that bound him felt like soft plastic. Unlike plastic, however, this material refused to give when he pulled against it. His struggle against the bindings had succeeded in drenching his shirt with sweat and rubbing his wrists raw, while failing to distress the material.

Setesh clapped a hand on Bob's shoulder. The pseudo-god curled his lips in the barest suggestion of a smile.

Bob asked, "Why haven't you killed me?"

Setesh chuckled.

Bob glanced at the box weapon on Setesh's belt. Though he wore clothes suited to a casual business affair in London or New York, he carried the weapons of his culture. The juxtaposition gave Bob a headache.

"Do not worry," Setesh said, releasing Bob's shoulder, "you shall join your friend presently. Once we have found the Book, that is."

A gust drifted sand over Charlie's body.

Bob set his jaw. No one else would die tonight.

Except, perhaps, him.

The thought no longer bothered him. Charlie must've transferred his martyr complex to Bob before he died.

Setesh strode toward the cliffs several hundred feet distant. The guards shoved Bob forward after their master. The other three men followed them.

A red light glanced overhead. Bob looked up. Pinpoints of red, half a dozen of them at least, shone in the cliffs above their heads. What the...

He faced forward. No point in worrying about it.

Someone shouted. Setesh spun around. Bob twisted his head to look back.

One of Setesh's minions sat on his buttocks in the sand. A figure cloaked in a sand-colored fleece dashed away into the night. The figure carried a load over its shoulder. As the shape retreated into the darkness, Bob saw Charlie's head and arms drooping down the figure's backside.

Someone had taken Charlie.

Some*one*? The being had stood over seven feet tall. Charlie, who was shorter than his son yet six feet tall himself, had appeared small over his captor's shoulder. The fleece Bob had taken for a coat or suit might've been hair covering the body of a massive primate. A Sasquatch.

Hairy hominid. Katy Bergren called them hairy hominids.

While he'd accepted her assertion that such creatures indeed existed, and admired her vow to keep their location a secret to protect the creatures, in the recesses of his mind he never quite believed it. After living on a UFO for a week, he'd lost the luxury of denial. Sasquatches existed. One had stolen Charlie's body. What next, a mothman swooping down from the heavens?

Setesh bellowed orders in Kemetian. His minions bowed their heads. Setesh turned north and followed the cliffs. The procession meandered after him.

Five minutes later, Setesh stopped. He knelt near the cliff. Touching his fingertips to the ground, he drew a line with his gaze from the spot he had touched into the darkness ahead of them. He brushed the dirt from his hands.

Setesh rose. He issued commands in Kemetian. Four guards hurried past him, weapons wielded. Setesh traipsed after them, with Bob and his guards close behind. As Bob passed the spot where Setesh had stopped, he glanced at the ground. His heart hammered.

Bootprints.

"I'll go after her," Warner said. Popping the clip out of his Glock, he frowned.

"No ammo?" Katy said.

"Two rounds. I used the spare clip earlier." He snapped the clip back into place. "I have more ammunition in my pack. It's two miles southeast of here in my jeep."

"Useful."

"I can still go after her. Someone must."

Rick glanced at the opening 20 feet above their heads. "I don't think they'll drop a ladder for you."

"I can use the same entrance as before," Warner said.

Rick stared up at the cave. Warner fiddled with the Glock as if he could make extra ammo materialize inside its clip by concentrating on the gun.

Katy looked out across the desert. The glow from Setesh's camp had gone out. She averted her gaze to the cliff face.

When the hairy hominids had abducted her last year, they took her into their subterranean network of tunnels and chambers. Slab doors plugged the exits. Boulders sealed the trapdoors. Stuck in a cave. No way out. Dark. Cold.

Charlie, a prisoner of the creatures himself, had found her there. She hadn't been alone. Aset was alone.

"Okay," Rick said, peeling his gaze away from the cave, "we'll all go."

Warner shook his head. "Find the tomb before Setesh finds you."

"You can't go alone. You need backup."

Katy touched his arm. "We're almost out of ammo too, remember?"

Rick said nothing. Her heartbeat ticked off the seconds, a timer counting down the moments until detonation.

"Go," Rick said. "And be careful."

Warner dropped into a crouch. His boots made no sound as he hurried away into the night. If anyone could handle the hairy hominids without massive firepower, Warner could do it. He knew how to sneak around, how to track, and he understood the hominids' nature.

But taking out a hairy hominid demanded more than intellect and stealth. It required a truckload of ammunition.

Rick clicked on the flashlight. Red light flooded the cliffs.

234

Katy ripped it from his hand, punching the power button. The light evaporated.

"Being followed, remember?" she said.

"Oh." He ducked his head and mumbled, "Sorry."

"It's okay."

Rick led her northward along the base of the precipice. At each wedge of darkness in the cliffs, they risked flashing the light into the crevice. Unless luck had completely abandoned them, Setesh and his gang wouldn't notice the dim, red flashes.

Each crevice disappointed them. Too narrow. Wrong direction. Too shallow.

Goosebumps dimpled her skin. She glanced over her shoulder. Nothing. Setesh and his men were back there. She felt it, like a stranger staring at her from across a room.

Everyone had sixth sense. People could sense someone watching them, even if the watcher hid behind a wall. Studies had demonstrated the human mind's ability to sense the danger. So why did Rick find it impossible to accept that they shared a paranormal bond?

Ahead of her, Rick segued into a trot. His longer legs carried him faster than hers could convey her. She sped up into a fast jog to keep pace with him. Her breaths came in gasps. Sweat beaded on her forehead, her neck, trickled down her spine. The wind blew a chill over her, turning the streams of sweat oozing down her back into rivulets of glacial meltwater. The sweat stung her eyes, leaked salt into her mouth.

A strip of darkness ruptured the cliffs ahead. They slowed as much as she dared. In the instant Rick powered up the flashlight, he swerved its beam toward the strip.

A fissure split the cliffs from west to east.

Snuffing out the light, he swerved into the fissure. Katy darted through the opening an arm's length behind him. Twenty feet in, the fissure narrowed. A foot separated her from the rock on each side.

The fissure dead-ended.

She halted with a hop, a millimeter from crashing into Rick's back.

Between huffs, he said, "Dead end. Dammit."

Click. The flashlight bathed the rock wall in front of them in red. Rick explored the walls around them with the light, over the rim above their heads, up the face of the cliff straight ahead of them. Six feet off the ground, a hole sucked the beam into its depths.

Three feet wide, two feet tall. The hole would accommodate a person.

"Boost me up," she said. "I see a way in."

"Oh no you don't."

"Would you rather stay here and wait for Setesh?"

Bending his knees, he cupped his hands in front of him. She set her foot inside his hands. He pushed up, straightening, and she soared toward the hole. She grabbed at the hole's edge. When she pulled, he pushed. Her head and torso cleared the opening. Rick no longer held her foot. She hauled herself deeper into the hole until her feet cleared the opening. She wriggled around to face the opening. The walls scratched at her as she executed the turn.

She rose onto hands and knees. Her head bumped the ceiling.

"Ouch." Rubbing her scalp, she poked her head out the opening. "Your turn."

The tunnel opened at eye level for Rick. Thrusting his arms up and over the edge, he pulled his body off the ground into the opening.

"Damn," he said. "My backpack won't fit."

"Ditch it."

He dropped onto the ground. Unzipping the main compartment of his backpack, he fished out two boxes of ammo—one for the Taurus, the other for the .45. He tossed Katy the boxes.

Again, he threw his arms up and into the tunnel. Katy grasped his hands as he heaved himself through the opening up to his shoulders. She pulled, scuttling backward.

Rick flopped into the tunnel. His feet dangled outside the opening.

Katy squirmed until she'd rotated around to face into the tunnel. The channel extended ahead of her into darkness.

No light at the other end. She tried not to take it as a sign.

"I should be in front," Rick said.

"Okay, I'll lay down and you can crawl over me."

"Not enough room." He groaned. "I should've climbed in first."

"Shut up and give me the flashlight."

He passed her the light. She turned it on and attached it to her waistband.

With the beam igniting the tunnel in red, she crawled forward. The tunnel stretched out in front of her beyond the flashlight's reach. The rock chilled her hands and knees. The flashlight bobbled on her waistband. She crept onward.

The flashlight flickered. She thumped the heel of her hand against it.

The beam wavered.

She whacked the flashlight good.

The beam extinguished. Darkness inundated the tunnel.

A shudder rattled her teeth.

"Batteries?' she asked.

"Think they're dead."

She shot him a look she knew he couldn't see—luckily. "I meant do you have extra batteries."

"Yeah. In my backpack."

"Never mind."

She kept crawling. And crawling. And crawling.

Her hands hit empty space. She plummeted out of the tunnel.

Katy struck the ground flat on her stomach, face down. The breath burst out of her lungs. Sand got mashed into her mouth, up her nostrils, into her eyes.

The darkness lightened a fraction of a percent upon her exit from the tunnel. When Rick jumped down beside her, he appeared as a shadow half a shade darker than the night around him. She heard his boots collide with the ground a few feet from her, sensed him bending near her, blocking the breeze.

Rick lifted her onto her feet. She spat mud, snorted sand, and blotted away tears of sand.

She rasped, "Should've let you go first."

"Stay here," he said. "I'll see what I can dig up for making a torch."

"This is the desert, there aren't any trees."

"The creatures found enough vegetation to make ropes."

Her eyes had adapted to the dark. However, when Rick strode off into the night, she lost sight of him within a few seconds. He could've traipsed into the maw of some monster that shut its mouth behind him and she wouldn't know. She heard him rooting around amid rocks, which clattered against one another. His footfalls crunched on the pebble-strewn sand.

How had the creatures made ropes?

The hairs on her neck prickled. She twisted toward the cliffs behind her, to the south of the tunnel. Intuition lured her gaze upward.

Red stars twinkled in the cliffs above her.

"Psst," she murmured in the direction of Rick's noises.

His noises stopped. His footsteps crunched toward her. Beside her again, he leaned close. The fabric of his jacket scritched against that of hers.

Red pinpoints winked on one by one in the cliffs. The creatures congregated in four groups, each separated from the others by 15 or 20 feet.

A growl reverberated through the chasm. Other voices joined the first.

Rick mumbled near her ear. "How many times do we have to kick their butts before they get the picture?"

"Maybe we won't have to."

The pairs of red stars bobbled in rhythm with grunts. Her throat tightened. She hated to repeat herself, but she could think of only one thing to do that might stop the creatures. It had worked before.

Katy took three steps away from the tunnel, toward the cliff that housed the cave.

The growling muted into a hush so deep Katy felt herself sliding into it.

She craned her head back, opened her mouth, and roared. Her voice ricocheted off the cliffs. The echoes folded in on themselves, giving the illusion of many voices.

Snarling and hissing, she stamped her feet.

Rick stamped his feet too, and grunted like an ape.

The red eyes withdrew into the caves.

Rick trotted to her. "You think—"

A noise above them silenced him. They looked up at the cave mouths.

Red eyes.

Splat. Splat-splat. Sounded like fat raindrops pattering around them.

A dark sliver whizzed down and past them. *Thwock.*

Across the fissure, a flaming arrow stuck out of the wall.

Something tickled her calf. Katy shook her leg.

Thwock. Thwock. Twin arrows hit the wall next to the tunnel. Their flame unleashed tides of yellow light on the cleft around them.

Something tickled her thigh. She looked down, reaching out to scratch her leg.

She yanked her hand back.

A scorpion climbed up her thigh.

Rick batted it off her leg.

The sand around them moved. Dozens of scorpions skittered around their feet, up the rock wall in front of them, out across the cleft behind them.

A scorpion crested the peak of Rick's shoulder. He flicked it off.

They ran for the far end of the cleft.

Flaming arrows punctured the sand behind them.

Rustling. Soft grunts. Crackling.

She opened her eyelids a fraction. The light from a small fire, which burned a dozen feet from her, stung her eyes. She squeezed them shut, and reopened them a fraction of a fraction.

A creature knelt near the fire. The female warmed her hands over the flames.

Aset shifted her arm. Her hand, pinned beneath her, chafed against the reed mat on which she reclined. Ropes trussed her hands behind her back. Her head throbbed, beginning at the back, stabbing straight through her brain into her eyes. Her scalp felt tight at the back of her head.

Aset rolled onto her side.

The creature barked at her. The beast bared her teeth while growling under her breath.

Aset glanced at her vest, which had fallen open. The sheath for her knife was empty. She recalled, hazily, losing the knife as she sailed through the air, propelled by the hands of a creature.

The hominid resumed warming her hands. Aset's knife lay on the floor near the creature's foot.

The air had taken on a chill. How long had she lain unconscious?

Past her head, a doorway accessed a corridor. The firelight licked at the shadows beyond the doorway. What awaited down the corridor remained a mystery. A pile of sticks near the door must serve as kindling for the fire. None had the weight or girth to act as weapons.

She could grab a smoldering stick from the fire and use that as a weapon. First she must free herself from the bindings.

The creature rose into a crouch. The ceiling, six feet overhead, prevented her from rising to full height. She waddled out of the room.

Grunts echoed in the corridor.

A creature outside grumbled, "Oogah."

"Oogah-oogah," responded another.

The female creature had assembled rocks into a pile, over which she had lit the fire. Rocks had edges.

Aset sat up. Her head throbbed. The room gyrated. When the dizziness subsided, she scooted closer to the fire. Most of the rocks had smooth edges, or at least edges that lacked the teeth to bite through rope. She kicked a few stones away from the fire to reveal those behind them. She noticed a stone with a sharp, jagged edge. With the toe of her boot, she kicked the stone out from under the coals. She pushed it away from the fire.

On her knees, she turned her back to the rock. She bent backward. Her right hand grazed the rock. Heat scorched the back of her hand. She winced. The pain wrung tears from her eyes. Blinking them away, clenching her teeth, she lowered the rope to the rock gently. The heat radiated from the stone. She took care to keep her hands away from the rock's surface as she rubbed the rope across its edge.

Creatures' voices grunted down the corridor. Distant. But approaching.

Aset rubbed harder. Her hand slipped, trapping her index finger between the rope and the rock. She choked off a cry. Extricating her finger, she raked the rope against the rock. Fibers snapped. The rope loosened a little.

Outside the doorway, grunts resounded closer.

She grated the rope on the rock. Leaned all her weight into the task.

The rope split. She cast it onto the fire.

Shadows distended outside the doorway.

Aset flung herself onto the reed mat. She tucked her arms under her body, hands clasped under her back.

The creatures marched past the doorway. They continued down the corridor.

When their voices faded, Aset leapt up.

Footfalls slapped in the corridor. A single creature.

No, the sound was different, crisper. Boots?

Setesh. Her inner voice screamed his name.

She retrieved her knife from the floor and ran to the doorway. Her back to the wall, she hugged the rock beside the opening. She brandished the knife.

A shadow fell across the doorway.

A man leaped through the doorway. He whirled toward her, gun raised at her face.

Warner dropped his arm. The Glock pointed at the floor.

"Where are we?" she asked.

"Tunnels in the cliffs. A creature brought you here. I have no idea why they let you live."

"As with humans, some are good and some are evil." She slid the knife into its sheath. "And some cannot decide which to be."

"The decision is simple."

"Fear complicates the matter."

"Are you suggesting the creatures are afraid of us?"

"Not us."

He arched an eyebrow at her.

"My people are afraid," she said, "to stand up to Setesh. Though many would turn against him if they had a leader to follow, on their own they feel too powerless. Perhaps it is the same with these creatures. They wish to stand up to their gods but feel powerless to do so."

"I thought the Sons of Horus challenged Setesh."

"No. They preserve the knowledge of Djehuty's book, do what they can to prevent Setesh and his kind from harming Low Ones, but they are few in number. They cannot affect great change alone."

"I see."

Feet slapped on the earthen floor somewhere down the corridor.

Warner exited the chamber. Aset tiptoed close behind him. She grasped his sleeve.

They reached a bend in the passage. Warner bent forward. With the left quarter of his face exposed to the corridor, he peeked in the direction from which the footsteps resounded. Aset leaned around his left shoulder, peering rightward down the corridor.

Torchlight shimmered on the walls 50 yards distant. Hominid voices grumbled, grunted, and muttered. Their shapes jostled in the torchlight like bats stirring in the moonlight.

Aset whispered, "We must find Katy and Rick."

Warner glanced at her, then returned his attention to the cluster of creatures further down the corridor. Hues of red and yellow flickered over the creatures as they waved arms, elbowed comrades, and ululated between grunts.

"What are they doing?" she asked.

"Shut up."

The creatures sprinted down the corridor toward Warner. He dragged Aset back down the passage, through the doorway into the chamber where the fire still burned. They huddled to the left of the opening. No time for leaping onto the mats to feign unconsciousness.

The footfalls thundered ever nearer. Torchlight overtook the darkness outside the doorway. In the muddle of words the creatures uttered, Aset discerned three syllables she recognized. Figures rushed past the doorway and vanished into the recesses of the caves. The torchlight retreated with them.

"Setesh," she said. "They spoke of the gods returning to reward them."

"Reward them? For what?"

"I do not know."

Warner stepped away from the wall, his back to the doorway.

Behind him, a growl resonated within a massive chest.

Over his shoulder, a pair of brown eyes squinted at Aset. Above the eyes, hair covered a heavy brow. The female who had abducted her blocked the doorway.

In her right hand the creature clasped a wooden club. In her left, she grasped a canopic jar with a stopper sculpted into a jackal's head. The creature peeled her lips back to bare yellowed teeth.

Warner whirled on the creature. He swung his gun up in the beast's face.

The creature threatened him with the club. Stiff and inert as a statue, Warner maintained his aim on the creature's head.

The creature grunted words.

"She calls us destroyers of life," Aset said.

The creature raised the canopic jar, shaking it. Her fingers slid apart. Between her digits, hieroglyphs became visible. The symbols spelled out a name, Wesir.

The beast grumbled a phrase.

"We have angered the gods," Aset translated. "We must be punished."

The creature backed into the corridor. She snarled out another phrase.

"What did she say?" Warner asked.

"It makes no sense," Aset told him. "She says we must be sent away."

Warner adjusted his grip on the gun. He narrowed his eyes at the creature.

"You know what it means," Aset said.

"Yes." He pursed his lips. "She intends to hand us over to Setesh."

The name struck her like a fist. She had to instruct her lungs to breathe, for they refused to act on their own.

The creature shrieked.

Warner fired his gun. Blood flowed from a hole in the creature's forehead.

The creature collapsed with a report that echoed down the corridor. The canopic jar shattered on the floor.

Though canopic jars normally contained the mummified organs of the deceased, this jar had been empty. Wesir had neither died nor undergone mummification.

Footfalls pounded in the distance, an legion of drums advancing on them.

"They won't be happy," Warner said.

They fled down the passage in the opposite direction. Around the bend. Away from the thunder of bare feet.

A creature clomped out of a doorway in front of them. The female jumped.

Aset yelped. Warner shoved her behind him and raised his gun.

The creature whimpered. Locks of gray hair streaked her coat.

"It is her," Aset said. "The creature who led us to your friends."

Warner lowered the gun. "I think you're right. She's the one Katy called Beset."

Behind them, footfalls thundered.

Through the doorway, a fire crackled inside a small chamber. Katy had instructed Beset to guard Chin, yet the traitor was nowhere within the creature's sight.

"Where is your prisoner?" Aset asked the creature. "The bad man your goddess entrusted to your care?"

"In the sanctuary. With the dead."

The creature headed down the corridor. She beckoned them to follow her.

They obeyed.

In the sanctuary with the dead. Beset must have incarcerated Chin in Wesir's tomb.

Behind them, the footfalls pounded louder and louder.

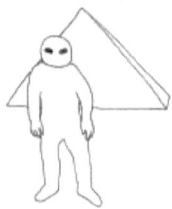

CHAPTER TWELVE

The wind descended into the crevasse from above. Sand swirled around them. Stars hung motionless in the sky. Her hair blew over her face. Katy brushed it away.

The scorpions climbed the wall across the cleft from them, at a diagonal to the corner into which they'd escaped. The flames on the arrows had died. No red eyes gazed down on them.

Rick cleared his throat. A single arrow, its flame waning, jutted out of the ground at his feet.

Katy relaxed. A little.

"Better start looking for the tomb," she said.

"I'm wondering why the creatures left. They could've hit me with the next arrow."

"Let's be glad they didn't."

"Okay," Rick said, "then may I ask how in hell we're going to find the tomb in the dark?"

"Always the optimist, aren't you, honey?"

She stretched her arms out in front of her and tiptoed forward. Probing the air with her fingers, like an ant feeling with its antennae, she searched for the wall she knew must lay ahead of her. She found it a few seconds later.

With no light save for the starlight to guide her, she skimmed her hands up and down the rock wall. While she explored vertically, she crept sideways away from the adjoining northern wall.

"What are you doing?" Rick asked.

"Looking for the tomb."

She practically heard the frown creasing his features.

"The entrance," she said, "ought to feel different than the surrounding rock, right?"

"I guess."

Hands flat on the rock, she paused. "Turn around, put your arms out, and walk until you meet the wall. Then start looking."

The rock felt cold against her skin. She tucked her hands in her armpits for a few seconds. Rick's boots scuffled in the sand as he obeyed her orders. His silhouette skirted the rock wall to her right as he searched the northern wall. She laid her hands on the rock.

"Ouch!"

"You okay?" Katy asked.

Visions of a scorpion stinging him played in her mind. She held her breath. Egyptian scorpions could kill you.

Rick grumbled, "Fine. Hit my elbow, that's all."

She released the breath that had caught in her chest. With her hands, she hunted for an opening, a doorjamb, a big bump, anything.

Her boot crunched on something. Not a rock. The object squished under her foot. *Don't think about it.*

"Hey," Rick said, "Think I found something."

"What?"

"I don't know, I can't see it in the dark."

"Maybe the flashlight'll work now," Katy said.

"Yeah, if it magically recharged its batteries."

A fireball streaked downward from high above. The fireball struck the ground a dozen feet from Katy. It was attached to a piece of wood. A torch.

Scorpions scurried away from the flame.

A voice called down to them, "Will that help?"

"Warner?" Katy said. "Is Aset with you?"

"She is. The female creature who helped us earlier came to our aid again. Her brethren aren't far behind us."

Katy backed away from the cliff. "Can you get down here? We need help finding the tomb."

Rick trotted to the torch. He nabbed it and hustled back to the cliff face before the scorpions got over their fright.

Clomping away from the cliff, Katy turned around. She looked up at the area from which Warner's voice resounded. A torch banished the darkness from the cave. Within the glow, Warner leaned partway out of the cave while Aset slouched behind him. She peeked around his shoulder.

Warner said, "There is a way down, but not here. The creature has agreed to take us, though I can't say how long the journey will take. These caves are quite extensive."

"Always are."

"We'll try to find you," Warner said, "once we're out of the caves."

"No. Find Setesh. Slow him down, stop him if you can."

Warner nodded. He strode deeper into the cave.

Aset tarried at the cliff's edge. The torchlight waned behind her.

Lit by veins of yellow, striped by shadows, Aset said, "You must find the Book. It is your birthright."

"What?"

"Use care." Aset shuffled backward. "Wesir's tomb is the most guarded secret since the birth of man. Your passage will not be easy."

Katy watched Aset's silhouette ebb on the tide of torchlight. Soon darkness filled the cave.

Aset's voice echoed soft as the fluttering of a falcon's wings. "Our ancestors watch over you."

Katy's muscles refused to move. She stared into the cave for a minute, maybe longer, after Aset and Warner disappeared into its depths. *Our ancestors watch over you.* The hairs on Katy's neck prickled. *It is your birthright.*

She joined Rick at the wall.

He stood before a section of rock that gleamed brighter in the torchlight than the rest of the cliffs. Its surface was smoother as well. The rectangle covered eight feet in height, five feet in width. The section had ragged edges.

Katy stepped closer to the cliff. She ran her hand over the edge, where the paler material fanned out into the surrounding rock.

"It's plaster," she said.

Rick pointed at the rectangle's top. "Something up there."

Raising the torch, he moved closer. The something he had seen clarified as the torchlight struck it—an inscription. Painted as outlines, the hieroglyphs had suffered the ravages of three millennia exposed to the elements. The red paint had faded. Bits had chipped away. The symbols remained legible.

A cartouche encircling the phrase "Sons of Horus."

The seal crossed the border between plaster and rock. After the Sons of Horus had broken into the tomb and deposited the Book of Thoth, they resealed the entrance. The cartouche acted as an official seal, to ensure no one would violate the tomb. Of course, such seals rarely worked. In the Valley of the Kings, cartouche seals had failed to deter generations of tomb raiders. The Sons of Horus, however, had employed a further deterrent.

The creatures.

Strange that the Egyptians seemed to have known of the creatures yet never spoke of them in tomb or temple inscriptions, papyri, stelae, or tablets. Well, if the gods had warned them against mentioning the creatures, nobody would argue.

"Shoot," Rick said, "I should've gotten the pickaxe out of my pack before I ditched it."

"Plenty of rocks around."

Rick looked at her. He nodded his head slowly.

Years of wind tunneling down into the crevasse had drifted sand into the corners. Handing her the torch, he rummaged through the dunes in search of a rock hefty enough to do the job. A minute later, he returned with a rock twice as big as his hand. The oblong stone tapered at one end.

He waved her away from the cliff. The torch in both hands, she trundled backward.

244

Rick swung the rock back. He slammed it into the plaster. A crack burgeoned out from the point of impact. Rick hammered the rock into the plaster. Chunks of plaster sprayed out around him. He hacked at the stuff until he'd cleared a three-foot hole.

The torchlight licked at the stone inside the hole. A granite block—set into a recess in the cliff, its surface smooth except for the percussion marks from Rick's hammering—barricaded the tomb's entrance.

With his fingernails Rick pried away what plaster clung to the granite. Bits that resisted his efforts he chopped out with the rock. In a few minutes, he'd cleaned away all the plaster.

Only the eight foot block of granite barred their entry.

Rick swung the rock back for another blow.

Katy grabbed his arm. She shook her head. "Remember the last time you tried that?"

He let his arm drop. Sweat beaded on his brow and the bridge of his nose. He wiped his sleeve across his forehead.

"Got a suggestion?" he asked.

"This tomb was built by the Planners."

Shoulders slumped, he twisted his lips in a half frown.

"The Planners," she said. "The people who built prefab caves for the hairy hominids in Michigan. The culture that operated UFOs and kept people in suspended animation for twelve thousand years."

She alternated her gaze between Rick and the slab.

He tossed the rock away.

She rolled her eyes toward the slab.

Hands on his hips, he said, "I get it, they have advanced technology."

Realization spread across his face in the guise of a closed-mouth smile.

She said, "There must be a mechanism to open the door."

The smile vacated his face as quickly as it had moved in. "Except they didn't want anyone to find the tomb. Which I'm assuming means they didn't want anyone to get inside it either."

"When they built the tomb, the Book of Thoth wasn't hidden in it."

"But Osiris was. If we believe Aset, her father swore the tomb would stay a secret forever."

Katy felt the hope slipping away from her, dragging her spirits down with it.

Rick knelt at the slab. "Worth a shot, I guess."

Katy stooped beside him. If the Planners had built a mechanism into the slab, one that opened the multi-ton door, some portion of that mechanism should be visible. A switch. A button.

They would've needed to protect the mechanism from the elements. Back when the Planners constructed the tomb, no plaster sealed the doorway. The slab itself, and any releasing apparatus, had endured the elements for thousands of years. The Planners would live up to their name and shield the mechanism. How?

Crazily, she thought of her toothbrush.

Not so crazy. She'd bought an electric toothbrush a few months back. Its design flashed in her memory. The power button was molded into the body to prevent gunk from building up around it and clogging the mechanism.

The slab was sunk into the cliff face. A four-inch jamb bordered it. She laid her hand flat on the jamb, a foot above the ground. As she slid her hand up the jamb, she unbent her knees. Halfway up the door's eight-foot height her fingertips bounced over a series of grooves. She skated her hand over the grooves three times.

Rick stabbed the torch into the ground. He squatted behind her, intent on the slab.

She glided her hand down until her fingertips rested just below the grooves. The edges had worn down in places, and dirt had crusted over the indentations. With her fingernails she picked at the encrustation. The grooves became shapes. She blew away the rest of the debris. A hieroglyph surfaced. The symbol depicted a jackal perched on a standard.

The hieroglyph represented the god Wepwawet, the Opener of the Ways.

Katy fingered the area surrounding the hieroglyph. The rock felt smoother. She shifted her hand down, to an inch below the hieroglyph. The rock was rougher. Using the tip of her finger, moving it by the millimeter, she slid her index finger across the limestone toward the hieroglyph. Half an inch from the symbol's lower edge, she felt it. A perimeter.

In the space of a few millimeters, the rock transformed from limestone that felt hard and cold under her skin to a substance both smoother and slightly warmer, as well as softer. If she pressed on the stuff, it might give under her finger.

Like a button. Or a release mechanism for a door.

She set her finger on the hieroglyph.

Rick tugged her sleeve.

She pulled her hand away and looked at him.

He held his hand on the opposite side of the jamb. His fingers framed a hieroglyph he'd freed from its encrustation. The hieroglyph depicted the god Amen, seated with a staff in his hand.

"What do you think?" Rick asked.

She knocked on the stone below the Wepwawet hieroglyph. "I've got one too."

Her hieroglyph represented Wepwawet, the Opener of the Ways. Rick's represented Amen, king of the gods. She felt certain both symbols marked buttons. One opened the door. The other could be a trick to trap the unworthy. Amen's name meant the Hidden One.

The Opener of the Ways should open the door.

"Push it," she told Rick. "The hieroglyph's a button."

"You mean push yours," he said.

"No. Push yours."

"Are you sure? "

"As I'll ever be."

He pressed the heel of his hand onto the Amen symbol.

A thunk resonated deep within the rock. The slab door trembled. The tremors bled into the jamb, the cliffs, the ground.

Rick grabbed her arm. Stumbling backward, he pulled her with him.

They stopped halfway across the crevasse.

Stone ground against stone. A mechanism within the rock chattered. The slab jerked up and out of its slot. Sand cascaded over the granite plug from above. The great door, swiveling as if mounted on a hinge, inched leftward out of the opening.

The cascade of sand petered out.

The slab ceased moving.

The granite block, a foot thick, reduced the opening to four feet in width. Beyond the doorway awaited a darkness that radiated cold by its very gloom.

The ground no longer shook. An ankle-high dune had formed where the sand had decanted onto the ground.

"You were right again," Rick said. "How did you know? Opener of the Ways sounded right to me."

"Wepwawet was too obvious. Amen's name means the Hidden One. We're looking for Osiris, who's been hidden inside his tomb for twelve thousand years."

Rick pulled out the .45. "Ammo."

She'd stashed the ammo boxes in her fanny pack. Now she unzipped the pack, levered the boxes out, and passed them to Rick. Once he'd reloaded the .45 and her Taurus, including the speed loaders, he stuffed a handful of rounds for the .45 into his pocket. He discarded the ammo boxes.

Katy tucked the Taurus inside the fanny pack.

Rick yanked the torch from the ground. He strode toward the doorway.

She trod after him.

Crossing the threshold, Rick said, "Wonder what happens if you push the other button."

Katy stopped for a second, looking at the Wepwawet symbol. A shiver coursed through her.

A long, neck-less shadow flitted past the doorway.

She hurried after Rick.

Beset halted.

The corridor ended at the rim of a precipice. Waving the torch at the opening, the hominid grunted syllables.

"This is the way out," Aset translated.

"How do you understand her?" Warner asked. "I thought the creatures spoke a later form of ancient Egyptian."

"It is Kemetian, not ancient Egyptian. And the creature speaks the older form that my people taught her kind long before the advent of Egyptian culture. Apparently, the contact her tribe had with Merenptah's men, and the Sons of Horus, was insufficient to alter their speech."

"Apparently."

Warner edged closer to the precipice. The torchlight dissolved before touching the ground below. Although his knit cap shielded his head, the wind gusted cold against his face.

"Ask if there's another way," he said.

Aset spoke to the creature. Beset shook her head vigorously. The motion chopped off the syllables hidden within her grunts.

"No," Aset told him, "she says all ways but this one are blocked because the others have crowded together to see the god."

"Which god?"

Aset asked the creature, who bulged her eyes in response. The hominid mumbled.

"They do not know," Aset interpreted. "They believe the Day of Awakening has arrived. The gods have come to revive Wesir and reclaim the earth."

"Setesh hasn't come to revive Osiris."

"I know." Her eyes glistened. She blinked away the moisture. "The creatures know only what they were told."

"Tell the creature that Setesh has come to destroy the world. We must find our friends and stop him."

Aset relayed the message to the creature.

Beset growled.

Aset pointed at herself. In a harsh voice, she said, *"Neteret Aset."*

The creature scrunched her nose and shook her head.

"Neteret Aset," she repeated, gesturing at her green eyes.

"Wadjat," Beset mumbled.

"Tiu." Glancing at Warner, Aset said, "My son Horus also had green eyes. These creatures have seen a representation of the Eye of Horus which displays the correct color, rather than the later version which is brown."

Beset bowed her head. Shoulders hunched, she grunted.

Aset translated, "She will take us to the tomb."

The creature handed Warner the torch. She knelt on one knee, bent forward with her left hand on the floor. Warner directed the torchlight at her. Beset squatted beside a niche in the wall, carved out at floor level. When she plunged her hand into the niche, the muscles in her shoulder flexed as she groped within the hole. She pulled out a wad of rope. The wad overflowed her arms.

On her knees, she scooted toward the precipice. She unfolded the rope, and he realized it was a ladder. The ropes had been woven together to form rungs. At one end of the rope, the first rung had loops on either side. Beset hooked the loops over two protrusions in the floor, at the edge of the precipice. The lips of the protrusions held down the rope.

Beset pitched the ladder over the edge. The rungs unfurled into the abyss.

On her feet again, she waved at the ladder.

Warner told Aset, "Ask her from which direction the gods are arriving."

Aset spoke to the creature. Beset extended her arm at a 45-degree angle from the opening, pointing back into the caves.

Holstering the Glock, Warner leaned out over the precipice. When he found the North Star, he estimated the direction the creature had indicated as southwest.

Warner approached the ladder. "Then that is where we must go."

"I do not think so."

Aset's eyes widened, her jaw quivered. She squeezed her hands into fists.

Warner knew from her reaction the identity of the speaker. When the man moseyed out from behind the creature, situating himself between Aset and the hairy hominid, Warner bolted upright.

A throng of creatures, dozens at least, flocked around their "god."

Beset cowered against the wall, head down.

Setesh caressed Aset's cheek. "*Neferet*, I warned you. No one can escape me."

She slapped him hard. A red ghost of her hand haunted his cheek for several seconds.

Setesh rubbed his jaw. He raised his arm above his shoulder and snapped his fingers.

Two of his minions scampered out from inside the throng of hominids. One seized Aset's arm. The second, snaring Warner's arm, tore the Glock from its holster. The man proffered the gun to his master.

Setesh cradled the Glock in both hands. He curled his upper lip.

"Disgusting," he said. "So primitive. So...low."

"Give it back," Warner said. "Then you won't tarnish your holy flesh by touching it."

A laugh, contained by his sealed lips, grumbled in Setesh's chest.

Aset kicked her captor in the groin. The man cried out, letting go of her. She ripped her knife from its holster under her vest and slashed it at Setesh's throat.

The other minion deserted Warner, jumpimg at Aset. He clubbed her hand with his. She shouted.

Warner dove at Setesh. His head rammed into the man's gut, knocking him backward. Setesh hit the floor on his back with Warner on top of him.

Aset flailed the knife at her attacker. The blade slit his shirt across his chest. Blood brimmed from the cut.

Warner nabbed the Glock and smacked it into Setesh's head.

Aset's attacker wrestled the knife from her.

A hairy hominid grabbed Warner's shirt. The creature hoisted him off Setesh. He socked the beast in the jaw, the eye, the nose. He clobbered the hominid's chest with his feet.

The creature let go. As he fell toward the floor, the hominid caught him by his neck.

Aset's captor reclaimed his prisoner. He grasped both of Aset's arms behind her back.

The hairy hominid throttled Warner. He gasped, gurgled, clawed at the beast's hands.

Aset screamed at the creature in Kemetian.

Beset shrieked.

The other creature dropped Warner. His feet struck the ground, buckling his knees, and he collapsed onto his side. His shoulder landed on the knob that secured one side of the rope ladder. Aset's captor detained her behind Warner.

The creature turned around with a hop. He growled at Beset.

"Kill him!" Setesh commanded.

The male creature snarled at Beset. His lips fluttered.

Setesh nabbed the Glock from the floor. He aimed it at Warner and pulled the trigger. *Click*.

Warner chuckled. The hoarse laughter transitioned into hacking.

Setesh hurled the gun away. It banged into the wall, bounced back, and spun across the floor into Setesh's foot.

Setesh punted it out the opening, over the cliff.

"You are too late," Aset said. "Katy and Rick have found the Book."

"You are mistaken. I will have the Book before the sun rises." Setesh patted the arm of a nearby creature. "My servants have tracked their progress. How fortunate that the Sons of Horus convinced them you were evil. The creatures began to worship me instead."

The man who'd restrained Warner still held Aset's knife. Setesh plucked the blade from his minion's hand.

"With the Revered Ones' help," Setesh said, "when the Bergrens uncover the Book, I shall take it from them."

He took a step toward

Beset flew across the passage. She slung Aset over her shoulder and leapt off the cliff.

Warner wrapped his hand around the rope and jumped after them.

The torchlight laminated the walls in molten gold. The flickering of the flames produced the illusion that the limestone rippled.

They trudged side by side, Rick with the torch in his left hand and the .45 in his right, Katy with the Taurus in her right hand. If anything roared out of the depths of the tomb to attack them, they could perforate it with lead right before they doused it in flames.

They had traversed a dozen feet into the tomb when the earth beneath them quaked.

They froze.

Behind them, rock groaned. The sound bled into the walls. The shaking intensified. Chunks crumbled from the ceiling.

Katy spun around. Back at the entrance, the granite slab grated against its jamb. The door was closing.

Rick sprinted for the door.

The great slab thunked into its slot. Rick stared at the door. The tremors petered out. He kicked the slab. Silence answered him.

He stomped back to Katy.

"Must be another button," he said, "to open the door from inside."

"I'm just hoping there's enough air."

Rick raised a hand palm-out in front of his face. He tilted his hand left and right.

"Feel that?" he asked.

She licked her index finger and held it up before her. One side felt cooler.

The side facing into the tomb.

"A draft," she said. "There's airflow."

The walls buzzed. Lights blinked on overhead.

Katy looked up. The lights were recessed into the ceiling at the juncture between walls and ceiling. The flat, oval bulbs curved over the joint. They emitted a glow comparable to a midsummer day dulled by thin clouds.

Rick snuffed out the torch but held onto it.

Why expend more oxygen than necessary? The draft suggested the tomb had ventilation, yet they had no way of knowing for sure.

Rick strode past her. "Since we're locked in, might as well take a look around."

They journeyed deeper into the tomb. Some of the lights, maybe a third of them, had failed to activate. The further they ventured, the more shadows battled the light fixtures for dominion over the passageway.

The walls bore no inscriptions. The corridor at first sloped downward, then gave way to stairs. If the tomb adhered to New Kingdom traditions, they'd find the first carvings in the corridor that succeeded the stairs. Osiris had been buried over 9,000 years before the birth of the New Kingdom's first pharaoh. Why should his tomb follow their traditions?

The New Kingdom pharaohs might've abided by the Planners' traditions.

They knew Merenptah had encountered his gods—a.k.a. the Planners—since they had informed him how to find the tomb. Sworn to secrecy by the gods, other pharaohs would've kept quiet about their divine encounters too. Of course, the so-called religious texts scholars interpreted as myth might well recount the contacts between the ancient Egyptians and their gods, exactly as the texts claimed. The ancient Egyptians clearly believed the Planners were deities. The Planners not only let them believe it, they encouraged the idea. As they had with the hairy hominids, the Planners derived power from permitting the ancient Egyptians to turn them into gods.

The Planners despised the Low Ones, yet they needed to control them. The hunger for domination led them to influence the culture of the hairy hominids, as well as that of the pharaohs—or whoever happened to be around when the Planners got bored with hiding at the bottom of the ocean reveling in their superiority.

Not all of them felt superior. She sensed no hankerings for godhood from Aset.

But the woman was hiding something.

Katy and Rick exited the stairway, through a gateway of sorts, into a corridor. The gateway consisted of a three-foot section where the walls narrowed, the floor rose, and the ceiling lowered, all by a measure of inches. In the corridor beyond the gateway, the floor sloped downward into the bedrock at a moderate angle. Inscriptions on the walls retained their paint, though some colors had flaked off. The inscriptions, hieroglyphs accompanied by renderings of deities, were carved as raised relief.

"Spells invoking the god Amen-Ra," Rick said. "In New Kingdom tombs, the spells would talk about the sun god, Ra."

"Ra was Aset's grandfather. Amen-Ra is the god of the Planners."

"Amen merged with Ra to become the supreme god Amen-Ra. They're the same being."

"Not according to Aset. Remember, sweetie, we're dealing with actual people who inspired the myths of ancient Egypt."

"Don't remind me. I'm confused enough."

Another gateway conducted them into a second corridor that slanted downward more steeply. Niches cut into the walls housed statues of gods and goddesses, portrayed life-size.

"The different forms of Ra," Rick said. He indicated each statue as they wandered past it. "Khepri, the morning sun. Atum, the evening sun. Horus, Osiris, Isis…"

"Looks exactly like her. But, um, I think those are the grandchildren of Ra not—"

"Fine, great, whatever."

She hesitated in front of the statue of Atum. "Who are Atum and Khepri, though? Aset didn't mention them."

"She kept information from you. What a shock."

They both stopped at the statue of Isis. The figure had green eyes. A black wig covered her hair, the tresses draping down over her chest. Her lips curved up at the corners in a placid expression. A diadem, a kind of tiara worn by royalty in ancient Egypt, encircled her head. On the diadem's front, a cobra reared its head. In her right hand she grasped an *ankh* over her abdomen. Her left hand she held down at her side. The sculptor had carved her garments in such detail and delicacy that they appeared to drape over her body like real linen. The fabric, thin as gauze, revealed hints of the contours beneath it.

The statue of Osiris showed him in human form. Normally, the Egyptians had portrayed Osiris as a mummy, since he served as the guardian of the afterlife and lord of the dead. Here, though, the sculptor had represented him as a man.

More than that. As a pharaoh.

Osiris wore a kilt with a wide belt, his cartouche carved on the gold buckle. The double crown, perched atop his head, covered his hair. He held his arms down at his sides. In his left hand he clutched the crook and in his right the flail, both signs of kingship. Rather than portraying his features with the anonymity of later tradition, the sculptor had carved them with an individuality which corresponded to one person—Wesir, king of the Planners.

Beside Osiris, Isis complemented him as queen. Next to her, the statue of Horus depicted the royal son as a young man of 18 or 20 striding forth in the posture that, in Egyptian art, signified the living. Isis and Osiris stood with their feet together, posture of the dead. Or the living dead.

Horus had lived on as pharaoh, according to Aset.

The sculptors had represented Isis and Osiris as humans, not as gods. Only in the afterlife would they become immortal beings, *akh* spirits, the effective dead. Thousands of years sifted away before the ancient Egyptians remade them as gods.

Rick contemplated the statue of Isis. "Actually, that looks kind of like you. Aset looks kind of like you."

They'd both shared the same thought when they discovered Aset's hair and contact lens. With green eyes and brown hair, Aset would resemble her.

Our ancestors watch over you. Aset's voice replayed in Katy's mind. *It is your birthright.*

"She thinks I'm her descendant," Katy said. "Which is baloney."

"How do you know?"

"Because—it can't—I mean, come on."

Rick tipped his head down to gaze at her through his eyelashes.

"Don't say it," she told him.

"You took to ancient Egyptian like it was your first language. What if the aptitude for a certain language is coded into our genes? That would mean you have Planner DNA."

"Which should mean I can speak Kemetian too, right? The language of the Planners. I can't, by the way."

"Your genes can't give you the knowledge of a language. You have to try to learn it. Your DNA must give you an edge, though, to make it easier to absorb the information."

She chewed the inside of her cheek.

Rick shrugged. "Face it, Katy. You're a Planner."

She whirled on her heels, facing into the tomb. "I am not related to those blood-sucking, self-righteous, homicidal sons of—"

"Horus?"

He smiled just like Aset.

Katy stamped down the corridor of gods, through a gateway into a third corridor that slanted the steepest of all. Rick loped after her. When he'd caught up, he said nothing. The torchlight shimmered on blank walls. The limestone had chipped, conferring upon the once smooth walls the raggedness of stucco.

Rick hustled past her down the corridor. They passed through another gateway which, unlike the others, stretched for 20 feet. Rather than rising, the floor sank by six inches while the ceiling stayed level. The walls bulged outward a foot on either side. While a straight boundary separated the gateway from the incoming corridor, its perimeter curved as it stepped up into the next corridor. The gateway was cartouche-shaped, an oval with one end flattened.

The next corridor comprised stairs leading downward. Images from the books of the netherworld, of which the ancients Egyptians had composed several, decorated the walls in raised relief.

The Egyptians had even patterned their religious texts after the Planners. Boy, that must thrill the scumbags.

The artisans had mixed images from different books together. Here a passage from the Pyramid Texts, the earliest known book of spells for the deceased, unfolded alongside an hour from the *Amduat*, a book which described the 12 hours of Ra's nightly journey through the underworld. Next a spell from the Book of the Dead accompanied a section from the Book of Gates. The hodgepodge of spells and imagery continued as the corridor opened onto a pillared hall. The chamber offered enough room for two rows of full-size pickups five deep. Four pillars, each decorated with more spells and excerpts from various books of the netherworld, hunkered in the center of the room. The walls hosted carvings that illustrated Wesir's journey to the afterlife.

Strange, considering he hadn't gone to the afterlife. But then, what else could his people do? They had no traditions for how to decorate the tomb of a man condemned to live out eternity in suspended animation.

To the left, a doorway accessed another corridor.

Katy meandered around the pillars to view their backsides. On the back of the pillar nearest the doorway, she found a relief of Wesir dressed as pharaoh. A man wearing the garb of an Asiatic knelt before the king. Wesir gestured with his hand as if bidding the man to rise. The relief occupied one third of the pillar. Hieroglyphs crammed into every inch of the remainder, including the spaces along the sides of the relief. Katy read the text.

"Rick," she called, "get over here."

He gave up his perusal of the far wall to join her by the pillar.

"Look," she said, sweeping her hand over the text that bordered the relief, "this tells how Wesir traveled the world for ten years cementing alliances with foreign tribes. Aset told the truth. While most of the Planners despised the Low Ones, Wesir thought of them— us—as his brothers and sisters. He even forbid anyone from using the term Low Ones."

"Guess they reverted after he got frozen."

"It says although his people had terrorized the other inhabitants of the Second Land, he sought to end the conflict."

"No wonder Setesh tried to kill him."

Much of the text dealt with Wesir's building projects within Kemet. He had erected the first temple, at Karnak, followed by a second temple at the same site and others sprinkled throughout the Two Lands. The walls of the temples contained reliefs that narrated the history of Kemet, preserved for eternity in stone. Wesir had never envisioned his historical libraries becoming religious sanctuaries, the Planners depicted in the reliefs getting transformed into gods, the tales recounted on the walls mutating into myths. The pharaohs of ancient Egypt had usurped the library temples for their own glory. They hacked out inscriptions to make way for new ones. They ravaged history because they'd lost the knowledge that it *was* history.

If Wesir had foreseen the fates of his libraries, he might have changed his mind about the Low Ones.

Of course, the Planners shouldered much of the blame for the loss of their history. They knew the Egyptians had turned them into gods, and they relished it. Aset said the Planners erased their own historical records to protect the Book's location. They cared nothing for truth.

She tapped a segment of the text. "Listen to this part. Atum, the first of the living, creator of all things, shall one day return. In preparation for this great day, Wesir has reunited the Two Lands of Kemet within the Second House of Man. The First House of Man ended one thousand million years ago."

"I've heard that phrase before."

"Seen these symbols before too."

The inscription was arranged in horizontal registers, with each symbol matching her palm in size. The second to last register, which mentioned the Second House of Man, concluded with a strange symbol—a circle, painted blue, mottled with green. A final register, flush with the floor, completed the inscription. On the last register, the sun-sand-mountain-pyramid formation preceded the star and sky glyphs. The four hieroglyphs were lined up at an angle, tilted up from the horizontal plane on which the balance of the text sat. The register wrapped up with a symbol comparable to the one on the register above it—a circle painted blue, mottled with green. This circle, however, had a slightly different pattern of mottling.

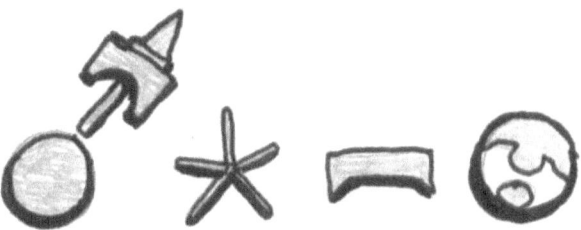

She bent down to scrutinize the lowest register. Her forehead nearly touched the floor. Hieroglyphs at the ends of words or phrases often served as determinatives, symbols that refined the context of the word or phrase. A circle with an X inside it told you the word referred to a town. A scroll hieroglyph meant the word symbolized an abstract concept.

But a mottled blue-and-green circle?

She dropped onto her belly and scooted closer to the pillar. Her nose bumped into the rock. She tipped her head side to side in the hopes a new angle might resolve the mystery of the circle glyphs.

"I can't figure out these symbols," she said.

Rick flopped onto the floor beside her. With his cheek mashed against hers, he scrutinized the symbol.

"Basketballs," he said.

"Come on, they must be determinatives. But I don't recognize them."

"Me neither."

"Thanks for the insight."

"That's what I'm here for."

Head tilted sideways, she touched a squiggle inside the circle hieroglyph next to the "Second House of Man" text. She traced the squiggle with her fingertip. The hairs on her head electrified.

She murmured, "Oh my God."

"What do you see?"

She retraced the line. "Look at this shape. Think back to high-school science. When you learned about continental drift, and the teacher showed a picture of the continents the way they looked before separating..."

"You're talking about Pangaea. The supercontinent."

"Yes. Now look closely at the circle glyph."

Rick squinted at the blob of blue and green.

He blinked.

"It's Earth," she said. "About two hundred million years ago."

Rick rapped his knuckle on the second circle. "What's this?"

"Another planet."

"Which one?"

"I have no idea."

The notion she'd seen the sun-sand-mountain-pyramid formation before niggled her brain. She had seen it, in a context that had nothing to do with ancient Egypt or the Planners.

"I hate to disturb you," Rick said. "But shouldn't we find the Book?"

Katy pushed off the floor onto her feet. Rick got up and, grabbing her hand, escorted her to the doorway. They entered another corridor which, predictably, sloped downward. At its end, a step 18 inches high brought them into a square room half as large as the pillared hall.

Katy froze. Her breath lodged in her throat. She gaped, unblinking, at the sight before her. A few feet in front of her, Rick had stopped as well. He shuffled in a circle to study the entire vista.

On the walls, artisans had recreated the Giza plateau. Instead of hieroglyphs positioned around stylized representations of the structures and landscape at Giza, the artisans had painted a mural that spanned the four walls. Where a doorway split the right-hand wall, the artists had incorporated the opening into the painting. The doorway acted as the pylon of an enormous wall surrounding the palace complex that had once graced Giza. On the far wall, the triad of pyramids nestled amongst trees, grass, and green slopes. The Sphinx with its temples and causeways reclined inside its enclosure on a grassy plain at the banks of the Nile. The river flowed in its old course closer to the monuments. The sun burned high in the sapphire sky, almost on the ceiling. Clouds wisped away from the disk, across the junction of wall and ceiling.

Katy swiveled left. The landscape spread out before her as if she'd alighted on a knoll high above the plateau, gazing down upon a green plain dotted with homes. When she tiptoed further into the room, turning toward the corridor from which she'd come, the panorama encircled her. The plain sloped up into a hill. Situated atop the hill, the palace nudged its head above the enclosure walls. Flags, one blue and one white, fluttered on poles attached to the pylon. Each flag bore the cartouche of Wesir: the blue flag carried his birth name, Wesir, the white, his throne name, Khentiamentu-Wenennefer.

Tiny figures frolicked in the grass, carried baskets, splashed in the river, or tended crops. Some gazed upward with hands shielding their eyes.

Outside the village limits, hairy hominids grouped around campfires or hiked up the hillocks. A handful loitered outside caves.

Rick tapped her arm. He pointed at the ceiling.

She tilted her head back. Above her, the sky arched its body across the curve of the barrel ceiling. Painted on the ceiling off-center, sparkling in the sunlight, hovered a silver disk. Smaller ovoid and spherical craft buzzed around the disk.

The mural recorded a moment in time, with an accuracy usually reserved for photographs. The pharaoh's people had accompanied him into his long slumber.

Rick ducked through the doorway. Katy trotted after him. Two steps conducted them down into a rectangular chamber.

Another mural recreated a nocturnal landscape from southern Egypt. On the right-hand wall, Karnak temple jutted above the greenery. Its walls and ceiling intact, the temple gleamed so white in the moonlight that it seemed luminescent. Paintings on the temple walls took on the appearance of shadows. In front of the temple, moonlight shimmered off the sacred pool, a rectangle of water fed by a canal from the Nile. Smaller temples clustered around the great temple.

On the opposite wall, the mural resurrected Luxor temple.

Katy looked up at the ceiling. Stars peppered the night sky. The full moon perched near the junction between wall and ceiling. A silver disk soared among the stars, alone.

"I don't get it," Rick said, eyeing the image of Karnak, "these temples have carvings that show which pharaohs built them. They can't be any older than the dynastic period."

"Pharaohs liked to usurp old monuments, right?"

"Yeah." He scratched his neck. "Guess I still have trouble shaking all the indoctrination about civilization starting five thousand years ago."

She patted his arm. He frowned at the painting of Luxor temple. She'd gotten used to his relapses. The conventional history of humanity was hard to give up, especially cold turkey as Rick had done. Most people—especially, in her experience, men—needed the conventional, the normal, the accepted. To venture outside the mainstream equated with rolling naked in a fire-ant mound.

For the first two years she'd known Rick, he took his daily injections of propaganda with, if not a smile, at least a sigh of relief. Their adventure in the woods had forced him to reject that indoctrination. Abruptly. She forgave him for backsliding now and then.

While Rick reflected on the mural, she faced the far wall. On its surface, the artisans had painted the pyramidal mountain that towered over the Valley of the Kings. Dead center of the wall, they had hacked a rectangle out of the floor—three feet in breadth, five feet in length. Shadows, pooled in the chasm, concealed its depth.

On the side walls, adjacent to the corners, the mural depicted the River Nile snaking through the grasslands of Luxor—Waset to the ancients. The river vanished into the floor. The chasm would've lain in the riverbed, if the artists had carried their mural onto the floor.

Katy crept to the chasm's edge. She leaned over the hole. Granite blocks walled in the chasm. Sheets of rose quartz an inch thick, which formed the floor of the chamber above the hole, capped the granite blocks.

Rick, striding up beside her, stooped at the chasm's edge.

"Think I found the burial chamber," she said.

Rick sat forward on his knees. He braced his hands on the chasm's rim, and dunked his head down into the chasm. He swung his head left and right.

"Nothing in here," he said. He pulled himself out of the hole. "I can see a light, though. Might be a chamber on the other side."

He got to his feet. Katy peered into the emptiness.

Rick jumped into the chasm. His boots whomped onto the floor.

"Floor's granite," he said. "Just like up there."

Katy stood and leaped in after him.

When her feet hit the bottom, she let her knees bend a bit. The granite fought back. Paints shot up her calves, through her knees into her thighs, straight into her hips. Her knees caved.

She grabbed Rick's arm.

Steadied, she let go of him. The chasm opened into a corridor faced with granite blocks. The ceiling slanted downward until it leveled off at seven feet above the floor. A dim glow up ahead, which streamed down from above, guided them like a beacon. The walls were blank, the floor heaped with sand. They plodded through the dunes toward the light.

Thirty feet later, the corridor dead-ended. The ceiling vaulted upward. Light from a chamber above diffused into the chasm. A hole above the corridor's dead-end created a porthole six feet wide, three feet across, and 12 feet above the floor. Hewn out of the chasm's wall, straight ahead, a set of stairs stepped up into the chamber. A foot wide and three inches deep, the steps ascended at near vertical.

Rick crawled up the steps on hands and knees. He squeezed the toe of one boot on each step, while he dug his fingers into the steps above him for support. Katy scaled the stairs a few feet behind him. She used both hands to keep steady. When she reached the top, Rick pulled her onto her feet.

They found themselves inside a square chamber. The walls sported no inscriptions. Funerary equipment crowded into every corner—baskets of bread piled on offering tables, linen swathes draped over a lifesize *ka* statue, jars of wine stuffed under the tables. A chariot pushed into one corner overflowed with gilded, bejeweled boxes. The sarcophagus, as wide as the chamber, abutted the back wall.

Katy's heart thundered louder than the hooves of stampeding cattle. Her eyes burned, because she'd forgotten to blink.

The sarcophagus, hewn from red granite, jutted out five feet into the chamber. The stone box consumed the width of the room, long enough to accommodate Rick twice over. Goddesses embraced the corners of the sarcophagus with their winged arms. Hieroglyphs covered the remainder of the exterior. Katy approached the sarcophagus. On its lid, the goddess Maat knelt with winged arms linked above her head. Below Maat, twin cartouches spelled out the king's names. A scarab separated the cartouches.

Katy caressed the granite lid. Her fingers bumped over the inscriptions. She knelt to browse the hieroglyphic text incised on the sarcophagus. The text retold the tale of Setesh attacking his brother, Aset saving Wesir from near death, the panic that his "resurrection" had incited among the people of Kemet, and Geb's decision to end their lives without taking their lives. The text finished off with a sort of prayer, or perhaps it had been meant as a plea for forgiveness.

Wesir, lord of truth, father of the king, may Hathor nourish you in your eternal sleep.

Rick strolled to the *ka* statue, a representation of Wesir meant to embody his life force. In the statue, Wesir strode forth while grasping a spear in one hand. With his other arm he reached out. A gold chain, hung around his neck, disappeared beneath the linen that swaddled his torso and outstretched arm. Rick clasped the spear in both hands and pulled. The spear jiggled. He slid it out of the hand, exposing a hole between the fingers and thumb, which had constrained the spear.

Rick jammed the defunct torch into the statue's hand. He swung the spear, pretending to strike down an enemy.

With the spear under one arm, he sauntered to Katy. "Got any idea how to open the sarcophagus?"

"Push really hard."

"Everything else is mechanized, why not the sarcophagus?"

She drummed her fingers on the lid. "Another button?"

"Why not? Maybe the hieroglyphs explain how to open the thing."

"I read them," she said, "and they don't."

"What if the Book's not in the sarcophagus?"

She hopped backward a step. "The offerings."

Rick chucked the spear. Together they searched the contents of the burial chamber for a scroll, or a clue as to the Book's whereabouts. The gilded boxes in the chariot held jewelry. The *ka* statue had no hidden compartments. The linen didn't have the Book of Thoth scrawled on its underside. Behind the chariot, Katy uncovered a wooden chest. Its lid lay on the floor, smashed into shards. Inside the chest stood three canopic jars, their alabaster shattered. The lids, sculpted into jackal heads, sat on the debris.

While she crawled under the table in search of wine jars, Rick examined the bread loaves on top of the table. Katy pried the stoppers from the jars. Each contained wine. She struggled to open the last jar. As the stopper popped out, the jar slipped. Wine sloshed onto her hand.

Rick cracked loaves of bread against the table. After each report, an intact loaf sailed past Katy onto the floor. Talk about stale bread.

She crawled out from under the table. The wine lent a pinkness to her skin. She sniffed her fingers. Smelled like wine. She licked her fingers. Tasted like wine.

Rick clamped his hand around her wrist, wrenching her hand away from her mouth. He scoured her hand with his sleeve to expunge the wine. The fabric chafed her fingers.

She wriggled free of his grasp. "What are you doing?"

"That stuff could be poisoned."

"It's an offering. Nobody poisons their gods."

"The stuff's three thousand years old. What if it mutated?"

"It's wine, not anthrax."

He ran his hand through his hair. Eyeing the tomb's contents, he said, "The Book must be in the sarcophagus."

Setesh roared.

Bob raised onto his toes. The ropes that trussed his hands behind his back strained his shoulder muscles. He stretched his neck out as far as it wanted to go, but he couldn't see what had caused Setesh's leonine outburst.

Setesh threw his arms up. He flapped them at his minions and the creatures, who scurried out of his path. Setesh remained at the precipice. His face flushed tomato red.

The man and woman had disappeared.

Bob had no idea who they were, or how they had gotten here. They must work with Katy and Rick.

He turned to his left. Instead of Charlie, he found his guard staring at him.

No, he couldn't ask Charlie about Katy and Rick or who worked with them. He could no longer ask Charlie anything.

Electric eels squirmed in his gut. He took a deep breath.

A minion handed Setesh an eyepiece. The device must help them see in the dark, Bob surmised, since the men flipped the lenses up when they switched on their floodlights.

Donning the eyepiece, Setesh leaned out over the cliff.

With the knife he had taken from the woman, he chopped at the ladder. The rope fell over the cliff.

Setesh hurled the eyepiece at his minion. As the man caught it, blubbering apologies at his master, Setesh stalked through the crowd of hairy hominids away from the cliff. The creatures moved aside to open a path for their god.

His Kemetian order for the creatures to "stay" echoed off the walls. The minions flocked after Setesh, down the corridor. Bob's guard shoved him into motion, and they merged with the herd.

Three men carried floodlights. The fourth kept both hands free to jostle Bob if he dared slow his pace by a fraction.

The passage sloped down. Within a few minutes, they exited the caves into a fissure that restricted them to walking single-file. The floodlights deluged the fissure in a brightness tinged with blue. The rock pressed close around him, though it stopped short of rubbing against his arms. The night had begotten a chill. Despite that, pearls of sweat cropped up on his forehead. The droplets rolled down his temples onto the bridge of his nose, over the sides to spill down his cheeks.

The crevice narrowed. The minion ahead of Bob turned sideways to sidle through a crack. Bob's guard jabbed him in the back. Bob turned sideways and shimmied into the crack. Six feet further along, the gap broadened into a crevasse. Setesh and his men assembled there.

The crack tightened around him. Bob stopped. He breathed in gasps, his chest aching with each inhalation. His body refused to compress a millimeter more.

His guard edged into the crack beside him. The man jabbed his bony fingers into Bob's arm.

Bob labored to squeeze his body through the crack. His guard pushed against him with both hands and one foot. He burst out of the fissure. The floodlights created a bubble of sickly daylight within the crevasse. The mouths of caves gaped from the cliffs overhead.

Hairy creatures populated those caves. His gut twisted.

The guard slid out of the crack behind him. With both hands, the guard propelled Bob across the crevasse to Setesh. The pseudo-god stood before an enormous door set into the cliff face, a slab of limestone that barred entrance to…what?

The tomb of Osiris. The hideaway for the Book of Thoth.

Setesh cut the cord that bound Bob's hands. "Open it."

Bob rolled his eyes to look at Setesh. "What?"

"Open the door, Doctor. Our tombs always have locks."

"Don't you know how to open it?"

"There is also always a riddle. You must solve it."

"What if I can't?"

Setesh canted his head. "Doctor Bergren failed me. Would you care to join him?"

Bob examined the slab. No hints there. He skimmed his hands along the inside of the jamb. That was how he found the hieroglyphs, one on either side. Wepwawet on the one hand, Amen on the other. The Opener of the Ways versus the Hidden One. The hieroglyphs must denote buttons.

What happened if he chose the wrong one?

What happened if he chose the *right* one?

He glanced at Setesh. The eels in his gut zapped him with their electrified tails.

Amen or Wepwawet. Admittance or…

He punched the Wepwawet symbol. The button depressed beneath his fingers. When he yanked his hand away, the button popped up. A grumbling initiated deep within the mountain.

The slab door quivered.

Bob stumbled backward, straight into his guard. The man elbowed him away.

The ground trembled. Rocks, dislodged from the cliffs overhead, ricocheted off the walls. They tumbled into the crevasse.

The slab door rocked in and out.

The monolith toppled into the sand. The slab crashed down flat on its face with a thud that resonated through the crevasse. Sand plumed up around the slab. Bob's brain rattled against his skull.

The tremors dwindled.

Sand rained down over the foot-thick slab. As the dust settled out of the air, the opening of a corridor gaped behind the slab. He must've chosen the right symbol.

Damn.

The lights wavered.

The quake had fizzled out. In its aftermath, a new sound reverberated through the tomb. A gushing originated from within the corridor connecting the burial chamber to the rest of the tomb.

"Wind?" Rick said.

Together they faced the hole in the floor that accessed the corridor. The gushing wasn't wind. She recognized the sound.

"Water," she said.

They sprinted to the stairs. Water had filled the corridor to three-fourths of its height. The water swirled as it rose ever higher. Transfixed, Katy watched the eddies rise toward her. Where had the water come from? A hidden reservoir beneath the tomb? Out of nowhere, brought forth by magic?

Did it matter?

The water lapped at the top stair. The swirling calmed. The gushing subsided into silence. The corridor was flooded.

Below, Setesh and his men piled into the tomb.

The cliff embraced Warner from behind, while Aset hugged his right arm. The hairy hominid loomed on his left side, at the boundary of the ledge.

Warner clasped the rope ladder in his left hand. He'd snagged it as it fell past them.

The grunting overhead had gone away. He sneaked a glance up at the cave. No creatures.

"How did you know?" Aset asked him. "I thought the creature intended to kill me along with herself."

"I didn't know."

He had clung to the rope ladder, sliding down it to the ledge 15 feet below. No one, including him, could see the ledge from inside the cave. The rope obscured it, plus the cliff swelled out above it like a roof.

The creature had caught the ladder in mid fall. He'd spied her below him, dangling by one hand from the rope contraption. From there, Beset had leaped onto the ledge. He'd had to slide down, quickly, when he heard Setesh screaming at his men inside the cave. Rick had told him about the Planners wearing headgear that probably worked as night-vision scopes. If Setesh used such a device to check the ladder, Warner had no desire to hang out in plain view.

Beset reached for the rope ladder. Warner gave it to her.

As she knelt at the ledge's rim, the creature secured the ladder by coiling the rope around her hands. She grunted at them, tipping her head toward the ladder.

The creatures possessed monstrous strength. He'd have to trust this beast not to drop them.

Out of time. Out of options.

Warner climbed onto the ladder.

Katy shuffled away from the flooded chasm. "Somebody hit the wrong button."

"They pick the wrong button and we get trapped." Shaking his head, Rick tramped back to the sarcophagus. "That's fair."

Hands curled over the lid's rim, he pushed upward. His features contorted. The lid held. Next he pressed down on the sarcophagus lid with both hands, leaning his weight into the effort. He released the weight and swung his arms up. The lid stayed put.

"Need some dynamite," he said.

Katy met him at the sarcophagus. "We don't have much time."

"If the entrance caved in we do."

"You think it collapsed?"

"That was a hell of a rumble."

A slideshow of possibilities projected in her mind. The entrance clogged by tons of rubble. The corridors choked with debris. All exits blocked. All airholes sealed.

She swallowed.

On the bright side, if the entrance had collapsed, at least Setesh wouldn't be able to find the Book. Disaster averted. World saved.

Setesh would find another way to wreak his vengeance upon the world.

If the Book of Thoth did contain all the mysteries of the world, the knowledge of the beings who first populated Earth, they could use it to get the hell out of here. And stop Setesh. Surely a book as powerful as the Book of Thoth would bestow upon them the knowledge needed to perform those tasks.

In a crouch, she scuttled around the sarcophagus, examining the three sides to which she had access. She viewed the ends via six-inch gaps between the sarcophagus and the walls. The front, as she'd already determined, recounted the tale of Aset and Wesir. The ends showcased an unnamed goddess kneeling on the symbol for gold, a common illustration on sarcophagi. In dynastic times, the goddess was usually Nephthys. When the Planners had buried Wesir, though, Nephthys had existed as a living person rather than a god. The symbolism had come down to the Egyptians from the Planners. They named the goddess after a Planner. After their gods. Specifically, they had named the goddess after the Planner who saved Egypt from chaos after the Old Kingdom fell—Aset's sister.

Knowledge that didn't help her open the sarcophagus.

She rose to study the lid. It contained little decoration. The hieroglyphs spelled out Wesir's names. The image of Maat took up half the lid's length, which made the portrait larger than life-size, since the goddess knelt rather than standing straight. Maat wore a scarab amulet around her neck.

Katy withdrew the scarab amulet from inside her shirt. Its size matched Maat's amulet.

Rick said, "Do you feel a draft?"

She rubbed the scarab amulet. *Maat*, the force associated with the goddess, had brought her this far. If she believed Aset, she must believe everything from intuition to luck to her telepathic bond with Rick derived from *maat*. She ought to trust in *maat*, in her instincts, in herself.

Bent over the sarcophagus, she felt around the Maat figure for a button or lever.

Rick had turned his back to her. He scratched his neck as he made faces at the funerary equipment stacked against the wall.

Katy located no buttons, no levers, no release mechanism. She dragged a low stool from the nearest pile of offerings over to the sarcophagus and stepped onto it. A foot higher now, she gazed down on Maat.

Rick ransacked the funerary equipment.

She bent closer to the carving. The scarab amulet swung away from her chest. It thunked into the sarcophagus.

Bread loaves soared past her, clunking into the far wall. Rick was tossing the loaves over his shoulder in an effort to clear the offering table.

Maat's amulet was carved in sunken relief, whereas Maat herself jutted out from the rock in raised relief. Katy shifted her weight. The scarab amulet scraped across the granite.

She took the amulet in her hand. No, it couldn't be that simple.

Aset had given her the amulet. Aset's father Geb, who also buried Wesir, gave her the amulet. What if he'd intended for Aset to find the tomb? What if he sought to ensure no one but Aset possessed the means to open the sarcophagus?

Katy removed the necklace. She set the amulet face-down in the sunken relief and pressed down on it. Click. The lid stayed locked.

The amulet bounced out of the slot. She hooked it around her neck again.

"Aha!" Rick said.

He had heaved the offering table away from the wall. Behind where the table had rested, a portal four feet high by three feet wide admitted a draft.

Deep inside the sarcophagus, a mechanism chunked.

The lid sprang up. It flew off the sarcophagus at Katy. She flung herself backward off the stool. The lid thundered onto the floor while she landed on her buttocks, teetering at the chasm's edge. She threw her arms behind her to check the fall. Her fingers splashed in the water.

The lid rested at an angle, one corner caught on the sarcophagus.

Rick grabbed her hands. He pulled her onto her feet.

"What'd you do?" he asked.

"I opened the sarcophagus." She sidestepped the lid on her way back to the sarcophagus. "Might as well look inside."

They converged on the sarcophagus and, together, stared into the granite box. Gigantic springs and rods, forged from a dark metal, formed a network that both fastened the lid to the sarcophagus and propelled it out of its slot when the amulet triggered the switch. The Planners sure knew how to build stuff.

A gold coffin nestled inside the sarcophagus.

Katy planted both hands on the sarcophagus' rim. The granite box, which stood on a base as tall as her knees, rose to chest height.

"Give me a boost," she said.

Rick cupped his hands. When she deposited her foot in his hands, he hoisted her off the floor. She swung her leg over the rim into the sarcophagus. One foot in the box, she swung her other leg inside. The walls of the sarcophagus came to mid-thigh. She straddled the coffin near its feet.

Shaped as a mummy, the coffin had the face of a man hammered into the gold of its surface. The eyes stared straight ahead. The lips were parted. Below the face, hieroglyphs extended in five vertical registers toward the feet. The text began with a voice offering to Amen-Ra.

Katy read the last line of the offering aloud. "Give him life, forever, like Amen-Ra."

"You mean given life," Rick said.

"No, it says give him life."

Rick bowed over the sarcophagus. He skated his finger down the register until he found the text she'd read. His lips moved in silent recitation.

"You're right," he said, "it does say give him life. But it's supposed to say given life, meaning the offering to the gods has bought him eternal life after death."

"Maybe the scribes messed up."

"Or the tradition changed over time."

An object stuck out from under the coffin's left shoulder. She leaned forward and pulled out the object. A papyrus scroll, five inches thick, rolled tightly and bound with a linen ribbon.

She handed Rick the scroll.

He untied the linen ribbon to roll out a few inches of the scroll. "Herein lies the wisdom of Thoth, written down for the enlightenment of the pure."

He grinned at her. "We found it."

Katy leaped into his arms. Rick swept her out of the sarcophagus and kissed her. Her feet dangled six inches off the floor.

A growl resonated nearby.

They looked at the portal Rick had cleared.

A hairy hominid hunched just beyond the opening. He bared his teeth at them as another growl vibrated through his chest. Saliva glistened on his wolf teeth.

The lights flickered and dimmed.

The creature snarled.

Two men marched out of the tomb, taking up positions at either side of the door. Before entering the tomb, the men had left a floodlight in the crevasse's center. The rectangular light, glaring on the tomb's entrance, tinted the cliffs a bluish white.

Warner crouched inside the fissure from which Setesh and his men had emerged a few minutes earlier. Aset hid behind him. He neither saw her nor heard her breathing, yet he sensed her there. The creature, Beset, had crawled through a tunnel on the opposite side of the crevasse.

Although he'd salvaged his Glock, the clip was empty. He had expended the spare clip earlier. The guards had box weapons. He needed a weapon—any would suffice.

The guards would spot him the second he dashed out of the fissure.

He could work around that.

Contorting his body to lean toward Aset, he whispered his plan to her. She said nothing.

Warner rocketed out of the fissure, across the crevasse toward the guards.

The men fumbled for their box weapons, clipped onto their belts.

Warner tackled the first guard. He seized a handful of the man's hair and bashed his head into the cliff. The guard went limp.

The second guard lunged at Warner.

Whack.

The guard crumbled like an imploding building.

Behind him, Aset dropped the hand-size rock she'd employed as a bludgeon.

Warner released the other guard. The man fell into a lump on the ground.

Aset retrieved the box weapon from the guard she'd taken out. Warner took the weapon from his victim.

No Planner was a victim. Some, like Aset, strove to affect change within their ranks, to alter the Plannerian mindset concerning the Low Ones. The remainder endeavored to destroy the Low Ones. None of them deserved the title of victim.

Warner looked at the buttons on the box weapon.

"Tell me," he said, "how does this weapon work?"

The lights sputtered.

Rick whipped out the .45. He dropped the scroll.

The creature pounced at him.

Rick emptied the clip into the hominid. The creature splatted face-first onto the floor.

"That was easy," Rick said.

Through the portal, torchlight rippled over the floor and walls. Feet slapped on an earthen floor.

"Eh-eh-eh," hominid voices grunted.

Rick shoved the .45 into its holster. The spear he'd removed from the *ka* statue lay on the floor. He grabbed it. The tip looked sharp.

The spear had been created as artwork, not a weapon.

Katy picked up a two-foot-high gold statue from the piles of junk behind her. She wielded it in both hands.

The lights winked out.

Torchlight from the corridor brightened. A creature bobbed down and through the portal into the burial chamber. The male grasped a torch in one hand, a club in the other.

Rick wrapped both hands around the spear.

A man screamed.

Filtered through the corridor, the scream echoed as distant as a cry welling up from the fires of hell.

The creature froze.

In the corridor, his brethren murmured. Kemetian, she recognized that much.

"Did you catch that?" Rick asked.

"Something about the god arriving."

The creature who'd entered the chamber muttered over his shoulder. A voice responded. Shadows writhed in the corridor.

Katy said, "He asked why the god didn't meet them at the sanctuary."

"What sanctuary?"

Switching into Kemetian, she asked the creature, "What sanctuary?"

The creature glowered at her.

In the corridor, his brethren raced past the portal. The creatures no longer grunted. Even their feet met the granite in a hush. Each hominid carried a club or a handaxe, a stone sharpened into a blade. The second creature who darted past the portal paused to jam a torch into a sconce on the corridor's wall.

The creature inside the chamber departed to pursue his brethren.

Rick, knees bent, strode through the portal into the corridor.

Katy picked up the scroll. She tied the linen around it and followed Rick.

The corridor was as spacious as the others they'd seen. Torches roosted in sconces on the wall at six-foot intervals, alternating between the right and left walls. To the right, the corridor dead-ended. The ceiling had collapsed there. Limestone chunks littered the floor of the corridor. Dirt had fallen in on top of the limestone, burying a small table that snuggled against the wall.

To the left, the corridor veered into a 45-degree turn.

The hairy hominids must've gotten into the corridor from above. Whether they'd breached the ceiling or nature had triggered the collapse, the evidence gave no hint.

Rick marched to the left.

Katy trotted after him with the statue in her left hand, the Taurus in her right. The statue's head, that of a ram, sported the sun disk lodged between its horns. Amen-Ra. She was preparing to use the king of the gods as a bludgeon.

"Sorry, little guy," she told the statue, "you're all I've got."

Rick glanced back at her. "What'd you say?"

"Nothing."

Spear in hand, he swerved around the corner. The creatures had lined this passageway with torches too. The corridor slanted left. Rick accelerated, forcing Katy into a run. The passage jogged left again. Rick rounded the bend.

And stopped.

Katy tilted sideways to look around him.

The hairy hominids, five of them, gathered 20 feet ahead where the corridor ended at a doorway. The creatures tarried just inside the threshold, wide eyes fixed on the room beyond, a chamber 20 feet wide by ten feet across. A source of brilliant, bluish light illuminated the chamber from high above the doorway. Limestone rubble covered the chamber's floor. Shards, and chunks the size of coffee tables, lay scattered amid gravel-like debris. On one chunk sprawled the body of a man.

His eyes were wide, unblinking, his arms and legs outstretched. Blood stained the limestone beneath his head. His mouth had fallen open.

The creatures, however, did not stare at the dead man. Their gazes had zoomed in on a target far above the floor.

A voice echoed down. "Find a way across, Doctor, or you will join him."

Katy whispered, "Setesh."

Rick nodded.

"That must be the entrance corridor," she said. "It did collapse."

"And there just happened to be a chamber underneath it?" he said. "No, the builders must've planted explosives in the floor. Pick the wrong button and bam—instant well shaft."

"Well shaft?"

"New Kingdom tombs usually had a deep shaft near the entrance. Nobody knows why."

Bob Hanover's voice resonated in the shaft. "You knew about the door release. Don't you know how to cross the well?"

"This tomb is unlike the others I have seen."

Feet scuffled. Pebbles dribbled down into the shaft.

"Think," Setesh said. "Or die."

"The great god isn't omniscient after all," Bob retorted.

The creatures stirred. They murmured amongst themselves.

A gray creature grunted. The others silenced. The gray male skulked into the chamber.

A man cried out. Katy isolated the word "revered" from the content of the phrase. The man had noticed the creature, one of the species known to the Planners as Revered Ones.

The creature raised his arms, palms up. He kneeled and bowed his head.

Setesh chuckled. The sound multiplied as it echoed down the shaft.

The remaining creatures clumped into the chamber. They lined up behind the gray male, mimicking his posture.

Hairy hominids genuflecting before their god. Jesus, like Setesh needed a *bigger* ego.

"My children," Setesh called to them in ancient Egyptian, "I have come to free you. No longer will you serve flawed gods who value Low Ones more than you. Henceforth you shall serve your true master, lord of all that is and shall be, the perfect one, Setesh."

Rick muttered, "Oh brother."

"Rise," Setesh said, "and help me reach my brother Wesir. The Day of Awakening has come. We cannot allow Wesir to arise, for he will destroy *maat*."

Rick slunk to the doorway. Katy tiptoed behind him. At the threshold, Rick leaned forward, tilting his head up as he inched it through the doorway. One eye clear of the threshold, he stopped.

The gray creature grunted at his companions.

Two creatures stood up. They turned toward the doorway.

The duo shrieked. The others jerked their heads to look at the doorway.

The gray male pointed a stubby finger at Katy. "*Neteret Aset.*"

Voices whispered overhead. A floodlight swooped its brilliance at the doorway. Katy shielded her eyes with her hand.

Setesh switched to English. "That is not Aset, you stupid beast."

Rick shoved Katy out of the doorway. He backed away from the threshold.

In ancient Egyptian, Setesh shouted, "Kill them!"

Rick grasped the spear in both hands. "Run, Katy."

She didn't move.

He glanced at the scroll in her left hand, then her face. "He can't get the Book."

"I won't leave you."

"We've got six bullets, a decorative spear, and a gold statue against five hairy hominids. The best we can do is slow them down."

She clutched the statue until her hand ached.

"Go," he said. "*Please.*"

She offered him the Taurus. He shook his head. She held it out to him again.

He pushed her hand away. "Keep it. Won't help me anyway."

She handed him the statue and ran.

Rick watched Katy until she disappeared around a bend. Her footsteps thumped on the dirt, fading with each step.

He confronted the creatures.

Ten feet from him, two of the beasts fisted their hands. They gnashed their teeth. Muscles bulged in their shoulders. Their eyes smoldered red.

Setesh hollered a Kemetian word at them.

Kill him.

The creatures roared. They hurtled toward Rick.

He stabbed the spear at the nearest creature. The blade grazed the hominid's shoulder. The creature grabbed the spear. Rick pulled. The creature swung the spear, hurling Rick sideways into the doorway. His spine cracked into the limestone.

The creature ripped the spear from Rick's hands.

He kicked the beast's shin. The creature barked. His buddy clamped his hands around Rick's thighs and yanked. Rick's feet flipped out from under him. His head bashed into the floor. Lights burst in his vision.

The creature grabbed him around the neck and winched him off the ground. The monster threw him into the well chamber. He crashed onto a pile of rocks. Something in his pocket dug into his hip.

The gas canister.

He rolled his head to the side. The dead man's eyes stared back at him.

Rick sat up. The creatures had surrounded him. Their voices growled around him.

A voice yelled at the creatures. They silenced.

Rick squinted up the shaft. Setesh smirked down at Rick. He spoke to the creatures.

To Rick, he said, "I told them to crush your skull."

The creatures rushed at Rick.

Katy fled into the burial chamber.

Hide the Book, she must hide the Book and get back to Rick.

Hide it where? She twirled in a circle. Not the sarcophagus. Setesh would definitely think of that. Not in one of the gilded boxes. Too obvious. Not in the burial chamber.

She ran back into the corridor. The torches fluttered in the breeze her movements generated. She couldn't hide the scroll.

Burn the damn thing.

Katy dipped the scroll into the flame of the closest torch. The papyrus ignited. She pulled the scroll away from the torch. The papyrus blackened, crumbled to the floor as ash. She dropped the scroll.

The papyrus rolled out down the corridor. Flames consumed it from both ends.

After the initial few feet, the scroll was blank.

A decoy.

She took off down the corridor, back to Rick.

A man screamed. He stumbled over the edge.

He hit bottom inches from Rick. The man's throat was scorched.

The creatures hesitated.

Another cry pierced the air. In the corridor above, Setesh slithered onto the ledge that bordered both sides of the shaft. Another man fell. He landed belly-up at the chasm's rim. His head lolled to the side, bent backward over the edge.

Setesh wriggled toward the other side. The ledge disintegrated beneath his left foot. He retreated a step.

He shouted at the creatures.

Rick's head throbbed. He couldn't think to translate the order.

The creatures massed in a circle directly under Setesh. Arms outstretched, they linked their hands at the center of the circle.

No. They wouldn't.

Setesh jumped. The creatures caught him.

Rick pushed onto his knees. He struggled to his feet. His left boot slipped on the rubble. He kicked the dead man's hand. The fingers fell open. A box slid out of the dead man's hand.

A box. He'd seen those things before.

Rick nabbed the box weapon. He searched his memory for the moment, two years ago, when he'd seen the Planners use their weapons. They pressed a button.

The weapon had two buttons. One red, one blue.

The creatures lowered Setesh onto the floor. The bastard smirked at Rick.

One of the hominids held his hand behind his back. Setesh argued with creature in ancient Egyptian, their speech too swift for Rick to translate. Slowly, the creature brought out his arm.

The monster held a box weapon. Setesh took the weapon.

The creatures growled at Rick.

Rick aimed the box weapon at Setesh. He hit the red button. Nothing.

Setesh chuckled.

God, he hated that sound.

Setesh pointed his weapon at Rick.

Rick punched the red button again. A green light flashed on the device.

Setesh fired. Rick rolled away as the flash singed the floor where he'd lain.

Rick pushed the blue button. Lightning exploded. The blast bypassed Setesh to scorch a creature's arm. He pounded the button. The creatures swarmed in front of Setesh. Blasts charred their chests, shoulders, necks. Two creatures fell.

The beasts shrieked. They stampeded toward Rick.

He fired. A hominid crumpled.

Lightning from above slew two more. Setesh shot at the overhead attacker.

Rick's head pulsated. His vision blurred. He fired.

The last creature evaded the shot and took off into the corridor.

A familiar voice called from above, "Are you badly hurt?"

Rick stood. His vision had cleared. "I'll live."

He glanced at the doorway. Setesh was gone.

Katy.

She careened around a corner.

A man clenched her arm. He wrenched her to a stop. Her mind needed a second before it registered the face.

Katy tugged her arm. Setesh grasped it tighter. Capturing her other arm, he clutched her close to him.

"Where is the Book?" he demanded.

"I burned it."

He clucked his tongue. "Lies earn you nothing."

She rammed her knee into his groin. As he doubled over, she twisted free of him.

Katy bolted down the corridor, around the bend that preceded the doorway.

Rick caught her in his arms. Breaths gasped from her. She hugged him fiercely.

He pushed her away. "Where's Setesh?"

"Burial chamber, I'd say."

Taking the Taurus from her, he strode down the corridor toward the burial chamber. They passed a pile of ash interspersed with blank fragments of papyrus. At the portal to the burial chamber, Rick halted.

Clattering issued from within the chamber.

Rick ducked down and charged through the portal. Katy hurried through behind him. Once inside, Rick sprang to full height. He leveled the Taurus at Setesh.

The man bent over the stacks of boxes rifling through the contents of one. The statue lay face-down on the floor. In his right hand, Setesh held a scrap of papyrus, blank and scorched.

"Back up," Rick said, "and keep your hands where I can see them."

Setesh crumpled the papyrus. He pitched it at Rick.

"If you kill me," Setesh said, "my men will destroy you. My vessel waits outside to kill anyone attempting to flee the tomb."

"You're assuming I care," Rick said.

"Give me the Book," said Setesh, "and perhaps I will spare you."

"Sorry."

Setesh shrugged. "If you wish to die, I shall accommodate you."

He flicked his wrist.

A dark blur flew through the portal.

The creature tackled Rick, knocking him face-first onto the floor. The Taurus collided with the far wall, bounced onto the floor.

Setesh whisked out his box weapon.

The creature flipped Rick onto his back. Rick pulled the gas canister out of his pocket.

Katy fired at Setesh. The bullet walloped him in the shoulder. He dropped his weapon.

Rick sprayed the gas into the creature's nostrils. The beast blinked. Rick squirted him a second time. The gas spluttered. The creature's eyes rolled back into his head.

The hominid collapsed. Rick crawled out from under the unconscious beast.

Another creature barreled through the portal.

Katy booted the .45 toward Rick. He reached for the gun. The creature slugged him in the jaw. Rick pressed down on the canister. Nothing came out. The creature clouted him again. Rick went slack. His eyes closed.

Katy dove for the gun. Setesh flopped on top of her. She punched her elbow backward into his jaw. He grasped her head, his fingers over her mouth and nose. She bit him.

Howling, he let go. She cuffed him in the gut with her elbow. He stiffened. She wiggled out from under him.

The hairy hominid bent over Rick.

Katy reached for the gun. Her fingers closed around the grip.

Setesh clawed at her ankles. She kicked him, grasped the Taurus, and fired at the creature.

The beast dodged the shot. The bullet hit the wall.

Setesh ran for the portal. Katy fired at him. The bullet grazed his arm. He disappeared into the corridor.

The creature jumped up. He slung Rick over one shoulder.

Katy aimed for the head and tensed her finger to fire. The creature kicked her square in the gut. She flew backward. Her finger jerked, pulling the trigger. The bullet sheered a slice out of the ceiling. She splashed down in the water. Her head submerged. She twisted around in the water. Her arm bumped the stairs. She pawed at the steps, caught hold of one, and hefted herself out of the water.

The creature scampered out of the chamber with Rick over his shoulder.

Katy vaulted up the stairs, sped into the corridor. Empty. She ran to the hole in the ceiling, mounted the table, and poked her head through the hole. Nothing. Not even the sound of footfalls receding.

Hopping down, she raced back to the well shaft. Six bodies, two human and four hairy hominid, lay there. No Setesh. No Rick.

She fell onto her knees. Her fingers slackened. The Taurus slid onto the floor. Tears stung her eyes as she sucked in a breath. Her mind went numb. The image of the creature hauling Rick away repeated in her mind like a record skipping.

No, goddammit, *no*.

"How pitiful," a voice said.

She looked up at Setesh.

He shook his head. "You have lost your will."

He held a small package in his left hand.

"The beasts are quite loyal to me," Setesh said. "They have told me of the sanctuary."

He lobbed the package into the shaft. It plopped onto the floor a foot from Katy. A cream-colored block of clay. Strapped to the clay, a digital timer counted down the seconds. Not clay. Explosives.

She stared at the timer. 50. 49. 48.

"I believe you are familiar," Setesh said, "with this substance's effects."

"Go to hell," Katy said.

He knelt at the chasm's edge. "I suggest you pray for Wesir to guide you into the afterlife."

Rising, he walked away toward the tomb's entrance. His footsteps waned.

The timer counted. 38. 37.

Katy fled the shaft, down the corridor, to the collapsed ceiling. She pulled herself up through the hole. Seated in the earthen passage with her legs hanging through the hole, she froze.

A package of explosives sat on the floor several yards from the hole.

Its timer read 25, 24, 23.

She leaped through the hole, running into the burial chamber.

In her mind, the timer counted down. 14, 13, 12, 11.

Across the chamber to the farthest corner. Squeeze between the sarcophagus and the wall. On her knees, she bent her head down with hands linked over the back of her head.

The explosion rocked the walls.

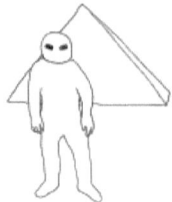

CHAPTER THIRTEEN

The earth shivered. An explosion rumbled through the mountain.

A cloud spurted from the tomb's mouth.

No one exited the tomb. No one had entered it either. Who set off the explosion?

Warner hunkered across the crevasse from the entrance. Aset had shut off the floodlight, which she cupped in her left hand while in the right she grasped a box weapon. They'd shot both of Setesh's men before the "great god" threw himself into the shaft. The guards remained unconscious.

Setesh had survived his leap, thanks to the hairy hominids. If he'd set off the explosion, how did he escape? Had he escaped?

The man would not trap himself inside the tomb.

Warner asked Aset, "Do your tombs have back entrances?"

"None I have seen did. However, this tomb is quite unusual."

"Then it might have another entrance." Warner stood up. "We must find it."

"How?" she asked.

"The creatures will know. Somehow they broke into the tomb."

"You intend for me to question them."

He marched across the crevasse to the tomb's door with Aset close behind him.

"I intend," he said, "to wring the knowledge from them by any means necessary."

She laid a hand on his arm. "They may be dead."

He shook off her hand.

Setesh had set off an explosive within the entrance corridor of the tomb. Yet he hadn't left the tomb, and when last Warner saw him he had been at the bottom of the 20-foot shaft. Setesh had found another entry into the corridor. Another entry meant another network of corridors.

A back exit.

The slab door rested on its face. He swiped the floodlight from Aset's hand. Switching it on, he clambered over the slab into the corridor. Debris cluttered the floor. He offered his hand to Aset. When she took it, he helped her over the slab and into the corridor.

The floodlight illuminated the corridor in false daylight. The entrance had suffered little damage. The debris, ejected by the explosion, had apparently funneled through the corridor to the entrance. They trotted through the sloping corridor, down the stairs, through a gateway, down the second corridor on whose walls artists had engraved inscriptions. Fifteen minutes earlier, most of the reliefs had boasted vivid paint. The explosion had scoured it away until slivers remained, dulled by dust.

A gateway channeled them into a third corridor, where niches along both walls accommodated statues. Warner trod past the statues. Ahead, past a third gateway, the corridor had collapsed.

Warner stopped.

Aset tugged his sleeve.

He glanced at her.

She pointed at a statue. It showed a man holding a scroll to his chest. The explosion had dislodged the statue from the wall, forcing its right half out from the wall at an angle. A six-inch gap separated the statue from the wall.

Warner shined the floodlight at the statue. The light plunged into the gap.

As he handed Aset the light, he crouched beside the statue. A semi-circular gouge marked the floor. The explosion hadn't jarred the statue out of position. Someone had swung it open like a door. He thrust his arm through the gap. The statue hid a cavity, perhaps a chamber. Or a corridor.

Leaning against the wall, he shoved the statue with both hands and one foot. The statue scraped across the floor an inch. He shoved harder. The statue scraped another four inches. He squeezed through the gap.

Aset squirmed through after him.

The floodlight inundated the cavity. It was a corridor. Torches affixed to the walls smoldered. The explosion must've snuffed them out.

To the left, further into the caves, a clapping started. He had heard a similar noise before, when hairy hominids knocked wood blocks together to communicate. Normally, they used the sound to triangulate their prey's position.

To the right, outside the statue door, wood rapped on wood.

The walls had stopped shaking. The debris had settled.

Katy clambered out of the corner. The chamber was dark. She shuddered.

The offering jars contained wine. Alcohol burned. If she could find them, she might have some light. She had the magnesium block in her pocket. She always carried it. So, if she found the jars, she had the means to start a fire.

The jars had been on the offering table. Rick moved them when he uncovered the portal. Moved them where?

Think. He picked up the jars and put them...

Beside the sarcophagus.

She thrust a hand out to her left. Her fingertips touched the wall. Good. Inching forward on her knees, she located the flooded chasm. From there, she turned 90 degrees right and crept on all fours toward the sarcophagus. Her hands bumped the lid, which still rested at an angle. She felt her way leftward along the lid. At its end, she crawled forward. Her head knocked into the sarcophagus' corner. She sat back on her heels.

With both hands, she explored the floor. When she found nothing, she crawled forward, felt around, crawled forward, felt around some more. She found a jar. On her knees, she pried the lid from the jar and dipped her finger inside. The liquid chilled her skin.

With the jar under one arm, she crawled sideways. Her free hand she held outstretched, like a cockroach feeling its way with its antennae. Her hand banged into the legs of the *ka* statue. She slid her hand down the statue's legs, over its hips, up the torso to the shoulders. The linen had gotten wrapped around the statue's neck when it fell. She followed the shoulder down to the arm and out onto the hand. The torch remained lodged between the fingers, though it had tilted, its handle on the verge of slipping from its perch.

Katy pulled out the torch and unwound the linen from the statue's neck. After wrapping the linen around the torch, she knotted the fabric. From the jar, she poured a liberal amount of wine over the linen, then dug the magnesium block out of her pocket.

A knife, she needed a knife.

She didn't have one.

Tears burned her eyes. She wiped them away. No crying.

You have lost your will.

Like hell she had. She might be trapped in a tomb hundreds of feet underground, with no light and limited air, but she'd be damned if she'd concede.

Okay, she needed metal.

The Taurus. She felt for the holster and found the revolver inside it. She must've picked it up without thinking about it before she fled the well shaft.

She held the Taurus and the magnesium block over the linen. She flipped the magnesium block to its flint side. When she struck the Taurus' barrel against the flint, a spark flitted off the stone. She struck the gun against the flint again, again, again, again.

A spark ignited the alcohol. A flame, tiny at first, gradually engulfed the linen. The torchlight chased the blackness from the chamber.

Debris blocked the portal to the corridor. Loose earth mixed with chunks of limestone and granite spilled from the blockage into the chamber. The slide had diverged around the *ka* statue into two slumps. A pair of hairy thighs protruded from beneath the slide.

The hairy hominid Rick had gassed.

276

Rick. Tears brimmed in her eyes. She blinked them away. No time for that.

She took a deep breath. The musty scent of earth filled her nostrils. Exhaling, she climbed the debris pile to make sure it completely blocked the portal. It did.

The Planners were smart. They would've considered the possibility the corridor might collapse. Earthquakes and floods had destroyed tombs in the Valley of the Kings. Surely the Planners had included escape routes. The front door looked like it hadn't been opened for thousands of years. Another route existed. She had no idea how to find it. If she could drain the chasm, she might get out that way and locate a hidden passageway branching off from the main corridors. Great, she had no idea how to drain the chasm either. She needed help.

From someone who knew the Planners' architecture.

She scrambled down the debris pile, righted the statue, and wedged the torch in the statue's hand. The stool she'd used to get into the sarcophagus before had splintered under the weight a limestone hunk from the ceiling. Lugging a big chest toward the sarcophagus, she mounted the box. The coffin rested in the sarcophagus as it had before, though the blast had showered limestone bits over the gold.

Give him life, it said. Instructions for setting Osiris free?

She looked at the *ka* statue. She'd noticed the gold chain around its neck earlier. When she removed the linen, however, she'd revealed an amulet that hung on the chain. The amulet was an *ankh*, the symbol for life.

Give him life.

Katy jumped off the chest. She ran to the statue, tore the *ankh* from its neck, and charged back to the sarcophagus. She hopped onto the chest. The face on the coffin had its mouth open. She'd taken the black gap for paint. Bending over the sarcophagus, she probed the mouth with her finger. The mouth was a slot. She inserted the *ankh* into the slot, straight end first. The amulet slid in a couple inches. She tried turning the amulet like a key, pushing it like a button, but nothing happened. She flipped the *ankh* over, this time inserting its looped end first.

The *ankh* slid into the slot. An inch of its straight end stuck out from the slot. Above the slot, a two-inch square panel whooshed open. The cavity hosted a shiny pad etched with a line drawing of a thumb.

Katy placed her thumb on the pad. Something pricked her skin. She recoiled. A droplet of blood oozed from her thumb pad.

The coffin clicked.

Steam hissed out the sides. The air chilled her hand. Not steam.

The coffin buzzed. She stumbled off the chest, onto the floor.

The frozen mist roiled up from the sarcophagus. The buzzing quieted. The mist fizzed from the sarcophagus.

The hissing stopped. The mist dispersed.

Thunk.

She tiptoed toward the sarcophagus, climbed onto the chest. A chill washed over her. She leaned over the sarcophagus. Though it remained closed, the coffin's lid had popped up an inch. She slipped her fingers under the edge, into the gap between the lid and the base. Cold air numbed her fingers. She lifted the lid. It rotated up on hinges.

Inside the coffin, swaddled in bandages with arms crossed over his chest, lay Osiris. Wesir. Whatever.

Her eyes burned. She had stopped blinking.

Katy shut her eyes. She inhaled deeply, slowly. Her hands trembled.

Opening her eyes, she stared at the mummy. No, he was not a mummy, because he had neither died nor been mummified. The bandages must protect him from the whatever-it-was that kept him frozen. She poked his arm. The flesh gave under the pressure. The bandages shrouded his entire body.

His chest heaved.

She jumped. Her foot slipped off the chest. She grabbed the sarcophagus. For a moment she hung there gasping. Then she pulled herself up.

Inside the coffin, Wesir breathed. His fingers waggled.

She peeled the bandages from his face. His eyelids remained closed, though the eyes themselves jiggled beneath the lids. She untied the linen strip which bound his hands together over his chest. The embalmers had wrapped each limb, each finger, separately.

Her heart revved like a racecar's engine. Despite the chill the coffin gave off, sweat trickled down her temples. She unwrapped the outer bandages from his legs. More bandages swathed each leg and toe. Was he wearing clothes underneath the bandages?

A blush heated her cheeks. Leave the bandages. He could move. She had freed him enough for that.

Katy straightened, hands gripping the sarcophagus.

Wesir's eyelids fluttered.

The stone dug into her fingers. She loosened her grip. Her ears rang. She bit her lip and tried to breathe normally. Didn't work.

He opened his eyes a smidgen. He squeezed them shut. As he opened them wider, revealing bloodshot blue eyes, he rolled his eyes left and right, up and down. His gaze crossed hers.

She attempted a smile. The effort twitched her lips.

She said, "Rise and shine."

He licked his lips. He raised an arm toward her. His arm quivered.

"Aset," he rasped.

"No." She leaned into the sarcophagus. "My name is Katy."

He squinted at her. His eyes watered.

Of course he didn't understand her. She had spoken English.

She repeated the phrase in his language.

He struggled to raise his head. She slid her hand under his head and lifted. He flailed a hand at the sarcophagus wall. She grasped both his hands. He tightened his fingers around her hands. She pulled him into a sitting position.

"Out," he said, in old Kemetian, the language the Planners had bequeathed to the Egyptians.

She spoke to him in the same tongue. "You want to get out of the sarcophagus."

"Yes." His voice cracked. He coughed. "Drink."

She helped him climb out of the sarcophagus. Seated on the chest, he slouched against the sarcophagus. He swallowed, wincing.

Thirsty, he was thirsty.

The wine jars sat beside the sarcophagus. Could you drink 12,000-year-old wine? The water that had flooded the chasm looked okay. Katy dug through the funerary equipment in search of a cup. She found an alabaster goblet, which she dunked into the water. She gave Wesir the cup. He sipped the water.

Katy hunched near the *ka* statue, hands in her pants pockets. The statue's face mimicked Wesir's. She shuffled away from the statue toward the flooded chasm.

Wesir sat up. He set the goblet on the floor.

"You are as beautiful as Aset," he said.

As color seeped into his skin, he rose from the chest. He towered over her, about the same height as Rick. Wesir stretched and yawned.

Rick's face flashed in her mind.

Her stomach lurched. The room swayed. She stumbled forward.

Wesir grasped her upper arm.

Steady again, she shrugged off his hand.

"I am indebted to you," he said, "for awakening me."

Each time he spoke, her skin prickled. She understood his words as easily as if he spoke English. Her grasp of the language had advanced too quickly for her to deny Rick's assertions anymore. She must have a genetic predisposition to learning the language of the ancient Planners.

She must be one of them.

The coffin had taken a sample of her blood before it unlocked for her. Testing her DNA?

The bandages she'd unwrapped from Wesir's head draped around his neck. While he spoke, he unraveled the linen from his shoulders.

"The coffin took a blood sample," she said, "before it would release its lock. You know anything about that?"

Wesir disposed of the linen in the sarcophagus. "While the embalmers prepared me for *mut ankh*, Anpu informed me of Geb's plan. Aset's father wished for us to be reunited. He installed my coffin with a device which samples the life code of whomever attempts to open it. Only Aset's code could unlock my coffin. After she awakened me, we would exile ourselves to another land."

"One of the cultures you befriended during your travels."

"Yes."

Life code. Sounded like DNA to her.

Wesir regarded Katy, his blue eyes radiant as jewels.

Her mouth had gone dry. Her throat too.

She said, "I may be related to you and Aset."

"Yes."

279

He took a step toward her.

She backed up to the edge of the chasm. Her heel knocked a pebble into the water. Splunk.

"If Aset was in mut ankh too," she said, "how did Geb think she could reach you?"

"He intended to wait one year, until the people had forgotten the tumult which ended my reign. Then he would awaken Aset, tell her where to find me, and we would be reunited."

"His plan failed."

Wesir nodded. He unwound the bandages from his upper chest. The torchlight shimmered bronze on his bare skin.

Katy held up her hands. "Whoa, Mister Godiva, in this millennium we cover our bodies in the presence of others."

He crinkled his forehead.

She'd spoken English. He had no clue what she'd said.

Katy repeated her phrase in ancient Egyptian—ancient Kemetian, really—using the nearest translation she could think of for the colloquialism.

Wesir recommenced disrobing. "I am clothed beneath the bandages."

"Oh." She folded her arms over her chest. "Good."

As he stripped off the bandages around his waist, the linen unveiled a wide belt, fastened by a buckle inscribed with his cartouche. The belt attached to a linen kilt. Once he'd unwrapped his entire body, bare feet and all, he jettisoned the bandages into the sarcophagus with the others.

His brown hair was cropped short. The redness had cleared from his blue eyes.

He scratched his scalp, rubbed his neck.

Katy tapped her foot on the floor. "I was hoping you knew the secret way out."

"Secret way?"

"You are a Planner. Your friends built this tomb."

He glanced at the rubble piled in the doorway. The flooded chasm. Katy.

She said, "Your brother destroyed the only doorway to this chamber. I hoped you had an insight on how to drain the water from the chasm."

"I do not."

"Then we slowly suffocate."

She strolled to the sarcophagus.

He tracked her movements with his gaze

Katy said, "Aset told me the Book of Thoth is my birthright."

He bounded two steps toward her, eyes wide, mouth ajar. "Aset lives?"

"Yes." The room gyrated. She clutched the sarcophagus. "Your friends awakened Setesh as well. He is about to find the Book."

Wesir smiled faintly. "You will not give in so easily, for you are the daughter of our *ka*. Aset never yielded, and neither shall you."

Katy slanted her head toward him. She gazed at him sideways.

Her face tingled. Her ears rang. Her vision darkened. Too much information too fast. Her CPU, a.k.a. her brain, threatened to crash from the overload.

Wesir leaned back against the sarcophagus.

Katy huddled by the debris pile, hands in her pockets. She explained the situation to him.

Standing in the presence of a god felt strange. But he wasn't a god after all, for the ancient Egyptians who came after him had elevated him to that status. She still felt weird standing there with, if not a god, at least a man who had been born 7,000 years before civilization began. According to the dogma. Which she rejected.

She was getting a headache. She flopped onto her butt on the debris pile.

"You must have seen tombs before," she said. "Is there another way out?"

"Tombs have no need of other ways out."

"But Geb wanted Aset to find you."

"She would have come through the entrance, as you did."

"Right." Katy kicked the debris, stumbled backward. "I have to find Rick."

The creature absconding with Rick. Setesh trying to rearrange her molecules with explosives. If Setesh got his grimy claws on the Book, the world would suffer. For a long, long time.

Wesir was right. She couldn't give up. For Rick, for the world, she had to get up off her butt.

She stood. "I will find another way out."

Wesir smiled at her—that same smile she'd seen on Aset's face. The one that irritated her beyond irritation.

She sensed Rick was alive, out there, in the hominid tunnels or above the surface. Wherever the beast had taken him, he breathed. He lived.

A way existed. A back door. A side door. Any kind of door or hole or crack through which she could escape. If she ever got out of the burial chamber.

She punted a limestone lump into the chasm. Sploosh.

"Goddammit," she said, "there has to be a way out of here."

Wesir scrunched his forehead. "Gaw-dam-it?"

She'd slipped into English.

"Never mind," she said.

English again. Forget about it. If her great, great, great-times-50 grandfather got a tad confused, he'd have to deal with it. Alone.

Katy marched to the chasm. The water was dark. Thirty feet separated her from the mural chamber on the other side.

She gulped in enough air to fill her lungs.

Then she jumped in.

Light. Blinding. In his eyes.

The blur of brilliance resolved into a disk of light that glowed within a dark crescent. Along one side of the crescent's rim, colored lights twinkled.

Rick blinked. That was no crescent. A disk-shaped craft hovered 500 feet overhead, its rim extending past his head. The cliffs concealed most of the craft, which created the illusion of a crescent-shaped object. He lay on his back inside a ravine. The walls, 20 feet apart, curved around him in an oval. A large boulder shaped like a camel's back blocked the entrance to the ravine. Or the exit. His head throbbed, and he moved to rub his temples. A rope around his neck dug into his flesh. His hands were tied behind his back. The cords that bound his hands were tied to the ones that shackled his feet, as well as to a noose that enclosed his neck. When he moved his hands or feet, the noose choked him.

Outside the ravine, voices resounded. Through the foot-wide breaks on either side of the camel rock he spotted figures, hairy and hairless.

He twisted his head to the side. Pain lanced through his jaw where the creature had slugged him. He grimaced. Behind him, something growled.

Rick sniffed. Ah, the aroma of rotted flesh in the evening.

Bare feet whapped on the dirt. The creature's shadow enveloped him before he could see its hairy bulk bent over him.

The craft's light bleached the creature's hair. He glared down at Rick, his lips fluttering as he growled. Spittle drizzled on Rick's face.

Rick screwed up his face. "Thanks a lot."

The beast grasped him under his arms and hefted him off the ground. Slinging Rick over his shoulder, the creature plodded toward the camel rock.

Outside the ravine, a familiar voice echoed. Bob Hanover said, "Kill me now, you daft fiend, I won't help you anymore."

Setesh's chuckle ricocheted off the cliffs. "I no longer need your help, Doctor."

"So kill me and get it over with."

"As you wish."

The creature bypassed the camel rock. The full brilliance of the craft assaulted Rick's eyes. He squinted until his eyes had adjusted. The hominid stormed through a line of Setesh's men, who scattered to the sides. The creature dumped Rick on the ground 25 feet from Setesh.

Box weapon in hand, Setesh looked over his shoulder at Rick. His weapon was aimed at Bob Hanover, who sat a few feet away with knees drawn up to his chest, arms locked around his knees. He looked ashen.

Setesh spoke to the creature.

"*Hetep*," the hominid replied, gesturing at Rick.

Offering. The creature was making an offering of Rick, to placate the god.

"Where's Dad?" Rick asked.

Bob squirmed. "I think—I think he's dead."

Mounds rose from the sands around them. For a second, Rick expected cobras to burst from the mounds. What emerged, however, could kill a man faster than any snake.

A dozen hairy hominids shook the sand from their bodies.

The creatures had formed a circle around them. Setesh chastised the creature who'd offered up Rick. The creature bowed his head.

Goosebumps prickled Rick's skin. His scalp tingled as if electricity had surged over him.

Setesh chuckled at the creature. "Yes, the Day of Awakening has come. But I shall awaken the power of the Book, not the body of my brother."

The creature grunted his response through bared teeth. "You must. For Atum."

"I do not obey animals. You shall obey me or die."

The creature growled.

Rick glanced around. "Katy?"

"She's not here," Bob said. "Setesh left her in the tomb."

In the tomb. Rousing as the hairy hominid hurtled through the tunnels. Upside down, suspended down the creature's back, he'd heard thunder. Close enough to jangle his bones.

Not thunder. An explosion.

Katy…

The creature muttered, "Reward us."

"For what?" Setesh chided.

"We guard. In your name."

"I did not ask that of you."

The creature's eyes ignited red. "Reward us. Or we hide Book."

"Where is the Book?" Setesh demanded.

The creature kept mum. Setesh glowered at the hominid. The creature failed to cringe at the ire of his god.

Setesh swapped his attention onto Rick. "Where is the Book hidden?"

"Ask Thoth."

"Your wife may yet live inside the tomb," said Setesh. "I will help you reach her. If you give me the Book."

"And after that, you'll kill us both. Great deal."

Setesh clenched his fists. *Tell me.*

A tremor initiated in Setesh's hands. The vibrations leached up his arms, through his shoulders, into his neck. As the tremor chattered his teeth, he bulged his eyes.

Setesh roared. "Tell me!"

To the black creature, Rick said in Kemetian, "He is not your god. If he were, he could turn the sand into water. Gods have power over all the elements."

The creature squinted at Setesh. "Make water."

"You will obey me," Setesh shouted, "and kill him!"

The creature didn't move. "Make water."

Setesh raised his box weapon and fired it at the creature. The shot singed the hominid's chest. The creature howled.

The hominid pointed a finger at Setesh. "False god."

A round of growls erupted in surround sound.

Setesh's men pulled out their weapons. The creatures' eyes burned red. Growls reverberated in their chests.

The creatures lunged at Setesh and his men. The Planners fired at the creatures. Some fell. Others, enraged by the pain, leaped onto the men. The air reeked of scorched hair and flesh. The hairy hominids beat the humans with their fists, bit the men's arms and hands. Men screamed. Shots coruscated. Hominids shrieked.

Bob stooped over Rick's feet. He fought with the knots that secured the cord.

Creatures knocked men to the ground, straddling them. The beasts roared like gorillas, thumped their chests, and slammed their fists into the men's ribs. Cries gurgled from the men's throats.

The men went limp.

Setesh hunched amid the carnage. He had lost his weapon.

Bob, fingers bloodied, undid the cord around Rick's feet.

The creatures circled around Setesh. They snarled.

Rick jumped onto his feet. He told Bob, "Run."

Bob hesitated. He reached for the cord around Rick's hands.

Beneath the snarls and apelike cries, Rick heard Setesh yell, "Fire! Kill them all."

Overhead, the craft buzzed.

Rick shook off Bob's hands. "No time, *run.*"

Bob bolted. Rick ran after him. His hands jerked. The noose cut into his throat. He choked and kept running.

Creatures shrieked.

Rick glanced back.

A beam lanced down from the craft. The weapon buzzed as it fired, hitting one creature after another. More powerful than the hand weapons, the beam pierced the creature's chests straight through their backs and out the other side. Smoke, rather than blood, seeped from the wounds. The beasts crumpled.

When the last creature had fallen, Setesh barked an order into his communication device. The craft buzzed.

The beam shot down at Rick.

Shockwaves undulated through the water.

Katy sprang out of the chasm. She slapped her hands on the chasm's lip and pulled herself up onto the floor of the chamber.

Panting, she combed wet hair from her face with her hands.

A single light flickered from the ceiling. Rubble dammed half the doorway's height. Through the three-foot gap, in the first chamber of murals, lights hummed and sputtered.

Wesir launched out of the water onto the floor. He landed flat on his belly, vaulting onto his feet.

Blasts rattled the mountain.

"We have to get out of here," Katy said. "Rick's in trouble."

"Even if we discover a doorway, we could not reach him in time."

"We *will.*"

She scrambled up the debris pile and through the gap.

Rick sat up. The rope pinched his throat. He threw himself up and onto his knees. Pain knifed through his leg. His knees gave. He collapsed onto his buttocks. As the rope tautened, he dropped onto his back.

Setesh halted a dozen yards away.

"I will find the Book," Setesh said. "You will not live to stop me."

"Katy burned the Book."

"Thoth boasted that he recorded all the knowledge of our people, all our power, in his book. The scroll she destroyed contained nothing."

"Maybe that should tell you something."

"You would be dead now if I wished it. Do you think my men have missed you with each shot through incompetence?" Setesh prowled closer. "I ordered they should wound you."

Rick lifted his head to glare at Setesh. The rope choked him. His wheezed.

Three yards from Rick, Setesh slipped a hand into his back pocket. He pulled out a switchblade.

He flicked open the blade. "Without the Book I can still summon the powers of chaos. I do, however, require a human sacrifice."

"You're insane," Rick croaked.

He rolled onto his side, pushed onto his knees. Though pain seared his leg, and the rope bit into his neck, he stood up.

A wind gusted past them, churning up a sand devil.

Setesh chanted in Kemetian.

Rick tried to swing his arms out in front of him. The cord yanked. The noose rasped against his throat, gagging him. He relaxed his arms. The noose slackened.

Setesh rushed at Rick. His chants escalated into cries as he kicked Rick's wounded thigh. Lights sparked in Rick's vision. He bashed his skull into Setesh's.

Setesh staggered backward.

Rick charged at Setesh. He rammed his head into Setesh's gut. He swung his head up under Setesh's jaw.

Setesh grunted. He dropped onto his knees panting.

Rick kicked at him. Setesh caught Rick's boot and thrust him backward. Rick stumbled, fell onto his butt. His hands got caught under his buttocks, wrenching the noose. The cord constricted around his neck. He freed his hands but the noose stayed tight. He raised his hands high behind his back.

The noose slackened.

Setesh dove at him.

Rick rolled out of the way. Setesh hit the ground on his stomach. Rick booted him in the head. An "uh!" exploded from Setesh. Rick belly-crawled away from him.

Setesh raised onto all fours. He shook sand from his head.

On his feet now, limping and wheezing, Rick hobbled toward the crevasse. Running away like a rabbit. He might find a rock to cut himself free so he wouldn't have to run.

Behind him, Setesh called, "You cannot escape a god."

Rick dodged the camel rock.

A man jumped out in front of him.

Chin waggled a finger at Rick. "Naughty, naughty."

Wesir bounded up the stairs. His bare feet spanked the floor.

"Wait!" Katy called. "The corridor is—"

He jerked to a halt, teetering on the precipice.

Scaling the stairs after him, Katy said, "The corridor is collapsed."

"I am aware."

The well shaft stretched 20 feet across. The lights spluttered, whipping shadows across the gap and onto the corridor beyond.

On the right-hand side of the shaft, a ledge skirted the gulf. The shelf, a foot wide at the extremities, narrowed to half that at its midpoint. From that point, the ledge widened again as it approached the opposite side.

Wesir climbed onto the ledge.

Katy mounted the shelf behind him. They crept across the shaft, backs flat against the wall, toes pointed at a 45-degree angle to their bodies. Rick would say Wesir was just like her. Reckless. Bullheaded. He'd be right too.

Rick. She stumbled, twisted, tipped over the edge.

Wesir grabbed her arm. He pulled her back onto the ledge.

"Thanks," she said.

They inched along the shelf. Their toes stuck out over the edge.

Wesir leaped into the corridor. He took Katy's hand to support her as she jumped off the ledge into the corridor.

Up the steep passage they ran, through the gateway, into the corridor of statues. Isis' head lay on the floor. Her decapitated body listed inside its niche. Katy hopped over the head.

Wesir had stopped in front of the statue of a man holding a scroll.

"Djehuty," he said.

The statue protruded from the wall about six inches. A draft emanated from the breach.

Wesir squeezed through the gap. Katy followed him through, into a corridor darker than the night outside.

Deeper into the corridor, a blue white light punctured the darkness

Katy ripped the Taurus from its holster. She scampered down the corridor. Her boots clip-clopped on the floor. She raised the gun in front of her.

The light swept toward her. Its brilliance stunned her, and she froze.

The light diverted to the wall. As the starbursts cleared from her vision, she aimed the Taurus at the figure who wielded the floodlight.

Relief ironed the wrinkles from Aset's face.

Katy lowered the Taurus. "Jesus, you scared me."

"I am sor—" Her face lit up as if a bulb inside her head had switched on. "Wesir."

Aset rushed to her husband. He swept her up in his arms and kissed her. When he set her down, she looped her arms around his waist. Tear tracks glistened on her cheeks. Wesir had enfolded both arms around her.

Behind the spot Aset had vacated, Warner stood stiff and stoic. He looked at Katy.

His lips twitched. Almost a smile. "We thought you might be dead."

"Glad to see you too," Katy replied. "But we have to find Rick. I think Setesh has him."

With a brusque nod, Warner led them down the corridor, around a corner, down another corridor that extended deep into the mountain. The floor inclined. They reached a dead-end.

Warner gestured at a the wall. Aset aimed the floodlight where he'd pointed. A slab as large as the one that sealed the tomb's entrance had pivoted aside to expose a portal.

Warner walked through the portal. Katy traipsed after him with Aset and Wesir behind her. Fifty feet down the passageway, they came to a pile of rubble where the ceiling had collapsed. The pile filled one-fourth of the passage's height, leaving a two-foot gap at the top.

Warner clambered up the pile.

Katy crawled after him. Once she'd wriggled over the rubble, Warner helped her hop over limestone shards that littered the passageway. Past the collapse, the corridor remained intact.

Twenty feet away, a hairy hominid loitered. The creature grunted.

Katy tore the Taurus from its holster. She leveled the gun at the creature.

Aset directed the spotlight at the creature. Katy saw the gray hairs that peppered the hominid's coat. Beset.

Katy holstered the gun.

"She is our ally," Warner said. "She convinced the others, the few who remain, that we mean no harm. She knows where Setesh took Rick."

The creature reeled 180 degrees. She loped down the corridor away from them.

Katy galloped after her.

Behind Rick, Setesh's footsteps crunched.

Chin bowed his head to the bogus deity. The traitor glanced up at Rick. A sneer warped his face into an ugly expression.

Setesh seized the rope behind Rick's back and yanked it down.

Rick winced. He gulped back a cry.

"My lord," Chin said, "I found the sanctuary where the Revered Ones hid the Book."

"Excellent." Setesh leaned close to whisper in Rick's ear. "I have no more use for you."

Setesh raised the switchblade to Rick's throat.

Rick bit Setesh's hand. Setesh howled. His fingers stiffened.

Chin punched Rick in the gut. Rick bit down harder on Setesh's hand. The tang of blood seeped into his mouth.

Setesh dropped the knife.

Chin ratcheted his hand back for another blow.

Rick drove his knee into Chin's groin. The man lurched backward.

Rick spun around and kicked at Setesh.

The man darted sideways.

Rick's hands yanked the noose. The rope choked him. He raised his hands high behind his back. The noose refused to loosen. He jerked his hands higher. His shoulders blades pinched a nerve. Pain shot up his neck. He fell onto his knees.

Gagging, he collapsed onto his side.

Setesh bent over Rick. He placed one foot on Rick's side, just below the ribs. His boot heel jabbed into Rick's gut. Setesh picked up the knife.

Whomp! Setesh jerked. The knife slipped from his fingers.

Crack. Setesh jerked again. As he snatched up the knife, he whirled around.

Rick rolled over.

A head bobbed up from behind the camel rock like a prairie dog popping out of its burrow. Bob launched a rock at Setesh and ducked back behind the rock.

Setesh dodged the rock. It sailed toward Rick's head. He twisted sideways to evade it, and the noose cinched tight around his neck. The rock smacked into the ground above Rick's head.

Bob popped up. He cranked his arm backward to lob another stone.

Chin tackled Bob.

The noose strangled Rick. He gasped and gurgled. Darkness spotted his vision.

On his knees, Setesh straddled Rick.

"Go ahead," Rick croaked, "kill me. Katy will make sure you go to hell."

Setesh sneered. "No woman can stop me."

He sliced the knife downward.

A gunshot boomed through the cleft. Setesh froze. His eyes bulged. His face blanched. Blood hemorrhaged from his chest.

Footsteps crackled behind Rick's head.

"This woman can," Katy said.

The craft shed the light of ten suns on the ravine.

Katy fired three shots.

The first socked Setesh in the chest. His fingers opened and the knife tumbled from his grasp. The second shot slammed into his gut. He gaped at the blood on his chest. The third shot perforated his heart.

Legs bent under him, he slumped onto his back.

Rick pawed at the cord around his neck.

Katy flew across the ravine toward him. As she dropped onto her knees beside him, she snatched up the knife Setesh had dropped. She cut the cord. Rick pushed up onto his elbows. While she helped him sit, she snapped the cord around his wrists.

Between gasps, he said, "Help Bob."

She glanced around the cleft. "Taken care of."

Warner jumped to his feet behind the boulder. He hauled Chin up with him. The traitor looked dazed.

Bob rose from behind the boulder. Wesir and Aset lingered a few feet behind them.

Katy brushed dirt from Rick's face. He managed a weak smile.

The cord had scraped a red line into his neck. The thigh of his left pant leg was scorched. She touched the burn. He flinched.

"It's nothing." He glanced at Wesir. "Leave it to you to dig up a half-naked man."

"I didn't dig him up, I defrosted him."

Rick propped himself up on one arm. Katy took his face in her hands and kissed him. He laid his hand on her cheek, sliding his fingers through her hair, behind her head, to pull her closer.

Warner groaned.

Rick pushed onto his knees. Katy draped his arm around her shoulders. Together they got up off the ground. Behind them, hidden by shadows, lay the back entrance to the caves. Beset, who had refused to leave the caves while the great god Setesh lived, wandered outside.

"Setesh's ship," Rick said.

Aset walked to Setesh's body. She fished around in his pockets until she located the communication device. When she pressed a button, a light blinked on the device. She spoke into it. A man's voice responded.

Although Katy understood ancient Kemetian, she had no clue what Aset said now, since the woman spoke in modern Kemetian

Aset plunked the device into her pocket. "The ship awaits the arrival of Wesir. They will not attempt to harm us, for many of them prayed this day would come. Setesh ruled with fear. My people are free."

"Some wanted to follow Setesh," Katy said.

"They will be punished."

Aset returned to the others. Katy helped Rick hobble toward the humped boulder. His footing became surer as they walked. He un-crooked his knee, and leaned on her less and less with each step. When they passed the boulder, he no longer needed support.

Warner restrained Chin's hands behind his back. The traitor glowered at Aset and Wesir with a contempt hot enough to melt rock.

Beset grumbled.

Katy told the creature, "Show us the sanctuary."

Chin slammed his head backward into Warner's face. As Warner let go of Chin's hands, the man lunged at Wesir.

Aset ripped out her knife and thrust it into the traitor's chest. He crumbled.

The knife stuck out of his chest. His eyes stared up at nothing.

Katy checked for a pulse. Chin was dead.

Beset grunted. She trotted away from them.

Katy and Rick cantered after her. The rest of the gang chased after them.

They passed under the craft. The center light had gone out. The lights at its rim twinkled.

To the east, over the mountaintop, sunrise smeared across the sky. The sun nudged its head over the cliffs within a halo of reds and yellows. The creature shepherded them into a crevasse that sloped downward. Five minutes later the slope mutated into stairs, battered by the elements yet largely intact, carved from the limestone bedrock. The cliffs closed in around them. The stairs ended at a tunnel.

The creature bent her knees, leaned forward at the waist, and tromped into the tunnel.

Rick, Warner, and Wesir stooped as they entered the tunnel, whose roof dipped within an inch of Katy's head. The tunnel slanted downhill. Warner switched on the floodlight. The creature led them down, down, down through the conduit to the *duat*.

Ahead, just beyond the floodlight's reach, honey-colored light tinged the darkness.

The creature strolled out into a jungle. The sun, low overhead, poured golden rays on the landscape. Warner shut off the floodlight.

The tunnel had deposited them on a ledge that overlooked an oasis. Vines curled over the ledge's rim. Trees, 80 feet tall, towered 35 feet above their heads. A mist swaddled the treetops. Birds squawked, chirped, and cawed while, in the distance, a monkey hollered. Somewhere below, masked by trees, water gurgled. The oasis stretched half a mile across, a little more in width, seated inside a bowl enclosed by 500-foot cliffs. On the far side, a waterfall cascaded from halfway up the cliffs. A bird flitted up from the trees only to dive into them seconds later.

The hairy hominid headed for another staircase hewn from the cliff, at the left side of the ledge. Humans in tow, she descended into the forest.

The trees spread their arms wide around a stream. Fronds overhung the stream's banks, along which reeds grew in waist-high clumps. Fish darted in the stream over a bed of sand. Pebbles blanketed the shoreline.

Katy and Rick ambled to the stream's bank. She dipped her boot in the water. The stream flowed clear and fast, six inches deep at its heart. Rick settled his hands on her shoulders.

Katy asked Beset, "Who made this place for you?"

"Sons of Horus," the creature said.

"The torches and ropes," Rick said. "This is where the creatures got the wood for them."

"Now we know why the creatures believed everything the Sons of Horus told them. Who else but gods could create a place like this, in the middle of the desert?"

"If we promised to worship the Planners, think they'd make us an oasis?"

"Get a grip, honey." To Beset, she said, "Is this the sanctuary?"

The creature shook her head. She sauntered into the trees, following the stream.

The humans hiked after her with Katy and Rick in the lead.

After ten minutes the creature veered away from the stream, through the trees, into a clearing. At the far end of the clearing squatted a stone building overgrown with vines. Hieroglyphs wallpapered the exterior of the shrine. Its walls, chiseled from rose granite, glowed a deep pink in the sunrise. A large slab blocked the doorway. The slab was carved into a false door, complete with a faux knob.

The creature approached the doorway. She heaved the slab inward. The door swung on wooden pegs embedded in the top and bottom of its left side. The pegs rested in depressions in the jamb.

The hairy hominid stepped away from the door. She bowed her head, hands clasped behind her.

Light flickered within the shrine. Through the doorway, Katy spied torches set in sconces on the walls.

Katy asked the creature, "Who keeps the torches lit?"

"Our elders," the hominid responded. She kept her head bowed.

Rick and Katy entered the shrine.

The building was 15 feet wide. The room extended 12 feet back into the structure, though from the outside the building appeared longer. The corbelled ceiling soared 18 feet high. Along the back wall, a trio of gold statues strode forth from the wall. A six-inch-high dais supported each statue. Aset and Djehuty accompanied Wesir, who carried the crook and flail crossed over his chest. The double crown of Kemet perched atop his head. Thoth and Aset each carried a staff. Aset grasped hers in the right hand, while Djehuty clutched his in the left. In her left hand, Aset held out an *ankh* as if offering it to someone. Djehuty, in his right hand, carried a scroll.

Not a real scroll, of course, but one fashioned from gold.

Inscriptions on the walls commemorated milestones in Wesir's reign—his coronation, his marriage to Aset, the birth of their son, his journeys around the world to befriend other peoples. One relief recreated his *heb-sed*, a celebration of 30 years on the throne.

A shadow eclipsed the doorway.

Katy twisted her torso to look back.

Wesir stood in the doorway, hands linked behind his back.

He nodded at the coronation relief. "I was fifteen years past my birth when I became king. I served for thirty-one years before my brother's treachery condemned us all to the *mut ankh*."

According to the text, he'd married Aset during Year Four. They'd been married for 27 years.

More like 12,027 years.

Horus had arrived in Year Six. He must've taken the throne, upon his father's "death," at age 25. How long had he ruled? How many children had he fathered? What woman had he wed? Which seeds of his family tree grew into hers?

Rick frowned. "What's he saying?"

She translated Wesir's words for him. His frown lingered. He meandered to the left-hand wall, where he crouched to trace his fingers over the inscriptions.

"Listen to this," he said. "The Sons of Horus did create the oasis. They dug springs, laid plumbing in the cliffs to create waterfalls, planted trees, brought wildlife. They wanted the hairy hominids to protect the tomb, so they made a home for them."

Katy knelt before the statues. The floor was marble, one huge sheet of it cut to fit the shrine's dimensions. The statues sat on the marble, freestanding. Their bases were wood gilded to hide the seams where the side planks linked at each corner. The base for Djehuty's statue, however, showed two seams in front.

Rick read more of the hieroglyphic text. "Behind this wall is a geothermal power station. It uses 'eternal power' to fuel the pumps that keep the waterfalls and springs going."

The front panel on Djehuty's base was gilded separately from the rest of his statue. Maybe it had jostled loose over the eons.

"Can you imagine," Rick said, scooting across the floor toward her, "machinery that runs reliably for thousands of years?"

"Fascinating," Katy mumbled.

She picked at the panel with her fingernails. It wouldn't move.

Beset grunted, "We fix."

Katy nailed her gaze on the creature. "You what?"

"We fix," the hominid said. She gestured at the wall. "Priests fix god's heart."

God's heart. Of course. The Planners had taught the creatures how to maintain the power station, which the hominids had labeled the God's Heart because it kept the oasis running. Or perhaps the Planners had christened it the God's Heart. They did love their metaphors.

She returned her gaze to the statue's base. "Warner, can I have your knife?"

His boots clomped on the marble floor behind her as he entered the shrine. He leaned over her and held the knife in her face.

Taking the knife, she wedged the blade into the crack where the front and right side panels met. She pushed.

The front panel popped out an inch. Giving Warner his knife, she pried the panel free from the base then plunked it onto the floor beside her. The panel had concealed a cavity within the base. The cavity housed a five-inch-thick papyrus scroll, bound by a gold ribbon.

She picked up the book—carefully. The scroll was heavy, wound into a tight roll with only a tiny space at its core. Katy undid the ribbon. She rolled out two feet of the scroll. Multi-colored hieroglyphs crammed into every inch of the papyrus.

"Herein lies the wisdom of the creators," she read, "recorded by I, Djehuty, overseer of priests at Karnak and Mennefer, overseer of scribes, protector of knowledge. All that we know and have known, since the time of Atum and the first gods, I chronicle in this book."

"The real Book of Thoth," Rick said. "Those sneaky weasels hid it."

"That's the Planners for you."

They glanced at Wesir and Aset.

"We are not offended," Aset said. "Some of our people have been…sneaky weasels."

Katy caressed the book's cover. "Hundreds of people died protecting this book."

Hugging the Book to her chest, Katy bent down to peer inside the cavity that had hidden the scroll. A mass of dark fabric was lumped into the back.

Katy handed the Book to Rick. She lowered onto her belly, legs outstretched behind her, and snaked her hand into the cavity. Snagging the fabric, she slid it out onto the floor. Metal clanged against metal.

The fabric fell open. Half a dozen objects, devices for unknown and alien purposes, sat on the fabric. A flat, round object—white as the moon, streaked with pale pink and lavender—corresponded with Aset's description of the moonstone she'd used to reanimate Wesir's heart.

Katy picked up the moonstone. It did feel soft and warm from her touch, like Aset had described. The assemblage included a blue faience jar and silver wand too, the devices Aset had employed to heal Wesir's wound. The purpose of the other objects remained a mystery. Their appearance gave no clues.

"Wesir and I must go," Aset said. "Our people are in turmoil."

"We should go too," Rick said.

Katy stood. She squeezed between the Aset and Wesir statues.

At its center, the rear wall imitated a doorway. Katy started to turn away. She looked back at the false door. A sliver of darkness divided the door from the rest of the wall. A faint light flickered through the gap.

A real door.

She grasped the knob and pushed. The door refused to budge. She gritted her teeth and strained against it. The door swung on its hinges, grating the wooden pegs against the marble. The door was an two inches thick, compared to the six-inch thickness of the main door Beset had opened for them.

Through the doorway, a torch lit a small chamber. A man lay sprawled on the floor, on his back. Blood matted his shirt. His face had paled to match his gray beard.

Charlie.

Katy ran to him, falling onto her knees and sliding the last few feet to his side.

"Rick!" she shouted.

No, no, no.

The blood had coagulated into a scab around a deep wound. She thrust her finger into Charlie's neck. No pulse. She flattened her ear to his chest. No respiration, no heartbeat.

Rick sprinted into the chamber. He dropped down beside her, gasping.

Tears streamed down her cheeks. Her jaw quivered. Rick slipped his arm around her shoulders, and she buried her face in his neck. Sobs shook her body.

Footsteps clapped outside the chamber.

Rick kissed the top of her head. As he murmured wordless sounds, he rocked her in his arms.

The footsteps pounded behind them.

"Quickly," Aset said, "there is still time. But we must *hurry.*"

Katy lifted her head. Through a haze of tears, she gazed at Aset.

The woman's face was flushed, her hair wild. In her hands she clutched the moonstone and the silver wand. Next to her, Wesir gripped the little blue jar.

Katy looked at Rick. She saw his lips moving, but her heart pumped the blood through her arteries so fast the noise drowned out his words. She sucked in a breath. Her body still trembled, though for a different reason.

Rick's voice broke through the clamor inside her head. "Can we really heal him? He's dead."

Aset knelt behind them. She proffered the moonstone and wand to them.

"I questioned the beast," Aset said. "She informed me your father's heart ceased beating less than three hours ago. Little time remains."

Rick took the devices from Aset. He flipped the stopper out of the jar.

"Not much left," he said.

"It'll be enough," Katy said. "It has to be."

Rick dispensed the gel onto Charlie's wound. A few tablespoonfuls poured out. With the wand, he scraped out the inside of the jar, wiping the gel off onto Charlie's wound. He raised the wand over the wound, pressing its sides between his thumb and forefinger.

A sliver of light beamed down from the wand's tip into the wound. Above the background of soft buzzing, the device hummed an arpeggio of tones reminiscent of music.

Rick swept the beam back and forth over the wound.

The gel fizzed as if Rick had poured carbonated water onto it. Charlie's wound sewed itself together from the inside out.

The wand vibrated, shaking Rick's hand. He wrestled to maintain his hold on the device.

The tissues in Charlie's chest knit together. The skin sealed itself. The scab, and the blood matted in Charlie's shirt, remained.

The beam shut off. The buzzing and humming quieted.

Rick set the moonstone over Charlie's heart. He pressed the heel of his hand down on the device. The moonstone clicked.

Charlie's body twitched. His chest inflated, ounce by ounce, taking in a breath. As his lungs expelled the air, Charlie's eyelids fluttered.

He opened his eyes and squinted up at Rick.

"Welcome back," Rick said.

Charlie glanced at the moonstone on his chest. Crinkling his forehead, he pushed up onto his elbows. Rick took his arm and helped him sit up.

The moonstone slid off onto the floor.

Charlie fingered the tear in his shirt, the scab, the dried blood on his shirt.

"I distinctly remember dying," he said.

"We fixed that," Rick said.

"Fixed...?" Charlie glanced from Rick to Katy. "What did you do?"

Katy hugged him, smacking a kiss on his cheek. "Long story."

Father and son considered each other for several seconds, then hugged as quickly as a hummingbird flapped its wings.

They all rose. Rick pocketed the moonstone and the wand. He clasped Katy's hand. She twined her fingers with his.

Charlie slapped Rick's arm. "So you finally smartened up and married her."

"Dad," Rick groaned. "That's all you have to say after a year?"

"What about grandchildren?"

"Dad!"

Katy grinned.

Rick rolled his eyes.

Charlie bounced on his toes. He fought to suppress a smile.

Rick squeezed Katy's hand. "Let's go home."

They filed out of the chamber into the sanctuary. Bob and Beset stood near the front door.

Charlie pecked at the blood dried onto his shirt. "I hope you whooped Setesh's behind. This was my favorite shirt."

"Katy got him," Rick said.

Charlie smiled at her. "You go, girl."

"Please, Charlie," she said. "Don't try to be hip. It doesn't suit you."

"Call me Dad."

The group marched out of the sanctuary into the jungle outside. The others started into the trees, down the trail along which Beset had brought them. The creature tagged along after Aset.

Rick and Katy lingered a moment outside the shrine's doors.

Katy sighed. "Another great discovery we can't tell anyone about."

"We have to protect the creatures," Rick agreed.

She tapped the scroll, which he'd tucked under one arm. "Maybe the Book will tell us about Warner's skeleton."

"Warner's what?"

"You remember. The half-a-billion-year-old skeleton he found in Canada, buried in the Burgess Shale."

"The one the Planners blew up when we tried to excavate it."

"That's the one."

Ever since Warner had shown them the skeleton, and especially since Intef/Setesh had blown up the find, she'd wondered how a human being carrying an Eye of Horus amulet had gotten into Canada. Western Canada had lain under an ocean during the Cambrian Period, the era to which the Burgess Shale belonged. Perhaps the answer awaited them in the Book of Thoth.

They jogged to catch up with the group.

While Beset guided them back through the jungle, they lapsed into silence. Up the stairs, through the tunnel, up more stairs and sloping crevasses they traveled. Eventually they wound up under the disk-shaped craft.

"We can take you to your friends," Aset said. "We must retrieve Jed in any case."

"Our friends?" Katy said. She glanced at Charlie, Bob, and Warner.

"The archaeologists who brought you in their aircraft."

Ethan and Theo. She'd completely forgotten about them.

"Sounds like a plan," Katy said.

Wesir motioned for them to gather around him and Aset. Once they had, Wesir spoke into the communication device.

The wattage of every light bulb on the planet flared around them.

They disappeared from the desert, leaving the hairy hominid to gape at the spot where they had congregated.

A minute later, Beset sauntered toward the entrance to the caves.

Light glinted on the DC-3's fuselage as the beam unloaded them onto the ground half a dozen yards from the plane. The main door was open. Jed, stationed in the precise spot he'd selected when they left the trio there, almost smiled when he saw Aset and Wesir.

Jed descended the steps, skipping off the last step onto the sand.

Ethan leaned out the door. The kid rubbed his eyes and yawned. On this side of the cliffs, the sun had barely peeked over the mountaintops. Clouds unfolded from the horizon in ribbons of pink, yellow, and orange.

A light shined straight down on Ethan's head.

Squinting, shielding his eyes with one hand, he looked at the source of the brilliance. His mouth gaped. He let his hand drop.

The craft hovered 500 feet overhead. Its center light cast a cone of illumination that dispersed over the DC-3.

Transfixed, Ethan exhaled in spurts.

Theo squeezed past Ethan. As he deplaned, he glanced up at the UFO. He puckered his lips, said "huh," and walked to Katy and Rick.

"Nice ride," he said.

Ethan staggered down the steps. He tripped on the last step, plummeted into the sand—landing on his butt—and, still gawking, climbed onto his feet.

Katy pointed out Wesir and Aset. "They were kind enough to give us a lift."

Ethan turned his gape on the two Planners. "Are you aliens?"

"No," Aset laughed. "We are not the aliens."

Ethan asked Katy, "You make the great discovery?"

Rick answered. "Yeah, but we can't tell anybody. And we need your promise you won't tell anybody where you brought us."

Theo raised his right hand. He jabbed Ethan in the ribs. The junior archaeologist raised his right hand as well.

"We swear," Theo said. He told Ethan, "Help our friends board the aircraft."

Ethan waved for them to follow as he trudged toward the main door. Warner, Bob, and Charlie followed him. He waited for them to climb the steps, while he stared up at the disk-shaped craft, before he mounted the stairs himself. Theo boarded next.

Katy and Rick ambled halfway to the plane. They faced Aset and Wesir.

"Thank you," Aset said.

"No problem," Rick responded.

"You will not see again us for quite some time. The moment for revealing ourselves has not yet arrived."

"You don't think we're ready," Katy said.

"On the contrary. It is *we* who are not ready."

"The Planners aren't ready to meet the Low Ones?"

"Precisely. That we persist in using such terms means we are not ready."

Aset murmured to Wesir. He spoke into the communication device.

"We must go," Aset said. "My cousin's book belongs to you now."

Katy waved.

Aset returned the gesture. Wesir slipped his arm around Aset's shoulders. As the beam enveloped them, Aset smiled.

Katy and Rick boarded the DC-3.

As the engines sputtered to life, Ethan's voice echoed across the desert.

"Yeehah!"

50,000 feet above the Pacific Ocean

Katy thrummed her fingers on the armrest of the seat. On the table before her, the laptop computer displayed a web page.

In the seat beside her, Rick gazed out the window. Warner snoozed on the sofa down the aisle from them.

Bob had stayed in Cairo with Ethan, Yves, Theo, and Tony. The hospital had released Tony, but the doctors warned him against traveling for awhile.

Katy lifted the computer onto her lap. She'd navigated to Symbols.com, a website that cataloged every kind of glyph imaginable, from ancient Egyptian hieroglyphs to astronomical symbols. The astronomical variety had her attention now.

She'd seen the sun-sand-mountain-pyramid formation of hieroglyphs before, in a context unrelated to ancient Egypt. Since the text in Wesir's tomb contained circle glyphs that represented the Earth and another, unnamed planet, she surmised the glyph formation must have something to do with astronomy. She must've seen it in a magazine or textbook.

The website allowed users to search for symbols based on their shapes. Her search had validated her hunch. The results included astronomical symbols.

On the screen, the web page listed the results of her search. Tiny thumbnails showed the symbols. She scrolled down the page.

A symbol jumped out at her. She clicked on the link. A larger version of the symbol, accompanied by text explaining its meaning and purpose, loaded on the screen.

"Oh my God," she said.

Rick leaned over her shoulder to look at the screen.

He met her gaze. "Are you serious?"

"I'm serious." Katy cleared her throat. "The First House of Man was on Mars."

She set the computer on the table. From her suitcase, which slouched against her seat, she retrieved the scroll. Rolling it out on the table, she read the opening text. Because she'd browsed the Book earlier, she knew what the text said. But only now did she understand.

The First House of Man ended one thousand million years ago, in the Desert of the Sun Mountain, where Atum and his brothers erected the first monuments.

Sun. Sand. Mountain. Pyramid. The pyramid glyph served as a determinative, perhaps because Atum and his "brothers" had built pyramids on Mars. Early photos of Mars, taken by the Voyager probe, seemed to show pyramids on the planet's surface. Desert of the Sun Mountain must be the name Atum and his kind gave to their homeland. Scientists speculated that, in the distant past, Mars had boasted rivers and seas.

The Book explained how a catastrophe had forced Atum's people to abandon Mars. The climate changed drastically within a few decades. Rivers dried up. The desert overtook the planet. Earthquakes, volcanic eruptions, and floods had decimated Atum's people. To save the remainder, Atum located another planet, a young world still suffering from growing pains. They could flee to the new world.

And they did.

Earlier, Katy had stopped reading at that point in order to search for the identity of Atum's home world. Now she continued reading from there.

Rick snapped his fingers in front of her face.

Her eyes burned. Her ears rang.

"Breathe, Katy," he said.

She took a deep breath.

"What is it?" Rick asked. "You look like you saw the ghost of Setesh."

"No, I…"

She stared at the text, certain she'd read it wrong. She hadn't.

"It, um, says…" She laid her hands on the scroll. "In a cave in the Sinai, Djehuty found texts from Atum's time. With the texts, he discovered a likeness of Atum. From the words he uses, I'd guess it was something like a photograph."

"And?"

"Well…he doesn't sound quite human." She skimmed her finger over the text until she found the relevant passage. "Djehuty describes Atum as 'like a man, yet also like a god, with aspects not seen in kings or men.' He goes on to say Atum had very pale skin and sunken eyes."

"But the First House of *Man* was on Mars. Which means Atum had to be a man."

"We call the ancient hominids, like *Homo erectus*, humans. They don't look much like us."

She scanned the next registers of hieroglyphs. Djehuty had explained a lot more than where humanity's ancestors had arisen.

"Listen," she said. "Djehuty says Atum's people came to Earth but they were going extinct. Since they had only a small population to work with, their DNA had become corrupted. They needed new blood."

Rick fidgeted in his seat. "Don't tell me."

"They blended their DNA with the DNA of creatures native to this world. First they created the hairy hominids. But they couldn't interbreed with Atum's race. So, next, they created us."

Rick's expression darkened. "They interbred with us?"

"No. Both experiments failed, from their viewpoint, and Atum's race died out. We and the hairy hominids are their legacy."

Djehuty explained how he had stumbled across an ancient text that mentioned how remnants of the technology created by Atum's race littered the earth. The text also talked about the cities of Atum's people. From that information, Djehuty had deduced the locations of several of the cities. There, he'd found the "wisdom" he recorded in his book.

Ancient Egyptian mythology named Thoth as keeper of the gods' archives. Djehuty had been the world's first archaeologist.

Since Atum's time, Djehuty said, human cultures had attained advanced technology—then been annihilated by cataclysms, war, disease. The cycle had repeated countless times. As for the separation between Planners and Low Ones, Djehuty understood its origins too.

Early in the Planners' history, a disagreement had broken out. Some of them wanted to teach the hairy hominids, elevate them to the level of human culture, while others wanted no part in cavorting with filthy animals. The disagreement bred rivalries, the rivalries gave birth to splinter groups who became exiles, and the exiles eventually turned into the Low Ones.

Later on, a mysterious figure who called himself Amen-Ra came to the Planners. He decreed that hairy hominids be treated as children of the gods. The Planners obeyed.

"Does it say anything," Rick asked, "about Warner's skeleton?"

"Actually, it does. When Atum's race came here, one of their ships crashed into the ocean in the northern hemisphere."

"How could the Planners read these ancient texts written by aliens?"

"Amen-Ra taught them the language and gave them advanced technology. That's all Djehuty says."

Atum's race had died out millions of years before the Planners coalesced into a society. Yet someone named Amen-Ra had taught them the language and technology of Atum's people. Who was Amen-Ra?

When Ethan asked Aset if she was an alien, the woman had said no. But the phrasing she'd used had bothered Katy. *We are not the aliens.*

The aliens.

Katy looked out the window. The stars sparkled in a sky unpolluted by the moon's brilliance. Below the jet, a smattering of clouds streaked past.

A light flashed to the northwest. She looked in that direction. The light pulsed larger. When it reached the size of the moon, it paused.

We are not the aliens.

The light zipped north out of sight.

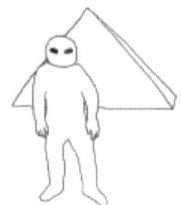

Epilogue

Anameka, Michigan
Wednesday, December 10

Outside the window above the sink, a shape shifted amongst the trees. Katy leaned forward. Through the kitchen window, she spotted Garfield.

The hominid raised a hand, palm out. She waved back at him.

Garfield moseyed up the hill behind the house.

Katy trotted to the desk. She pulled out a drawer. Inside it nestled a GPS unit. She'd programmed the unit with the coordinates Warner had taken them to last year, where he'd shown them the skeleton of Atum's brethren. Back then, they thought the skeleton was human. She knew better today. The bones may have resembled a human skeleton because Atum's race looked similar to humans—or perhaps because the skull had been crushed, obscuring its shape, and they'd expected the skeleton to be human anyway. They'd know the answer soon enough.

Her wheeled suitcase leaned against the sofa, its main compartment unzipped. She crossed over to the sofa, stuffed the GPS unit inside the suitcase, and zipped up the main compartment.

A rapping at the front door gave Rick an excuse to stomp across the living room. Katy heard the door click as he opened it.

"Howdy, pard'ner," Ethan called.

Ethan and Theo stood on the front porch. Out the windows, Katy glimpsed a Hummer squatting in front of the house. The huge vehicle consumed the entire width of the circular drive. Alongside the vehicle, Warner, Bob, Yves, and Tony Edwards chatted and gestured, all smiling—even Warner. A pretty young woman, a little older than Katy, stood beside Warner. The woman was Ankhes, a Planner sent by Aset and Wesir to learn the ways of the Low Ones—kind of a cultural immersion program. Ankhes would also teach them about the Planners.

Rick asked Ethan, "Got the equipment?"

"You betcha. Even got us a real, live permit to excavate."

Katy arched an eyebrow. "And what did you claim we're excavating?"

Ethan winked at her ."Fossilized fishies, of course."

Rick wheeled their suitcases out the door, across the porch. The wheels clunked on the steps as he dragged them down into the front yard.

Rick reappeared in the doorway. Shutting the drawer, she jogged to him.

He pulled her close. "What do you say we go dig up a spaceman?"

"Our destination isn't exactly precise. Might take years to find another skeleton."

"Maybe. But it'll be a hell of a ride getting there."

Footsteps pounded on the stairs to the basement.

Katy looked to her left. Charlie, his jacket in hand, sprang off the top stair into the living room.

"Heard the door," he said. "Are we going or what?"

"We're going," Rick said.

Charlie followed Ethan and Theo into the front yard. Katy and Rick walked out the door behind them, hand in hand.

Katy ignored the urge to look back into the cabin. Their future waited outside.

The future of the whole world rested in their hands. They could rewrite history.

Rick shut the door.

COMING SOON

the adventure continues!

ANCIENT
ONES

 Book Three in the Human Origins Series

Unlocking the door to humanity's past unleashes an ancient enemy whose wrath may destroy the world…

Navigate to

www.SlipdownMountain.com/origins/

for the latest on the Human Origins Series, or to

∞ order Book One, *The Hunt for Bigfoot*;
∞ read the Strange Origins blog;
∞ find out how to learn more about the real subjects
  discussed in the Human Origins Series;
∞ and more!

LISA A. SHIEL has turned a long-time interest in archaeology, alternative history, and the paranormal into gripping fiction based on her own unique interpretation of events that have fueled curiosity worldwide. In 2005, she established the Michigan Upper Peninsula Bigfoot Organization (MUPBO). As a recognized Bigfoot expert, Lisa has been interviewd by big city newspapers and drive-time talk radio hosts. She's currently at work on the third book in the Human Origins Series. She has a master's degree in Library Science.

Coming Winter 2006!

BACKYARD BIGFOOT
THE TRUE STORY OF STICK SIGNS, UFOS, AND THE SASQUATCH

by Lisa A. Shiel
with a foreword by Nick Redfern

Based on her own first-hand experiences and original research, *Backyard Bigfoot* sheds light on ignored evidence to tell the real story behind the world's most mysterious creatures—giant ape...or something else?

Keep up with our new releases and special offers by visiting us on the web at:

www.SlipdownMountain.com

OR

Sign up for our Book News email updates by sending an email to:

BookNews@SlipdownMountain.com

with

"Subscribe Newsletter"

as the subject.

www.ingramcontent.com/pod-product-compliance
Lightning Source LLC
Chambersburg PA
CBHW030026180626
46810CB00001B/230